Tunnel Vision

Linda Rich

iUniverse, Inc.
Bloomington

Tunnel Vision

This is a work of fiction. All of the characters, names, incidents, organizations, and dialogue in this novel are either the products of the author's imagination or are used fictitiously.

iUniverse books may be ordered through booksellers or by contacting:

iUniverse
1663 Liberty Drive
Bloomington, IN 47403
www.iuniverse.com
1-800-Authors (1-800-288-4677)

ISBN: 978-1-4502-7626-9 (sc)
ISBN: 978-1-4502-7627-6 (ebk)

Printed in the United States of America

iUniverse rev. date: 11/30/2010

Also by Linda Rich

CASEY'S WALL
REMEMBERING HOME

The envelope was waiting in his mailbox when he got home from work, nestled between his electric bill and an advertising circular. At first glance he'd been startled by the word "summons," but when he took a closer look he saw that it was nothing to worry about. He was just being called for jury duty.

He pictured himself sitting on a jury, like he'd seen on television, and found the idea appealing. While he might not get paid for the time he missed from work—he couldn't recall offhand what the company policy was—losing a few days' pay was no big deal. He had a modest but secure income from his grandmother's estate.

He'd been quite pleasantly surprised to find out she'd left him everything: not mega-millions, maybe, but still a nice piece of change. He smiled, recalling how sure Chad had been that he'd somehow managed to do the old gal in.

He hadn't, of course. For starters, it would have broken one of their most important rules: *Don't shit where you eat.* No, her death had been a completely natural one. She'd been standing in line at the grocery store when she simply toppled over. According to the autopsy report, she was already dead when she hit the floor.

And besides, he'd been truly fond of good old Gram. She'd taken him under her wing when nobody else would, when even his own mother had shown him the door. It had turned out pretty well for him, all things considered. It was in Milwaukee, where he'd gone to live with Gram, that he'd been reunited with Chad, his boyhood comrade.

He'd learned a trade—two trades, actually, counting the tech-school course Gram had paid for—and all the rules Chad, his mentor, had drummed into his head: *Be patient. Preparation is everything. Don't be greedy. Always keep your day job.*

Still, he'd begun to be wary of the association with Chad, instructive and profitable though it had been. After Gram's death he'd returned to Illinois and found the all-important day job; not a great one, but good enough to let him live quietly, under the radar, until a better opportunity came along.

He removed the documents from the envelope and leafed through them. One was a paper badge with his name printed on it, and a number: 118.

Jury duty. The more he thought about it, the more interesting it sounded.

A fast-moving storm front had come barreling out of the Great Plains shortly before noon, burying most of north-central Illinois under a fresh coating of snow. By the time Jill McKinnon's workday ended and she headed north out of town, the desolate late-winter landscape lay flat and featureless beneath the darkening sky.

The snowstorm had moved on to the east except for a few lingering flurries. Snowflakes driven by a frigid west wind floated and danced in the headlights of Jill's Chevy Impala, creating a diaphanous curtain that clouded her view of the narrow county blacktop. She watched for the warm yellow lights of the Cameron place, then slowed in anticipation of the sharp right turn into her own driveway a quarter-mile past Camerons'. The familiar sign greeted her: *McKinnon Farm Est. 1892.*

Instead of pulling into the detached garage twenty feet behind the house, she parked as close as possible to the side door of the shabby, old-fashioned farmhouse and let herself in, noting with a moment's annoyance that Jessica had left the door unlocked yet again.

Jessica McKinnon was standing at the stove with her back to the door, stirring a pot of chili. A short, sturdy woman of seventy, she wore her wintertime uniform of denim stretch pants and turtleneck sweater. She greeted Jill without turning around.

"Hey," she said. "I hope chili's okay for supper."

"Perfect weather for it, that's for sure." Jill set her briefcase down and took off her coat, hanging it on a peg near the door.

"Some mail for you," Jessica said, gesturing toward the kitchen table. "Looks like you're being called for jury duty."

Jill crossed to the table and picked up an envelope with the word "summons" printed in boldface type below her name and address. She opened the envelope and quickly scanned the contents. Included with the summons was a questionnaire and a return envelope addressed to the Remington County Jury Commission.

"When's it for?" Jessica asked.

"April." Jill consulted the calendar hanging on the side of the refrigerator. "The second week."

"You can probably get out of it."

"Why would I want to do that?"

"Most people do, from what I hear."

"Well, I don't."

"Up to you," Jessica said with a shrug. She set out a green salad and dished up the chili, which they ate with a minimum of conversation.

The air around them was heavy with the tension that had developed between them since Kevin's death six months earlier. Jill and Kevin McKinnon had been married just three years when his National Guard unit was deployed to Afghanistan. Four months into his tour, he was killed by an improvised explosive device on a desolate stretch of road near the Pakistani border. For the first several weeks afterwards the two women had been nearly immobilized by the loss of Jill's husband, Jessica's only son. Since then, their relationship had grown increasingly strained.

After they finished eating, Jessica got up and went to the kitchen counter. She returned bearing a ruby-glass plate containing several large heart-shaped sugar cookies decorated with pink frosting and cinnamon red-hot candies.

"Would you like dessert? I made cookies."

Too much to hope for, Jill reflected, that Jessica would just let the holiday pass. She forced a smile. "They look delicious. Almost too pretty to eat."

"I thought you might enjoy them. Remember how Kevin always loved my heart cookies?" Jessica's voice quavered as she spoke Kevin's name. "He could eat a whole batch all by himself. Go ahead, have one."

Jill eyed the cookies, which were huge. She picked up one of the cookies and broke it apart. She raised a fragment to her lips, leaving the remaining pieces on the plate.

"I don't see why you won't eat the whole thing," Jessica protested, sounding fretful. "You're too thin, and besides, I made them for you."

No, you didn't, Jill wanted to say. *You made them for Kevin.* "I'll eat the rest of it later. I'm too full of chili to enjoy it right now."

"All right, then." Jessica helped herself to a cookie. "So how was your day?"

"Well, the bank wants the cost projections for the next phase of Tommy's condo project. So I spent most of the morning working on those. And—"

"No, I meant how was your *Valentine's* Day."

Jill sighed. There was no point telling Jessica about the fiasco at the office earlier in the day. Jill shared a large open workspace with the boss's executive assistant, Karen, and their desks were on opposite corners with potted ficus trees strategically placed to create the illusion of privacy. Still, there'd been no way for Jill to remain unaware when Kelly, the receptionist, had come in bearing a vase of red roses and placed them on Karen's desk.

"Look what you got. You are so lucky," Kelly gushed.

Karen flicked a glance at Jill, who had looked up when Kelly entered their office. "Thank you," Karen said quietly. Then she resumed tapping away at her computer keyboard, but Kelly failed to take the hint.

"You are *so* lucky," she said again, "Now, how many years have you and Don been married?"

"Thirty-two. Maybe you should go back to your desk? You know Tommy doesn't like the front office left unattended."

"That is amazing," Kelly chattered on, oblivious. "So few couples stay married these days. Just making it to your second anniversary, let alone your *thirty*-second—"

"*Kelly,*" Karen hissed, and the girl's lips formed a soundless "O" as she realized her gaffe. The year before, Jill had also received roses on Valentine's Day; but there would be none for her today.

Clasping her hands in front of her chest, Kelly turned toward Jill. "I'm so sorry." Tears formed in the girl's eyes and slid down her cheeks. "I'm sorry," she repeated.

"It's all right. Don't cry." Jill reached for the tissue box she kept on her desk and offered it to Kelly, who pulled out a handful and then dashed off in the direction of the ladies' room.

"Oh, Lord," Karen moaned. "She's such a twit. Why Tommy keeps her around I'll never know."

"Because she's good on the phone, and the guys love her." 'The guys' were Tommy Adair's myriad business contacts. "Anyway, don't worry about it. It's no big deal."

"Yes, it is. When I think of—" Karen's voice cracked, and she fumbled for her own box of tissues.

Oh, wonderful, Jill thought. *Now they're both in tears.* She stood up and pulled her coat from the nearby rack. "Listen, I have to meet Tommy over at the bank. He wants me to bring the updated figures for the Juniper Ridge project. Call me on my cell if you need me for anything."

She hadn't returned to the office until shortly before five o'clock, staying only long enough to check her emails and shut down her computer. As she left the building, the snow flurries and biting wind seemed like a fitting end to a difficult day.

Now, looking at Jessica over the plate of Kevin's favorite cookies, Jill just shrugged. "Like any other day at the office. I crunch numbers and try to keep the bankers happy."

A crafty smile curved Jessica's lips. "Oh," she said. "I thought maybe you might have got some flowers from somebody."

Jill stared at her. "Why in the world would you think that?"

"Because you're so careful about staying thin, and you always put on makeup and look so nice when you go to work, I just thought maybe…"

"You know," Jill said, trying to keep her voice pleasant, "my job involves meeting and working with influential members of the community. I'm expected to look professional and dress appropriately."

"Well, I just thought…"

Jill reached across the table and grasped Jessica's hands. "Now, listen. I'm not ready to start dating again. Most of the time I feel like I'll never be ready. But if and when that day comes, I'll tell you. I promise."

Jessica looked down at the table, refusing to meet Jill's eyes. Disengaging her hands from Jill's, she stood up and went into the living room.

Jill carried the dirty dishes over to the sink, rinsed them and loaded them into the dishwasher. She was wiping down the kitchen table when she saw the jury summons still lying at the far end. She picked it up and put it into her briefcase. She would deal with that tomorrow. She reached for the light switch and flicked it off. Only then did she realize that Jessica was standing in the living room doorway, watching her.

"I've been thinking about what to do with the farm," Jessica said.

Jill slipped her key into the office door, opened it, and turned on the lights. It was not quite seven-thirty, and even Tommy, usually the first to arrive, hadn't come in yet. She shrugged out of her coat and hung it up, then entered the tiny kitchen area and started a pot of coffee.

At her desk, she booted up her computer, pulled the jury summons out of her briefcase, and noted the dates in her Outlook calendar. That accomplished, she unfolded the questionnaire and began to read it.

The first few questions were basic: name, age, occupation, employer, marital status. She lingered over that one, wondering whether it would be acceptable to check the "single" box even though "widowed" was listed as an option. She couldn't imagine what difference it would make. And besides, when new acquaintances found out her husband had been killed in Afghanistan they often felt free to express their opinions—sometimes stridently and at great length—about the war in general and the politics involved. Even when Jill agreed with the point of view expressed, such discussions were painful. She tried her best to avoid them.

Jill continued reading the questions. Are you or a relative a member of law enforcement? Ever a party to a lawsuit? Ever a crime victim? Ever convicted of a crime? If so, explain. Jill picked up a pen, then set it down again. The aroma of freshly brewed coffee wafted through the office. *Coffee first*, she decided. She was pouring coffee into a ceramic mug when she heard the office door open and looked around. Karen stood behind her.

"About yesterday," Karen began, "I feel so bad about what happened."

"Don't worry about it. It's water over the dam."

"Yes, but Kelly should have known better than to make a fuss over the flowers and how long I've been married. I feel awful about it."

"Just let it go, Karen. It's over and done with."

"Yes, but I feel so bad—"

"I don't intend any offense," Jill cut in, "but could we please just drop the subject?"

Karen looked as though she'd been slapped. "Well, all right, but I'm always here for you if you want to talk."

"And I appreciate that, but what helps me the most is to just come to work every day and focus on my job."

Karen filled a mug with coffee. "All right, then. Please excuse me for caring," she flung over her shoulder as she marched away.

Jill returned to her desk and sipped her coffee. She had realized shortly after coming to work for Tommy that his executive assistant was addicted to tragedy. She loved nothing better than to wallow in other people's misfortunes, vicariously sharing in their grief.

Jill picked up a pen and began to fill out the questionnaire. She had finished it, except for the question about her marital status, when Tommy came in. She caught his eye as he was passing her desk on his way to his private office.

"Can I see you for a minute?"

"Sure, come on in."

Jill followed Tommy into his office and closed the door, facing her boss across his desk. Nearing his fiftieth birthday, he was slightly above medium height and very fit. He'd been a star running back on the local high-school football team and liked to brag that he was still only eight pounds above his playing weight. Like several of his teammates on the 1979 team, the first-ever Drummond Dragons team to win an Illinois state championship, Tommy had fantasized about playing for the Bears or Packers. He'd been recruited by Notre Dame, but he'd eventually faced the reality that his future lay in the business world instead of professional football. So he'd returned to Drummond, married the most eligible young lady in town, and joined his father's company, which had grown substantially since Tommy had taken it over in the early 1990s.

Tommy focused warm brown eyes on Jill. "What's up?"

"I'll be out for a week the middle of April. Jury duty."

"Can't you get out of it?"

Jill thought it was interesting that Tommy and Jessica had responded the same way, both assuming she could get out of jury duty—and that she'd want to.

"Why? Don't you think I'd make a good juror?"

"The best," Tommy said with a smile. "It's just that I'm not sure I can spare you."

"It's only for a week, if that. And if you're worried about the tax work, I'll have everything done by the end of March."

Tommy drummed his fingers on his desk and studied her. "You really want to do this, don't you?"

"Yes, I do."

"Mind if I ask why?"

"Because I think they call it jury *duty* for a reason." Aware that Tommy might find this last statement overly self-righteous, Jill smiled to lighten the mood. "And besides, it sounds like a way to meet new people."

Tommy saw no point in further discussion, although he didn't believe that thing about wanting to meet new people. While Jill was outwardly personable, unfailingly pleasant with business associates and customers, she was also one of the most introverted individuals he'd ever known. "Okay, fine. Just put it on the office calendar."

"Thanks, Tommy."

"That's okay. Send Karen in, would you?"

Once Karen had entered Tommy's office and Jill could be sure of a few minutes of privacy, she dialed Roy Hanninen's number. Roy had been the McKinnon family's attorney for decades.

"Just a heads up," she told him. "You might get a call from Jessica asking for an appointment to talk about what she wants to do with the farm."

"You did tell her it's not hers to do anything with?"

"I only told her she should talk to you about it."

"You're letting me do the dirty work, huh?" The old man laughed. "So what brought this on?"

"I'm not sure, except she seems awfully hung up on the fact that her husband's branch of the McKinnon family died out with Kevin, and that the farm should stay in the family. 'Family' in this case meaning by blood instead of name."

"Ah. Joe's sister Carol and her boys."

"Yes."

"And your position is…?"

"I wouldn't be against selling it, if they're interested in buying it and the price is realistic. But it doesn't sound to me like Jessica wants to sell it. It sounds more like she was planning to leave it to them in her will."

Louise Engquist had known Jessica McKinnon since their school days, but they had become close friends only in recent years. Louise had grown up a mile north of Drummond on the large, successful Sorenson farm, while Jessica spent her childhood in town. Her father had owned and operated the local shoe-repair shop, and although the family never went hungry, money was chronically tight. Jessica had been intensely envious of her classmate Louise, who owned a beautiful bay saddle horse and was always at the center of a large group of friends. Long before she was out of her teens, Jessica had made up her mind to marry a prosperous farmer when she grew up.

Not that women had a lot of other opportunities at that time in Drummond, a farming community west of Chicago and south of Rockford. Advanced education was necessary to become a teacher or a nurse, and Jessica was an indifferent student. What else was left? Jessica had no interest in becoming a hairdresser, secretary, or telephone operator.

Reasonably attractive as well as determined, she eventually realized her dream by marrying Joe McKinnon, heir to a modest farmstead a few miles up the road from Sorensons'. That same year, Louise Sorenson finished nursing school, married Harold Engquist—a history teacher at Drummond High School who would eventually become its principal—and moved into town. While their paths crossed occasionally, Louise and Jessica rarely saw each other until Joe McKinnon entered hospice care in 2003.

Louise was Joe's hospice nurse and had been widowed just the year before. The bond she formed with Jessica was a strong one, forged from empathy and shared experiences, and still endured after several years.

Louise wasn't surprised to receive a call from Jessica, given how fragile her emotional state had been since losing her only child. What did surprise Louise was the undertone of anger in her friend's voice.

"Louise, can you come out and see me today?"

It was a brilliantly sunny day in late February, and the roads would be fine. Louise paid closer attention to road conditions now than she had before retiring a few years earlier. Back then she'd been fearless because her patients needed her, but not any more.

"Of course I can. Say, I haven't had lunch yet. How about if I stop and pick us up some sandwiches?"

"No, don't bother. I couldn't eat a bite. I'm too upset."

"But I could, and like I said, I haven't had lunch yet. You can put yours away for later if you're still not hungry when I get there."

Louise arrived at the McKinnon farm half an hour later, bringing two box lunches from Pinky's Café. Carefully balancing the boxes, she tapped at the side door of the house.

"It's open," Jessica called out. "Come on in."

"Hands are full," Louise shouted. "Let me in." And then, when Jessica swung the door open, Louise added, "You really ought to keep your doors locked, Jess. I know we never did in the old days, but we live in a different world now." She crossed to the kitchen table and placed the box lunches on it. Without waiting to be invited, she sat down.

"Everything good is long gone," Jessica said. "Would you rather have coffee or pop?"

"Coffee, if it's made. Now tell me what's wrong." Louise opened her box lunch and unwrapped a sandwich while Jessica poured coffee.

"I saw Roy Hanninen this morning about updating my will," Jessica began. "I thought it was time to make sure the farm stays in the family. Joe was his parents' only son, you know."

"Yes, I know," Louise said, trying not to sound impatient. "I grew up just a few miles down the road."

"He had two sisters, one older and one younger. The older girl—"

"Doris."

"—Doris went to college down in Normal to become a teacher. She met her husband down there, and they settled in Bloomington. They had two boys. One's an insurance executive, and the other's a college professor. Anyway, Doris and Floyd moved to Florida quite a while back. Floyd died six or seven years ago, and she's still down there but not in good health. And of course," Jessica said dismissively, "neither of Doris's boys ever showed any interest in the family farm. Now Carol, the younger girl, got married and moved to Rockford. When they got divorced she stayed up there, got a job, and bought herself a nice little condo. She has two boys, Chris and Mike, and I remember her saying they'd bounced around from one thing to another and never found careers they were happy with." Jessica paused to sip her coffee. "Their last name is Gregory, but they're Kevin's cousins. They've got as much McKinnon blood as he had. And I thought they might be interested in taking over the farm."

"Do they know anything about farming?"

"Doesn't matter," Jessica said with a wave of her hand. "Before Kevin left for Afghanistan he set it up with the bank for their Ag Services division to manage our land. No reason why they can't keep on doing it." Jessica opened the white box that Louise had pushed toward her. "What kind of sandwich did you bring?"

"Ham and turkey club. Jess, tell me something. When you say 'take over the farm,' what exactly do you mean?"

"Just what I say. They'd take it over. Move down here and let Ag Services manage it till they get the hang of it—"

"And you'd continue to live here?"

"Actually, I was thinking more of leaving it to them in my will. But if they wanted to move down here sooner, I figured I'd get a little place in town. At my age, it might be a good idea not to live so far out in the country."

"I see. And what about Jill? Where would she live?"

"Well." Jessica took a bite of her sandwich and chewed it, watching Louise as she did so. The glint of malice in her eyes was unmistakable.

"Well?" Louise prompted her.

"Oh, she'll remarry and go on with her life. She's young, she's got a good job, why does she need a farm? And if she did remarry and have kids, why should they get this place?" Jessica demanded, her voice rising in pitch and volume. "They wouldn't be McKinnons."

"Okay," Louise said, "so you saw Roy Hanninen this morning about leaving the farm to Kevin's cousins. What was his take on it?"

"His *take* on it," Jessica spat, "was that I only own twenty-five percent of McKinnon Farm, Incorporated. And that *woman*, that Jill, owns the other seventy five percent. And she knew that! She knew it when I told her I'd been thinking about what to do with the farm, but she didn't have the guts to tell me. She just told me to talk to Hanninen about it."

"Is it possible," Louise suggested, "that she thought you already knew?"

"That's what Hanninen said. He showed me copies of some papers and asked me if I didn't remember signing them and him telling me what they all meant. He said he told me at the time, but I didn't—I don't remember."

Jessica's voice had begun to quaver, and Louise reached over and took hold of her friend's hand. "What papers, honey?"

"The farm is in a land trust. Has been for I don't know how long. And now the land is pledged as collateral for a loan the bank made to the corporation."

"You're going too fast for me, Jess. What corporation?"

"While Kevin was still in college, he and Joe decided they needed to modernize. First of all, they wanted us to have our own grain bins, which we never did before. And then they bought a lot of new equipment, with GPS technology and all that stuff Kevin was learning about in ag school. Well, of course they needed an expanded line of credit to do all that. So Roy Hanninen advised him to set up the farm—the business, I mean, not the land—as a corporation. Joe and Kevin each had a fifty-percent interest in the corporation, and they put up the land as collateral for the loan."

Louise was beginning to see where this was going. "Then what?"

"Before Joe died, he transferred half his interest in the business to me and the other half to Kevin, which gave him seventy-five percent. He also appointed Hanninen as trustee of the land trust, with Kevin as the beneficiary. Roy showed me a paper I signed years ago. He called it a homestead waiver." Jessica wrapped her half-eaten sandwich and replaced it in the box. "I can't eat now. I just can't. I never gave it a thought, Louise. Kevin was our son, and it was going to be his eventually anyway. But before he left for Afghanistan, he and Hanninen put their heads together to transfer it all to Jill. His interest in the corporation, everything." Jessica was silent for a moment, turning her head to gaze out the kitchen window. "I own twenty-five percent of the business, so I get a share of the income from it. And of course I got Joe's and my joint bank accounts and everything, so it's not like I'm broke. But when it comes to this land, I have no rights at all. No say in what becomes of it after I'm gone."

"Jess," Louise said, speaking softy, "you do understand, don't you, that Kevin was only trying to provide for his wife in case he didn't come back? And besides, she's very knowledgeable about business affairs. Between her and the Ag Services guys at the bank, the property couldn't be in better hands."

"But it's not fair," Jessica burst out. "She's young. She'll get married again, and she and her new husband will have this place. And if she has children, then the children will have it. It was supposed to be Kevin's. Over my dead body will that woman get my boy's farm."

Louise heaved a deep sigh. Jessica probably wasn't in a frame of mind to see reason, but Louise felt compelled to make the effort.

"When you lost Joe," she said, "I promised I'd never tell you how to grieve. I hated it when other people tried to tell me, and we all have to deal with it in our own way. I also understand you're feeling a lot of anger right now, and that's natural. You've lost your son, which goes against everything that seems right and proper. Our children are supposed to bury us, not the other way around."

"Don't talk down to me, Louise. Not you, of all people."

"I'm sorry if it sounds that way, because I don't mean to. But I need you to explain something to me. Why is so much of your anger directed toward Jill? She didn't cause Kevin's death. It would make a lot more sense to me if you were mad at the people in Afghanistan who planted the roadside bomb, or even at the government that sent him over there. They're the guilty ones, not Jill. So why are you mad at her?"

"Because my son is dead, and she's alive." Jessica's voice was roughened by grief. "She'll probably live another fifty years, with a husband, with children, with grandchildren. I don't have any of those."

"So you don't want Jill to have any of the things you did have? You shared this place with Joe for over forty years. And then when you'd been married for so long and almost given up on ever having a baby, you finally had Kevin. He was the light of your life. You would wish for her to never experience any of that? What has she done that you think she deserves such an empty life?"

Jessica had begun to sob. "You don't understand," she managed to say, shaking her head.

Louise got up and went around the table to stand behind her friend, placing her hands on Jessica's shoulders. "Try to direct your anger where it belongs, Jess. It'll take a while to spend itself, and maybe it never will. Not entirely. But try not to be angry at Jill. She hasn't done anything to you."

"Yes, she has." Jessica reached for a paper napkin and blew her nose. "She took my son away from me."

"I have two sons," Louise said, squeezing Jessica's shoulders. "They're both married to lovely girls, but it still hurt when they got married because I'd been the number one gal in their lives for so long. It's like I said before, though. Why would I want to deny my sons the kind of happiness their father and I had?" Louise picked up the coffee pot and refilled their cups. "Why don't I sit with you for a little while? Maybe you'll be able to finish your sandwich."

Jessica drew a long, shuddering breath. "I'll try."

She ate the rest of her sandwich, washed down with another cup of coffee, but as she watched Louise pull out of the driveway and head south toward town, Jessica's anger at Jill remained undiminished.

Pinky's Café had been a fixture in downtown Drummond since the 1920s. Flanked by the Remington County Bank across the alley to the south and a gift shop to the north, it enjoyed a steady stream of customers from early morning until closing time at 7:00 p.m.

Nearly all the buildings on both sides of lower Main Street, beginning with the bank at the corner of Main and First, were of late nineteenth-century vintage. Beyond Pinky's and the gift shop were a ladies' clothing store and a shoe store. On the other side of the street, directly opposite the bank and its neighbors, were a bakery, a travel agency, a bar—the Dragons Den, its name paying homage to the local high school's mascot—and a shop selling linens and other accessories for bedroom and bath.

These businesses, with their high ceilings and old-fashioned charm, had changed little since Stack Ridgeway's boyhood. One of Stack's earliest memories was of his father bringing him to Pinky's for a cheeseburger. It looked pretty much the same now as it had then, except for one thing. About ten years earlier, the granddaughter of the original owner had taken over the café from her parents and had ripped down the old grease-spotted wallpaper. She'd then commissioned a local artist to paint expansive murals of Drummond in the old days, complete with horse-drawn carriages. That was the only change she'd made, though; the menu remained nearly the same as in her grandfather's day. Pinky's still served good American comfort food, and plenty of it: perennial favorites like burgers, fries, cole slaw, and grilled cheese sandwiches, all at bargain prices. Breakfast was available all day.

Other dining opportunities in downtown Drummond were limited: a little hole-in-the-wall place two blocks farther up Main Street that sold tacos and burritos, and a newly opened delicatessen a block west of the courthouse on First Street. Several chain restaurants in varying price ranges bordered the two interstate highways that bracketed the town to the east and south, but truly discriminating customers with a taste for *nouvelle cuisine* preferred the locally owned Chez Marie on the newer, upscale north side of town.

In the three decades since Stack had graduated from high school, Drummond—once a sleepy little farming community—had nearly quadrupled in area and population. The nuclear power station had come first, with construction beginning several miles south of town in the late 1970s. By the time the plant had actually begun generating power in the 1980s, most of its large workforce had settled in and around Drummond. The majority purchased homes on the north side, of course, since even they didn't want their families to live *too* close to the nuclear plant. Next had come a large truck terminal and distribution center, drawn by reasonable land prices and proximity to two interstate highways, and a farm implement manufacturer.

As the industrial base expanded, so did Drummond's population. Predictably, this growth drove increasing demand for other services such as shopping centers, medical and dental care, and, of course, housing. Stack's high-school teammate, real estate developer Tommy Adair, had profited hugely from the growth in the housing market. Most of Drummond's expansion, though, was on the booming north side. Pinky's and the other businesses along Main Street remained frozen in an earlier—and, for many longtime residents, more comfortable—time.

Stack's real first name was Starnsworth, after his maternal grandfather; he had been christened "Stack" by Tommy Adair's father. The elder Adair, an athlete in his youth, was a tireless booster of Drummond sports and self-appointed surrogate father to Tommy's teammates. The Adairs' spacious Victorian house on the near west side of town was their favorite weekend hangout.

"Starnsworth!" Thomas Senior had railed. "What kind of candy-ass name is that for a quarterback? We'll call you Stack." Then, as an afterthought, he had renamed the team's starting wide receiver, Steve Berglund, "Stick" because of the boy's height—and because it went well with "Stack."

Stack's senior year had been a golden one for the Drummond Dragons. Under the guidance of Diogenes Pappas, the young head coach hired just three years earlier, they had made it all the way to the state finals and captured their first-ever 4A championship. They had demolished the top-seeded Maxwell Raiders by a score of 42 to 14, dethroning the defending champions and establishing Drummond—and Coach Dio—as a force to be reckoned with in high-school football.

Like Tommy Adair, Stack had briefly dreamed of achieving professional football stardom. But, also like Tommy, Stack had soon come to terms with reality. Deciding on a career in law enforcement, Stack had majored in criminal justice at Illinois State University and returned to Drummond after graduation to join the local police force. Although he'd climbed steadily through the ranks, Stack had never aspired to becoming Chief of Police. He was happy with his job as Captain of Detectives, which allowed him to do actual police work while his boss coped with the politics and the press.

Stack had claimed his table of choice, the one in the front corner by the window. From there he could see most of the 100 block of Main Street. This was his domain, and he enjoyed watching over it while he waited for Barb, the waitress, to bring his club sandwich. He stifled a groan when he saw Steve Berglund come up the sidewalk and turn into Pinky's narrow entryway. Steve was alone, which meant he'd probably be looking for a lunch partner. Stack turned his face away from the door and leaned closer to the window, hoping Steve wouldn't see him and would go pester someone else instead.

Stack had already noticed that Coach Dio was absent from his usual stool at the counter, which was located at the far end of the café by the cash register. The recently retired Coach liked that particular spot because all the patrons had to come to the register to pay their bills, giving him the opportunity to greet them and chat for a few minutes. Coach's favorite pastime was keeping up with all the latest gossip and ongoing local dramas, and he could usually be counted on to take Steve off Stack's hands.

No such luck today, though. Steve stopped just inside the doorway, turned, and looked directly at Stack.

"Hey, how's it going? Mind if I join you?" Without waiting for permission, he sat down across from Stack and arranged his long legs under the table.

Barb, the waitress, had seen Steve come in and brought a dog-eared menu to their table along with Stack's club sandwich.

"I'm fine, Stick. How about you?" Stack had always liked his own high-school alias, and by now hardly anyone in town knew his real first name. Even his wife called him Stack. Steve, however, hated his nickname and had spent years trying to get his classmates to drop it. Most had, but not Stack. He continued to address the man who now sat across the table from him as "Stick," partly from habit but mostly to annoy him.

While it was uncommon for a small high school to have a strong ground game as well as a good passing game—usually it was either/or—the Drummond Dragons had possessed both in the fall of 1979 thanks to a gifted young coach and three promising players. Running back Tommy Adair was nimble, hard-charging, and even late in the fourth quarter possessed a seemingly bottomless reserve of strength and stamina. Stack Ridgeway was a capable quarterback with a decent arm, a natural leader endowed with a generous amount of what Tommy's dad referred to as "football smarts."

Tall, thin Stick Berglund, the wide receiver, was possibly the most talented of the three. Despite an awkward, loose-jointed running style, Stick was deceptively fast. He also had great hands. He could dash downfield with remarkable speed and effortlessly snag Stack's passes out of the air, even those that were imperfectly thrown. Despite his stellar prep performance, though, Stick never dreamed about playing for the NFL. He viewed football solely as a ticket to college and, eventually, a successful career in a major city.

Things went well for him initially. He earned his bachelor's and then a law degree from the University of Illinois and, as might be expected by an undistinguished young lawyer ranked in the middle of his class, was recruited by an undistinguished, middle-sized Chicago law firm.

Although he passed the state bar examination in due course, Steve Berglund possessed neither unusual legal talent nor personal charisma. His billable-hour production was not that great, either, and he was tersely instructed to increase it. An unspoken but strongly implied "or else" had hung in the air at the end of that conversation.

It was his father, service manager at a Drummond auto dealership, who guided Steve toward the next phase of his career. The elder Berglund listened attentively as his son described his frustration, then spoke a name.

"Walt Jacobs."

"Who?"

"Walt Jacobs. He brought his car in for maintenance the other day. Said he's been thinking about hiring an associate. He's getting on in years and needs someone to help him out."

Steve laughed. "You can't be serious. Walt Jacobs is a friggin' ambulance chaser."

His father gave him a long, steady look. "Maybe so, Steve, but he's got more work than he can handle. He does all kinds of stuff besides personal injury. Family law…even criminal defense cases sometimes."

After a series of meetings with Jacobs, Steve Berglund had joined and eventually taken over Jacobs' practice, currently known as Berglund Law Firm, P.C., and married a local girl, more or less happily. While not as successful as his classmate Tommy Adair, a millionaire many times over, Steve earned more even in his leanest years than Stack Ridgeway. But the satisfaction with life that Tommy and Stack both enjoyed had stubbornly eluded Steve.

He looked across the table at Stack. "I guess you heard," he said.

"Heard what?"

Steve glanced at Barb, who had approached to take his order. "Gimme a grilled cheese, side of slaw, and iced tea. Please," he added after a moment, feeling Stack's eyes on him. He waited until she moved away before continuing. "Phelan's going to trial with that date-rape case. I tried to talk her out of it, but she wouldn't listen. Shit, she can't possibly win."

Denise Phelan, Assistant State's Attorney for Remington County, had been planning to grab a sandwich at Pinky's. But, catching sight of Steve Berglund at the window table, she kept right on walking north on Main Street until she reached Consuelo's. The spicy Tex-Mex food suited her mood today. A natural redhead who wore her flaming hair very short and spiky in a style that accentuated her upswept brows and pale blue eyes, she always looked ready for a fight despite her petite stature.

As she munched on a burrito, Denise reflected on the case that would pit her against Berglund. In her opinion he was a conceited jerk, a big duck in the little pond that was Drummond, Illinois. But he had also lived here forever and knew everyone in town worth knowing. More to the point, he was in sync with the mood of the community in a way that she, transplanted from an affluent northern suburb of Chicago, could never be.

Denise was aware of her reputation as arrogant and overly ambitious. Well, so be it. She was sick of Drummond's small-town, good-old-boy atmosphere and would do everything she could to change it, especially when the law was on her side. Still, it would be a challenge. Acquaintance-rape cases always hinged on whether the jury believed the defendant's or the accuser's version of events.

The facts as she knew them were these: Katie Putnam had run into former boyfriend Brian Briggs at a party. They had talked for a while, then left together. At that point, however, their accounts of the episode diverged. She said he'd offered her a ride home, which she'd accepted because the female friend who had brought her had disappeared and it was too far to walk. He said she'd asked for the ride, then invited him in for a drink when they reached her apartment. She said yes, she'd wanted to talk with him for a while longer, so she'd offered him a drink. But only a drink, and nothing more. He said she'd offered plenty more. And so forth.

Superficially, at least, Katie was more credible than her alleged attacker. She was a soft-spoken young woman with a full-time job at a local discount store, where she was assistant manager of the children's clothing department, and lived alone in a small apartment on the blue-collar southeast side. As far as Denise could determine, Katie had never been in any kind of trouble.

Brian Briggs, on the other hand, had a history of minor offenses including disturbing the peace and driving with a suspended license. He'd also been unable to keep a job for more than a few months at a time. He alternated between living with his mother and a succession of girlfriends. Katie Putnam had been one of these, but they'd split up several months before the incident in question.

In discussions with Denise, Katie had admitted to occasional binge drinking but swore that was all in the past. She now drank only rarely, she claimed, and never to excess. More disturbing to Denise was a chance remark Katie had made about being in counseling. She'd been evasive when Denise had tried to follow up, refusing to divulge any details. Denise hoped to God that Steve Berglund never got hold of that particular tidbit, but there was no reason to think that Berglund had a clue.

The police work underlying the state's charges seemed solid, too. Denise's boss, Terry Lankowski—State's Attorney for Remington County—had reassured her on that score.

"Stack Ridgeway runs a tight ship," Lankowski had said, tapping the case file with a forefinger. "His detective division does things strictly by the book, so I don't think there's a chance in hell that any of this will get thrown out." But, while he'd given Denise his blessing to proceed with prosecuting Briggs, Lankowski had cautioned her strongly on the subject of jury selection.

"I've been doing this for a long time, so trust me on this. Your best bet is young women and older men. The young women will look at

Putnam and put themselves in her place. The older guys will look at her and think of their daughters, and any guy who takes advantage of daddy's little girl is automatically a scumbag. But the young guys, well, that's obvious. They'll identify with the defendant, which is not a good thing."

"What about the older women? Wouldn't they identify Katie with their daughters as well?"

"Here's the problem with that. They'll think she should have known better than to invite the scumbag into her apartment. Didn't Mama always warn her about that? Stupid girl, it's her own fault. What else did she expect?"

"But the law says she has the right to say no, even if—"

"We both know what the law says," Lankowski interrupted. "But I can absolutely guarantee you this. When you stand up in front of those potential jurors and quote the law, when you ask if they understand it and if they're willing to apply it, they'll look you right in the eye and tell you they can. But if you believe that, you're dreaming."

"That sounds pretty cynical, Terry."

"Oh, some of them will do their best to apply the law as it's written, even if they don't agree with it. But some of them won't. And even if it's only one person, that one person can hang the jury."

Lankowski rose from his desk and pushed the file toward Denise. "Do I think we've got a solid case? Yes. Otherwise we wouldn't be taking it to trial. But can we get a conviction? Frankly, I think it's a crap shoot." He paused. "And if we get a hung jury, I'd have to think long and hard about spending the taxpayers' money on a second trial."

The last Saturday in March was unseasonably warm. Jill turned left out of her driveway, headed toward town, and lowered the rear windows of her Impala so she could enjoy the fresh scent of the awakening countryside. She reached the turnoff to the Commons at Juniper Ridge, a shopping center Tommy Adair and some other local businessmen were developing adjacent to Tommy's newest condo project. The first stores were slated to open by late summer, and so far, at least, the project was right on schedule. But for now, although there was a large mall in a nearby town, the best shopping opportunities in Drummond were still downtown.

Fifteen minutes later, Jill pulled into the city parking lot next to the courthouse and nosed the Impala into the first available space. Because she worked on the prosperous north side and lived even farther to the north, she'd never spent much time in downtown Drummond. But each spring and fall she freshened her wardrobe at Mason's, which offered a good selection of women's clothing. The familiar brand names were moderate in price and style, appropriate for conservative downstate tastes.

Jill crossed First Street, walked up Main past the bank and Pinky's Café, and entered Mason's. After several trips into the fitting room she was finally satisfied with her selections and paid for them. Laden with plastic bags containing her purchases, she moved on to the shoe store next door.

She was seated in a chair trying on a pair of high-heeled pumps when a woman approached and spoke to her.

"Jill?"

She looked up and saw Jessica's friend Louise Engquist standing nearby, a tentative smile on her face.

"I thought that was you," Louise said. "It's so nice to see you."

"It's nice to see you, too." She barely knew Louise, so she was surprised when the older woman consulted her watch and asked if she'd had lunch.

"No," Jill said. "Now that you mention it, I haven't."

"Well, look. Why don't you join me at Pinky's? We've never had a chance to sit down and chat, just the two of us."

Jill hesitated. Her relationship with Jessica was becoming rockier by the day, and surely Louise must know that. But, as Jill looked into Louise's pleasant, weathered face, the expression she saw there was hopeful, almost pleading.

"That would be nice. Just let me pay for these shoes."

"Seems like we beat the rush," Jill said as they entered the café a few minutes later. Only four of the tables were occupied.

"It's a lot busier during the week. Most of the courthouse crowd eats here, and of course my dear brother-in-law."

"Who?"

"Dio Pappas, my kid sister's husband. She still works, but he's retired. So he's in here almost every weekday to have lunch with his cronies and keep up with the local gossip. He's really a good guy," she said with a smile. "It's just that every once in a while he needs to be reminded to get over himself." The smile broadened. "And that's my job."

They seated themselves in a booth near the back of the café. A very pregnant waitress appeared with menus and glasses of ice water.

"My goodness, Melissa," Louise exclaimed. "You're still working? When is that baby due?"

"Nine more days," the young woman said. "But I feel fine. And I'd rather keep busy than sit around at home just waiting."

"Yeah, right," Louise murmured after the waitress was out of earshot. "More likely, she can't afford to take the time off from work. The poor little thing will be back here like a shot as soon as the doctor says it's okay. That no-good boyfriend of hers can't hold a job, so he sends her out to work to support him. That's the problem with living in a small town all your life like I have. You get to know way too much about everyone else's business."

Jill looked directly into Louise's blue eyes. "Including mine?"

"Actually, I don't know much of anything about you." Louise gestured toward the menu lying on the table in front of Jill. "So why don't you decide what you're going to have, and then tell me about yourself?"

An hour later, on her way home, Jill reflected on her conversation with Louise. It had felt so good to talk about herself. Not about her problems with Jessica. Not even about Kevin, although there were times when she longed to talk about him, especially with someone other than Jessica. But just about herself: what her life had been like before meeting Kevin, before going to work for Tommy, even before moving to Illinois.

Jill's parents' marriage had been brief and unhappy. Her father, already forty years old when he'd married her mother, had had no intention of settling down until his girlfriend of the moment, the daughter of a business associate, had become pregnant. So, because Suzanne was a pretty girl who was excited about the coming child, and because his professional reputation would have been damaged otherwise, Alan Carmichael did what was expected of him. He married Suzanne in a quickie Las Vegas ceremony and set up housekeeping with her in San Diego, where his company was based. But, while he was an astute and successful businessman, he wasn't cut out for domesticity. He spent more and more time on the road, while Suzanne, who hungered for a normal home life and a husband whose fidelity she could count on, became increasingly unhappy.

Her parents divorced when Jill was four years old. She was seven when her mother remarried, this time to a mid-level civil servant who could provide the conventional lifestyle she craved. By the time Jill reached her middle teens she was half-sister to three young boys, including a set of twins, who were the center of their parents' existence. While Jill got along well enough with her stepfather, it was apparent to her by this point that her primary value to the household lay in her unpaid babysitting services and the support checks that her father scrupulously mailed every month.

Meanwhile, Alan had climbed several rungs on the corporate ladder and relocated to Chicago. He had also remarried recently, not a shotgun wedding this time but a genuine love match. Or at least, as his much-younger second wife would later comment, as close to genuine love as one could expect from a man as self-centered as Alan Carmichael.

During the summer before Jill's junior year in high school, she got out of bed one Sunday morning wearing what she always wore to sleep in—a cotton tank top and panties, but no bra—and wandered half-asleep into the kitchen. Her mother and Bill, Jill's stepfather, were sitting at the table drinking coffee. Bill's eyes lingered too long on his stepdaughter's developing figure, and Suzanne caught him looking.

"Jill," she snapped. "For heaven's sake, go put some clothes on."

At that moment Jill had become, at least in her mother's mind, a rival. Suzanne called Alan later that day and told him it was time for him to take more responsibility for Jill. Specifically, she wanted to send the girl to live with him and Serenity, his new wife.

Encouraged by Serenity, who assured him she would welcome his daughter, Alan arranged for Jill to move to Chicago before the next school year started. And because he'd seen her occasionally, whenever his business took him to San Diego, he wasn't surprised by his daughter's lack of social skills. But Rennie, as she was known to family and friends, was appalled.

"The poor little thing," she said to Alan during Jill's first week with them. "She must have been a regular Cinderella! Never allowed to go out and have fun because she had to stay home and take care of the little boys. No after-school activities, no nothing. And you allowed it? Shame on you!"

"How was I supposed to know? Suzanne said she was doing fine, and her grades were always great. I saw her report cards. Besides, I was in no position to raise a kid, on the road all the time…"

"Well, it's different now. You've got me. And *she's* got me."

Looking back on the two years she'd spent with her father and Rennie before going away to college, Jill would always be grateful to her loving stepmother and friend. Generous, free-spirited Serenity was the daughter of two flower children who had met in San Francisco during its 1967 Summer of Love. Serenity's father was a vagabond and had disappeared before his child's birth, but her mother came from solid

Chicago money. She had returned home to her family, where she and her infant daughter were warmly welcomed.

Rennie had done her best to ease Jill's transition from the modest San Diego neighborhood where her mother lived to her father's home in the fashionable suburb of Hinsdale, and to teach her the social skills she lacked. But, while Jill was able to copy Rennie's technique for making small talk, she never attained her stepmother's effortless, kind-hearted charm.

What Jill did possess, though, was her father's flair for business. She decided to major in accounting, and early in her senior year of high school she applied to and was accepted by Western Illinois University in Macomb. But eighteen months later, in the spring of her freshman year, she received some devastating news: Rennie had been diagnosed with breast cancer.

By the time Jill returned home for the summer, Rennie had already had her left breast surgically removed and was undergoing chemotherapy; and as soon as Jill arrived, Alan moved out. His beautiful wife was damaged goods, and her illness was more than he could deal with. Jill could take care of her now. And she did, staying with her stepmother through the summer instead of joining her father at his new condo unit in a downtown high-rise overlooking Lake Michigan.

When Jill returned to school in the fall Rennie seemed to be doing well, but the cancer recurred the following year. Although she put up a gallant fight, she died halfway through Jill's senior year; and, because Rennie and Alan had never divorced, he inherited her money. It was only a small fortune, but a fortune nonetheless. Shortly after his wife's funeral, Alan retired to Florida.

Upon receiving her degree Jill was recruited by a regional accounting firm that was expanding into the growing Drummond marketplace. As soon as she was eligible, she sat for and passed the CPA exam. The partner in charge of the local office promptly assigned Jill to work with some of his newer clients, one of whom was Kevin McKinnon. Another was local developer Tommy Adair, who was quick to recognize Jill's talent. During one memorable week shortly after her twenty-fourth birthday, she received a marriage proposal and a job offer. She accepted both.

Now, less than five years later, Jill was a widow. This was not the path she had expected her life to take, but after a great deal of soul-searching she had decided that it was time to begin moving on. Despite the loneliness, despite the grief, there was only one way to go, and that was forward. She parked the Impala by the side door of the old farmhouse that had once felt like home but no longer did. She retrieved her purchases from the trunk and stepped inside.

Jessica was sitting at the kitchen table, reading the newspaper. She looked up when Jill came in. Jill set her packages on the other end of the table and sat down across from Jessica. Much as Jill hated confrontations, there was no avoiding this one. She came straight to the point.

"It's time for me to move out. I need to get my own place."

Jessica blinked. "Move out? Why in the world would you do that?"

"For starters, because you don't want me here. You tolerated me because of Kevin, but now that he's gone—"

"That's not fair, Jill. You've always been welcome in my house." As soon as the words left her lips, Jessica realized what she had said. *My* house. "I mean," she added hastily, "of course it *was* my house, but..."

"It's okay. Actually, Kevin always knew how you felt. He and I planned all along to build our own place on that little parcel up the road. It's why—"

Jessica's eyes widened with shock. "What parcel?"

"The two-acre parcel his father gave Kevin when he turned eighteen. It was deeded out of the land trust into Kevin's name. It starts just the other side of that line of evergreens and fronts on the road—"

"I had no idea," Jessica cried out. "Joe never told me."

Jill wondered if this was actually true. She had learned early in her marriage that Jessica's memory could be highly selective. But she also knew, based on what Kevin had told her about his father, that Joe had not always involved Jessica in his decisions.

"I'm sorry you didn't know," Jill said. "But the point is, Kevin and I always planned to build. It's why we held off having a baby, so I could keep working full time and save my salary toward a new house."

"No!" Jessica protested. "I don't believe it. He never would have left me here all alone."

Jill stood up and retrieved her shopping bags. "Then there's something I need to show you," she said. "Let me take this stuff upstairs. I'll be right back."

She returned a few minutes later and spread a set of house plans on the table in front of Jessica. She pointed to the date in the lower right-hand corner of the top sheet. "We had these drawn up right after we got married," Jill said softly. "It was our dream house. I haven't decided yet if I want to go ahead with it. I might buy a place in town instead. But in the meantime, I can move into a short-term rental. I'll start looking next week."

"I'll be all alone if you move out," Jessica said mournfully. "If your only reason for leaving is because you think I don't want you here..."

Jill leaned across the table, looking directly into Jessica's eyes. "But it's not the only reason. I've reached a point in my life where I need a home of my own. One that's just mine. I've never really had one, you know, except for that little apartment I rented when I moved here right after college."

"So I guess your mind is made up?"

"About moving out? Yes." Jill rolled up the plans and slipped a rubber band around them. "You'll be fine on your own, you know," she added encouragingly, then headed toward the staircase. She had almost reached it when Jessica fired her parting shot.

"You probably want your own place so you can have your boyfriend sleep over."

Jill stopped and turned around. She bit back an angry retort, reminding herself that it wouldn't accomplish anything.

"Maybe someday," she said. "If and when I have a boyfriend. But it won't be any time soon." She went up the stairs to her bedroom and shut the door firmly behind her.

Jessica got up from the table, crossed the kitchen and looked out the window over the sink. Planting would begin within a month. When she'd come here as a bride, they'd been thrilled to harvest 75 bushels of corn per acre. Now, though, thanks to the new hybrid varieties, they could expect yields that were more than twice as large.

Jessica remembered reading in the local newspaper that the average age of Remington County farmers was 56. Men like Joe McKinnon were truly a dying breed. How he had loved this land, this rich, bountiful earth! Kevin had, too, in his own way, although in recent years he'd seemed more focused on the commercial aspects of farming. That was Jill's influence, no doubt. Jill, the so-called businesswoman. Jill, the number-cruncher.

"Oh, Kevin," Jessica whispered. "How could you do this to me?"

Upstairs, Jill opened her bedroom window to let in the unseasonably mild breeze. She noticed, not for the first time, that the old single-glazed windows needed replacing. The condition of the roof was questionable, too, and the plumbing was terribly outdated. Kevin, surprisingly unsentimental about the family homestead, had told her shortly after their marriage that it would probably be easier to tear it down and start from scratch than try to renovate it.

"I'd do it in a minute," he'd said, "but Mom would never stand for it. She loves this old place just the way it is." It was at that point that they'd decided to build a house of their own.

Jill turned away from the window and looked at the framed picture of Kevin that gazed back at her from its place on her bedside table.

My mom can be a real pain sometimes, Kevin had said before he left for Afghanistan. *I know that. And she's not the sharpest knife in the drawer, either. But she's still my mother. So do the best you can to take care of her if anything happens to me.*

"I'm sorry," she whispered as tears streamed down her cheeks. "I know I promised you that I'd try to take care of her. But I just can't live with her any more."

On Monday Jill went to the First Bank of Drummond over her lunch break and accessed her safe deposit box, from which she removed a small velvet-lined box containing a ruby-and-diamond ring. She slid the ring onto the third finger of her right hand.

The ring had been a gift from Rennie shortly before she died. "It belonged to my grandmother, who gave it to me when I turned twenty-one," Rennie had told her. "She called it my coming-of-age ring. And now I want you to have it."

Though Jill had treasured the ring, she'd rarely worn it. She'd thought it was too old-fashioned for a college student, too ornate for a young businesswoman. But now, Jill reflected, she seemed to have grown into it. She stretched out her right hand to admire the ring. Then, hesitantly, she removed the wide gold wedding band from her left hand and slipped it into the little velvet box. It felt strange. But, as with Rennie's ring, the time seemed right.

When she got back to the office, she approached Tommy for advice about selecting a good builder. She'd decided to go ahead with the house she and Kevin had planned.

"All the builders I work with are good," Tommy said. "Otherwise, I wouldn't work with them. Pretty ring," he added casually. "Is it new?"

"Thank you. It's a family heirloom."

"What I'd recommend is that you hold off on building for a while," Tommy said. "At least until fall. The builders will be hungrier for work heading into the off season." He fidgeted with a pen and gazed out his office window, deep in thought. "Meanwhile," he continued after a moment, "why don't you move into one of the Juniper Ridge villas and see how you like it? We can work something out about the rent. And we've got a lot of furniture we shift around among the model units, so you can use some of that until you get your own. If you decide the villa suits you and you want to buy it, I can promise you a good deal. But if fall gets here and you still want to build, then go for it. I'll help you out any way I can."

Apparently, Jill thought, Tommy subscribed to the conventional wisdom of waiting a year after your loss before making any big decisions. Well, maybe he was right. And the offer of a furnished rental in his new Juniper Ridge development, an upscale condo community, was very generous.

"That would be wonderful, Tommy. Thanks very much. Can I move in after I'm done with jury duty?"

"Sure. Sounds like a plan."

The Remington County Courthouse and Law Enforcement Annex and the adjacent parking facility occupied the entire city block bounded by First Street on the north, Oak and Main Streets on the east and west, and Prairie Street on the south.

Earlier that morning, as she'd been directed in her information packet, Jill had called the telephone number provided to verify that her services were still needed. She listened to the recorded message telling her to report by 8:30 a.m., then drove into town and found a parking space on the third level of the city parking deck. Referring to her instructional pamphlet again, she read that cell phones and all other electronic devices would be prohibited in the jury assembly room. Court officials would collect them and hold them until jurors were released for the day.

Jill had left her laptop at home, but her cell phone was in her purse. She turned it off and stowed it in the glove compartment. She locked her Impala, went down the steps to street level and crossed a narrow courtyard to the courthouse entrance.

A burly security guard instructed her to put her purse on a conveyor belt to be x-rayed, while a second man gestured her toward a metal detector. She stepped through it and retrieved her purse from the guard.

"Thank you. Where do I go for jury duty?"

"Take the elevator to the basement and follow the red arrows. Have a nice day."

When Jill reached the basement she joined a line of several people being admitted to the jury assembly room, which was huge. When her turn came, she produced her summons and watched while the clerk consulted a list and made a check mark by her name. Another clerk handed Jill a plastic holder and a safety pin.

"Tear off your juror badge," the woman said, indicating the perforated bottom portion of Jill's summons, "put it in this holder, and pin it on. You'll be called by number, not your name." Jill looked at the badge. Her number was 22. "Do you have a cell phone?" the clerk continued rapidly, reading from a checklist. "Laptop computer? PDA? Any newspapers or other reading material?"

"No, nothing."

"Okay, go ahead and have a seat."

The room contained row after row of molded plastic chairs—Jill estimated about a hundred and fifty of them—arranged to face a lectern. She selected a seat in the middle of the fourth row and settled herself as comfortably as possible.

She watched as prospective jurors kept arriving, many wearing what Jill considered totally inappropriate clothing even though the Juror Handbook had given specific guidelines regarding attire. She saw both men and women in jeans, ratty t-shirts and flipflops, despite the chilly mid-April temperatures. Many of them sported tattoos and body piercings. Jill, who wore a conservative beige suit and ivory blouse, was beginning to feel distinctly overdressed.

After about ten minutes a woman entered the room, stepped to the lectern, and gave a brief explanation of the morning's procedures. There were, she said, two cases on the calendar for which juries were expected to be empanelled.

"I have a list of numbers for the first case. If your number is called, you'll be taken to the courtroom for examination. If not, you'll wait here for the time being." She picked up a sheet of paper and began to read the numbers.

The second number she called out was Jill's.

Jill was part of a group of about forty people shepherded along the corridor by an ancient female escort named Edna, who nudged them into numerical order as they entered Courtroom #1 and took their places in the spectators' area. Almost immediately, the first fifteen were called to occupy the jury box.

"You six, all the way to the end, front row," Edna instructed them in an authoritative voice. "The next six, all the way to the end, second row. Last three, third row."

Jill sat, as directed, in the second chair in the first row. She'd never been in a courtroom before except when she'd married Kevin.

This wasn't the judge who had married them, though. She read his nameplate: Benjamin J. Meyerhoff. He looked stern and magisterial, with rimless glasses and wispy gray hair that he wore in a bad comb-over, but he greeted the prospective jurors with a smile and thanked them for coming. He quickly got down to business and pointed out the defendant, who was accused of sexual assault.

The defendant, the judge explained, had a prior relationship with his accuser. He, Judge Meyerhoff, would briefly interview each prospective juror in open court. The attorneys for both sides would have an opportunity to ask additional questions. Prospective jurors were instructed to answer all questions truthfully and without mental reservations. It was anticipated that a full panel of twelve jurors and three alternates would be selected that morning.

"There are two very important commitments I will ask you to make," Judge Meyerhoff began. "One is to set aside any preconceptions you may have about the defendant and the accuser based on their race, sex, age, and most especially whether you approve of their lifestyles. You are to be guided strictly by the laws of the State of Illinois as they will be communicated to you. The other commitment you must make is to keep an open mind throughout the proceedings. As prescribed by law, the defendant is presumed innocent until proven guilty." He paused and fixed the fifteen prospective jurors with what he often referred to as "the hairy eyeball" before continuing. "I would ask each of you to examine your consciences very carefully and be sure you can make both of those commitments. If not, please don't hesitate to say so. And finally, I should warn you that some of the testimony you will hear may be very graphic. That is, unfortunately, necessary in order for you to have a complete knowledge and understanding of the case."

Oh, yuck, Jill thought. Nearby, juror number 118 had a different reaction: *This is going to be interesting.*

Throughout these preliminaries, Assistant State's Attorney Denise Phelan had been scrutinizing the fifteen individuals seated in the jury box. One, the wife of a local attorney, was already known to her and would almost certainly be excused. The remaining fourteen were strangers: a mixed bag of male, female, white, black, and brown. The age range was, she estimated, early twenties to senior citizen. The same diversity was reflected in the other members of the jury pool still seated in the spectator area. Chances of getting a jury consisting mostly of older men and younger women, as Terry Lankowski had advised, seemed remote. But then, selection of a jury completely favorable to the defense seemed equally unlikely.

A level playing field, Denise told herself. *That's all I need, just a level playing field.*

"Well, let's get on with it. Number seventeen," the judge intoned, and began to interview a forty-something woman named Tracy Kahler. She was married, employed by a local hospital as an ultrasound technician, and her husband worked at the nearby nuclear power plant. The judge went through the items on the questionnaire the woman had previously filled out, confirming her responses. Nothing in her answers raised any red flags for Denise. She glanced at Steve Berglund, seated at the defense table next to his client. Apparently he had no concerns about Mrs. Kahler, either.

The judge consulted his list. "Number twenty-two."

Denise turned her attention to a slim, dark-haired woman in a beige suit. She was young, somewhere between twenty-five and thirty, and attractive in a prim kind of way. Denise listened attentively as Judge Meyerhoff rattled through the questionnaire. The woman's name was Jill McKinnon. She was single, worked as an accountant for a business called TBA Enterprises—Denise noticed the way Berglund's head popped up when he heard that name—and was not acquainted with anyone involved in the case. No family member was employed in law enforcement. She had never been a crime victim. Never a party to a lawsuit. Et cetera. This girl would make a good juror, Denise decided. She was a bean counter, the type who could dispassionately evaluate all the evidence despite what Terry Lankowski described as the "ick factor" inherent in sexual-assault cases. Denise was curious about Berglund's reaction and wondered if he would pose a follow-up question, but he didn't.

Meyerhoff worked his way through the thirteen people remaining. The lawyer's wife Denise had spotted earlier stated she was acquainted with both attorneys present, the judge, and several members of law enforcement, and admitted she would have difficulty remaining unbiased. There were also two other individuals who, Denise thought—based on their responses to the judge's questions—didn't belong on this or any other jury.

When Meyerhoff had finished interviewing the first fifteen prospective jurors he nodded at Edna, who led her charges out of the courtroom through a rear door to the left of the judge's bench. They moved down yet another corridor and into a room marked Jury Room #1.

"Sit down at this table," Edna boomed. "In numerical order, starting here." She indicated a chair at one end of the table. She pulled on the arm of a decrepit-looking colleague who had been waiting just outside the jury room and had entered at the rear of their little procession. "This is Lonnie. He'll stay with you while I'm gone. Do not discuss anything pertaining to this case or what you've seen or heard thus far." She indicated a stack of tattered, months-old magazines. "You can read if you like. The rest rooms are there in case you need them." She pointed to two doorways at the back of the room.

Edna vanished, then returned a few minutes later and read out three numbers. "You are excused from service on this jury," she announced. "Go back to the Jury Assembly Room. They'll tell you if you need to stay. Lonnie will wait here with the rest of you while three more jurors are picked. Then we'll go to lunch." Although Edna hadn't spelled it out, the three jurors yet to be selected would be the alternates. The twelve people in this room would, in all probability, be the actual decision-makers.

Dio Pappas pulled open the front door of Pinky's Café and immediately noticed that all the tables in the middle of the café had been pushed together in a single long line and held a "reserved" sign. Positioned between the two rows of wall-hugging booths, the tables were usually set up for parties of four. Their current arrangement could mean only one thing: a jury would be escorted here for lunch.

Dio walked past the jury tables and took his usual seat at the counter, near the cash register. He was approached by the plump red-haired girl who was filling in for Melissa—his favorite waitress, now on maternity leave—although without Melissa's level of skill.

"What can I get for you, sir?"

"I'd like a turkey club, no mayo, and a cup of soup." He watched as the girl wrote laboriously on her pad.

"What kind of bread for your sandwich, sir?"

"Sourdough."

"And what kind of soup? Today we have"—she pulled a list out of her pocket and consulted it—"vegetable beef and cream of broccoli."

"Vegetable beef."

"Anything to drink, sir?"

"Just water. Everyone calls me Coach," Dio added, but the girl had already turned her back and moved away. He wondered idly what kind of soup and sandwich he would actually receive. He'd learned the previous week that just because she wrote something on her order pad, it didn't necessarily correspond to what he'd asked for. Not that it mattered too much, because he wasn't a picky eater. The extra pounds he'd gained since coming to Drummond as an athletic young buck in the 1970s were proof of that.

Dio swiveled sideways on his stool so he could see the front door. You could just about set your watch by Edna, and here she came. Right on time.

Dio always enjoyed watching the interaction among the jurors. Very early in his career he'd learned the importance of observing facial expressions and body language, especially when, as on the football field, he couldn't hear what was being said. The kids had no idea how transparent they were; nor, he'd found, did many adults.

As he watched, Edna gave her usual spiel: they could order whatever they wanted as long as it didn't cost over seven dollars—which here at Pinky's meant anything on the menu—plus coffee, tea or soda. There was the predictable mutter of protest when she informed the jurors they wouldn't be allowed to use the restroom here. If nature called, they would have to wait until they were back in the jury room. At least they didn't have to sit in their assigned order here, so there had been some jostling among the men to score seats near the younger ladies.

During the short walk from the courthouse Jill had chatted with a young African-American woman she'd recognized as a hostess at Chez Marie, where she occasionally ate lunch. The woman's name tag identified her as Courtney Singleton, juror number 43. As they entered Pinky's, one of the male jurors—Derrick Reese, also African-American—adroitly slid between the two women. Courtney caught Jill's eye and gave her a wry smile as if to say, *That's a man for you.*

Jill followed Derrick into the café and took the seat to his right. The chair on her other side was immediately pulled out by another young man who asked her permission—rather diffidently, she thought—to sit there.

"Of course," she said, responding with the easy, smiling courtesy she'd learned from Rennie. "Please do." According to his name tag he was Brett Petersen. Although slender, he had the soft, under-exercised look of a man who worked at a desk all day. And, she guessed, judging from the naked gratitude in his expression as he seated himself next to her, he was no stranger to rejection by the opposite sex.

At the end of the table, Edna called out yet another instruction. "Remember," she said, "there is to be *no* discussion of the case at this time."

Directly across from Jill, a tall, solidly built man of about thirty had removed his mirrored blue sunglasses and was putting them into his shirt pocket. "Give me a break," he said to no one in particular. "I don't see how we can discuss it when we don't know anything about it yet." He pulled his lips into a smile that failed to reach his eyes.

Jill glanced at his name tag: Ryan Carlyle. *What a jerk,* she thought, and turned her attention back to Brett. "So, Brett, what kind of work do you do?"

At the back of the café, Dio Pappas was making his own assessment of the fifteen people—nine women and six men—on this particular jury. Three were black and at least two appeared to be Hispanic. The women's ages were anywhere from twenty-something to about sixty. The group was a pretty good cross-section of present-day Drummond, Dio reflected, which was much more diverse than when he'd first moved here. There was just one thing that didn't fit the local demographic: all but one of the men appeared to be under the age of thirty-five. Dio's gaze lingered on the solitary older man, who was white and in his fifties, with a pleasant expression and erect, authoritative carriage. *Unless he's one of the alternates,* Dio thought, *he'll wind up being the foreman.*

He heard a clattering sound behind him and turned around to see that the waitress had set a bowl of soup on the counter. It was cream of broccoli. That was all right, though. He actually preferred it to the vegetable beef, which he'd ordered only because it was lower in fat and calories. He would go ahead and eat the cream of broccoli, just to keep from making a fuss. And maybe, despite his "no mayo" request, there would be mayonnaise on his club sandwich when it arrived. If there was, he wouldn't send it back. After all, the girl was still learning.

Besides, he didn't want to come across as one of those demanding, obnoxious customers he'd encountered in his youth. His immigrant parents had owned and operated a popular eatery in Chicago's Greektown called Flame of the Acropolis, which was now managed by Dio's younger sister and her husband. Dio had labored in the kitchen washing dishes when he was still so small that he had to stand on a stool to reach over the edge of the sink, and his parents had expected him to take his place in the family business when he grew up. Those plans had been derailed, though, when Dio discovered the sport that would give meaning and purpose to the rest of his life: football.

As a fifteen-year-old sophomore, Dio was already six feet fall and weighed a muscular 190 pounds. The football coach had spotted the strapping dark-haired youngster on the first day of school and urged him to try out for the team. Dio promptly agreed, but Andreas and Despina Pappas were initially reluctant to grant permission. They soon relented, though, and eventually became their son's biggest fans.

Dio had an outstanding high-school career, playing middle linebacker with single-minded ferocity, and by his eighteenth birthday had grown to six-feet-three and 220 pounds. His football prowess earned him an athletic scholarship to the University of Illinois, where he played in nearly every game until a knee injury in his senior year ended his hopes for NFL glory.

After graduation he came home from Urbana and, to his parents' delight, took a position at a Chicago high school where he taught social studies and served as assistant football coach. Two years later, still a bachelor despite his mother's best efforts at pairing him off with a suitable Greek-American girl, he was offered and accepted the head coaching position in downstate Drummond.

It was in Drummond that he fulfilled his goal of sharing his passion for football with succeeding generations of high-school boys and, in the process, instilling in them a solid work ethic. It was also in Drummond—a town where, in that era, most residents were of northern European descent and no other Greek-Americans lived—that he met and married Margaret Sorenson.

The knee injury still bothered him, and the principal's wife, Louise Engquist, had recommended that Dio consult Dr. Ram Patel. Her younger sister was the doctor's office nurse, Louise had said, and he was by far the best orthopedist in the area. Because Louise was also a nurse and Dio trusted her advice, he made an appointment. At the doctor's office the following week, the handsome Greek-American football coach and the willowy, brown-haired nurse locked eyes over the front desk. The rest, as they liked to say, was history.

Margaret was the descendant of Swedish immigrants who had come to America in the middle of the nineteenth century. Her great-

great-grandparents had walked from Chicago to the fertile prairie of north-central Illinois, where they had broken the virgin soil with crude hand tools and then bequeathed their homestead to succeeding and increasingly prosperous generations. Unlike Dio, who had been born only a year after his parents' arrival in America and spoke Greek as fluently as English, Margaret considered herself wholly American. It would never have crossed her mind to refer to herself as Swedish, or even Swedish-American. Although she accepted Dio's fierce pride in his heritage, she had never fully understood it. Still, their marriage had not only endured; it had flourished.

Dio ate his soup, glancing over his shoulder now and then to check on the jurors. When the waitress set his sandwich on the counter in front of him, it was exactly as he had ordered it: no mayo. *That's the breaks*, he thought. At least Margaret—still slim despite giving birth to two children, and still fully engaged in her nursing career—would be happy to know he'd followed her advice and eaten the sandwich without mayonnaise.

Denise Phelan had prepared her opening argument thoroughly. She took two deep breaths, approached the jury, and waited until all fifteen sets of eyes were firmly focused on her before she spoke.

"This morning," she began, "Judge Meyerhoff instructed you to set aside any preconceptions you might have about the defendant and his accuser because of their race, sex, age, or lifestyle. He instructed you to be guided strictly by the laws of the State of Illinois. By the laws of the State of Illinois," she repeated. "That's very important. Not by the laws of conventional wisdom. Not by the laws your mother taught you about how nice girls behave. And most definitely," she said, speaking slowly and with careful emphasis, "not by the laws of the locker room."

She paused and scanned the jurors' faces for any flicker of expression—surprise, disapproval, amusement—that might help her gauge their response to her last statement. She saw one of the older female jurors nodding thoughtfully, which was a good sign, and another—the young woman in the beige suit—glancing at the defendant as though to observe his reaction. But from the corner of her eye she'd also noticed an unpleasant smile curling the lips of the guy at the end of the first row. By the time she shifted her gaze to look directly at him, though, his expression was studiously neutral.

Seated at the defense table, Steve Berglund was also watching the jurors. You had to give Phelan credit, he thought, jumping right in with that locker room reference. It was definitely an attention-getter. Risky, though, judging by the nasty but quickly controlled smirk he'd observed on the face of one of the jurors. While Steve considered it a good omen, he hoped the guy never played poker. He was much too easy to read.

Denise Phelan began to lay out the case against Brian Briggs, who sat stolidly at the defense table, his eyes downcast. She described his prior relationship with the accuser and the chain of events leading up to the assault: their meeting at the party, his driving her home, her inviting him in for a drink.

"Katie Putnam only wanted to talk for a while. They were in a relationship last spring, and then they broke up, but she still wanted to be his friend. When they talked at the party, it sounded like he was having problems at work. And she thought she could help him with them. But instead," Denise said, turning and pointing at the defendant, "*this* man took advantage of her generous impulse to help him. *This* man chose to misinterpret her offer of simple friendship. *This* man," she continued, "pushed her down onto her living-room sofa, pulled off her pants, and had sexual intercourse with her against her will. *Against... her... will*, ladies and gentlemen."

Denise moved closer to the jury box, standing only a few feet from the jurors seated in the first row. "So when the defense tells you that it was consensual sex, which they will, and they point to her lack of resistance as *proof* that it was consensual, which they will, here's what you need to remember." She prowled along the railing, fixing uncompromising blue eyes on each of the jurors in turn. "Under Illinois law, Katie Putnam was *not* required to fight back. She was *not* required to scream. She was *not* required to physically resist. Her sole obligation was to say 'No,' which she did. Not just once, but repeatedly. The absence of a struggle, the lack of defensive wounds, the fact that none of her neighbors heard her cry out, none of that matters. None of that makes Brian Briggs any less guilty. Because under Illinois law, penetration through the use of force or threat of force—simple *threat* of force, ladies and gentlemen—constitutes sexual assault. And of that crime, Brian Briggs is guilty as charged."

Denise bowed her head for a moment and dropped her voice almost to a growl. "And we will prove it." Then she returned to her chair at the prosecution table.

Steve Berglund was acutely aware of Brian Briggs seated beside him in a cheap polyester suit. He could smell the pungent odor of the man's perspiration, the scent of his fear. He wished he could tell his client that yes, Denise Phelan was a good prosecutor. Yes, she had correctly stated the law. Yes, she was passionate, forceful and idealistic. And despite all that, she was probably going to lose. But of course he couldn't say that, at least not right now. Instead, he stood up and strode confidently toward the jury.

Now it was Denise Phelan's turn to silently observe the jury's response to Berglund's opening statement. Predictably, it consisted of characterizing Katie Putnam as a clingy, pathetic woman who had been a willing participant in their sexual encounter; had, in fact, been the one to initiate it. She'd only claimed "rape" after the defendant showed no interest in resuming their prior relationship. The spurned woman had retaliated in the most vicious, damaging way she could think of.

Denise paid little attention to Berglund. He was a small-town hack, and she'd known what he was going to say before he opened his mouth. But she paid very close attention to the members of the jury. Most were politely attentive to the defense counsel, as they had been to her, but gave no indication as to where their sympathies lay. And realistically, if they were to do their job properly, they shouldn't have decided yet. Denise fixed her gaze on the man she'd seen smirking earlier. He was watching Berglund intently, his lips slightly parted, as the defense counsel concluded his opening argument.

"I know you all want to see justice done here," Berglund said, gesturing with open arms to include the courtroom at large. "And justice demands that my client be found not guilty of the crime with which he has been charged. If he is guilty of anything, it is only of being naïve enough, *trusting* enough, to believe that the sexual encounter he was offered—I repeat, *offered*—came without strings attached. And I know that after you have heard all the facts of this case, you will set Brian Briggs free." Berglund turned toward the defense table and gestured toward his client.

This was a prearranged signal for Briggs to face the jury, but he failed to pick up the cue. *Look this way,* Berglund wanted to shout. *Look at me, you friggin' moron! If you want them to believe you're innocent, you have to let them see your face!* But Briggs kept his head down, his gaze fixed on a spot on the floor in front of the defense table, until his lawyer came over and sat down beside him.

The judge nodded toward Denise Phelan. "Call your first witness."

"The State calls Patrol Officer Jason Williams."

A clean-cut uniformed officer came forward to be sworn. The jurors sat up a little straighter in anticipation of hearing some actual testimony, and several held their court-provided notepads and pencils at the ready.

Denise consulted her notes. "Last October 12, at 1:18 a.m., you were dispatched to 1712 South Wentworth Street, Apartment 1D. Is that correct?"

In the jury box, juror number 118 made a note of the address.

"Yes, ma'am."

"Would you please tell us why?"

"Ma'am, a 911 hang-up call was received from that address."

"Which means what?"

"Ma'am, someone at that address dialed 911 and then hung up before the dispatcher could find out the nature of the call."

"And what is the normal procedure when that happens?"

"Ma'am, the dispatcher calls the number back to determine if emergency services are required." The officer, though young, was already experienced in giving testimony. He answered only the immediate question, then waited for the Assistant State's Attorney to pose the next one.

"So the dispatcher called back, and what was the outcome of that call?"

"Ma'am, the dispatcher reached a female. She was reported to be crying and incoherent, so I was dispatched to investigate." The officer paused, and the Assistant State's Attorney encouraged him with a nod.

"Go on."

"While I was en route, the dispatcher kept the female on the line. Then she stated that she'd been sexually assaulted."

Aware of the impact of this last statement, its effect magnified by the officer's crisp, unemotional delivery, Denise Phelan let the silence stretch out for a few seconds before following up.

"When you arrived at the address in question, what happened next?"

"Ma'am, I rang the doorbell and identified myself. A female came to the door and asked me to come in."

"Can you please describe the young lady's demeanor?"

"Ma'am, she was crying. After she let me in, she went over to the couch and sat down. She had a blanket that she wrapped around herself, and then she curled up in a ball, almost in a fetal position."

Denise paused, ostensibly to consult her notes, but actually so the jury would have time to formulate the image of a badly traumatized young woman. "What was your course of action at that point?"

"Ma'am, first of all, since she'd stated she'd been assaulted, I confirmed that the individual was no longer on the premises. Then I asked her if she was injured, and she said she wasn't. Then I asked her if she wanted me to call a female officer to assist her in getting medical attention."

"And did she?"

"No, ma'am. She just kept saying it didn't matter, and that nobody would care what happened to her."

"'It didn't matter, and nobody would care,'" Denise repeated slowly. "What did you do next, Officer Williams?"

"Ma'am, I explained to her that since she had reported the commission of a crime, we were required to follow up. I called Dispatch and asked that the on-call detective be notified. Then I took a brief statement from her while we were waiting for him to arrive."

"Did she tell you the name of her alleged assailant?" Denise was careful not to emphasize the word "alleged," knowing it would antagonize Judge Meyerhoff. He had once threatened to hold in contempt of court an attorney who had drawn air quotes around that very word.

"Yes, ma'am, she did."

"And that name was…?"

"Brian Briggs, ma'am."

"Thank you, Officer Williams. I have no further questions."

Smiling pleasantly, Berglund approached the young patrolman. "Good afternoon."

"Good afternoon, sir."

"Could you tell us, please, when you entered the complainant's premises, were there any signs of a disturbance or a struggle?"

"No, sir."

"Nothing at all seemed out of order?"

"Sir, not that I observed."

"So you're telling me that your decision to involve the on-call detective was based solely on the young lady's claim that she'd been assaulted?" Berglund avoided undue emphasis on the word "claim." Like Denise Phelan, he was aware of the judge's intolerance for such theatrics.

The patrolman hesitated fractionally, giving the prosecutor opportunity to object if she so chose. When she didn't, he responded. "Yes, sir."

Berglund waited as long as he dared, hoping that Williams would feel compelled to speak into the silence and expand on his answer; but he sat calmly—and mutely—awaiting the next question.

Hoping to goad Williams into defending or justifying his actions, Berglund tried again. "So, based on absolutely *nothing* that you observed, no *evidence* of a crime having been committed, you decided to involve the on-call detective."

Recognizing that the defense attorney had made a statement rather than asking a question, Williams remained silent.

"Does that accurately describe your course of action, Officer Williams?" Berglund persisted. Anything Williams said that would make him seem unsure of himself, anything that would suggest he might have overstepped the bounds of his duty, could only help the defense and undermine the prosecution.

Denise Phelan, poised to object on the grounds that the question had already been asked and answered, took a calculated risk and held her silence. Then, when her witness responded with a simple "Yes, sir," she wished she could jump up and give him a high five. Officer Williams had just left Berglund with nowhere to go.

Berglund turned on his heel and did his best to sound disgusted. "No more questions for this witness." He resumed his seat at the defense table.

Denise was instantly on her feet. "Redirect, please, Judge?"

"Go ahead."

"Officer Williams, the course of action you followed, and to which you have just testified, is that the exact procedure established by the City of Drummond Police Department in those particular circumstances?"

This time the answer came quickly. "Yes, ma'am."

Denise allowed herself a brief smile. "Thank you, Officer Williams." Then, to the judge: "No more questions."

"Witness may step down." Meyerhoff glanced at the clock on the rear wall. "Let's take a twenty-minute recess."

After the judge swept out of the courtroom, Edna shepherded her charges toward the jury room. Two pitchers of ice water and a stack of paper cups had been placed on the long table in the center of the room.

"Grab yourselves a drink, if you want one," she said. "And I hate to sound like your mother, but you'd better take a potty break now. You may not have another chance before we adjourn for the day." Then she vanished.

Juror number 118 had jotted down several bits of information on his court-provided notepad: Officer Jason Williams' name, the date, and the time of his arrival at the woman's apartment, all as camouflage for the one item that was important to him. Seated at the oblong table, he focused on the woman's address for a minute or so, committing it to memory: *1712 South Wentworth, Apartment 1D.* Then, leaving the pencil and notepad at his place, he rose and got in line to use the men's room.

When his turn came he entered the restroom, which had only a single toilet and sink, and locked the door. He pulled a pen out of the vinyl protector in his breast pocket, wrote the address on one of the small sticky notes he habitually carried, and replaced both items in his pocket. Then he relieved himself, washed his hands, and exited the washroom, smiling politely and holding the door open for the next occupant as he did so.

He'd been back at his seat for about five minutes, making small talk with a few of the other jurors, when Edna returned.

"Court is in session," she bellowed. She eyed their badges, making sure they were all in numerical order, before leading them back into the courtroom.

Detective Scott Allison was the State's next witness. *Timing is everything,* Denise Phelan reminded herself as she approached the witness stand. She knew from past experience that Allison would be meticulously prepared. He was older and bulkier than Williams, but equally clean-cut. His muscular shoulders strained the fabric of a dark blue off-the-rack jacket, and his brown hair was cropped very short. Despite his intimidating appearance, though, his manner was low-key and his voice was mild.

Denise's task this afternoon would be to lead him through the first portion of his statement—a detailed description, including photographs, of Katie Putnam's apartment and what he had found there upon his arrival—at just the right pace. It needed to last until court adjourned for the day and, ideally, convince the jury of the thoroughness of his initial investigation. On the other hand, she couldn't allow him to be so long-winded as to put the jury to sleep. Her plan was to finish laying the necessary groundwork today, and then start fresh the next morning with the much more dramatic phase of Allison's testimony: the account of his initial meeting with Brian Briggs at the Drummond police station. The interview had been videotaped, and the tape would be shown to the jury. Denise could hardly wait.

She quickly established that Allison had been the on-call detective at the time of the incident. Next, she asked him about the layout of the small one-bedroom apartment. He obligingly produced a chart showing Putnam's unit, which was located at the end of the building farthest from the parking lot. Her windows overlooked a lightly traveled residential street in front and a green space in back. The common wall between her apartment and the one next door separated the two bedrooms, not the living rooms, and the sofa where the alleged attack had taken place was located at the farthest point from that common wall.

Jill McKinnon, who worked with house plans and plat maps all the time, had immediately grasped the obvious implication: even if the girl had cried out, her next-door neighbor would probably not have heard her. And neither would anybody else.

A few feet away, juror 118 paid particular attention to the charts presented by Detective Allison. He was tempted to make sketches on his notepad, but decided against it. Instead, he would make detailed drawings as soon as he got home.

Stealing a glance at her watch, Denise asked Allison if he'd taken photographs. He had, of course, and they were already set up for display on a video monitor. By the time all the photos had been shown and their significance described, it was 4:30 p.m. Denise's timing was perfect. Judge Meyerhoff tapped his gavel and adjourned for the day.

"Please remember," the judge instructed the jurors before dismissing them, "you are not to discuss this case with anyone, including each other. And you are not to read any accounts of this trial that may appear in the newspaper."

The jurors filed back to their deliberation room to round up their belongings. "Leave your pads and pencils here," Edna said. "You won't need them, and they'll be right here under lock and key until tomorrow morning."

Juror 118 wondered if Edna would examine the notes they'd taken. Probably not, he decided, but he was still glad he hadn't made any sketches.

Jill trudged wearily up the stairs to the third level of the parking deck. The day had been more tiring than she'd expected. As always, she held her keys at the ready and waited until she was only a few feet away from her car to click the remote door-lock control.

She slid behind the wheel and locked the doors once more, then retrieved her cell phone from the glove compartment and turned it on. Joining the slow-moving queue of vehicles leaving the parking deck, she checked the phone for messages. There were none. Next, she speed-dialed Tommy Adair's private number and, predictably, got his voice mail.

"Tommy," she said, "it's Jill. I'll be serving on a jury, not sure for how long. Probably the next few days. I can't make or receive calls during the day, but I'll check my office voice mail and email every evening. If there's anything that needs to be taken care of right away, I'll pass it on to you. Thanks. Bye."

It would be a good idea, she decided, to leave an absence-alert message on her office phone. Not that anyone would pay attention to it, of course. She still remembered returning to the office after Kevin's death and retrieving petulant messages from local businessmen demanding to know why she hadn't returned this or that urgent call.

Kevin was rarely far from her thoughts, especially with his birthday approaching. Last year, they'd celebrated a few days ahead of time because of his imminent departure for Afghanistan. It was his thirtieth birthday, an important landmark, and they'd slipped away to the plot of land where they intended to build their dream house.

"Next year," Kevin had said, "when I get home, we need to get started on that house. And on a family, too."

Tears slid down Jill's cheeks as the memories washed over her. She drove north out of town, passing the turnoff to Juniper Ridge on the left and, on the right, the old Sorenson homestead. Most of the Sorenson land had been sold off piecemeal to Tommy Adair and other developers, but the Victorian-era farmhouse remained. It sat on a one-acre lot, looking forlorn and out of place among the bland, cookie-cutter tract houses surrounding it on every side. White or buff two-story houses predominated, with a few ranch-style homes scattered into the mix. Their roofs were either brown or charcoal gray, and shutters and trim were painted forest green or colonial blue.

As Jill passed the northernmost subdivision and approached the Cameron farm, she was seized by a sudden impulse. Instead of turning into her driveway, which was a quarter-mile beyond Camerons', she continued on past a line of evergreens to the next crossroads. She turned right at the intersection, then almost immediately right again onto a barely-visible track about a hundred feet long.

She stopped the engine and got out of the car. The air was chilly even though the sun was still up, so she reached into the back seat for her all-weather coat and put it on. Stepping carefully to avoid soiling her high-heeled shoes, she made her way to the little wooden bench Kevin had placed there three summers ago. This had been their special spot to come and talk, away from Jessica's hovering presence, and to dream. The bench was green with moss, but the coat was washable so Jill sat down on it anyway. Hugging herself for warmth, she listened to the breeze whispering through the evergreens. The deciduous trees were just starting to leaf out, and she could hear birds chirping among the branches.

Yes, she told herself, *I will definitely build a house here.* It might not be exactly the house she and Kevin had planned on, and she wouldn't have him to share it with, but she would still build. She'd picked out one of the Juniper Ridge villas to rent in the meantime and would move into it as soon as she was done with jury duty.

Startled by a flash of movement at the edge of her peripheral vision, she turned to see a boy and a dog standing a few yards away. She had been so lost in thought that she hadn't heard them approach.

"Hello, Mrs. McKinnon."

She recognized the boy as Ethan Cameron. He had his mother's coloring, with soft dark hair that fell untidily over his ears, and although he seemed small for his age—around twelve, if she remembered correctly—his hands and feet looked too large for the rest of him. He was on the cusp of adolescence and would most likely experience a growth spurt soon. An image of her young half-brothers flashed into her mind. She kept in touch with them through occasional emails, but she hadn't seen them in several years. *Maybe someday,* she thought wistfully.

"Hello, Ethan." She looked at the dog, which was of indeterminate breed and had a thick, brindle-colored coat. It boldly returned her gaze, its eyes golden brown and oddly unsettling. She remembered Skipper, the Camerons' ancient terrier mix, but this dog was unfamiliar to her. "I haven't met your dog. Have you had it long?"

"Ever since we had Skipper put to sleep back in January. Mom hated to do it because she'd had him forever, even before she married Dad. But he was seventeen, and the vet said..." The boy's voice quavered and threatened to break, drawing a worried glance from the dog. "Anyway," he went on, "she couldn't stand not having a dog around, so she went over to the Humane Society and got Rowdy. He's only a year old, so he should be with us for a long time."

"Is that his name? Rowdy? What breed is he?"

"Don't know. The vet told us he's got some chow, for sure. See the shape of his head and the way his tail curls up over his back? And he's got black spots on his tongue, too. But he's got ears like a collie. The vet called him an all-American."

"Well, he's a very handsome fellow," Jill said with a smile, but she didn't try to approach the dog. She guessed that he weighed close to fifty pounds, and his eyes were still fixed on her face. She remembered reading somewhere that if a dog tried to stare you down, you should break off eye contact and keep your distance.

As if he'd read her mind, Ethan said, "He looks kinda scary, but he's really friendly." He tweaked the leash he held and moved toward Jill, the dog obediently following. Reaching into his pocket, the boy removed a dog biscuit and handed it to her. "Here, give him this."

The dog had sat back on his haunches and was regarding Jill intently. "He's learned he has to sit to get it," Ethan said proudly. "Now go ahead and give it to him. He'll be nice."

"Good boy," Jill murmured. "Nice Rowdy." As she extended her hand she noticed the dog's large white teeth and wondered if he would devour a few of her fingers along with the treat; but he took it from her gently, almost delicately. After he had swallowed it he fixed his eyes on her expectantly, making a rumbling noise in his throat.

"It sounds almost like he's growling," Ethan said, "but he's not. That's just the noise he makes when he wants to play. He loves to run around and act crazy. That's why we named him Rowdy."

Jill scratched behind the dog's ears, noticing for the first time the patch of white beneath his chin as he pushed his head against her hand. Despite his strange amber eyes, he no longer seemed the least bit threatening. "He's a lovely dog. Were the two of you out for a walk?"

"Well…" Suddenly aware that Jill might think he was trespassing, Ethan hastened to explain. "I'm working on a merit badge for Scouts. The Nature badge. And since there's a lot of trees and ground cover, and nobody lives here, I thought this might be a good place to watch for birds and squirrels and stuff. If that's okay with you," he added anxiously.

"Of course it is. But aren't you afraid Rowdy will scare the squirrels away?"

"Oh, I won't usually bring him with me. Today I was just trying to find good spots to look for plants and animals. Anyway, I should get home. It's almost time for dinner, and Mom'll be wondering where I am."

"Nice seeing you, Ethan. Tell your mother hello for me." Jill watched as they moved away, thinking how wonderful it would have been to have a son with Kevin, a son with two parents and a comfortable home out in the country. And a dog, too, if he wanted one. She wondered if Ethan's parents realized how lucky they were.

The sun was sliding toward the horizon, and she could just make out the bulky shape of her house beyond the trees that obstructed much of her view. Except it wasn't really her house, she reminded herself. It was Jessica's house, and Jessica was welcome to it.

The jurors assembled at eight-thirty the next morning in the deliberation room, where Edna was already on guard. While she didn't actually frisk them for cell phones or other electronics, Jill had the impression that she would have liked to. Once they were all present, Edna left the room. She locked the door behind her.

Jill took her assigned seat between Tracy Kahler and Courtney Singleton. The note pads they had left lying haphazardly at their places the previous afternoon were now lined up with military precision, and the pencils had been freshly sharpened. The jurors traded inconsequential pleasantries while they waited for Edna to return.

They heard a key in the lock some five minutes later. "Court is in session," Edna bawled, and took her place at the head of the procession leading them to the courtroom.

The trial resumed quickly and with few formalities. Detective Scott Allison was recalled to the stand, this time to testify about his interrogation of Brian Briggs. Prompted by the Assistant State's Attorney, Allison explained that all such interviews were videotaped to ensure an accurate record was kept.

Steve Berglund could see that his opponent was practically salivating. He knew why because he'd already viewed the tapes, which portrayed his client—who steadfastly denied any wrongdoing—as arrogant, profane, and not very bright.

On the plus side, introduction of the tapes as evidence would probably eliminate any expectation that he'd put Briggs on the stand.

Conventional wisdom held that the jury always wanted to hear the accused testify in his own defense. If he didn't, it would count against him despite any instructions from the judge to the contrary. In this case, though, it was clear that there was nothing Briggs could add in the courtroom to what he'd already told the police: the sexual encounter with Katie Putnam was consensual. End of story. Besides, it would be unutterably stupid to give Phelan a chance at him. She'd be ten times rougher on him than the soft-spoken Allison had been. And if she provoked him into an outburst, the result could be disastrous.

All things considered, it was probably better to take a few lumps now and hope to score some points when Katie Putnam took the stand. Unlike Briggs, she would *have* to testify.

On the large television monitor that had been set up at the far side of the courtroom opposite the jury box, Brian Briggs was displayed in living color. Slouched low on his tailbone in a molded plastic chair beside a wooden table, he tapped one foot nervously while Allison read him his rights.

"I ain't done nothing wrong," he said, brushing his stringy dark hair out of his face. "Wha' do I need a lawyer for?"

"Do I understand that you are waiving your right to legal representation at this time?"

Briggs snorted. "Yeah, fine. You wanta get on with it?"

Allison sat down opposite Briggs and leaned forward, his forearms on the table.

"Three days ago, on the evening of October 11, you were at a party at a friend's house. You ran into Katie Putnam there. Then what happened?"

Briggs shrugged. "Nothin' much. Had a couple drinks…next thing I know, she says the girl who brought her musta left, and would I give her a ride home when I was ready to go." He shifted his position, sitting up straighter. "How come? What does *she* say happened?"

"I just want to get your side of things for now. So you left the party together?"

"Yeah, she just lives a couple blocks from me. I didn't mind giving her a ride."

"So you gave her a ride home. What happened when you got there?"

"She asked me to come in, have a drink." He paused, regarding Allison with a sly smile. "Not rocket science to figure out what that meant."

"What did it mean?"

"Oh, come on, man. *You* know. We used to live together, but I dumped her after a couple months. Anyway, I figured she wanted to get me into bed. She wanted to be my girlfriend again."

In the jury box, Jill McKinnon was both amused and disgusted by Brian Briggs' obvious belief in his own irresistibility. Nearby, juror 118 was feeling sympathetic. *Poor bastard,* he thought. *Girl leads you on, then screams bloody murder when you try and take her up on the offer. Believe me, buddy, I can identify.*

As the videotape played out, the jurors watched while Allison painstakingly evoked Briggs' account of the evening's final events. They'd had sex, Briggs said, but she had initiated it—he'd just gone along.

"Shit, man, wouldn't you?" he'd asked with a grin. "And she wanted it." Then, as if finally becoming aware of why he was being questioned about the incident, he leaned forward and glared into the detective's face. "I don't care what she says. *She wanted it.* And now I want a lawyer before I say anything else."

Assistant State's Attorney Phelan aimed the remote control toward the video setup and clicked it off.

"Detective Allison," she began, "subsequent to his arrest, Mr. Briggs has remained in custody at the Remington County Jail, is that correct?"

"Yes, ma'am. He wasn't able to make bail."

"Has he made any phone calls from the jail? Other than to his attorney, that is."

"Yes, ma'am."

"Those calls are recorded, are they not? And the inmates are aware of that fact?"

"Yes to both questions, ma'am."

At the defense table, Berglund drew a deep breath. He knew what was coming. The State was preparing to introduce the transcript of a phone call from Briggs to his mother. In it, he had described Katie Putnam in terms that Berglund could barely imagine a man saying to any woman, let alone his own mother. It was bound to have an impact on the jury.

Denise turned toward the judge. "Brief recess while we set up, please, Judge?"

"Twenty minutes." Meyerhoff banged his gavel, and Edna led the jurors out of the courtroom. When they returned, an audio system with two large speakers had replaced the video equipment.

"Portions of the tape you're about to hear aren't very clear," Denise began. "That being the case, we've provided written transcripts for your use."

She handed a sheaf of documents to Edna, who carefully counted out the correct number of copies at the end of each row of jurors. "Pass 'em down," Edna stage-whispered.

Jill accepted her copy of the transcript and began to read, barely aware of the courtroom formalities playing out before Judge Meyerhoff's bench. Then a voice boomed out of the speakers: Brian Briggs. She shifted her attention back to the beginning of the document so she could follow the printed version of his spoken words.

"You gotta get me outta here, Mom. Maybe if you go see her, you can talk her outta this shit."

"I don't know if I should do that," a female voice responded. "Wouldn't that be against the law?"

"It ain't against any law I know of. Just talk to her, tell her—"

"But if there's a trial, she's going to be a witness. I don't want to get in trouble. Wouldn't they call that witness tampering or something?"

"I don't give a shit what they call it. You tell that psycho bitch to back off, or else she'll be sorry."

"Now, Brian," his mother said in a wheedling voice, "you don't mean that."

The mom sounds smarter than the son, Jill reflected. It's like she knows she's being taped, but he doesn't. Or if he does know, he doesn't care.

"That stupid cunt is gonna cost me my job," he ranted. "I don't show up for work pretty soon, they're gonna fire my ass. I'm on thin ice over there already. And I don't have to remind you what it means if I lose my job."

"Well, yes, I know..."

"Then it's all on you. You better take care of this, or else the shit's gonna hit the fan."

"You're sure, Brian? You didn't really take advantage of her, did you?"

"Nah, no way. It's like I told you. She invited me in. No girl does that unless she expects to spread her legs. I don't care what she says, then or later."

Then or later. Jill focused on those words. Had Katie said something to him *then,* at the time of the incident? Had he known all along she didn't want sex? Jill scribbled the words on her notepad and underlined them, just in case the jurors were not allowed to keep the typed transcripts for reference.

The defendant's voice on the tape went on. "And besides, she was drunk. All that goody-two-shoes bullshit she lays down is just that. It's bullshit. She drinks like a fish and fucks like a rabbit. Now you listen to me. You need to make this go away. Otherwise you and her are *both* gonna be sorry."

After the recording ended, Denise Phelan waited a minute or two before speaking into the silence. She wanted to be sure the jurors absorbed the full force of Brian Briggs' rage, his violence, his lack of regard for anyone except himself. Then she turned to Detective Scott Allison, who was still on the stand.

"About how long after Ms. Putnam's initial 911 call did you arrive at her residence?"

"I was only a couple of miles away when Officer Williams paged me, ma'am. So I was there within five minutes of the page. That would have been about twenty minutes after the 911 call."

"I noticed that in his taped telephone conversation, the defendant told his mother that Ms. Putnam was drunk. But when you interviewed Ms. Putnam, did anything about her demeanor lead you to believe she was under the influence of alcohol or any other substance?"

"No, ma'am." Allison spoke with obvious conviction. "She definitely was not drunk. In the course of our interview, she told me she'd had two drinks at the party a couple of hours earlier. That was along with some snacks. Then she fixed one apiece for herself and Mr. Briggs after they arrived at her apartment, but she only had a sip of hers. Nothing I observed gave me any reason to doubt what she told me."

"You sound pretty confident of your judgment in that regard," Denise said with a smile.

"Yes, ma'am. Before I was promoted to Detective, I spent twelve years in uniform. During that time I conducted, I would estimate, an average of ten field sobriety tests every week."

"I see. So that's—please help me with the math, Detective."

"Five hundred a year, give or take, times twelve years, is six thousand."

"Six thousand field sobriety tests. Well, I think that makes you a pretty good judge." She turned to Berglund. "Your witness."

Berglund rose. He didn't have much to work with, but he had to make the attempt. He approached Allison and smiled. "Detective."

"Sir."

"You're convinced that Ms. Putnam was sober when you reached her apartment?"

"Yes, sir."

"Well, I bow to your expertise in that regard. Conducting six thousand field sobriety tests is an impressive accomplishment indeed."

Accustomed to the baiting of defense attorneys, Allison waited impassively.

"And yet, wasn't she described as 'incoherent' at the time of the 911 call?"

"I can't speak to someone else's description, sir. I can only tell you that by the time I arrived, she was quite coherent."

Berglund tilted his head and raised his eyebrows in an exaggerated display of surprise. "But she *was* crying hysterically, isn't that correct?"

"Sir, she wasn't crying when I got there, although I could see that she had *been* crying. I would also say that crying does not always equal hysteria."

Jill noted the gleam of a gold wedding band on the detective's left hand. *You've just scored points with every female member of the jury,* she thought. *Your wife would be proud.*

Berglund spun on his heel and walked away. "No further questions."

Denise Phelan consulted her watch. It was a few minutes after eleven o'clock. She wondered if Meyerhoff would call for a recess or an early lunch, but he did neither. Instead, he curtly instructed her to call her next witness.

"The State calls Katherine Putnam."

The double doors at the back of the courtroom swung open and Katie Putnam moved forward. She was petite and small-boned, clad in tight-fitting ivory slacks and an equally snug knit top, bright red in color, which was cut low enough to expose a generous amount of cleavage.

Denise stared. *Oh, God.* The girl had been casually but not immodestly attired during their preliminary meetings. What in the world had possessed her to dress this way today?

At the defense table, Steve Berglund barely managed to conceal his glee. He'd seen Phelan's eyes widen in shock, and, as soon as he'd registered the reason for it, he'd immediately turned his attention to the jury. Disapproval was clearly written on the faces of several jurors, particularly the older women, while the younger men were openly ogling the prosecution's main witness. Berglund's gaze swung back to Phelan. *Good luck, lady. You're gonna need it.*

Juror 118 watched as Katie Putnam stepped up onto the witness stand. *What a slut,* he thought. He was reminded of the incident up in Farleyville some years earlier, the one that could have totally screwed up his life. It probably would have without Gram's intervention—and his stepfather's clout. His eyes flicked toward Brian Briggs at the defense table. *Don't worry, pal. I've got your back.*

Denise Phelan, meanwhile, had taken a deep breath and tamped down her anger. The last thing she needed was for the girl to get rattled, and there was nothing to be done now about her dreadful choice in clothing. Smiling in what she hoped was a reassuring way, Denise approached the witness stand.

"Hello, Katie."

The girl's voice was barely audible. "Hello, Ms. Phelan."

"Would you please state your full name for the record?"

"Katherine Marie Putnam." She was twenty-three but looked younger, with round blue eyes and a childlike face that was in stark contrast to her voluptuous body.

"I would like you to please tell the court about your relationship with Brian Briggs."

"He was my boyfriend for a couple of months last spring."

"By 'last spring,' you mean…?"

"Most of March, all of April, and the beginning of May. This was last year."

"I see. And was it an exclusive relationship?"

"Well, it was supposed to be. He moved in with me." Katie's voice had grown stronger.

"Supposed to be," Denise repeated. "But was it?"

"It was for me. Not for him, though. He wasn't working back then, but I was. And sometimes when I was at work he'd bring other girls to our apartment. *My* apartment, I mean. When I found out about it, I told him he had to move out. I said it was okay if he wanted to see other girls, but he couldn't do it while he was staying at my place."

"I see. And how did he react?"

"He was mad. He called me names."

"What kind of names?"

"He called me a whore," Katie said in a tremulous voice. "And he called me a stupid, selfish bitch."

Denise took a step back and folded her arms across her chest. "Let me see if I understand this. Mr. Briggs moved in with you. During the time he lived with you, you didn't see anyone else. Only him. Is that correct?"

"Yes."

"But he saw other girls during this time. Is that also correct?"

"Yes."

"So *he* was the one who cheated, not you, but he called *you* those names?"

"Yes."

"Hmm. And after he moved out, did he remain angry with you?"

"Yes, for a while. He used to hang around and watch me. When I left for work, when I came home, a lot of times I'd see him just watching me. And if he knew I saw him, he'd flip me off."

"I'm sorry?"

"You know, flip me the bird." Katie raised her hand as if to illustrate, but, to Denise's enormous relief, stopped short of extending her middle finger.

"And how long did that go on?"

"Most of the summer. But then I stopped seeing him around, and I heard he got a job at the truck terminal. I was happy for him, too. Even if I was done with him, I was still glad for him to catch a break."

"So after that, when was the next time you saw Brian?"

"At the party. It was at a friend's place, someone we both knew. So it turned out he was there, too, and we started talking. I asked about his job, and he said it wasn't going too good because his boss was a jerk. Only that's not the word he used. And I said something like, you know, the boss usually is a jerk no matter where you work. But you just have to let it roll off and not bother you, and you'll get along a lot better that way. And he was like, 'That's easy for you to say. You get along with everybody.' And I'm like, 'Yeah, but I work at it.' So we talked about work for a while longer, and how it might help if he tried being nicer. And then pretty soon he sees me kind of looking around, and he asks me who I'm looking for. And I told him I got a ride to the party with a friend of mine, but she must've hooked up with some guy and left because I hadn't seen her for a while. Then he said he was back living with his mom again in the trailer park next to my apartment complex, and he had her car. So he could give me a ride home if I wanted."

"And you accepted?"

"Sure. I was tired because I worked all day, and he seemed like he wasn't mad at me any more. Then on the way home, I was telling him about this training course we had at work on how to handle irate customers. I thought it might help him deal with his boss when he was being a jerk. And it just seemed natural to ask him in for a drink so I could finish telling him about it. I never thought—I never meant—" Katie faltered to a stop, raising both hands in a helpless gesture.

Jill McKinnon, in the jury box, was amazed at Katie's total lack of judgment but convinced of her sincerity. Nearby, juror 118 was evaluating the girl's testimony in a completely different light. *What an incredible crock of shit. She's a lying little tramp.*

"You never meant what?" Denise pressed.

"I never meant it as some kind of invitation. I didn't want to sleep with him."

"Even though you had in the past?"

"Sure, when we were together, but I was way past that."

"Can you tell us why?"

"Because all he ever did was use me. He stayed at my place and never helped with the rent. He ate my food and never bought any himself. And of course there were the other girls." For the first time that morning, she looked directly at Brian Briggs, who refused to meet her eyes. "And I knew he was never going to change. If there was something I could do to help him in his job, to be a friend to him, then fine. But that's all it was, because I was *totally* over him."

Denise noticed Judge Meyerhoff glancing at his watch. He was getting ready to recess for lunch, and before that happened she wanted to reinforce the jury's image of Katie as a victim instead of a clueless bimbo.

"So you invited him in. You fixed drinks. Then what happened?"

"I came in from the kitchen with a drink in each hand. Rum and Coke. I put them on the coffee table. He was sitting on the couch. I sat down beside him and reached for my drink. And then he grabbed me." She took a deep breath and lowered her head, as though to compose herself before going on.

Denise closed her eyes for a moment. *Recess for lunch, Judge. Come on. Do it now.*

As if he'd heard her, Meyerhoff spoke. "I think this would be a good time to take a lunch break. Recess until one-thirty." He banged his gavel and exited the courtroom.

Edna had been babysitting juries for more years than she cared to count, and she could tell by the expressions on their faces—especially the women's—that they were bursting to talk about what they had seen and heard that morning.

"I would like to remind all of you," she said in her most authoritative voice, "there is to be absolutely *no* discussion of the case at this time. You'll have plenty of opportunity to talk about it when the judge sends it to you for deliberation. And like I told you yesterday, if nature calls while we're in the restaurant then you'll just have to hold it until we get back here. So I recommend that you use the rest room here before we go to lunch. Even if it's just to wash your hands."

Juror 118 obediently got in line to use the men's toilet. There wouldn't be anything to write down this time, no need for secret notes about Katie Putnam. He already had all the information he needed about her. He glanced around at the other jurors, whose faces he had read as easily as Edna had. Maybe it was time to start making notes about *them*, especially the three young, unmarried female jurors. He knew their names, but that was all. Now it was time to find out more.

He fell into step behind Jill McKinnon and Courtney Singleton, close enough to overhear what they said without giving the appearance of eavesdropping. He'd observed that women were usually less guarded in their speech when talking among themselves than when conversing with men.

The current topic of conversation was of little interest to him, though. They were talking about food, specifically the new items recently added to the menu at Chez Marie. His attention had begun to wander when, just before they reached the entrance to Pinky's Café, Courtney made reference to her working hours at the restaurant. Finally! Some information he might actually be able to use.

He was amused to see Derrick—one of two black men on the jury—pulling the same stunt as he had the day before, slipping into the café just behind Courtney and grabbing the seat beside her. Meanwhile, Jill had taken a few steps in the other direction and was now engaged in conversation with a short, fifty-something woman with frosted hair.

Jill intrigued him. He'd already noticed that, unlike the other women on the jury—especially the older ones, who blabbed interminably—Jill encouraged her tablemates to talk about themselves while revealing nothing about herself. He turned his attention to Amy Morrison, the third of the young female jurors. She was blonde, a little pudgy, and, he guessed, about twenty-five. She was sitting across the table from him and down two places, between Rob Lynch, the middle-aged white guy, and a round grandmotherly type, Mary Jane Dunn.

Directly across from him, on Mary Jane's other side, sat Cheryl Lemay. She was loud, opinionated, and nearing sixty. Beyond her were the two Latinas. They had initially been conversing in English; but when they lapsed into Spanish, Edna quickly reprimanded them.

"English only, please, ladies. I need to be sure you're not discussing the case between yourselves."

One of them—Ernestina Castaneda, the alternate—gave Edna an angry look, but Lucrecia Zuñiga smiled apologetically. "Sorry," she said.

He kept his head down, pretending to study the menu, while keeping his ears open for any interesting conversational tidbits from the younger women. He was stuck near the bottom of the table among the other men, sandwiched between Derrick Reese and Aaron Allen, the African-American alternate. But if he listened carefully, he might pick up something on the way back to the courthouse.

He was unaware of Coach Dio, watching the jurors from his usual place near the cash register. Coach had read in that morning's *Drummond Observer* that of the two cases for which a jury had been selected, one had been resolved through a plea bargain. This, therefore, must be the jury for the sexual assault case, events of which had been described in the dispassionate style of the *Observer*'s veteran courthouse reporter. It was interesting, the coach reflected, that the jury's lunchtime seating arrangement seemed to be coalescing into its demographic components.

As Dio observed the jurors' interactions, his attention was drawn to one individual in particular. While he couldn't remember the name—although he was sure it would come to him, probably just before he fell asleep tonight—he clearly recalled the unpleasant, hulking kid who had tried out for football several years earlier. Dio had cut him from the team almost immediately. While the youngster had size going for him, he'd had no aptitude for either the game itself or the teamwork it required. And, judging by the facial expressions and gestures Dio noted today, the guy's personality hadn't changed much.

Dio's gaze slid over the remaining jurors. While he didn't recognize any of the others, as a matter of habit he scrutinized each of them in turn. They were an interesting mix, and he would love to be a fly on the wall when their deliberations began.

When the trial resumed after lunch, Denise Phelan led her principal witness into the next phase of her testimony: describing the actual assault.

"You told us you made two drinks, brought them into the living room and set them on the coffee table. And when you sat down beside the defendant, he grabbed you. Then what?"

"He pushed me down so I was laying on my back. He put one hand on my shoulder and pushed up my skirt with the other. Then he pulled down my pants and laid on top of me." She paused and took a deep breath.

"Did you say anything to him?"

"I asked him what he was doing."

"And he said…?"

"He laughed and said, 'Like you don't know.' He was wearing jeans, and he must've unzipped them while I was in the kitchen and pulled his sweatshirt down to hide it. Because when he pulled up his sweatshirt he already had it out."

"By 'it' you mean…?"

"His cock." She flushed. "I mean, his penis. It was already hard. But when I told him I didn't want sex, he got mad and asked me what kind of game I was trying to play. And I told him it wasn't a game and to get off me, but he wouldn't. And when I tried to sit up and get out from under him, he made a fist like he was going to hit me. And I said, 'No, don't.'"

"Did he respond in any way when you told him, 'No, don't'?"

"He told me to be quiet."

"Were those his exact words?"

"No."

"What *were* his exact words?"

"What he really said was, 'Shut up, you fuckin' bitch.' And I started to cry. By that time he was already inside me and going at it pretty hard. He was hurting me."

In the jury box, Jill McKinnon shifted her gaze from the witness to the defendant, who, during most of Katie's testimony, had been staring at the floor in front of the defense table. At that moment, though, he lifted his head and looked at the girl with such loathing that Jill was startled.

"Did you tell him he was hurting you?"

"Yeah. I said something like, 'That hurts, cut that out.'"

"And he responded how?"

"He kept saying, 'You like it. You know you like it.' And I was saying, 'No, no, stop,' but he started doing it even harder. And then he came."

"By that you mean he reached orgasm?"

"Yes. And then he just laid there on top of me, and he was really heavy. I asked him again to get off me. I asked him a couple of times, and he finally got up and went into the bathroom."

"Did he say anything to you at that point?"

"He said I had a filthy cunt and he had to wash my stink off of himself."

It was clear to Jill by that point why the judge had warned the jury to expect graphic testimony. Rather than shock, though, she felt only sympathy for the girl on the witness stand.

"Just so we're clear," Denise said, "were those his exact words, as best you recall, or are you paraphrasing?"

"Those were his exact words. I'll never forget him saying that to me."

Denise paused momentarily, giving the jury an opportunity to absorb what the witness had just said. "All right. And then what did he do?"

"He came out of the bathroom, picked up his drink from the coffee table and chugged it down. Then he left."

"Did he say anything else to you?"

"No. He just walked out and slammed the door."

"And what did you do?"

Katie brushed a strand of hair back from her forehead. "Nothing for a few minutes. Then…this might sound weird, but I picked up his empty glass and went to the sink and washed it. I took a sip of my own drink, but I felt like I might throw up so I dumped it down the sink. Then I went into my bedroom and took the blanket off my bed and wrapped myself up in it. I was so cold I started to shake."

"Was that when you called 911?"

"Yes. But after I dialed, I remember thinking it was a stupid thing to do. So I hung up."

"Why did you think it was stupid?"

"Because it didn't matter. Nobody would care. And besides, the police have better stuff to do."

"And do you still feel that way?"

Katie tilted her head, considering. "Sometimes. But most of the time I don't."

"Why not?"

"Because he had no right to do that to me. He had *no right*."

"Thank you, Katie," Denise said quietly. "Nothing further."

Steve Berglund stood and approached slowly, a slight smile on his face. "Good afternoon, Ms. Putnam," he said respectfully.

She regarded him warily. "Good afternoon."

"I wonder if you could tell us a little bit more about the party. You said you went with a female friend, is that correct?"

"Yes."

"And you testified that your friend hooked up with some guy and left? Is that also correct?"

Denise shot to her feet. "Objection. That's not what she said."

Before the judge could rule, Berglund raised his hands in a gesture of surrender. "I'll rephrase. You said you hadn't seen your friend for a while, and you *thought* she had hooked up with some guy and left. Is that your recollection?"

"Yes."

"Okay. Now, for those members of the jury who are of a different generation, it might help if we define the term 'hook up.' It's my understanding that 'hooking up' means finding someone to have sex with. Is that generally correct, or do I have it wrong?"

Oh, crap, Denise thought. She'd been hoping Berglund hadn't picked up on Katie's use of the term "hook up." But he had, and because she had said it he was entitled to ask her to define it.

"Well, I guess that's what some people mean by it. But I only meant that maybe she met up with someone she knew and they decided to go somewhere else."

"I see. So is that why you two young ladies went to the party? To find guys to hook up with?"

Denise was on her feet again.

"Withdrawn," Berglund said quickly. "Although by your own definition, that *is* what happened. You met up with Brian Briggs, and then you left with him. Isn't that true?"

"Yes, but..."

"But?" Berglund inquired politely.

"I didn't go to the party to hook up with anyone. I only wanted to see my friends and have a drink or two. Just relax a little."

"Of course," Berglund said, although his mocking tone of voice and condescending smile made it clear that he didn't believe her. "Now, I do have just one or two more questions about the evening in question. You testified that the relationship you had with Mr. Briggs last year ended because you were unhappy with the way he treated you. You said he failed to contribute to household expenses. Correct?"

"Yes, that's right."

"You also said he had other girlfriends while sharing your living quarters. Correct?"

"Yes."

"And that he seemed to be angry with you for at least a while afterwards. Correct?"

"Yes." Katie, suspecting a trap, was beginning to sound apprehensive.

"And yet, after all this, you invited him into your home for a session of career counseling?" Berglund's facial expression and tone of voice telegraphed amused disbelief.

"Yes."

"Because you still wanted to be his friend, I believe you said." Berglund crossed his arms and tilted his head. "I hope you'll forgive me, Ms. Putnam, but I find that hard to understand. A man treats you badly, at least you *say* he treated you badly, and yet you still want to be his friend? How in the world can that be?"

Katie looked down, twisting her hands in her lap.

"Please explain, Ms. Putnam. I'm sure I'm not the only one who doesn't understand. Why would you want to have a person like that as a friend?"

Mutely, the girl shook her head.

"Answer the question, Ms. Putnam," the judge prompted her.

Finally, she looked up. "I don't know," she whispered.

Berglund cupped his hand behind his ear. "I'm sorry, but I can't hear you."

"I don't know," she said more loudly. "I just don't know."

"May I suggest a reason? Maybe you find that attractive in a man. Some women do, you know. Maybe you *enjoy* being treated badly." He approached and stood very close to her. "Maybe it turns you on. Maybe Brian Briggs had it right, and you *were* playing a game with him. Is that the way it was?"

"Objection," Denise shouted, but Steve Berglund had already turned his back on the witness and was striding toward the defense table.

"No more questions," he flung over his shoulder.

Denise Phelan was nearly beside herself with fury. She was so enraged that she was barely aware of the judge dismissing Katie Putnam and declaring a twenty-minute recess. Breathing deeply to calm herself, Denise turned and saw Katie making her way to the back of the courtroom where Dawn Martin was waiting.

Dawn, Denise's contact at the Women's Justice Coalition, had been there most of the day to provide moral support for Katie, take her to lunch, and make sure she returned to the courthouse on time. Catching Dawn's eye now, Denise could only shake her head and shrug. With any luck, the jurors would see Berglund's last question for what it was: an outrageous attempt to shift the blame from perpetrator to victim. As Denise watched, Dawn wrapped an arm around Katie's shoulders and led her out of the courtroom.

Denise slipped away to the ladies' room. She found her reflection startling. Her cheeks burned bright pink, and her pale blue eyes still blazed with anger. She splashed cold water on her face, then blotted it dry with paper towels and touched up her lipstick. *Focus!* She exhorted herself. You can still put away that bastard Briggs, but you have to *focus*.

The State's final witness was Tiffany Cruse. A large, self-assured woman in her thirties, she was the department manager of the discount store where Katie Putnam worked selling children's clothing.

"Ms. Cruse," Denise began, "on the afternoon of October 13, did an individual approach you and ask if Katie Putnam was in the store at that time?"

"Yes."

"And is that individual present in the courtroom now?"

"Yes, he is. That's him right there." She gestured toward Brian Briggs.

"Let the record show that the witness indicated the defendant. And was Ms. Putnam present at that time?"

"No, she wasn't working that day."

"And you communicated that to him?"

"Yes, I did."

"What was his reaction?"

"He said," Cruse related calmly, "that I should tell her to keep her lip zipped if she knew what was good for her."

"And how would you describe his demeanor when he made this statement to you?"

"Angry. Aggressive. He had his hands balled up into fists. I told him we did not tolerate threats and he should leave, or I'd call the police. He mumbled something I couldn't make out, but he did leave at that point."

"I see. Now, you're sure about the date? It was October 13?"

"Positive. It's the anniversary of an important event in my life."

"I see," Denise said again. "Now, at this time were you aware of what had taken place two nights before at Ms. Putnam's apartment?"

"No, I'd had no reason to speak with her. She wasn't scheduled to work until the fourteenth."

"When she returned to work the following day, did you tell her about the incident at the store?"

"Of course I did. First of all, there's always a concern when an employee's personal life affects the store in any way. Because obviously, we don't want people coming in and making a scene. And if there was any kind of danger, to our customers or to Katie personally, I needed to know about it."

"Quite so. And how did Ms. Putnam respond?"

"She told me about what happened the night of the eleventh. Well, actually it was the morning of the twelfth. She thought the police might be planning to pick him up for questioning."

"Which, in fact, they did," Denise said. "Although according to the record, that was not until"—she made a show of consulting her notes—"the morning of October 14. So clearly, Mr. Briggs was already anticipating that possibility." Then quickly, before Berglund could object, Denise turned to her witness. "Thank you. I have nothing further."

Steve Berglund had already decided against cross-examining Cruse. It would serve no purpose except to draw additional attention to his client's bad temper. Instead, he would treat her testimony as unimportant. He looked up and smiled briefly.

"No questions."

Judge Meyerhoff looked at Denise. "Miss Phelan?"

"The State rests, your honor."

"Mr. Berglund?"

"Defense rests."

The judge glanced at the large clock at the back of the courtroom. The time was just after 3:30 in the afternoon. To nobody's surprise, he adjourned for the day after firmly instructing the jury not to discuss the case or read any news items about it. Closing arguments would be heard the next morning.

Back in the jury room, Jill shrugged into her all-weather coat, picked up her purse, and left the building as quickly as she could. A chilly drizzle had begun to fall, and she hunched her shoulders as she crossed the courtyard to the parking deck. She'd already climbed the first flight of stairs when she heard the street door bang open and a male voice calling out to her from below.

"Jill? Could you wait a minute, please?"

She stopped and looked back. Brett Petersen was hurrying to catch up with her. "I thought maybe I could walk up with you," he said. "What level are you on?"

"Three."

"Me, too." He followed her up the second flight. "You can't be too careful, you know. People sometimes hang out in these stairwells."

"So I've heard. But I try to watch out."

"Yeah. Um…I know this might not be a good time to ask, considering some of the stuff we heard today, but…well, I was wondering if maybe I could call you some time? Just for coffee or lunch or something."

They were nearing the top of the third flight of steps. When they reached the landing, Jill stopped and turned to face him. While he seemed nice enough, she didn't want to encourage him. On the other hand, he'd only suggested coffee or lunch. It was hardly an indecent proposal.

"I have kind of a crazy schedule," she said after a moment's hesitation. "So it might be better if I call you. Do you have a card?"

"I'm not important enough to have business cards." He reached into his shirt pocket and pulled out a pen and a pad of brightly-colored sticky notes. He hated the gaudy things—he much preferred the plain yellow ones—but his female coworkers at the bank insisted on them. And it was cheaper to use the bank's than to buy his own. He smiled apologetically as he handed her a neon green sticky note on which he had written his name and phone number. "Here. Very professional, huh?"

Jill couldn't help smiling in return. "It's fine." She opened her purse and dropped the sticky note into it, then removed her car keys. She pushed open the door to the third level and hurried toward the haven of her Impala, only a few yards away.

"I'll see you tomorrow," she called over her shoulder.

Brett Petersen kept walking toward the far end of the deck. When Jill had backed out of her parking spot and turned the corner out of sight, he reversed direction. Returning to the stairwell, he ascended to the fourth level where his own car was parked.

He wondered if she really would call him. He knew it wasn't likely, because he'd seen her brief hesitation and knew what it meant. She was probably just being polite when she asked for his number. She had class, he could tell. There was the way she dressed, for starters: conservative and ladylike. The beige suit she'd worn yesterday was nice, but he really preferred today's gray slacks and pale yellow sweater. Yes, he really hoped she'd call him, although it was hard to believe she'd be interested in someone like him. Still, you couldn't blame a guy for trying…could you?

Juror 118 tossed his keys onto the kitchen table along with the contents of his mailbox and went to the refrigerator for a Pepsi. He retrieved the mail—a solicitation from a local charity and his cable television bill—and carried it and the soda upstairs, where he sat down at his computer and turned it on. While he waited for it to boot up he fed the fund-raising letter into the small crosscut shredder beside his desk.

He was always punctual about paying his bills. It was an important part of the facade he'd cultivated in recent years: quiet, good-humored, dependable, the last guy in the world who'd cause any kind of trouble. He smiled, recalling how completely his grandmother and all her old-biddy friends had been taken in. For a couple of them, their mistake had turned out to be fatal.

He logged onto his bank's website and clicked the bill-pay tab. Selecting the appropriate payee, he entered the amount and clicked "submit." When the confirmation number was displayed he made a note of it on the cable bill and tucked it away in a file drawer. Then he shredded the empty envelope.

His rented townhouse had two bedrooms, and he'd converted this one, the smaller of the two, into his office. As he'd learned from Chad, he kept everything neat, well organized and sanitized. That was what the shredder was for. That was also why every scrap of unneeded paper went into it, creating mounds of chaff to obscure the few mangled bits of actual information. Not that it was necessary, at least not yet, but a person had to think ahead. If he formed the habit now of taking precautions, he'd be less likely to make a sloppy mistake later.

The computer, for example: he used it to manage his finances, check the news and weather, and order movies online (crime dramas and suspense films, but never porn even though he enjoyed it; it wouldn't fit his new persona). He occasionally used the computer for email, too, although he was vigilant in keeping his electronic correspondence innocuous. Nobody from his old life had his new email address, not even Chad. He and Chad now kept in touch only by phone. Not via his full-featured mobile, which he used in place of a land line, but the other one: the prepaid throw-away.

He also avoided social networking sites, partly to guard his own privacy but mostly because he'd never cared about other people, never felt the urge to mingle. Everything he needed for recreation was right here in his townhouse. He had a treadmill and some free weights for keeping in shape and a wide-screen plasma television for watching his movies and favorite shows. Outside of work he was totally his own man, with no need to ask anybody else what they wanted to do, or eat, or watch. "Lonely" was not a concept he understood.

He logged off the bank website and pulled up the online version of the *Drummond Observer*. Skimming through it, he came to an item posted just minutes earlier about the Briggs trial. Disregarding the judge's instructions, he began to read it.

The story was brief and antiseptic by most readers' standards, but he found it so heavily slanted toward the prosecution that he could barely stand to finish it. Why hadn't the writer described how the so-called victim had shown up dressed like the tart she obviously was? And claiming she'd invited the poor guy home out of "friendship" to offer him "career advice"? How lame was that! She was no better than a whore. No, she was actually worse. With a whore it was a simple business transaction, not some sick game that could land your ass in jail.

He'd already decided that he would, if necessary, prevent a conviction through an unwavering "not guilty" vote, even if the other eleven jurors voted to convict. But now he realized that he wanted to do more. He wanted to punish the trashy bitch. Just like he would've punished that fat little slut up in Farleyville, except his mother and her prick of a husband had packed him off to Gram's house in Milwaukee before he'd had the chance. He'd promised himself that someday he'd track her down and shut her up permanently, but at present he had other priorities.

He shut down the computer and opened the file drawer on the left-hand side of his desk. He pulled out the chart he'd drawn from memory the previous evening, the one that showed the layout of Katie Putnam's apartment. He'd copied the address at the bottom of the page, then shredded the sticky note on which the information had originally been written. With the sketch in hand, he headed down the stairs and grabbed his car keys.

He returned an hour and a half later. He'd thoroughly acquainted himself with the area surrounding Katie Putnam's apartment complex, paying close attention to entrances, exits, side streets, and the best locations to sit and watch her unit with minimal risk of being observed himself. The chart he'd drawn was now superfluous. He ran it through the shredder.

A few miles to the north, Jill was sitting in the farmhouse kitchen with Jessica. Jill had stopped by her office on her way home and spent an hour retrieving messages and returning calls. By the time she'd arrived home, Jessica had had dinner on the table: homemade rolls and a hearty broccoli salad. Probably because of Jill's imminent move to Juniper Ridge, conversation was even more strained than usual.

Jill spoke into the heavy silence. "Delicious salad. What's in it?"

"Just what you see," Jessica responded, sounding impatient. "Sliced broccoli, bacon bits, chopped red onion, a handful of raisins. The dressing's mayonnaise with some sugar and vinegar stirred in. By the way," she added after a brief pause, "I saw an article in this morning's paper about the trial. I saved it for you."

"I appreciate that, but I'm not supposed to read it. No need to, anyway, since I was there. I know what happened."

"Well, I was hoping you might at least be able to tell me if what's in the paper is accurate or not."

Jill sighed. "Sorry, but I can't help you there. I'm not supposed to read *or* talk about it." She stood up and carried her dirty plate and silverware over to the sink. She noticed that Jessica was having a large second helping of the salad and had already consumed several rolls slathered with butter. The older woman, always stocky, had gained a lot of weight since Kevin's death. *Emotional eating*, Jill reflected. *Too bad she can't find some other way of consoling herself. But heaven knows, she'd never listen to any advice I tried to give her.* Returning to the table, she gestured towards Jessica's plate.

"Are you done? I can take that if you are."

"Not yet, no."

"Okay, well, I should go on upstairs and get a little more packing done. I'll finish clearing up the kitchen later." She had already reached the bottom of the stairs when she heard Jessica's voice behind her.

"Will you be taking the truck?"

"To move, you mean? Sure, I was planning to use it this weekend to haul my stuff down to the new place."

"What I meant was, were you planning on keeping it at your house?" Jessica's voice began to take on a threatening tone. "Because if you were—"

"Oh, for crying out loud." The three-year-old Ford F-150 had been Kevin's ride, but it was registered to McKinnon Farm, Inc. "Of course I won't keep it. I'll bring it back here as soon as I'm done with it." Without waiting for Jessica's response, Jill continued up the stairs to the upstairs hallway. Then she stopped, gasping in shock.

The hallway walls, which had been lined with family photographs just this morning, were now nearly bare. Pale rectangles marked where pictures of Kevin—as a baby, a little boy, an adolescent—had been so proudly displayed. Gone, too, were Kevin's awards from his years of involvement in 4-H and Future Farmers of America. All that remained were the few recent photos that included Jill.

She rushed into her bedroom. Surely Jessica wouldn't have dared…! Thank God, the framed picture of Kevin in his uniform still stood on her bedside table. But Jessica had her own copy of it, so she would have had no need to take Jill's. Struck by another thought, Jill picked up the album that lay nearby. She and Kevin had begun putting it together shortly after their marriage. Taking a deep breath, she opened it and leafed through it, only to find that many of the snapshots had been removed: all the early ones of Kevin, some of which had included his parents as well.

Jill sat down on the bed, struggling for calm. Jessica was becoming unbalanced, she truly was. The business about the truck was mere bitchiness—nothing unusual for Jessica these days—but the removal of the pictures from the upstairs hallway was more troubling. And the outright theft of the pictures from Jill's room could not be tolerated.

Jill walked down the stairs, through the living room and past Jessica, who still sat at the kitchen table wearing a belligerent expression. Jill went straight to the wall phone, picked it up, and consulted the emergency contact list that hung on the side of the refrigerator a few feet away. She found the number she wanted and punched it in. Only when the party at the other end answered did Jill fix her eyes unwaveringly on Jessica.

"Louise?" she said. "This is Jill McKinnon. I hope I didn't catch you at a bad time, but I need to ask you for a very important favor."

Jessica's eyes widened at the mention of Louise's name, but she said nothing.

"I need you to help my mother-in-law get copies made of some photographs she has. She knows which ones. Go with her if necessary. I'll pay all the costs involved, but it's very important for this to be done as soon as possible."

Louise agreed, as Jill had been sure she would. After ending the call, she copied Louise's number onto a note pad. Then she went and stood in front of Jessica, who refused to meet her eyes.

"I never would have taken the pictures from the upstairs hallway," Jill said. "But the others were mine. You can have the copies, but I want the originals back."

20

At a few minutes past nine the next morning, following the judge's reminder that closing arguments were not to be considered evidence, Denise Phelan faced the jury. She took nearly an hour to summarize the state's case against Brian Briggs, buttressing her argument with a carefully organized PowerPoint presentation. As she advanced the slides and addressed each bullet point in turn, she spoke with authority and conviction. She was careful, though, to avoid appearing overly emotional. She had learned very early in her career that while men could get away with that, women—if they wanted to be taken seriously—could not.

It was ten o'clock when she pointed the remote control at the video screen and turned it off. She approached the jury and stood before them, a small figure in a bright red suit.

"Here's the bottom line," she concluded. "This was *not* consensual sex. No obvious physical injury? Doesn't matter. No evidence of a knock-down, drag-out struggle? Doesn't matter. It doesn't matter, ladies and gentlemen, because the State of Illinois does not require a victim to risk life or limb by resisting or fighting back if an assailant uses force. Or even if he *threatens* to use force. All that matters—the *only* thing that matters—is that Katie Putnam said no. She said no, and Brian Briggs refused to take no for an answer. Instead, he used his much greater size, his much greater strength, to force himself physically on Katie Putnam. Logic requires a guilty verdict." She paused briefly and looked directly into each juror's eyes, challenging them to disagree. "And *justice* requires a guilty verdict. I know that, and you know it, too."

As Denise returned to her seat she was satisfied that she had given this case her very best. Whether it was good enough remained to be seen. She wasn't overly concerned about Steve Berglund's closing argument. It would undoubtedly be a recap of his opening statement alleging a consensual encounter between his client and a game-playing bimbo.

No, Berglund's closing didn't worry her that much. What really bothered her was what she had seen when she looked into the jurors' eyes at the conclusion of her own summation. While most of the jurors had telegraphed agreement, a few had not. One had appeared skeptical, another downright hostile. The gaze of a third had met hers with disturbing opacity. She wished she could get inside their heads and know what they were thinking.

Denise sat motionless as Berglund delivered his closing argument, which lasted barely fifteen minutes. His efforts to portray Brian Briggs as the victim in the case—disadvantaged and misunderstood, who might be full of bluster but wouldn't hurt a fly—filled her with disgust. She watched the jury intently, trying to see if any of them might actually buy the load of manure that Berglund was peddling, but it was impossible to tell from where she sat.

Following Berglund's closing argument, Judge Meyerhoff dismissed the alternate jurors and sent the remaining twelve to the jury room to begin their deliberations. Denise Phelan stared at their retreating backs, willing them to return a "guilty" verdict. And quickly.

Nearby, her opponent snapped his briefcase shut. He stood up and took a step in her direction.

"Nice job," he said. "I mean that sincerely. Considering what you had to work with."

She swallowed an unpleasant retort and responded calmly. "Thank you. But of course, what I had to work with was a guilty defendant."

Berglund shrugged. "Maybe, and maybe not. It's all up to the jury now." Smiling, he turned away. "See you soon."

Inside Jury Room #1, Rob Lynch—a 54-year-old customer service manager for the local electric company—was quickly selected as foreman, just as Coach Dio Pappas had foreseen.

Lynch immediately took charge. "What we should probably do first is get a sense of where we all stand right now. I'd like each of you to please tear a piece of paper off your notepad and write either 'guilty' or 'not guilty' or 'undecided.' Then fold it up and pass it over to me."

As the slips of paper were pushed in his direction he gathered them into a pile, waiting until he had everyone's attention before unfolding and reading each of them aloud. Lucrecia Zuñiga, who sat next to him, tallied the votes as they were announced and then turned her scratchpad so he could read it.

"Eight guilty," he announced. "Two not guilty. And two undecided. I think," he went on after a moment's thought, "it might be helpful to hear from the undecided folks first and see what their thoughts are. Anyone want to jump in?"

Tracy Kahler, the ultrasound technician, tentatively raised a hand. "I will," she said. "It's a very serious charge, sexual assault. It could put this guy in prison for a long time, and it seems like…well, it seems like the girl wasn't hurt all that much. I mean, she wasn't beaten up or anything. She didn't get pregnant or catch an STD—"

"That we know of," an older female juror put in.

"Well, still. The episode—"

"The crime, you mean," the other woman interrupted. Her name tag identified her as Cheryl Lemay.

"Ms. Lemay," Rob Lynch said gently, "Please let Ms. Kahler finish making her point. We'll all get the chance to be heard here."

The older woman sat back and folded her arms across her chest, her lips puckered disapprovingly. "Fine," she said with a snort.

"Thanks," Kahler said, "but I was almost done anyway. I was just going to say that based on what we heard earlier it seems like—well, it *could* have been a misunderstanding, at least to start with. I don't think he actually meant her any harm."

"That could be true," Jared Snow said in a soft voice. He was in his middle twenties, lean, and of medium height. "I don't mean to make light of what he did, but it's not like he's attacking women on the street or anything. So it's kind of hard to know what's right." He shrugged. "I'm just saying."

Courtney Singleton, the restaurant hostess, spoke up. "But the penalty isn't our concern. That'll be up to the judge. Our only job here is to decide if he did what he's accused of and broke the law he's accused of breaking. And it seems pretty clear to me that he did."

"Of course he did," Amy Morrison put in. "What you two have described," she went on with a nod toward Tracy Kahler and Jared Snow in turn, "is exactly what date rape *is*. There's a reason it's called that. It starts out as a date, or maybe just meeting up at a party or something. And then it progresses to rape, which is sex against a woman's will. Being beaten up or attacked by an intruder doesn't need to be involved. I'll grant you, it would make it easier to recognize the crime for what it is. But it's not a necessary component."

From the end of the table, another man spoke. "I'll tell you the problem I have with all this. It's just a matter of 'he said, she said.' We weren't shown any real *proof*. None at all. Why didn't they present DNA evidence? Why no fingerprints? It looks like a pretty sloppy investigation if you ask me." He surveyed the table at large. "By Drummond's finest," he added sarcastically.

Jill leaned forward, trying to read his name tag, but couldn't see around the intervening jurors. "Mr.—"

"Carlyle," he supplied. "But call me Ryan."

"I don't understand why there would need to be DNA or fingerprints. Brian Briggs admitted to his presence in the apartment, and he never denied having sex with Katie Putnam."

"But that was after he was picked up. They should have collected it earlier."

"Actually," Jill said, "if you'll recall the photos the detective showed us, they had bagged several items including the washcloth Mr. Briggs used just before he left her apartment. Assuming there was biological evidence on that—"

"Sperm, you mean. Why don't you say what you mean?"

Oh, jeez, Rob Lynch was thinking. Guiding this jury to a decision was going to be like herding cats, and the hissing and clawing had only just started. "Now, folks," he put in, but Amy Morrison, at the other end of the table, came to Jill's defense.

"The correct scientific term," she said, "is semen, not sperm. And by definition, that's biological evidence."

Ryan Carlyle bowed in her direction. "I stand corrected," he said with exaggerated politeness. "But I still think the investigation was unforgivably sloppy. The cops decided this guy was guilty, and they obviously expected a jury to rubber-stamp their decision. And I'm here to tell you, I am nobody's rubber stamp. Plus the fact, the girl's a tramp. You could see that just by looking at the way she was dressed. And getting back to the 'he said, she said' thing, even if she did say no, she didn't mean it for a minute. She only said it so he wouldn't think she was too easy."

"Oh, please," Amy Morrison shot back, rolling her eyes in disgust. "If that isn't the most chauvinistic thing I ever heard. A woman never means 'no,' she only means 'coax me.' For crying out loud! Do you hold women in that much contempt?"

There was a rap at the door and the sound of Edna's key in the lock. She swung the door open. "It's time to take a break now. We'll be leaving for lunch in ten minutes."

Juror 118 entered the rest room and locked the door. Enjoying the momentary privacy, he pondered the jury's preliminary vote. Even though not all of the jurors had spoken yet, he had a pretty good idea who had voted which way. Not that it mattered too much. He had it in his power to keep this jury from convicting Brian Briggs. He wouldn't enjoy being the lone holdout, but he would do it if he had to. It was unlikely that all the "guilty" voters would change their minds, though, so the best Brian Briggs could hope for would be a hung jury. And if that happened he would stand trial again, quite possibly without a sympathetic juror to protect him. It was time to think about a permanent solution to the problem.

21

When the jurors entered Pinky's Café and sat at their usual table, Dio Pappas noticed immediately that the group was not only smaller, but also whiter and younger. The day before there had been two black men and two Hispanic women. Today there was only one of each, so the others must have been alternate jurors. And, if he recalled correctly, one of the older white women was also missing.

Dio's gaze lingered on the juror he'd cut from the football team a dozen or so years earlier, the one whose name he hadn't remembered the day before. As he'd expected, it had come to him several hours later: Ryan Carlyle.

The kid was indignant at being cut and had made it plain that his father, a prominent local businessman, would be displeased. "You'll be hearing from my dad," he'd warned Dio. "Count on it."

The elder Carlyle had in fact telephoned Dio the next day, but after a brief and courteous conversation he had accepted the coach's decision without further argument. The incident had stuck in Dio's memory only because he'd been at a point in his career—universally regarded as the dean of downstate high-school coaches—where his judgment was rarely questioned, even by the biggest movers and shakers in town.

It had been a very different story when he first arrived, of course. He was an outsider with a strange name, the meaning of which he'd explained to his players on the first day of practice.

"My name is Diogenes Pappas," he told them. "But you can call me Coach. Now, have any of you heard the name Diogenes before?"

Not surprisingly, none of them had. A pity, he thought to himself, that high schools didn't teach the classics any more. "Diogenes was a Greek philosopher who carried a lantern throughout the world, looking for an honest man. Now I'm looking for some honest football players. Honest with me, honest with your teammates…and honest with yourselves, because sometimes that's the hardest." He paused to make eye contact with each of the boys in turn. "Stick with me, give me the best you have to offer, and I'll make you winners. Not just on the field, but off it, too."

Initially, of course, there had been challenges to his authority. But they had become increasingly rare as the years had passed, which was why the Carlyle boy's had been such a surprise. Now, studying the adult Ryan, Dio couldn't help noticing the young man's exaggerated gestures and the way those seated close to him reacted by pulling away.

Dio's gaze roamed over the other jurors, finally settling on one in particular. *There's an odd one*, he thought. *Very hard to read.* He watched for a few more moments, but the man's face and body told him nothing at all.

A few yards away from Dio's stool at the counter, Juror 118 had scored a seat next to Amy Morrison. He accepted a menu from the waitress but set it aside. He already had it memorized. As a matter of courtesy he waited until Amy had also put her menu down before speaking to her.

"So, Amy. Where do you work and what do you do there?"

"At the Walgreens on the west side. I'm a pharmacy technician, and I go to community college two nights a week."

"Interesting. What are you studying?"

"Psychology. It's nothing to do with my work, really. I just think it's fascinating."

It was amazing, he thought, how easy it was to get most people to talk about themselves. Especially women. And even more especially, women who wanted to impress you with their intelligence, education, whatever. Just ask a few simple questions, and you could get any information you wanted. He let her ramble on for a while about her interest in psychology before posing another question.

"So you work on the west side, but the college is on the east side. Do you live closer to work or school?"

She smiled. "Neither, really. I live about twelve miles north of here. You know those apartments you can see from the interstate?"

He pretended to search his memory, although he knew exactly where she meant. "I think so, yeah. A few miles before you get to the rest area?"

"Yes, on the right-hand side. The rent's a lot lower than in town because they're so far out. I still come out ahead even if I have to spend more on gas."

Now he knew where she worked, where she lived, and had a pretty good idea what her schedule was like. Time to change the subject before she remembered it would be polite to show an interest in him, too. He saw the waitress approaching. "What are you having? Not that there's much to pick from."

"No, and most of it is pretty unhealthy. It's way too high in fat and calories—" Perfect. She was off on another tangent. He nodded and murmured "Mm-hmm" at intervals until the middle-aged woman on her other side chimed in about the food. Taking advantage of the distraction, he turned his head to listen to the foreman and the black guy, Derrick, talking about the Chicago Cubs. Now, if only he knew more about Jill McKinnon. But she was sitting too far away for him to talk to, and time was running out.

Walking back to the courthouse, Jill lagged near the end of the procession. She was engaged in conversation with Lucrecia Zuñiga, who was also a native Californian. Approaching the building, Jill saw Ryan Carlyle holding open the outer door. He motioned her in with an expansive wave of his arm. As she passed him and entered the building, his lips stretched into a smile. But his eyes, hidden behind his mirrored sunglasses, were impossible to see. The effect was oddly chilling. Remembering her manners, she returned the smile and thanked him. *That guy gives me the creeps*, she thought.

When Edna had locked her charges into Jury Room #1 once more, Rob Lynch promptly reasserted control. As they emerged from the restrooms and took their assigned seats at the table, he suggested it would be helpful if they all gave their names and occupations so they'd be better acquainted with each other. And they should write their first names on a piece of paper—he passed out blank sheets folded into makeshift tent cards—so they could address each other informally without having to squint at the small print on the juror badges.

"I'll start," he said. "Rob Lynch, customer service manager, North Counties Electric Company." His name card read ROB in large block letters. He turned to his right and smiled encouragingly.

"Lucrecia Zuñiga. I work in the cafeteria at Meadowlands School."

Introductions continued around the table.

"Jared Snow, shift manager, PDQ Print-N-Copy."

"Derrick Reese, United States Postal Service."

"Brett Petersen, loan processor, Remington County Bank."

"Amy Morrison, pharmacy tech, Walgreens."

"Tracy Kahler, ultrasound technician, Community Hospital."

"Jill McKinnon, accountant, TBA Enterprises."

Juror 118 made a mental note: TBA Enterprises. He was familiar with many of the businesses in town but had never heard of that one. He'd need to check it out.

"Courtney Singleton, hostess at Chez Marie."

"Cheryl Lemay, payroll administrator, Grimm Industries."

"Mary Jane Dunn. Retired."

"Ryan Carlyle. I'm responsible for the day-to-day management of several businesses my father owns." He might have said more, but Rob cut him off. "Okay. Thanks, everyone. Now," he went on, "I think one more vote would be a good idea before we resume deliberations."

This time the count was nine guilty, two not guilty, one undecided. *Moving in the right direction*, Rob reflected. "I'd like to hear the thoughts of the not-guilty voters." He looked at Ryan. "I'm assuming you're one? I think we have a sense of your opinion, so may we please hear from the other?"

"That's me," spoke up Mary Jane Dunn in a soft voice. "I think the girl was lying when she told the 911 operator she'd been raped. Maybe she didn't mean to, at least not at first. Maybe she was just exaggerating. Then when the police got involved, the whole thing was out of her hands. By then it was too late. She got caught up in it and didn't know how to get out."

Jill tilted her head to look at Mary Jane, seated at the far end of the table. "When you say she was exaggerating, what exactly do you mean? I don't understand."

"Well, sometimes...sometimes a woman might not really *want* to, you know, but she might decide to go along just to please the man. But then afterwards, she might feel like she was used or taken advantage of, and that would make her mad. Since she didn't refuse, she has only herself to blame. But she might in her own mind try to shift the blame to the man. Do you see what I mean?"

Ryan Carlyle was nodding agreement, but Jill wasn't convinced. "I can see how that might happen in some cases, but I don't believe that's what happened here. She was pretty definite about telling him no."

"Now, yes. But remember how she tried to backtrack when that young policeman came? She said it didn't matter, but he wouldn't let it drop."

Juror 118 regarded Mary Jane thoughtfully. While she was an unexpected ally, he wondered if she would cave in when pressed by the others.

"It wasn't his fault," Derrick Reese put in. He was sensitive to the implied rebuke of the patrol officer, who was also black. "And anyway, she didn't backtrack. She may have said it didn't matter, but she never said she wasn't assaulted. And besides, the officer was only following procedure."

Carlyle waved a dismissive hand. "Oh, sure, the usual excuse. He was just following orders. But he's at the bottom of the food chain. You ask me, it was that prosecutor who decided the kid was guilty. Easy to see she's a real man-hater."

"And you're a woman-hater," Cheryl Lemay said angrily. "I think you have a real problem."

Rob Lynch privately agreed with her, but such accusations couldn't be allowed to keep flying. Smiling, he held up his hands in a time-out signal. "Discussing personalities is off limits, folks. We need to stick to the facts and whether the prosecution proved its case."

Discussion continued throughout the afternoon. Topics ranged from what constituted "threat of force"—did simple size and strength advantage suffice, or did an actual gesture or spoken threat need to be made?—to the nature of the relationship between accuser and defendant, and, inevitably, the way Katie Putnam had been dressed during her court appearance the previous day.

"She was dressed like a tart," Cheryl Lemay said. "I'll give you that. But if you go to the mall, you see all the young girls dressed that way. When I was at the bank the other day, even the teller that waited on me was showing cleavage."

"More to the point, it doesn't mean that any guy who wants to has the right to jump her bones," Courtney Singleton said.

Rob Lynch consulted the clock. It was after four, and they didn't seem to be getting anywhere. "How about one more vote?"

As before, Lucrecia tallied and Rob read the results aloud: ten guilty, two not guilty. He looked at Ryan Carlyle and Mary Jane Dunn for a long moment before speaking.

"Is there any chance that either of you will change your minds?"

"No way," Ryan said forcefully.

"No." Mary Jane spoke more quietly, but with conviction. "I won't change my mind."

Sighing, Rob stepped to the door and tapped on it to summon Edna. "We're deadlocked," he told her. "Ten guilty, two not guilty."

She nodded. "I'll tell the judge." A few minutes later she returned. "Court is in session."

Once the jurors had filed into the courtroom and taken their assigned seats, the judge regarded them solemnly. "I'm told that you're deadlocked," he said. "Is that correct?" He sat impassively as they indicated assent.

"All right, then. I want you all to go home and consider the evidence that was presented and the testimony that was given. Think very carefully, and then sleep on this matter. Maybe things will look different in the morning."

Juror 118 sat quietly in his place. *Maybe,* he thought, *but I hope not.*

Jill dawdled behind the other jurors as they filed out of the jury room, then lingered in a secluded alcove of the main lobby until she had seen them all leave the building, particularly Brett Petersen. She'd filed away the post-it note with his name and number but had no plans to call him. While he seemed nice enough, the plain fact was that he didn't appeal to her.

Equally unappealing was the thought of returning to Jessica's, which she no longer thought of as home. Besides, she'd already told Jessica that she'd grab a bite in town and not to expect her for supper. She waited another five minutes before leaving the courthouse and heading for the parking deck.

Then she remembered about the pictures. When she reached her car she retrieved her cell phone from the glove compartment and rummaged in her purse for Louise Engquist's telephone number.

Louise knew exactly why Jill was calling. "Not to worry," she said. "I drove up to Jess's this morning and took her downtown to that camera shop on the corner of Third and Main. They do everything there. Restoration, duplication, you name it. I was afraid she'd get up on her high horse and give me a hard time, but she didn't. She's a decent old gal at heart, Jill. She knows what she did was wrong."

"Well, that's good news. But I'll feel better when I actually have those pictures in my hands. I owe you big time for helping me out."

"Tell you what. I've been dying to check out those condos at Juniper Ridge. Soon as you get settled in, I'd like to stop over. For drinks or just to chat."

"Deal. I'll call you in a week or two."

Next, Jill checked her office voice mail and returned a couple of calls. Finally, she left a message for Tommy to update him on the progress of the trial. That done, she started the engine and backed out of her parking space.

Three levels below, a black Ford Explorer had just exited the parking deck. Juror 118 had walked quickly from the courthouse to his vehicle and descended to street level, where he'd found an empty space near the exit. He'd pulled into it and had left his engine running while he watched for Jill, hoping to follow her home at a discreet distance, but after nearly ten minutes he still hadn't seen her. He must have missed her. Maybe he'd have better luck tomorrow.

23

Judge Meyerhoff wasted little time when the jurors reassembled the following morning. "I hope you have all clarified your thoughts overnight and can come to a verdict this morning," he rumbled. "Please continue your deliberations with that goal in mind."

Inside Jury Room #1, the table tent cards bearing the jurors' first names were still set up. Rob Lynch walked around the table and picked them up. "I don't see any reason for us to keep on sitting in the same places, so long as we get back into order before we go into the courtroom. Maybe if we mix things up a little, it will help us see things from a different perspective." As he spoke, he shuffled the tent cards in his hands. Then he made a second trip around the table, distributing them at random. "Grab your note pads and then find your new seats." Smiling to soften the authoritarian tone that had crept into his voice, he added, "And thanks for indulging me. Now let's take another vote."

The new seating plan had placed Rob between Jared Snow and Courtney Singleton. Rob carefully collected the slips of paper, glancing at them before passing them to Jared, who sat on his right, to be counted.

Jared slid the tally back to Rob. "No change," he said quietly. "Ten guilty, two not guilty."

Rob tapped the stack of ballots and placed them in front of Courtney, on his other side. "Would you verify that, please?"

She carefully sorted the votes and counted them. "That's correct. Ten and two."

"Okay. Any new insights?" the foreman asked the group at large. "Does anyone have anything more to offer?"

Cheryl Lemay spoke up from her new spot at the end of the table, between Derrick Reese and Amy Morrison. "You," she said angrily to Ryan Carlyle, "have obviously got a big problem with women. And I think you should have owned up to that when we were being interviewed, because you obviously do not belong on this jury with an attitude like yours. And you," she added more gently, turning to Mary Jane Dunn, "are simply blaming the victim. I wish you could understand that."

"Except she's not a victim. She's just going along with the people trying to make her *look* like a victim." Mary Jane folded her arms across her chest and looked at the other jurors. "The police and the prosecutor don't like Brian Briggs. They think he's a lowlife. And he might be, but that doesn't make him guilty of rape. He's not guilty, and I won't change my mind."

"He's guilty," Cheryl shot back. "And I won't change my mind, either. Not now, not ever."

"*Not* guilty," Ryan Carlyle insisted.

"Guilty," Amy Morrison put in, and half a dozen other jurors murmured agreement.

Rob Lynch motioned for silence. "Well, I guess that's that." He rose and went over to the door, calling out for Edna. "We're deadlocked," he told her. "For real. There's nothing else we can do."

Judge Meyerhoff had no choice but to declare a mistrial. He privately believed the defendant was guilty as sin, and he had little patience with the two jurors who were too obtuse to agree with him. Still, this was the system of justice he was sworn to uphold, and which he wholeheartedly loved despite the occasional unfortunate outcome. He banged his gavel and dismissed the jurors with a smile and his thanks.

Denise Phelan, the assistant state's attorney, followed the jurors as they returned to the jury room to gather their belongings. She was desperate for their feedback. Had she failed in some way? Should she have approached the case differently? Could they tell her something—anything—that might help her in a future trial?

As Denise stepped into the jury room, Amy Morrison confronted her. "He's not going to get off, is he?" She sounded on the verge of tears. "Are they going to let him go?"

"A mistrial is not the same as an acquittal," Denise said, choosing her words carefully. "All that's needed is to set a new trial date, probably a few months from now, and retry him on the same charges." Whether that actually would happen was open to question, but Denise didn't want to go there. "So what I'm hoping is that as many of you as have the time will stay a while and give me your thoughts on how I can present a more convincing case next time around."

Ryan Carlyle ignored her request. "Will there be press outside?" he demanded.

"No, I shouldn't think so."

"Good. I need to guard my privacy." He put on his mirrored sunglasses and shrugged into a lightweight jacket. "I'm outta here."

With the exception of Rob Lynch, the rest of the men left quickly, too. Denise wasn't surprised. Most men disliked post-mortems, while women could and sometimes would hash over every detail for hours. What did surprise Denise was that one of the women had also slipped away, and that the level of tension in the room diminished noticeably after she had gone.

"What I found out," Denise reported to Terry Lankowski later that day, "is that an older gal on the jury was absolutely convinced that Katie went along with having sex, even though she didn't especially want to. And she only decided after the fact that she'd been forced. Even then she tried to recant, except the police wouldn't let her because they had it in for Briggs."

Lankowski drummed his fingers on his desk. "Hmm. So that was one of them. Weren't there two?"

"Yeah, a guy. He thought Katie was a lying tramp. Said he could tell just by looking at her. Consensus was, he had a warped attitude toward women and shouldn't even have been on the jury."

"But he was. How do you suppose that happened?"

"Obviously, he wasn't honest about keeping an open mind. He—"

Lankowski held up a hand to silence her. "I hate to say 'I told you so,' but I told you so. People are gonna lie like rugs when you ask 'em if they can pay attention to the law instead of their own prejudices. And when it comes to date rape, it's the narrow-minded old ladies and the horny young guys who'll do you in every time."

Denise grinned. "That's not *exactly* what you told me, Terry."

"Yeah, but you see what I mean. And it's like I said before: we've got a finite budget to last the rest of the year. We have to consider how much of a threat this guy is to the general public, compared to all the other perps out there that we might have to bring to trial."

"So you're going to ask the judge to cut him loose?"

"Not yet, no. I'll wait as long as I can before I make that call."

Jill removed the film cover from the veggie platter she'd bought at the grocery store, then spooned dip from its original deli carton into a glass dish. She carried both items into the great room, where she set them next to a plate of crackers and cheese on the slate-topped coffee table. There was also a bottle of German white wine chilled and waiting. It was nothing elaborate, but Jill didn't think Louise would mind.

"I got a call that your pictures were ready, so Jess and I went downtown to pick them up," Louise had said when she'd phoned the day before. "She paid for them, but she asked me if I'd deliver them. And of course I said I would. I'd love to get a peek at your new place."

Jill surveyed her small domain. Much of the furniture was on loan from Juniper Ridge Subdivision, Inc., along with some accessories also owned by the company. The windows featured built-in blinds, so no curtains were required. The overall effect was impersonal, almost sterile, and certainly not what she would have chosen.

Still, there would be plenty of time to decorate the rooms on the lower level to her own taste if she decided to buy the unit. In the meantime, she'd purchased an oak bedroom suite for the large rear bedroom on the second floor and set up her home-office equipment in the smaller front bedroom.

"Nice," Louise said as she stepped into the two-story foyer and handed Jill a large plastic bag containing her precious photographs. Louise's gaze was drawn upward to the open loft and lingered on a grouping of two chairs upholstered in leopard print and a table designed to look like a tribal drum. An arrangement of artificial pampas grass in a tall ceramic jar stood next to a large carved-wood giraffe. "Although," she added apologetically, "it does look kind of *decorated*, if you don't mind my saying so."

"As it happens, I agree with you. But I can live with it for now." She led Louise into the spacious great room and gestured toward the leather sofa, which was strategically placed across from a gas fireplace. "Have a seat." She poured wine into crystal glasses and handed one to Louise along with a cocktail napkin.

Louise sipped her wine and nibbled a cracker. "Can I see the upstairs?"

"Of course," Jill said with a smile, amused to hear the eager note in the older woman's voice. As she led the way up the carpeted stairs and across the loft, Jill gestured toward the leopard-print chairs and carved giraffe. "I feel like the only thing missing up here is a vine to swing from."

Louise grinned. "My thoughts exactly." Then they entered the master bedroom suite, with its simple mission-style oak furniture and muted pastel furnishings. A tall window overlooked the rear deck and green space beyond, and Jill's clothing and shoes were neatly arrayed in the walk-in closet. "Now this looks like you," Louise said. Stepping into the bathroom, she stared at the oversized whirlpool tub. "Wow, this is *nice*. Absolutely top shelf."

She gave barely a glance to the second bedroom and hallway bath before returning to the loft and looking down on the great room below. "You did good, kiddo. Have you decided if you're going to buy it?"

"I like it a lot, especially that tub. It's definitely a step up from Jessica's house. But…I don't know, Louise." She gestured toward the leopard-upholstered chairs. "Even if I got rid of the safari look, I don't think it would feel like home. For now, though, it's great. Come on, let's go back downstairs. I want to take a look at those pictures you brought."

Later, as the women lingered over wine and snacks, Jill asked the question that had been on her mind all day. "How's Jessica doing? Has she adjusted to living by herself?"

"Well, she did make a point of telling me she's never lived alone before. She was with her parents until she got married, and by the time

Joe died Kevin had already finished college and was back home. I think she's kind of nervous about being on her own."

"I feel like I did the right thing by moving out, but I still worry about her. Mother's Day is next weekend," Jill added after a brief pause. "Chez Marie has a nice brunch every Sunday. Do you think Jessica would go with me if I invited her?"

"I think so. At least I hope so. One thing is for sure, you won't know unless you ask her." Louise shrugged. "Worst case, she'll say no and you'll be off the hook. Or maybe," she amended with a smile, "that's the best case."

"Okay, now another question. Any gift suggestions?"

"As a matter of fact, yes. If you're up for the expense, I think one of those emergency pendants would be ideal. You've probably seen them advertised on TV."

"Of course, and it's a wonderful idea. Do you think she'd go for it?"

"She might need a little convincing, but yes, I think she would. Just leave it to me."

Dusk had fallen by the time Louise left Juniper Ridge and headed south toward town. A few miles away, Katie Putnam was unaware of the black Ford Explorer with tinted windows that had taken up station in the parking lot of the apartment complex across the street. There were no assigned parking spaces, and no resident stickers were required on vehicles parked there, which made this lot ideal for the purpose at hand.

In a far corner of the lot, the driver of the Explorer slouched down behind the wheel and unwrapped the sandwich he'd bought at a nearby Burger King drive-through. He had a clear view of Katie Putnam's front door and the bus stop nearest her apartment. He knew that she didn't own a car and rode the bus to and from work and for routine errands. As he watched, a cab pulled up near her end of the building.

He'd already learned a lot about her routine, and he was beginning to suspect that she used a cab for only one purpose: to visit a bar. She had gone out exactly two weeks ago, also a Friday evening, which probably meant it was her payday. And when she came home, also by cab, she was very drunk.

He'd followed the cab two weeks before and noted the name of the bar where she'd been dropped off. He had driven on by, of course. To have stopped and entered, and risked her recognizing him, would have been foolish.

He watched as Katie got into the cab, then started the Explorer's engine and backed out of his parking space. As before, he followed at a distance and was pleased to see that the destination was the same as it had been two weeks earlier: a large tavern on the right-hand side of the road. And a crowded one, too, judging by the number of vehicles in the parking lot.

He drove past, then turned left on the next street. He had a good sense of the Putnam girl's routine by now, and it was only a matter of time before he put his plan for her into action. In the meanwhile, he had other prey to stalk.

Settling into a booth at Chez Marie, Jessica gazed at the family groups at nearby tables. It had been a mistake to accept Jill's invitation for Mother's Day brunch, and she wouldn't have done it if Louise hadn't bullied her into it. All these people, Jessica reflected, had their children by their sides. They had grandchildren, too, or would have them someday. *All of them…except me.*

As Jessica looked around, she saw Louise's sister Margaret and her husband, the former football coach, along with the couple's two grown children. Jessica recalled Louise telling her that the girl was a recent college graduate who taught physical education at a high school in Joliet. Christina was her father's own daughter, Louise had commented. She was already showing great promise as a volleyball coach. The boy, Nick, was an agronomist down in Bloomington; but, according to Louise, he was looking for something closer to home.

Across the table, Jill had said something and seemed to be waiting for an answer.

"What? I didn't hear you."

"I said, do you want to order off the menu or visit the buffet?"

"Oh…the buffet, I guess."

Returning to their table after a trip around the lavish buffet, Jessica ignored Jill and instead concentrated on her well-laden plate. She ate quickly and, she realized, probably too much. She'd had an awful time finding something to wear this morning. She hardly ever dressed up these days, and the few appropriate outfits in her closet had suddenly become much too small. Luckily she'd found a pair of black knit slacks with a forgiving elastic waistband tucked away in the back of her closet and had topped the slacks with a beaded sweater that still stretched far enough to cover her middle. By the time she had finished dressing she was bathed in sweat from the exertion of putting on and taking off so many pieces of clothing.

To make matters worse, even her dress shoes seemed to have shrunk. They pinched almost unbearably, and she would have taken them off under cover of the nearly floor-length tablecloth if she'd thought she'd be able to wedge her swollen, aching feet back into them when it was time to leave.

Jessica stole a glance at Jill's plate. Why, the girl didn't eat enough to keep a bird alive! But she was paying the tab, and if she didn't care about getting her money's worth then that was her problem.

"Going back for dessert?" Jessica asked.

"No, I've got this." Jill tapped a small dish of fruit salad with her fork. "It's all I need."

If you only knew, Jessica thought irritably, *how smug and self-righteous you sound.* "Well, if you'll excuse me, I'm going to get some of that carrot cake. It's my favorite."

When she returned, there was an envelope lying on her placemat. She shoved it aside and began eating her cake.

"That tells about the emergency pendant and base unit I'm getting you," Jill said, gesturing toward the envelope. "Louise told me she'd talked to you about it, and you thought it might be a good idea. She has one, too."

"If it makes you feel better," Jessica said, tucking the envelope into her handbag. "Less guilty, that is." She forked another bite of cake into her mouth.

Jill sighed. Obviously Jessica was willing, maybe even happy, to receive the pendant, especially since she didn't have to pay for the equipment or the monthly monitoring fee. If she wanted to pretend she was doing Jill a favor by accepting it, so be it. There was no point in rising to such obvious bait. Instead, she reached across the table and touched Jessica's hand. "Happy Mother's Day."

"Pardon me, but aren't you Mrs. McKinnon?" Both women looked up, but the young man who stood beside their table was addressing

Jessica. "I don't know if you remember me, but I'm Nick Pappas. I was two years behind Kevin in school. We were in FFA together. I just wanted to tell you how sorry I was to hear about…well…I'm sorry." Seeing the tears well up in Jessica's eyes, Nick quickly turned toward Jill. "We haven't met," he said, and held out his hand.

After a fractional hesitation—just long enough to remind Nick that he should have waited for the lady to offer hers first—Jill reached up and shook his hand. "Jill McKinnon."

Belatedly, Nick remembered that Kevin had been married at the time of his death. So this must be his widow. "I'm sorry," Nick repeated, still holding Jill's hand and gazing into her face.

The nerve of this kid, Jessica was thinking. He couldn't care less about consoling *me*. Coming over here was just an excuse to get next to Jill. And she's eating it up.

Snatching up her handbag, Jessica scooted clumsily out of the booth. "Excuse me, but I have to go." Without another word, she turned away and walked out of the restaurant.

Nick watched her go. "Did I do that? I didn't mean to upset her."

"It's not your fault. She can be a little touchy."

"She didn't leave you stranded, did she? Will you need a ride somewhere?"

"Thank you, but I have my car. I offered to pick her up, but she wanted to meet me here." *What a nice guy*, she was thinking.

"Would you care to join us?" Nick gestured toward a nearby table, the occupants of which were watching with undisguised interest.

"That's very kind of you," she replied, smiling, "but Mother's Day is a family occasion. I wouldn't want to intrude." She picked up the leatherette folder that held the restaurant check, glanced at it, and pulled some bills from her wallet. She tucked them into the folder and laid it on the table.

"I thought I knew all of Kevin's friends, so meeting you was a pleasant surprise." She slid out of the booth. "Enjoy your lunch." She smiled at him once more before walking away.

Nick returned to his family's table, where his father grinned at him. "Struck out, huh?"

"Dio, hush," his mother scolded. "The girl's a recent widow. Louise has told me all about her."

Nick resumed his seat. "Aunt Louise knows her?"

"Of course she does," Margaret said. "Now, Nick," she added after a moment, "don't…"

"Don't what?"

Margaret sighed. Her son was young, good-looking, and—much as she hated to acknowledge it—very aware of his appeal to the opposite sex. "Just don't."

Out in the parking lot, Jill got into her Impala and fastened her seat belt. *What wonderful eyes he has,* she thought. *At first I thought they were brown, but they're really blue. Very dark blue.* She wondered, just for a moment, if it would have been too forward of her to give him one of her business cards. Then she remembered Kevin and felt a moment's suffocating guilt. Her eyes filled with tears. She started the engine, jammed the car into gear, and drove away.

Eighty-year-old Ethel Lindsey opened her front door and nearly collided with the man who was sweeping the long common balcony in front of her apartment and the three neighboring units.

Hunched over, wearing a John Deere ball cap, sunglasses, and a threadbare, too-large jacket over rumpled khaki pants—clothing items he had carefully selected at a thrift shop many miles away—he quickly averted his face and mumbled what Ethel took to be an apology.

"Hello," Ethel said brightly. "I haven't seen you around here before."

The man edged away, sweeping as he did so. "Nah."

"Where do you live? Here in the building?"

"Nah," he said again, and gestured vaguely toward another building in the complex. "Over dere. Wi' my ma."

Retarded, Ethel thought. *Poor soul.* "I see. Did you just move in?"

"Stayin' wi' my ma. Dey close d' place I stayin' before. She lookin' fer 'nudder place f' me to stay."

He'd followed Amy Morrison home from work the previous week and had managed to catch a glimpse of her unlocking her front door, so he knew which apartment was hers. Unfortunately, though, the adjacent parking lot offered no good vantage point to watch and wait.

The alternative was to become part of the landscape, part of the background, without drawing undue attention to himself. But now he'd have to be on the lookout for this nosy old cow as well as for Amy

Morrison. "I be'r go." He ducked his head and shuffled away, cradling the broom in the crook of his arm.

"Well," Ethel called after him, "you have a good day." She turned and walked in the opposite direction, headed toward the open staircase that led to the ground level parking lot. Her heart went out to the man. What would become of him when his mother could no longer care for him?

The steps seemed to grow steeper every day, and when it rained they could be treacherously slick. But, as she emerged from the shadow of the stairwell, she relished the warm late-afternoon sunshine. *This is the day the Lord has made,* she told herself. *Let us rejoice and be glad.*

The staircase had a twin at the far end of the balcony, but instead of descending it he watched as the old woman crossed the narrow parking lot and got into a battered green Pontiac. She reminded him of one of his grandmother's friends, the one with the obnoxious little dog. He and Chad had managed to get rid of that stupid dog as well as its mistress, and recalling how they had done it gave him an idea.

As soon as the Pontiac was out of sight he began sweeping once more, moving back in the direction he'd come from. His progress was slow, his steps tentative, but from beneath the cap and dark glasses he was paying close attention to the windows facing the balcony. All had either shades or curtains drawn for privacy.

When he reached the staircase—the one just beyond Amy Morrison's front door—he stayed in character, sweeping each of the stair treads. They were concrete, he observed, and the railing was wrought iron. It was a long flight: he counted eighteen steps. At the bottom of the staircase he turned slowly in a circle to survey his surroundings. *Perfect.*

He passed through the breezeway that separated the north wing of the building from the south and continued on, holding the broom close to his body, until he reached the Explorer. He had parked it behind the cinder-block enclosure where the complex's dumpsters were kept, beyond the south end of the parking lot. Chances of anyone spotting it were remote, and he had already begun taking precautions regarding the license plates. Still, it wouldn't hurt to look for a different place to park next time.

He removed his jacket and the John Deere cap and tossed them onto the floor of the back seat along with the broom. It was an old one he'd found behind a supermarket, its bristles curved and worn from long use. He would come back in a few days and do some more sweeping, next time on the balcony of one of the other buildings. He didn't mind if Amy Morrison saw him once or twice, so long as it was from a distance. Actually, he hoped she would. That way, she was unlikely to be alarmed by his presence when the time came for him to make his move. As with Katie Putnam, it was only a matter of time. He repeated his mantra: *Be patient. Preparation is everything.*

Instead of driving directly back to the Interstate, he took a more roundabout route and found a nearby side street, out of view from the apartment buildings, where he could park the Explorer on his next visit.

By the time he accelerated onto the Interstate and headed south toward Drummond, his Explorer was once more displaying its valid license plates. He checked the time on the dashboard clock. He would have time to go home and change clothes before the end of happy hour at Katie's favorite tavern, although she wouldn't be there. At least, he hoped not. But if she was, he'd keep his distance, have a quick drink, and leave as soon as he'd scoped the place out.

He briefly considered wearing a ball cap—a different one this time, one that would go with another of his carefully crafted personas—while he was in the bar, but decided against it. It might not be considered appropriate there, and he wanted to make sure he didn't break that or any other unwritten rule. The fewer people who noticed him, the better. He parked in one of the few available spaces and left the Milwaukee Brewers cap on the passenger seat.

He walked past several smokers clustered several feet from the front door as prescribed by state law and entered the tavern. It was crowded and noisy, and, he noted, several of the men were wearing ball caps.

"Coors Light," he told the bartender, and tossed a five-dollar bill onto the bar. There was a Cubs game playing on the nearest television screen. There were three others, all tuned to different stations. He drank his beer and glanced idly around, scanning the building layout. There didn't seem to be any security cameras. And if there were, so what? He wasn't doing anything unusual, just having a cold one on a warm afternoon. On his next visit, he would be wearing his cap and keeping his head down.

He finished his beer and left, the change from the five still lying on the bar. Nobody had paid the slightest attention to him. Even the bartender, busy with his many customers, had barely acknowledged his presence. *Excellent*, he thought. This was proving to be a very productive day.

He checked his watch. Courtney Singleton's shift at Chez Marie wouldn't end for another hour. Whistling softly, he drove to a nearby Subway and bought a sandwich to go.

By the time he reached the popular north-side restaurant, the dinner rush was just beginning. And the Singleton woman—he knew, because he'd heard her tell Jill McKinnon—would have been on duty since lunchtime and would be glad to see her successor arrive. Knowing she would almost certainly leave via the employees' entrance, he parked behind the restaurant in the large lot belonging to the neighboring strip mall. He settled down to eat his sandwich and wait.

A little after eight o'clock, a figure emerged from the rear door. There was still enough daylight for him to see that it was indeed Courtney Singleton. As she got into her car, a white Chevrolet Cobalt, he started the Explorer's engine. He'd tried to look her up in the phone directory, but she wasn't listed. He had no idea yet where she lived. He'd have to stay fairly close to avoid losing sight of her, but not so close that she'd realize she was being followed.

He kept the Chevy in view until it turned onto a four-lane state highway, then briefly lost it in the congested traffic of the busy shopping district on the southeast side of town. A few minutes later, though, he saw it pull into a driveway on the right and vanish behind a small frame house.

He had no choice but to drive past. *This is not good*, he thought. There was no on-street parking, and this was a black neighborhood. He'd stick out like a sore thumb. He turned right at the next street, wondering if there might be an alley running parallel to the state highway. There was, but he didn't turn down it. Instead, he continued on to the next intersection and turned right again, backtracking to a through street that would intersect the highway. Two more right turns had him back on the state route, and as he passed Courtney Singleton's driveway a second time he began counting the houses between hers and the end of the block. He turned right once more.

This time, he pulled slowly into the alley. It was now completely dark, and he hoped the Explorer's tinted windows would camouflage his white face if anyone happened to see him. He reached the fifth house—hers—and saw the Cobalt parked behind it. The gravel driveway ran all the way to the alley. There was no garage, just a small storage shed. No fence, either. Apparently she entered her driveway from the front, then exited via the rear alley instead of backing onto the heavily traveled highway

No point in stopping, he decided. He returned to the state highway a second time, scanning the fast-food places on the other side of the road, and spotted a Taco Bell. It was almost directly across from Courtney Singleton's house.

He turned around at the next intersection and entered the Taco Bell parking lot. He went to the counter, where he ordered a quesadilla and a soft drink. He didn't really want them, but he couldn't sit in one of the booths without buying something. He watched the house for a while, but there was nothing to see except the lights burning in both front windows. Well, he would think of something. *Be patient*, he reminded himself again. There was plenty of time.

He checked his watch. It was nine o'clock, and he had to be at work early. He got up, tossed the half-eaten quesadilla into the trash, and headed for home.

When he left work the next afternoon, he'd gone straight to the nearby Kroger store and bought a bouquet of white roses in a red glass vase. He went home, entered through the garage and set the vase on his kitchen counter, then put on the pair of rubber gloves he kept under the sink next to the oven cleaner. He carefully wiped down the vase with a cotton dishtowel and pulled the small blank card from its plastic spike.

He block-printed FROM GUESS WHO on the card and replaced it. Leaving the flowers on the counter, he removed the gloves, went upstairs to his bedroom and changed into a short-sleeved white polo shirt and black trousers. He studied himself in the full-length mirror, then added a plain black ball cap, mirrored blue sunglasses, and black driving gloves.

There was still something missing, though. He went into the smaller bedroom, the one he used as an office, and pulled a clipboard out of a desk drawer. He picked up a sheaf of papers—just the television listings he'd printed out earlier that week, but how would anybody know that?—and slid them onto the clipboard.

Back in front of the mirror, he checked out his reflection once more, head to toe this time. *Shoes.* The ones he had on were too casual. He changed into dress socks and shiny black loafers. Clipboard in hand, he went downstairs and picked up the flowers.

He made a detour past Chez Marie to make sure Courtney Singleton's car was still in the lot. He didn't want to take a chance on her actually being home when he tried to deliver the flowers. He spotted the white Chevy almost immediately, but took the extra step of checking the license number to satisfy himself that it was hers. *Preparation is everything.*

He drove to her house, turned into the empty driveway, and got out. Holding the clipboard in one hand, he removed the roses from the back of the Explorer with the other. He climbed the two steps to her small front porch, set the vase on the wide wooden railing, and rang the doorbell.

He pretended to study the sheets on his clipboard, but his attention was focused on the front door, which had a dead bolt. He wondered if there might be an easier way in at the rear of the house. In the meanwhile, it would be helpful to know if the woman had any nosy neighbors who would come over to find out who he was and what he wanted. Or, worse yet, did she have a dog? He hated dogs. The damn things were a pain in the ass, always barking and carrying on. He rang the bell again and picked up the roses. He silently counted to twenty, then thirty. At sixty he would leave.

When he reached fifty-one, the door was flung open by a large, angry-looking black man in t-shirt and shorts. "What?"

Sound bored, he admonished himself. Don't let the guy know he startled the shit out of you. "Flowers for Ms. Singleton."

The man glared at him. "Yeah, all right." He accepted the vase and slammed the door.

It would be suicidal to try backing onto the busy state highway. He drove straight ahead, passing within a few feet of the house. When he reached the alley he stopped and looked back, hoping the guy inside wouldn't notice him. The house was L-shaped, with what appeared to be a bedroom jutting into the back yard past a covered porch. There were two lawn chairs on the porch, and something else; he couldn't make out what it was. Not that it mattered, though. It was time to get the hell out of Dodge. He turned left into the alley and headed for home.

Obviously, disposing of the Singleton woman was going to be a challenge. He hadn't foreseen a man in the picture, probably because of the way she'd flirted with that poor dumb bastard of a postal worker when they were on jury duty. But then, that was how all women acted: ready, willing and available, even when they weren't. Even when they were just leading you on. He'd make her pay, though, sooner or later.

He'd figure out a way, and there was no hurry. Actually, a delay of weeks or even months would probably be a good thing.

As he drove, he thought about his grandmother's friends. Because they were old, and there were no signs of forced entry, and nothing appeared to be missing, it was just naturally assumed that their deaths were either natural or accidental. One had died in her sleep, the victim of an apparent heart attack. Another had fallen down the stairs—tripped over her dog, it seemed, who was also unfortunately killed when she landed on him—and broken her neck.

But Singleton and Morrison were young and healthy, and so was Jill McKinnon, whom he hadn't yet located. Too many deaths clustered together would surely draw attention. Besides, although he hated their guts, they were of secondary importance. The first order of business was to neutralize the Putnam bitch before she could testify against Brian Briggs again. Then it would be Amy Morrison's turn.

Katie Putnam struggled into wakefulness, trying to figure out what that ringing noise was. She groped for her alarm clock, picked it up and tried to turn it off, but the noise wouldn't stop. *What the hell…?*

She finally realized it was the doorbell. "Go away," she shouted. Or she meant to shout, but all that came out was a whisper. Relentlessly, the ringing went on.

"Oh, shit," she moaned. "All right, I'm coming." She put her feet on the floor and felt the room begin to spin. Putting a hand on the dresser to steady herself, she squinted at her reflection in the mirror and saw that she was wearing only a low-cut bra and thong panties. *Can't go to the door like this,* she thought woozily. She pulled the pink thermal blanket off the bed and draped it around her shoulders, then stumbled into the living room.

She opened the front door and saw a man wearing a ball cap and sunglasses standing there. As she opened her mouth to ask why the hell he was ringing her doorbell at this hour of the morning, he held out a key ring. It was hers.

"I'm sorry," he said. "I found this in my pocket this morning. I must've put it in there last night. You know, like a reflex."

"What?" She stared at him, uncomprehending, and he wondered if she had any idea how stupid she looked.

"I brought you home last night. In the taxi. Remember?"

Mutely, she shook her head. Damn, she needed to stop drinking so much. She didn't remember squat about last night.

"You were having trouble opening your door, so I helped you with your keys. And like I said, I must've dropped them into my pocket without thinking. Maybe I had a little too much to drink," he said, smiling in what he hoped was an ingratiating manner.

"Oh. Thanks."

"I'm sorry to wake you up, but—" He consulted his watch.

"What time is it?"

"Ten-thirty. Anyway, I'm on my way home and I've got a long drive ahead of me, so—"

"Where do you live?"

"Dubuque. I was just here visiting—"

"Dubuque? Where's that?"

What an ignorant bitch she was. "Iowa. And I didn't want to just leave your keys on your doormat. Anybody could come along and pick 'em up. Well, I better get going. Take care." He turned around and began to walk away.

"Thank you," she called after him, then realized she didn't even know his name. "Wait a minute."

He slowed momentarily, but didn't stop. "You're welcome." He reached the sidewalk and turned right. A few more strides carried him out of sight beyond the corner of the building.

Katie shut the door. Her purse was lying on the living room sofa, where she must have tossed it last night. She didn't remember. She put the keys in her purse and returned to her bedroom. She lay down on the bed, still wrapped in her blanket, and wondered if she was becoming an alcoholic. But no, that was impossible because she only drank at the bar, and only once every two weeks. She kept liquor around, just in case she had company, but she never drank alone at home. Not even when she wanted to, which was more and more often lately.

She closed her eyes, willing the queasiness to go away.

By the time she fell asleep, the Ford Explorer was back in its owner's garage. He reached into his pocket and took out the copy of Katie Putnam's front door key he'd had made two hours earlier. Then he dropped it into a kitchen drawer.

He owned her now. He'd need to wait a couple of weeks, until the bartender forgot all about the good Samaritan who'd taken the poor drunken girl home in a taxi. She'd been so confused when she couldn't find the money she always kept separate for her ride home, not realizing he'd seen her slide it into an outside pocket of the large purse she carried. It had been ridiculously easy to steal it. He'd made sure she always had a drink in front of her, too. He'd been ordering tequila shots for himself, but one way or another she'd wound up drinking most of them while he sipped a club soda. What an incredibly easy mark she was.

He'd been wearing his Milwaukee Brewers cap and a temporary tattoo of a dragon, the kind little kids sometimes wore, on the side of his neck. Funny how people focused on things like logos on caps or sunglasses or tattoos instead of faces. Not that his face was especially memorable, a fact that had always worked in his favor.

The cab driver would soon forget him, too. He was just another fare. After he'd escorted Katie Putnam to her apartment and palmed her keys, he'd had the cabbie take him back to the bar. He'd ordered a beer and engaged in a brief exchange of small talk with the bartender, less busy now that it was nearly closing time, who'd asked him if he was a Brewers fan. No, but his dad was and had given him the cap. It was a shame about the girl. He'd felt sorry for her because his sister had a drinking problem and was in and out of rehab. Man, his family sure was a mess. He'd come all the way down here to visit his brother, who lived over there—he'd gestured vaguely in the direction of the subdivision across the road—and damned if his brother and sister-in-law hadn't gotten into a fight. He had just walked over here to keep out of the way until he could be sure things had quieted down, then he'd go back to their place. He was headed home in the morning. Of course, he hadn't specified where "home" was.

Yes, he owned her now. Her next binge would be her last. And in the meanwhile, he would enjoy the long Memorial Day weekend.

Brett Petersen had been a mortgage loan processor for the Remington County Bank for nearly two years. He enjoyed his job, and the money was adequate, but it wasn't easy being the lone male in an otherwise all-female department. While most of his co-workers were conscientious and industrious, there were a few who would rather chat than work. He had become adept at screening out the sound of their conversations, but sometimes he'd overhear something that would get his attention. This time, the topic of conversation was whether it was acceptable for a woman to pursue a man she was interested in.

"What do you say, Brett?" one of them asked him. "Would you like it if a girl called you and asked you out?" She smirked and winked at one of the other women. He knew it was because she thought he was gay, which he wasn't, and most of the time it didn't bother him. Recently, though, it had begun to get on his nerves.

"I'd love it," he said with a smile, "assuming she wasn't an absolute troll….Has anyone seen the Gaylord appraisal?" he asked the group at large as he turned his attention back to his computer screen. "The closing's on the calendar for day after tomorrow, so we really need it." It was a not-so-subtle reminder to get to work, and he could picture his talkative co-worker rolling her eyes behind his back.

He wished that Jill had phoned him. It was now several weeks since the trial had ended, and he hadn't heard from her. He hadn't totally given up, though. Maybe, just possibly, there was still hope. She'd told him she had a crazy schedule, so maybe she was very busy with work and would call him when she had more time. Or maybe she had lost his number. Or maybe, he decided, *he* should try calling *her*.

He wondered if she might be a customer of the bank. He pulled up the internal database and searched on "McKinnon." Nothing. A few mouse clicks took him to the Remington County Recorder's website, where he ran another search. Still nothing, although the County had only been imaging documents since 2004. Finally he accessed the online white pages, where he found *McKinnon, J.* Now, there was a possibility. He might try calling the number after work. Maybe. But for now, he needed to concentrate on the task at hand. Mindful that his every keystroke was being recorded, he logged off the internet and reopened the loan file he'd been working on.

On the other side of town, Katie Putnam was reorganizing and tidying the children's clothing displays in her department. Because of the multitude of careless shoppers that had descended on the store's Memorial Day sale, the merchandise was all mixed up. Luckily things were quieter today. Her stomach rumbled, and she checked her watch. It was nearly time for her break.

As if on cue, Tiffany Cruse approached. "Go ahead and clock out for lunch. I'll cover." She watched as Katie moved toward the back of the store, where the employee lunchroom was located. It was odd, she thought, that even though the girl's face looked puffy, she seemed to have lost weight. She just hadn't been the same since that rape trial.

In the lunchroom, Katie bought a vending-machine sandwich and a soft drink. Spotting her co-worker Jennifer, from the jewelry department, Katie slid into the chair next to hers. "Hey."

"Hey. How's it going?"

"Okay. Listen," Katie said, dropping her voice to just above a whisper, "were you at the Sports Fan Friday night?"

"Yeah, I was there for a while with Jamie."

"I was there, too, right?"

"Shit!" Jennifer hissed. "Don't you remember?"

"No. I mean, sure, I remember most of it, I just don't remember a couple of things."

"I'm not surprised. You were pretty out of it. Somehow or other you even managed to drink up your cab fare home. I've never seen you do that before. Seriously, Kate, you need to slow down."

"But there was a guy, right?" She took a bite of her sandwich and looked at Jennifer expectantly.

"Yeah, there was a guy. He seemed nice enough, but while you were in the bathroom I told him he'd better not try taking advantage of you or he'd have me to deal with." What she'd actually told him was that the last guy who'd taken Katie home had wound up in jail accused of rape. She'd thought that sounded scarier. And besides, it was for his own good. "But he said his sister was struggling with a drinking problem, so he'd make sure you got home okay and I didn't have to worry."

Katie dropped her sandwich onto the table. "Is that what you think? That I have a drinking problem?"

"Well, it does seem like...since the trial, I mean..."

"I don't," Katie said. "I don't," she repeated more loudly, drawing glances from other employees seated nearby. She picked up her sandwich and soda and moved to an unoccupied table on the far side of the lunchroom. "I don't," she whispered.

30

The second Friday in June was lucky for Brian Briggs. It was the day Gary Carlyle bailed him out of jail and offered him a job. He didn't know Gary Carlyle from Adam, but so what? He accepted the job offer, acting grateful and polite even though the nature of the job had not been specified, because it might provide an opportunity to steal something.

"I'm only doing this because my son asked me to," Carlyle said. "He thinks you got a raw deal. Just remember one thing: you might be taking orders from him, but he takes 'em from me. I call the shots." He'd delivered Briggs to the reception area of a nondescript office suite in an equally nondescript building. "Let Ryan know his new employee is here," he told the blonde woman behind the desk. Then he left.

Briggs soon learned that the job consisted of outdoor maintenance work, mostly picking up trash in the parking lots at several businesses owned by the Carlyle family.

"A janitor," he complained to his mother that night. "I'm a fuckin' *janitor*. Minimum wage, no benefits, and it's only part time. Some job."

"It's better than you had before," she pointed out.

"I was makin' fifteen bucks an hour before, full time, at the truck terminal."

"But they let you go, Brian. So you weren't earning anything at all when you were in jail."

"I was in fuckin' jail because of that bitch Katie, and they fired me for absenteeism because of it. It's all her fault."

Tammy Briggs laid a hand on her son's arm. "I'm going to bed now, Brian. Promise me you'll work hard and stay out of trouble."

"Yeah, sure. I'll stay outta trouble."

He watched his mother disappear into the bedroom at one end of the mobile home they shared, then went to the refrigerator in hopes of finding some beer. There wasn't any, only a few cans of diet soda. "Why does she drink that shit," he grumbled under his breath. He picked up the telephone and punched in a number he knew by heart.

"Hey, Darrin? It's me, Brian. I'm out. Can you come pick me up?"

Half an hour later, Tammy was jolted awake when the trailer door slammed shut. She squinted at her bedside clock and saw that it was a few minutes after ten. She heard a car engine nearby, then a voice she recognized close to her bedroom window. Not Brian's, but Darrin Harvey's. He was bad news, and so was his brother, Sean. "Oh, Brian," she breathed. "Be careful."

Less than two miles away, at the Sports Fan tavern, Katie Putnam was sipping a margarita while she watched for someone, anyone, she knew. Several of the faces were familiar to her because they, like she, were Friday-night regulars, but she didn't know their names. And even though there were a few cute guys she wouldn't have minded getting acquainted with, none of them approached her. She'd begun to wonder if they'd heard about the trial. Maybe they were afraid they'd wind up like Brian Briggs, accused of rape if they tried to get friendly. She knew people were whispering about her at work. She'd considered calling Dawn Martin at the crisis center about resuming counseling sessions, but so far she hadn't followed through. It was just too hard: too hard to fit it into her schedule, and too hard to face the things they wanted her to talk about.

She gulped down the rest of the margarita. Now, that was easy. She went over and ordered another one from Josh, the bartender.

"Okay," he said, "but why don't you let me hold your cab fare for you? Just in case."

She pulled a ten-dollar bill out of her purse and laid it on the bar. "There's my cab fare." Then she dropped a twenty on top of the ten. "Now where's my margarita?"

Three hours later, after she'd switched from margaritas to straight tequila, Josh realized it was time to cut her off. He dialed the Round Town cab company and ordered a taxi for her, then called one of the waitresses over. "Just take her to the door and give this money to the driver. They all know where she lives."

Ruben Díaz helped Katie into the back seat of his taxi, then slid behind the wheel and drove to her apartment, praying she wouldn't get sick. She never had so far, but you could never tell. The first few times he'd taken her home she'd just been a little giddy, giggling like a schoolgirl. But lately, she'd seemed *muy borracha*.

He sighed with relief when he pulled up in front of her building, stopped the cab and opened the rear passenger door for her. Safely home, and no mess to clean up. She was unsteady on her feet but still upright when she reached her front door. He could see her clearly, illuminated by the porch light, searching for her keys in her oversized bag. Once she found them, she struggled to fit the door key into the lock.

"Okay, miss?" he called.

She tried again, successfully this time. She stumbled across the threshold and shut the door behind her. Ruben shook his head in dismay, wondering how many more steps she'd be able to take before passing out. As he pulled onto the street he passed within several yards of a black Explorer parked across the street, but he never noticed it. There was no reason he should. It was only one of many vehicles in the lot.

Slouched low behind the wheel of the Explorer, its driver watched the taxi's taillights until they were out of sight. Before leaving home, he'd turned off the dome light so it wouldn't go on when he opened the door. Then, still in his garage, he'd tested it not once but twice. *Preparation is everything.*

He waited to see if any lights went on inside or, equally important, if her porch light went off. Five minutes passed, then ten, and he saw no interior lights. The porch light stayed on, which was unusual. Always before, she'd turned it off shortly after returning home. So she'd probably forgotten about it. That was no problem, though. He'd meant to use the rear door to her apartment anyway.

Half an hour went by. *Be patient.* He needed to be sure she was totally out of it when he entered. As he waited, he remembered the first time he and Chad had killed someone. They hadn't planned to—hadn't even expected the old lady to be home—but afterwards, he was surprised at how little remorse he felt.

He took the key from his pocket and rubbed it, smiling. He'd been so compliant, so easygoing, so willing to house-sit for Gram's old-lady friends when they went on their Caribbean cruise. During the prior months he'd heard them chattering away whenever they got together over coffee and dessert at Gram's. One time, they'd talked about the fellow on television who'd said they should make sure to keep plenty of cash on hand. For emergencies, you know. He'd hovered out of sight, but not out of earshot, as they compared notes on the most foolproof hiding places. A few of them used fake food containers, but most favored ordinary plastic sandwich bags tucked into places that thieves would never look, or so they thought: at the bottom of a sewing basket, under a microwave oven, or beneath a stack of sheets in their linen closet. The ladies, all well off, also agreed it was a good idea to split up the money into several packets of not more than a thousand dollars apiece.

While they were gone on their tropical adventure, he'd methodically searched their houses and made notes on where they kept their cash and how much there was. He'd also duplicated all their keys. He had not, of course, taken a single dollar while they were gone. He could too easily visualize them rushing home and checking their stashes, first thing. No, it was just as Chad had always said: *Be patient*. And also: *Don't be greedy*.

It had been a wonderful plan. They would wait for one of the old biddies to leave town just for a day or two—not long enough to require his house-sitting services—and then they would slip in during the small hours of the morning and take a few bills from each of the baggies. It was easy money, and apparently it was never missed as long as the bags themselves remained in place.

Unfortunately, though, one of the old gals had changed her plans at the last minute and didn't leave as scheduled. She'd been asleep, but woke up when she heard them moving around. She had sat up in bed, turned on the bedside lamp and looked at him, then called him by name. That had sealed her fate.

"Lie down," he'd told her, "and we won't hurt you. I promise. Just lie down, close your eyes, and pretend we're not here." Small, frail, and terrified, she had obeyed. They had smothered her with a pillow, then carefully arranged her body to suggest peaceful repose. There were no signs of a struggle, and they locked the back door behind them when they left.

It was a decent payday. They had removed over eight thousand dollars from her various caches of money and left the other seven thousand there, so her heirs were none the wiser. Neither were the police. An eighty-three-year-old woman had died in her own bed, with nothing disturbed and nothing missing. Because her health had been declining in recent years, the post-mortem exam was cursory. Cause of death listed was as cardiac arrest.

He'd been lucky that time. Since then, he'd learned to make his own luck through meticulous planning and preparation. He checked his watch: ten minutes after three. He had waited long enough.

He backed away from the girl's lifeless body, tamping down the temptation to get the hell out and make a run for it. Instead he went to the front door, checking to make sure it was locked, and removed a small flashlight from his pocket. He swept its beam over the path he'd followed from there to the area around her bed, checking for any trace of evidence he might have left behind.

Satisfied, he turned off the flashlight and dropped it back into his pocket. He took a deep breath, slipped out the back door and locked it behind him. There were no lights on in any of the neighboring buildings. The street light half a block away provided the only illumination. He walked quickly around the corner of the building, crossed the street and got into his Explorer.

He followed a roundabout route home, keeping a close eye on his rearview mirror to make sure he wasn't being followed. At the end of his block, he pressed the remote control for his garage door opener. The door was fully up by the time he reached his driveway. He pulled in and had pushed the remote button a second time before he'd even turned off the engine. Someone would have had to be looking out the window at exactly the right moment to see him enter his garage.

Once inside his townhouse, he stripped to the skin and dumped everything into the washing machine, including his canvas sneakers. Moving into the kitchen, he took off his baseball cap and smoothed it over an inverted mixing bowl, which he placed on the upper rack of the dishwasher. As an afterthought he added the rubber gloves he'd been wearing. He selected the steam cycle and pressed the start button.

After a long, hot shower he lay down on his bed and closed his eyes. He wouldn't—couldn't—go to sleep yet, but he needed to rest for a while. He thought back over what he'd done so far, and what he still needed to do.

A little after eight that morning he drove the Explorer to a self-service car wash and spent half an hour meticulously cleaning the vehicle inside and out. When he returned to his townhouse he removed the rubber gloves, now thoroughly sanitized, from the dishwasher. *Epithelials*, he reminded himself. It was a term he'd learned from watching crime shows on television. He'd taken care to avoid leaving fingerprints or other evidence at the scene, and he couldn't afford to get sloppy now. He put on the gloves before collecting his clean laundry from the clothes dryer. He stacked it neatly on the Explorer's back seat, topped by the cap, then peeled off the gloves and tossed them onto the front passenger seat.

He started the engine and drove to a town fifty miles to the south, where he located a charity collection bin in a supermarket parking lot. He scanned the area for a security camera, but saw none. Satisfied, he put the gloves back on before depositing the clothing, shoes and cap in the bin.

On his way back to the interstate he spotted a McDonald's and realized he was very hungry. He purchased two sausage biscuits and a large coffee at the drive-through. He stopped at a nearby park and ate the sandwiches, then got out of the Explorer to stretch his legs and enjoy the nice summer weather. Off to the right he saw a porta-potty. *Perfect*, he thought. He went in and latched the door. Donning the gloves once more, he removed the key to Katie Putnam's apartment from his pocket, carefully wiped it down, and dropped it into the holding tank. As an afterthought, he dropped the gloves in too.

He knew from experience that the next day or two would be the most difficult to get through. It was vital to stick to his usual routine and maintain his normal demeanor. He'd found it especially tough the first time around. He still remembered the almost unbearable tension he'd felt while waiting for his grandmother to learn about her friend's death and to tell him about it. His response was calculated to convey just the right level of interest: *Oh, really? I'm sorry to hear that.* But he hadn't asked any follow-up questions. After all, he'd barely known her. It would have seemed odd if he'd shown undue curiosity about the circumstances of her death. Fortunately for him, Gram had felt the need to talk about it and, in due course, had shared the welcome news that the death was due to natural causes. The second time had been easier, especially since he'd learned that Chad's discretion was equal to his own.

This time—better yet—there was no one who shared his secret.

By Sunday morning, he was beginning to wonder when the girl would be found. He checked the online version of the Drummond newspaper. Nothing yet, but it was just a matter of time.

Stack Ridgeway was relaxing over coffee and the Sunday paper when his daughter Caylee approached him. She was thirteen, his youngest—his baby—and maturing into womanhood at an astonishing pace. She was nearly as tall as Heather, her sixteen-year-old sister.

"Look at my new sandals, Daddy. Mom bought them for me yesterday at the mall." She extended one foot for his approval. "Aren't they cute?"

The sandals looked pretty much like any other sandals to him. He dutifully admired them anyway, noting her dainty feet with their scarlet-painted toenails. "Very cute. Nice pedicure, too."

"Heather did them for me," she said with a grin. "She said you can't wear sandals without having your toenails done."

Stack was watching her dance away from him, still smiling, when his pager chirped.

Twenty minutes later, he pulled up in front of the apartment building at 1712 South Wentworth. He already knew what he would find there, and he was dreading it.

Stack was no stranger to sudden and violent death. During the early years of his career he'd responded to many motor vehicle accidents, some of which had been horrific. Later on, as a detective, he'd investigated a particularly grisly murder-suicide. Still, murders were sufficiently rare in Drummond that he had never become hardened to the human tragedy involved.

He parked his city-issued Dodge Durango behind a black-and-white unit and approached the doorway of apartment 1D. A heavyset fiftyish woman stood near the yellow crime-scene tape, her face tear-stained and ravaged by grief. She held a lit cigarette in one hand and a cell phone in the other.

"I don't know," she said into the phone. "They won't tell me anything." She paused and raised the cigarette to her lips, then exhaled a stream of smoke. "I only know Katie's dead. I found her myself."

It was one thing, Stack reflected, to have your loved one die in bed, often advanced in years and suffering from chronic pain or debility. That was hard enough. But this…this was something else. They couldn't be sure, at least not yet, that the girl's death was murder. That would have to wait for the coroner's verdict. But given what Scott Allison had told him on the phone, murder seemed likely.

The woman with the cell phone moved into his path. "I'm Katie's aunt. Harriet Gerston. Please tell me what happened to her."

"We don't know yet, ma'am," he said gently. "That's what we're trying to find out right now. Did you speak with one of these officers?" He gestured toward a pair of uniformed officers standing nearby, one of whom nodded in acknowledgment.

"Yes, when—after—" Unable to continue, she began to weep.

Stack touched her shoulder in what he hoped was a reassuring way. "I need to go inside now, ma'am." He ducked under the yellow tape and stepped over the threshold of Katie Putnam's apartment. The scent of death was faint but unmistakable. Just inside the door, Allison was conferring quietly with a crime-scene technician. Stack waited until the tech went into the bedroom before addressing Allison.

"Thanks for calling me, Scotty. What can you tell me?"

"The aunt said she talked to her earlier this week and she sounded pretty low. So they decided to get together this morning and go out for breakfast, maybe to the farmer's market or something. Aunt got here around eight and got worried when her niece didn't come to the door. So she let herself in—she had a key—and found the girl in bed. Said she didn't realize she was dead until she turned her over, and even then she wasn't sure. Didn't want to be sure is more like it, I think," Allison said with a shrug. "Anyway, the aunt called 911 and started trying to revive her, pounding on her chest like she'd seen on TV. The paramedics had to pull her off the body."

"The aunt thought the girl sounded low," Stack mused. "Any chance it was suicide?"

"Unless the blood work tells us something different, I'd say no. We didn't find any pills or empty bottles or anything else that would point in that direction."

The technician emerged from the bedroom. "Want to take a look before we bag her?"

"Yeah," Stack said, and moved toward the bedroom Then, addressing Allison, "Tell me again how she was found?"

"According to the aunt, she was lying on her stomach. Both hands under the pillow. Blanket up to her shoulders."

Stack approached the body, which was lying on its back on the double bed. Except for the unnatural color, there was nothing gruesome about it: no blood, no disfigurement, no mutilation. But, for some odd reason, that made its appearance even more disturbing. Thank God, Stack thought, she was wearing underwear. Skimpy, perhaps, but it covered her where necessary. He found it difficult to look at the dead girl's face, focusing instead on the pink blanket that covered her lower torso and legs.

"The aunt turned her over, you said."

"Yeah. She was trying to do CPR."

"Damn," Stack muttered. Then his gaze fell on the girl's left foot, which protruded from beneath the blanket. It was a small foot, the toenails meticulously painted with bright red polish, and uncannily similar to his daughter Caylee's. He felt a moment's suffocating rage. "When did you say that bastard Briggs made bail?"

"Friday morning."

"Take a couple uniforms and go pick him up."

Stack followed Scott Allison outside and took a deep breath of fresh air before approaching Harriet Gerston. He gently steered her away from the apartment door, hoping to spare her the sight of her niece being brought out in a body bag. He fumbled in his pocket for a business card, which he handed to her.

"I want you to know that we'll do everything we can, as fast as we can, to find out what happened to Katie. You can call me any time."

"I raised her," Harriet said, her eyes filling with tears. "Her parents weren't married. They were so young, they weren't ready for a baby. I wasn't married either, but at least I was a grownup. Her father was never in the picture, but every now and then her mom—my little sister—would show up and move in with us for a while. Just long enough for Katie to get attached to her all over again, then she'd get involved with some guy and take off. I never finished school, and I worked two jobs most of the time she was growing up just to make ends meet. After she graduated from high school she couldn't wait to get out on her own. I did the best I could for her, but..."

"I'm sure you did."

"She was a good kid, a hard worker. Anyone'll tell you that about her. But lately she—that trial really messed her up."

"Is there somebody we can call for you?"

"I already talked to my mother. Katie's grandma. She had problems of her own when Katie was little, and she's pretty sick with emphysema now, so..." Looking past him, Harriet began to sob. "Oh, God, my poor baby."

Stack turned around. The body bag containing the mortal remains of Katie Putnam was being loaded into the coroner's van.

Tammy Briggs was deeply worried about her son. She was pretty sure he had gone somewhere with Darrin Harvey after she went to bed Friday night, but she didn't know where or why. He had returned on Saturday morning to take a shower, shave, and change clothes, then he'd left again. She had no idea where he'd gone or when he would be back.

She said as much now to the detective who had come looking for him, even volunteering to let him search her trailer, although she omitted any reference to Darrin Harvey. He had served time in prison, and there was no need for the cops to know that Brian associated with a convicted felon.

The detective wouldn't tell her why he was looking for Brian, only that he needed to talk to him. "Leave me your number," Tammy said, "and I'll have him call you as soon as he comes in. He should be back by tonight. He's got a job now, you know. He works for Gary Carlyle," she said with a proud little lift of her chin.

"So I heard." Allison handed her a business card. "You'll be sure to call me as soon you hear from him, won't you?"

"I will. I promise. And now I need to get back to my sewing," she said apologetically, indicating a mound of fabric on a nearby table. "It's how I make my living."

As soon as she'd spoken the words, "I promise," Allison knew she had no intention of calling him. He was also pretty sure that the doll clothes she sewed and offered for sale at area flea markets were only a cover for the true source of her income. But believing something, or even knowing it, wasn't the same as being able to prove it in court.

He thanked Tammy Briggs politely and drove away. A few minutes later, he pulled into the empty parking lot outside a dental office and dialed Stack Ridgeway's cell number.

"He wasn't home," Allison said when his boss answered.

"Big surprise there. When did his mother see him last?"

"Yesterday morning, she said."

"You sure he really wasn't there? Or was mama just covering for him?"

"No, he wasn't there. But that's not to say she wouldn't cover for him, now that she knows we're looking for him."

Stack sat behind the wheel of the Durango, thinking about what to do next. Scott Allison was a good man. He'd already had the investigation well underway when he called Stack. There was one task, though, that couldn't be delayed any longer. Stack scrolled through his speed-dial numbers and clicked on Terry Lankowski's.

"Terry," he said when the State's Attorney answered. "We need to talk."

They met half an hour later in the parking lot of a Dunkin' Donuts and sat in the front seat of the Durango, sipping coffee.

"Am I correct in thinking you haven't told your boss about this yet?" Lankowski asked, referring to Drummond police chief Harry Whitesell. Whitesell was well connected locally—perhaps too well connected, Lankowski thought, and too inclined to focus on politics instead of law enforcement. He suspected that Stack Ridgeway agreed with him.

"That'll be my next call. I just wanted to give you a heads up first."

"I appreciate that, but we still need to be careful how we handle this business. First of all, we don't know for a fact that the girl was murdered."

"Not yet, but I'd bet money on it. She died lying on her stomach with her face buried in a pillow. At least that's how the aunt found her. And the tech noticed some bruising around her shoulder blades. Somebody could've straddled her back and forced her face into the pillow so hard she couldn't breathe. Probably with another pillow over the back of her head."

"Jesus."

"We won't know for sure until the autopsy's done, but like I said—"

"It could just be a coincidence, though," Lankowski broke in. "The timing, that is. Briggs makes bail Friday morning, and the girl dies... when?"

"Early Saturday morning, according to the tech on the scene. Most likely between three and five."

"Do we know his whereabouts at the time?"

"No."

"Okay. Evidence of forced entry?"

"No. The front door was locked, and it doesn't look like it was jimmied. Same for the back door."

"Anything to place Briggs at the scene? Witnesses? Physical evidence?"

"Not yet," Stack said, sounding impatient. "But we're still canvassing the area. And we've got our best technicians processing the scene."

"All two of 'em, huh?" Lankowski sighed. "Listen, I know you like Briggs for this. Actually, so do I. But until we know the girl—"

"Katie. Her name was Katie."

"Okay, Katie. Until we know for sure she was murdered, *and* we have some evidence that Briggs did it, we have no case. Just liking him for it gets us nowhere."

"Shit, Terry, you think I don't know that?"

"I only meant we have to tread carefully here. Briggs was bailed out by one of our town's leading citizens. If we even halfway suggest that Gary Carlyle was somehow responsible—"

"I'm not suggesting that for a minute. I can't claim to know him well, but he seems like a decent guy. Kind of a cold fish, maybe, but..."

"But still a decent guy. *And* a good friend of Harry Whitesell's." The State's Attorney drained his coffee cup. "Be sure to keep me in the loop." He got out of the Durango and walked over to his Lexus, already wondering how he was going to break the news to Denise Phelan. She'd been livid when she learned Brian Briggs was out on bail.

On Monday morning, he flipped on the television to catch the local news while he got ready for work and caught the tail end of a story about Katie Putnam's death. There was no video of the scene, just a couple of sentences spoken by the blonde, horse-faced anchorwoman. He raced to his computer and turned it on, then accessed the station's website. He quickly scanned the story, which described the death as probable homicide. The police were looking for Brian Briggs, who was described as a person of interest.

Too much to hope for, he thought, that the cops would be fooled into thinking the bitch had drunk herself to death. All the more reason to be glad he'd taken such pains to dispose of everything he'd worn at the scene, even though there was nothing unusual about of it: just common brand names that could be bought at any store, that anyone might own. And, while it was a shame that Briggs was under consideration as a suspect—that "person of interest" crap didn't fool anybody—the fact remained that there couldn't be any evidence against him, because he simply hadn't been there.

Across town, Tammy Briggs had seen saw the same news story. She rushed into Brian's bedroom, shouting his name. She'd heard him come in, very early that morning, but she hadn't wanted to call that nice young detective at such an ungodly hour. She had rolled over in bed, sleepily deciding that she'd call him later, if Brian was still there when she woke up.

"Brian!" She yanked at the sheet that covered him up to his waist. "Get up!"

He opened his eyes, staring at her woozily. "What the fuck?"

She pulled harder on the sheet. "Get up, Brian!"

He fought her for control of the sheet. "For Chrissake, let go. I'm naked!"

"I'm your mother," she shrieked. "You think I've never seen you naked? Get up and get dressed!"

"Calm down, for Chrissake." He sat up and swung his legs over the edge of the bed, leaning forward and folding his arms over his lap to hide his private parts. "Just lemme get dressed and I'll be right out."

Moments later, clad in jeans but still barefoot, he emerged from his bedroom to see his mother pacing around the trailer's small living area. He stood in front of her and grasped her upper arms to stop her pacing. "Okay, I'm here. Now what the fuck is going on?"

"What have you done?" she demanded. "That girl is dead and the TV is saying you did it!"

He stared at her, dumbfounded. "What girl is dead? I ain't done nothing. Jesus! You think I'd kill someone?"

Tammy sank down on the threadbare sofa and covered her face with her hands. "No," she muttered, wanting to believe it. "No," she said again. "You better sit down."

She told him about the detective's visit the day before, how she hadn't known what it was about—never dreaming it was about a *murder*, for God's sake. She'd thought it was about something trivial, like making sure Brian showed up for work on Monday. She rose and went over to the kitchen counter, where she picked up Scott Allison's business card. She held it out to Brian.

"Call him," she said. "If you don't, I will."

Instead of taking the card from his mother's outstretched hand, he reached around her for the telephone directory. "I need to call my lawyer first. I got rights, and I ain't done nothing wrong. Swear to God."

Two hours later, he was seated across from Steve Berglund at a table in a small, stuffy conference room in the Law Enforcement Annex of the county courthouse. "I didn't do it," he told Berglund. "As God is my witness, I didn't."

Berglund wasn't sure whether he believed that or not. It didn't matter, of course. Believing him would have been nice but was not a requirement of the job, which, at this point, was to make sure Briggs' rights were protected.

"When are they saying she was killed?" Briggs asked.

"Between three and five o'clock Saturday morning."

Briggs leaned forward, his eyes focused intently on Berglund's face. "What if I could tell you where I was and who I was with from somewhere around ten o'clock Friday night until seven the next morning? And what we were doing?"

"That depends. Can you?"

"Yeah, maybe so. *If* we can work a deal. 'Cause I was with some bad dudes, and we were doing some bad stuff. Not as bad as murder, though. Nothing that would hurt anybody," he said with a smile that was meant to be ingratiating, but it made Berglund cringe.

"It's worth a try. So who were you with, and what bad stuff were you doing?"

"*If* I was with these guys, then maybe—now, I'm saying *maybe*—we were riding along in their car down along Interstate 80, hitting some of those big 24-hour stores. You know, like Wal-Mart and Meijer stores."

"Hitting them," Berglund repeated. "Meaning what?"

"Let me put it this way. These guys, my friends, we go way back. So *maybe* we might walk out of the store with some stuff other people might want. And *maybe* my friends might know other guys to take it off their hands. And maybe I could even tell you who those other guys are." Briggs leaned back, looking pleased with himself. "So, do we have a deal?"

Berglund shrugged. "It's not my call. But I'll see what I can do."

Terry Lankowski listened impassively as Berglund made his pitch. "I'll think about it and let you know," he said, rising and moving toward his office door. This was supposed to be Berglund's cue to leave, but he refused to take the hint.

"When?"

"When I'm finished thinking about it. Now if you'll excuse me, I've got work to do."

As soon as Berglund was out the door, Lankowski phoned Stack Ridgeway. "Get over here as soon as you can," Lankowski said, chuckling. "You are not gonna believe what that dickhead Briggs is trying to pull."

"I know exactly who he's talking about," Stack said after Lankowski recounted his conversation with Steve Berglund. "His old buddies Sean and Darrin Harvey. One of my undercover guys is working on a joint task force with the State Police. They expect to take down the whole network before long. We don't need Briggs to bust the Harveys, even if he really was with them, which I doubt. Although he's right about one thing, they go way back. But the Harveys are nobodies. Bottom of the food chain."

Bypassing the elevators, Stack jogged down the three flights of stairs to the parking lot and got into his Durango. He knew Scott Allison had already left for the Briggses' trailer with some uniformed officers to serve a search warrant, and he wanted to be there before they finished. He punched Allison's mobile number into his phone. He had some additional instructions to convey.

When Stack arrived he found Tammy Briggs standing outside her mobile home, looking bewildered, and introduced himself.

"Mrs. Briggs," he said brusquely. "I need to speak with you right now. It's urgent." He saw the fear in her eyes and almost, but not quite, felt sorry for her. The woman was only weeks—possibly days—away from finding herself in some very deep shit that was unrelated to the death of Katie Putnam.

"What...what about?"

"About your son's whereabouts this weekend."

Tammy's mind raced. She struggled to remember what she'd told the other detective earlier that day. If she contradicted herself it would look very bad for Brian, and for her too. "He was still here when I went to bed Friday night."

"So he was here all night?"

"I don't know. He was gone when I got up the next morning. He came back not long after that, though."

Stack jotted the information in his notebook. "What time was that?"

"I don't know for sure."

"Well, what time did you get up?"

"I don't remember. I didn't look at the clock."

"Mrs. Briggs," he said, trying to sound more patient than he felt, "it won't help your son if you lie for him. Now, let me ask you again. What time did you get up?"

"Like I said, I didn't look at the clock. But I usually get up around seven. And he came in at maybe eight? Eight-thirty? He took a shower and put on clean clothes. Then he left again. Didn't even eat breakfast."

"And when did you see him next?"

"This morning. I didn't actually see him, just heard him come in real early. Might have been about three? But I don't know for sure. I went back to sleep."

"You promised Detective Allison you'd call as soon as you saw or heard from Brian. Did you call him?"

"No," she stammered. "It was the middle of the night."

He saw Allison beckoning to him from the doorway of the trailer, and shut the notebook with a snap. "Okay. Thanks for your time."

35

"Hello, Jackie."

The middle-aged blonde at the front desk jumped. She'd been working on the monthly bank reconciliations and hadn't heard him come in. "Good afternoon, Mr. Carlyle." She watched as he strode past her and flung open the door to his son's office, walked through it, then slammed it shut behind him.

She'd never seen the old guy really mad before, but, judging by the way he was yelling at Ryan, he was definitely pissed off now. She wondered why. Not that she cared, because she thought Ryan was a prick.

She kept her eyes focused on her computer screen and her right hand on the mouse, trying to make out the words of Gary Carlyle's tirade. It was useless, though. She had no idea what he was saying until he stormed out of Ryan's office, stopped, and turned around to face his son.

"You killed that girl," he shouted. "*You* did it. Don't try to tell me otherwise." Then he remembered Jackie's presence and looked directly into her eyes, which were round with astonishment. "And you," he said forcefully. "Mind your own business."

"Yes, sir," she breathed after a moment or two, but by then he was gone. She flicked her eyes toward Ryan's office door, which was already closed.

It wasn't until she went home and saw the evening news that she was able to put two and two together. Brian Briggs, the new employee

Gary Carlyle had brought to the office the previous Friday—and he hadn't looked too happy about it, Jackie now recalled—was being held on suspicion of murder. She didn't know how or why that made Ryan responsible, but the thought of being just a few feet away from an accused murderer gave her chills.

She wasn't the only one who watched the story. The Harvey brothers saw it, too.

"He's gonna tell 'em he was with us," Darrin said.

"Ya think?" Sean responded sarcastically. "Too bad he wasn't."

"No, wait, let's think about this. Somebody at the trailer park mighta seen us when we picked him up. Lights were still on in some of the trailers. So let's say we picked him up and brought him here to our place, just for an hour or two, and we had a couple beers to celebrate him gettin' out."

"Then we took him back to his mom's?"

"Yeah, but we didn't go all the way into the trailer park. We dropped him off at the entrance." In reality, they'd let him out of the car at seven o'clock Saturday morning in the parking lot of a 24-hour diner a quarter-mile up the road from the entrance to the trailer park. Brian had eaten breakfast there, paying for it with money he'd taken from his mother's purse. He'd lingered for another hour, hitting on the waitress, and then walked home. "This was at midnight, twelve-thirty maybe. Right?"

"Got it," Sean said. "What did we talk about? In case they ask us."

"We didn't actually talk that much. At least you and I didn't. But remember how he was bitchin' about Katie and the trial most of the night?"

"That won't sound good for him, if we tell the cops about that."

"That's his problem."

North of town, Jill also saw the newscast detailing the death of Katie Putnam.

"Oh, no," she murmured, sinking onto the leather sofa in front of the television set. When she'd lived in the Chicago area, murders were often in the news. But Drummond was different, or so she'd thought. Obviously, though, she'd been mistaken. She got up and went outside onto the small rear deck. She rested her forearms on the railing and gazed into the distance, acutely aware of her physical isolation from the rest of the world. Sometimes the need to be held and comforted was overwhelming, and there was no one she could turn to. She began to weep, for Katie Putnam and for herself.

36

A few minutes after eight the next morning, Terry Lankowski called Denise Phelan's extension. "Hey, Red. Come join me for coffee."

Two minutes later, she was in his office. "You sound pretty chipper this morning," she said. He only called her Red when he was in a very good mood.

Lankowski shrugged. "Yeah, I guess. Our old friend Steve Berglund is on his way over, and I thought you'd enjoy sitting in on our meeting. I just gave him the happy news that we'll be charging his dirtbag client, so he should get his ass over here or we'll go ahead without him."

"Charging him with murder?"

"Not yet. The ME confirmed it was murder, but for the time being we'll have to settle for possession of stolen property."

Denise poured coffee from the pot on her boss's credenza into a Styrofoam cup. "Explain."

"Stack's boys executed a search warrant yesterday and found a whole lot of interesting stuff in Brian Briggs' bedroom, including some jewelry and small electronics identified as stolen from local stores. They also found a key which did not fit the door to his mother's trailer. But guess which door it does fit?"

Denise's eyes shone with excitement. "Katie Putnam's?"

"Bingo. Unfortunately," he added, "that's all we've got to tie him to the murder, at least for now. And since he used to live with her, he'll just claim he never got around to giving it back."

"There's just one problem that I can see. Could Berglund argue that the stolen stuff in Briggs' possession was outside the scope of the warrant? If it's unrelated to the murder charge—"

"Except it's not unrelated. Briggs alleged—through his attorney, mind you—that he was in the company of two known felons all night Friday, and they were actively engaged in committing retail theft. So what we found, and seized, was potentially exculpatory evidence. But all the merchandise we found was stolen months ago, and we can prove it. And to nobody's surprise, the Harveys have categorically denied that Briggs was with them for more than an hour or so Friday night. They, of course, have no idea where he went after he left them."

"What I can't figure out is whether Berglund has an idiot for a client, or Briggs has an idiot for an attorney."

"You want my opinion? Both. Seriously, though, Berglund isn't a bad guy. The problem is just that he's underqualified as a criminal defense lawyer. He oughtta stick to real estate closings and drawing up wills." Lankowski drummed his fingers on his desk. "Let me ask you something. We both agree that Briggs is an idiot. So how did this *idiot* manage to enter Katie Putnam's apartment, smother her with a pillow, and get out again without leaving any evidence? No fingerprints, no nothing. Doesn't that seem weird to you?"

"Not really. Even an idiot could figure out he'd need to wear gloves. And besides, he made threats in the presence of witnesses. That's a matter of record. And she was killed within hours of him getting out on bail."

"That's all true. But we still need to be able to place him at the scene. And given that he's not the sharpest tool in the shed, *and* presumably killed her in the heat of the moment—at the very least without much advance planning—I'd expect to find *something*."

"What does Stack Ridgeway say?"

"What can he say? He says they'll keep at it. They're interviewing neighbors, re-interviewing them in some cases. They're also tracing the girl's movements over the past few weeks to see where she went and with whom."

"I don't see how that will help. We know Briggs was in jail until noon on Friday."

"It'll help a lot when we go to trial and Berglund asks if they even bothered to look for other suspects. Then Stack can honestly say they did. He's a thorough guy. And in the meantime, the techs are still processing the scene. You never know what else might turn up."

He was almost certainly safe now. Over two weeks had passed, and he'd been carefully monitoring the news coverage of the case. Other than a brief report of Brian Briggs' arrest on other charges, no developments had been reported. There was no hint that anyone had a clue about his involvement. And why would they? Even if by some mischance he'd left a fingerprint, which the gloves should have prevented, he'd never been fingerprinted or had a sample of his DNA taken. So, since there was nothing to connect him with Katie Putnam, there'd be no reason to suspect him. He'd been keeping a low profile lately—even lower than usual, he thought with a smile—but now it was time to proceed with his next project.

That was how he thought of them: as projects, not people. He didn't consider women in general as people, and certainly not these woman. In the course of the jury's deliberations they had demonstrated their arrogance, their approval of using sex as a weapon, and their utter disregard for the men thus victimized.

The married women who had voted to convict Brian Briggs were annoying, of course, but they had husbands—and, in some cases, children—who needed them at home. The others, though, were a different matter entirely. He repeated their names to himself: Amy Morrison. Courtney Singleton. Jill McKinnon. Of these, the one he hated the most was Amy Morrison. And luckily for him, he knew exactly where to find her.

He'd continued watching her covertly on an irregular basis since her evening classes had ended the previous month, just to be sure her schedule hadn't changed significantly, and it hadn't. Except for Fridays, her after-work routine was the same every week: she visited her health club on Mondays, Tuesdays and Thursdays, and grocery shopped on Wednesdays. Fridays were unpredictable, but that didn't matter. He already knew how he would proceed. It was just a matter of waiting for the right opportunity. He also knew where to find Courtney Singleton. It was fortunate, he reflected, that his workday ended earlier than that of both the Morrison and Singleton women.

Jill McKinnon had eluded him, though. She'd been extremely guarded while on jury duty, sharing no personal information that he could recall. His only lead was the "J. McKinnon" listing he'd found in the telephone directory. After leaving work on Monday, he drove north out of town and spent nearly an hour locating the address. It was a tedious process because the roads bore only numbers, not names. While it would have been quicker to access a computer program, it would also have left electronic evidence that he didn't have the expertise to remove. There were, he knew—thanks to his fondness for televised crime dramas—software programs that would allow law enforcement to retrieve deleted files. *The low-tech way was the safest way*, he told himself. It hadn't been one of Chad's rules, or at least it hadn't been articulated. But it was a principle they had followed, and with excellent results.

There! He saw the sign: McKinnon Farm. He drove past without slowing down. There were no vehicles visible, no sign of activity. He glanced at his watch. He remembered from the brief jury selection interview that Jill was an accountant, and though he remembered the name of her employer—TBA Enterprises—he hadn't been able to find an address or telephone number for the company. But accountants typically enjoyed a regular schedule and worked until five or so. If Jill lived here, she would probably be arriving shortly. Unfortunately, though, there was nowhere nearby for him to park and observe. He continued to the next crossroads and, because the McKinnon property was on the right-hand side of the road, turned right.

He missed the turnoff the first time he passed it. But when he turned around and drove back the way he had come, he saw the barely-visible track leading into a small wooded area. He turned into it and followed it until it dead-ended after about a hundred feet at a line of evergreens. He shut off the engine and, because it was very warm, lowered the windows. He could see the outline of the house through the trees and, behind the house, what looked like a garage. Beyond that were other outbuildings, all of which appeared deserted. He also had a good view of the road to the south.

It occurred to him that he needed a cover story in the unlikely event that he was discovered. He got out of the Explorer and pulled some license plates from their hiding place beneath the back seat. All of the plates—stolen, of course—had small magnets glued to the underside. He considered: should he go with Iowa or Wisconsin? *Iowa,* he decided, and affixed them on top of his valid Illinois plates. The Quad Cities. He was making a delivery and got lost. He was waiting for instructions from his home office. *Delivering what?* was the next question. *Don't know,* he would respond with a shrug. Just a package. A special order package. *From whom?*

He remembered that he had a John Deere cap in his vehicle. John Deere headquarters were located in the Quad Cities, but on the Illinois side of the river. Not to say they wouldn't use an Iowa delivery service, though. It sounded lame, he thought, but it would have to do. And with any luck, nobody would ask him to explain himself. He settled back to watch for Jill to come home.

Although days were long this time of year and the sun was still far from the horizon, he eventually saw a light come on at the back of the house, in what he guessed was the kitchen. So there was somebody home. He waited until after seven o'clock, but saw no sign of Jill. His stomach rumbling, he finally gave up and removed the Iowa plates, which he tossed into the back seat before driving home.

It occurred to him that, though Jill might not live there, she was probably related to the person who did live there: undoubtedly a woman, given the use of an initial only instead of a first name. *As if that would fool anybody*, he thought contemptuously. On the heels of that thought came another: a woman might enjoy an unexpected gift of flowers.

The next day was hot and dry. He left work promptly, made a quick stop at a Jewel-Osco—instead of Kroger this time, because establishing patterns of behavior made him nervous—where he purchased a bouquet of flowers from the refrigerated case at the front of the store. The vase was cobalt blue instead of red, and it contained a mixed arrangement rather than roses.

As with Courtney Singleton's delivery, he was careful to wipe down the vase and don gloves before writing out the card: FROM YOUR SECRET ADMIRER. He donned his delivery-man ensemble of black trousers, white shirt, and black baseball cap. The blue mirrored sunglasses were the finishing touch. He picked up the flowers and set off for the McKinnon farm.

When he pulled into the driveway he noticed that one side of the garage was open and there was a car inside. What if it was Jill's? *Too late to chicken out now,* he decided. He got out of the Explorer and, holding the flowers and his clipboard, approached the front door and knocked.

The woman who answered the door wasn't Jill; she was much older, and obese besides. She looked at him suspiciously. "Can I help you?"

"Yes, ma'am. I have a delivery for"—he pretended to consult the clipboard—"J. McKinnon. Would that be you, or is there another J. McKinnon living here?" he asked with a smile.

She hesitated and seemed about to say something, then caught herself. "No," she said firmly. "I'm the only J. McKinnon here." She reached out and took the flowers from him. He had just enough time to realize that there was a purse dangling from her wrist before she shut the door in his face.

"You're welcome," he said under his breath, still smiling.

The purse plus the open garage door might mean she was on her way out. Maybe he should wait around to see what happened next. He got into the Explorer and backed out onto the county road, then drove to the hiding place he'd discovered the day before and shut off the engine.

As he watched, the woman came out a side door of the house, carrying the flowers as well as the pocketbook, and disappeared into the garage. Moments later he saw a beige Lincoln Town Car emerge and turn south toward town. To deliver the flowers, perhaps? She knew Jill, he was sure of that. Her hesitation when he'd asked about another J. McKinnon had given her away.

He'd noticed that she hadn't locked the door behind her. Either she didn't expect to be gone long, or she simply wasn't in the habit. And, since he was well acquainted with the habits of elderly ladies, he was pretty sure there would be a key rack just inside the door, with—if he was lucky—a spare door key hanging on it.

He watched until the Town Car was out of sight, then drove back to the house. He tapped on the door, just in case somebody else was there; then, brandishing the clipboard, pushed the door open.

"Hello?" he called out. Nobody answered him. Then, again, "Hello? I need a signature." Still no response. Quickly, he surveyed the room he had just entered: the kitchen. And sure enough, there was the key rack. There were two key rings hanging from it, one of which contained a single key which, judging by its appearance, was a door key. The other ring held a set of car keys and a twin to the house key. He removed the single key, which was, he decided, much less likely to be missed, and slid it into the heavy, old-fashioned lock. It fit perfectly.

Bingo, he thought, and pocketed the key. Then, because the old gal might return at any moment, he quickly climbed into the Explorer and left. He'd keep an eye on the place and, when the opportunity presented itself, he would perform a leisurely search. If Jill lived here now, or had in the past, he'd find out. Not right away, maybe, but he'd find out. There was no hurry, and in the meantime there was Amy Morrison to think about.

38

Jessica McKinnon visited her son's grave several times a month. Initially she'd gone every day and spent hours at a time there, because leaving—even briefly—felt like abandoning him. But when winter had set in, the snow and bitter cold had kept her at home, indoors, and ended her lonely daily vigils. During that time she'd begun to imagine him following behind her, just out of sight, as she went about her daily tasks. She talked to him, too; not when Jill was around, but at other times. When they were alone together. And sometimes she could almost hear him answering her.

Now, entering the cemetery where Kevin was buried, she turned left, then right, then drove straight ahead on the narrow lane until she reached the place where she always parked. She got out of her car. Holding the vase of flowers, she approached his grave.

"Kevin," she said softly. "Look what Mama brought you, honey." She removed the flowers from the vase and placed them in the metal container next to his headstone, then poured in water from the vase, which she set aside. "Aren't they pretty?"

She had decided immediately that this unexpected bouquet should be given to Kevin, even though she strongly suspected that it had been meant for Jill. All the more reason, Jessica reasoned, that Kevin should have it. After all, she was no fool. And she certainly didn't have any secret admirers.

She dropped to her knees and leaned over Kevin's headstone. "Enjoy the flowers, honey. I'll be back to visit you soon." Almost as an afterthought, she turned to her husband's headstone. "And you, too, Joe." She struggled to her feet, breathing hard, and picked up the vase. She would keep that, at least for now. It was such a beautiful shade of blue.

Back at home, she debated with herself for only a few minutes before calling Jill, who was getting ready to leave work.

"I just wanted to let you know," Jessica said, "that your secret admirer sent you flowers."

"What?"

"Your secret admirer," Jessica repeated. "He sent you flowers."

"I have no idea what you're talking about." Aware that Karen, the boss's assistant, was listening avidly from her desk nearby, Jill lowered her voice. "Listen, I'm on my way out. I'll call you back from home."

"Problems?" Karen asked.

"No, everything's fine. I'll see you tomorrow."

Half an hour later, Jill settled into a comfortable chair and dialed her mother-in-law's number. "Now tell me about the flowers."

"You received a bouquet," Jessica said with exaggerated patience. "It was delivered at a quarter after four. The card said it was from your secret admirer."

"You're sure they were for me?"

"Yes. Well, to J. McKinnon, but I know the 'J' meant you. Nobody would send *me* flowers."

"But, Jess, anyone who knows me well enough to send flowers would know that I've moved. Even if they didn't know my new address, they'd know where I work and have them delivered there."

"Maybe it's not someone who knows you well. Maybe it's someone who just *wants* to know you well."

Jill sighed. "If you're so determined to find out who it was, why don't you just call the florist and ask?"

"How should I know which florist they came from?"

"Wasn't the name on the van?"

"No, it was just a plain black SUV."

"That's weird." Under state law, Jill knew, commercial vehicles were supposed to display some kind of identifying markings. "And you said the flowers came to J. McKinnon? No first name?"

"No first name," Jessica said defiantly. "But I still think—"

"Listen," Jill broke in. "Since the flowers came to your house, let's just assume they were for you and leave it at that. Enjoy them with my blessing."

"I took them to Kevin's grave. I didn't think you'd mind."

Unlike Jessica, Jill rarely visited her husband's grave. It seemed pointless to her, because she'd never had the sense that he was *there*. But she knew it gave her mother-in-law some measure of comfort. "That was a lovely idea. I'm glad you thought of it."

After ending the call, Jill considered the matter of the flowers. She knew that their friend Louise had been trying to involve Jessica in social activities, including the local senior citizens' group and the county historical society, and that she had actually attended a few meetings recently. Could she have caught the eye of some elderly gentleman? The thought made Jill smile. It would be interesting to see if Jessica received any more deliveries.

Stack Ridgeway's frustration was growing by the day. Despite their best efforts over the past three weeks, they'd made no progress in building a murder case against Brian Briggs. He'd had motive, means, and opportunity. He'd made threats; that was a matter of record. He had a key to Katie Putnam's apartment. And the timing was right. But the fact remained that they still had no evidence to place him at the murder scene.

It hadn't taken long to compile a detailed history of the girl's movements during the weeks immediately preceding her death. They'd taken statements from her friend and coworker, Jennifer Cade, and Josh Dooley, the bartender at the Sports Fan. They'd also questioned Ruben Díaz, the cabdriver, very closely. He was the last person they knew of who had seen her alive.

"Lo siento, señor. I'm sorry, but it was like I tell you before. She gets out, she goes to the door and unlocks it, she goes in. I drive away. That's all."

"You're sure nobody was hanging around? Hiding, maybe?"

"Seguro," the cabbie insisted. "I don't see nobody. And how could I see if somebody was hiding?" he added with an eloquent shrug. "That's why you hide, so nobody sees you."

Stack had to admit that the cabbie had a point. "That's true," he said with a smile. "Thanks for your time."

Stack kept a white board in his office on which he'd sketched out the timeline of the night in question and listed the names of all the people he knew of who'd interacted with Katie Putnam. He scrutinized the board, searching for any loose ends he'd failed to notice.

And loose ends, as he knew from experience, were bad news. A good defense attorney—or even a mediocre one like Stick Berglund—could pull on the smallest hanging thread until the entire case unraveled. Stack looked at the board again. There was one item they hadn't yet cleared, although Scott Allison had some uniformed officers working on it. Stack picked up his phone and speed-dialed Allison.

"Hey. Any luck on tracking down that guy from the bar? The one who took her home in a taxi two weeks before she died?" They'd already spoken to the driver—not Díaz, but another one—who had been no help at all. He couldn't describe the man who had walked Katie to her door and then asked to be taken back to the Sports Fan. Medium height and weight, he thought, but it was too dark for him to see the man's face. Hair color? The driver didn't know. The guy had been wearing a hat.

"Not yet," Allison said, "but we've still got some ground to cover." The subdivision across the road from the Sports Fan bar and grill was a rabbit warren of small single houses and duplexes with postage-stamp yards. They were cheaply built, and many of the residents were first-time homeowners. The rest were tenants who rented from a local management company. It was slow work, going from door to door asking if the occupants had out-of-town relatives who'd been visiting Drummond the latter part of May.

"At least half the houses we've been to so far, there was nobody home," Allison went on. "Most likely, they're at work. You know," he added, "we're spending a lot of manpower on this." There had been a rash of residential burglaries in recent days, and retail theft had been increasing too.

"I know," Stack said with a sigh. "But stay on it for the rest of the day, and then we'll move on. I realize it's probably nothing, but I'd like to find the guy just so we can rule him out."

It would be one less loose thread for Berglund to pull on, Stack told himself as he headed out the door on his way to lunch. It was only a four-block walk to Pinky's, and he was hoping to catch up with Coach Dio there and score an invitation to the coach's annual Fourth of July barbecue. It was a guaranteed good time, and Coach's cooking was superb. That Berglund might be at Pinky's, too, with the same purpose in mind, was a risk he would have to take. His old teammate seemed convinced of his client's innocence—although Stack couldn't imagine why—which had caused some tension during their last few meetings.

Luck was with him today. He found Coach perched on his usual stool next to the cash register, but Berglund wasn't around. After a pleasant lunch with his old mentor, Stack left with the hoped-for invitation.

A few miles away, Jill McKinnon was working at her computer when her telephone rang. It was Louise Engquist.

"I know it's short notice," she said, "but my sister Margaret is having a Fourth of July cookout, and she asked me to invite you."

"Margaret," Jill repeated. "Have I met her?"

"I'm sure you must have, some time or other. Almost everyone in town knows Margaret and Dio. Anyway, she knows you. She specifically asked me to bring you along."

"I wonder why?"

"What difference does it make? The food will be great. Dio's parents were in the restaurant business, and he's a wonderful cook. Margaret's no slouch, either. Please say yes. I'll be glad to swing by and pick you up."

"Tell me one thing first. Will Jessica be there?"

"No, Jessica will not be there. You have my word on that. Just come on out, have some good food, and meet some nice people. They're my relatives, so how awful can they be?"

Jill laughed. "When you put it that way, I can't refuse."

"Great. I'll pick you up at two o'clock on the fourth."

Officer Jordan Copeland knocked at the door of a duplex unit which, although only a few years old, already looked dilapidated. After a brief wait, a diminutive young woman opened the door.

"Yes?"

She sounded apprehensive, so he smiled to reassure her. "I'm following up on a case, ma'am. Just wondering if you may have had any houseguests during the past couple of months."

"Maybe," she said hesitantly. "Why?"

"As I said, I'm just following up on a case. Could I step in for a few minutes, please?"

"All right." She moved grudgingly away from the door and motioned him inside, but didn't ask him to sit down.

"Your guests," he continued. "May I ask who they were, and when they were here?"

"It was my husband's older brother, and I think he was here last month. He comes down a few times a year. He's not in any trouble, is he?"

"Not that I'm aware of, ma'am. You said he comes down here? From where?"

"Zion. What's this about?"

Copeland smiled again. He was young, with a disarming manner, and very aware of his good looks. "Maybe I should start at the beginning. Could I please have your name for my report?" He pointed to his name tag. "Mine is Copeland."

He was rewarded with a tentative smile in return. "Bethany Alvarez." She gestured toward a threadbare sofa. "Sit down."

"Thank you, Mrs. Alvarez. Now tell me about your brother-in-law."

"His name is Richard Alvarez, and he works for Amtrak. Every so often he grabs a ride on the westbound California Zephyr out of Chicago and gets off in Mendota. That's the nearest stop, so Tim—that's my husband—picks him up there. He stays for a few days, and then we take him back to Mendota to catch the eastbound train. The last time he was here was around Memorial Day."

"Okay." That would have been about the right time. He recalled that from the briefing he and his colleagues had received. "And he hasn't been here since then?"

"No, that was the last time." She was starting to sound worried again. "You still didn't tell me what this is about."

What this is about, Copeland thought, is wasting time traipsing around in ninety-degree heat, knocking on doors, when I could be out chasing real criminals in an air-conditioned squad car. "Just tying up some loose ends, Mrs. Alvarez. You said your brother-in-law works for Amtrak. What does he do, exactly?"

"He's a car attendant. He used to be on the Zephyr, but last year he transferred to the Empire Builder. He's a really nice person," she added, a pleading note creeping into her voice. "He likes people, likes helping them."

"I'm sure he does." That would fit with what the bartender had said, Copeland reflected. Taking the girl home in a taxi had been an act of kindness. The bartender had agreed with the cabbie that the guy was medium height, but thought he was a little on the thin side and about thirty years old. Now, that made sense. Mrs. Alvarez appeared to be in her early to middle twenties and, presumably, her husband was roughly the same age. That would put an older brother in the right age bracket. What else had the bartender said? The guy was wearing a Brewers cap. "By the way, does Richard like baseball?"

"How did you know? He's crazy about it."

"Me, too," Copeland said with a grin. "You said he lives in Zion, which is pretty close to the Wisconsin state line. So does he like the Cubs or the Brewers?"

"The Brewers." Actually, her brother-in-law was a diehard Dodgers fan, but that hadn't been offered as an option. She'd heard the hopeful note in the cute young policeman's voice when he'd mentioned the Brewers and had picked them because he seemed to expect her to. And besides, it couldn't possibly matter.

Copeland heard a baby's faint waking-up noises in another room. "One more thing. Do you have a phone number for him? We'll need to call him, see if he remembers exactly when he was here."

She reached for her phone and scrolled through the list of stored numbers until she found the one she wanted. She read it out to him.

Copeland wrote it down, thanked her politely and left, pleased to have found the mystery man. It had to be the guy, he told himself. After all, everything fit.

He had reached the sidewalk before he realized he hadn't asked the most obvious question. He stopped, turned around and retraced his steps. He tapped on the door once more.

"Mrs. Alvarez," he said when she answered, "I'm really sorry to bother you when you've got your baby to take care of, but I was wondering… does your brother-in-law ever visit the Sports Fan when he's here?"

"Sure, to watch the games. I don't like to have the TV playing late at night when I'm trying to sleep. I have to get up early with the baby."

"Great," he said with a smile. "I really appreciate your cooperation."

Bethany Alvarez watched him walk away. She could have told him that when Richard went to the Sports Fan, Tim went with him. In fact, it was usually Tim's idea. But he hadn't asked about Tim—only Richard.

Copeland relayed a slightly embellished version of his interview with Mrs. Alvarez to Scott Allison, who called his boss late that afternoon.

"There's good news and bad news," he told Stack.

"Good news first."

"We finished canvassing the subdivision across from the Sports Fan, and we're pretty sure we've ID'd the good Samaritan from the bar. The one who took Katie Putnam home."

"Okay, so what's the bad news?"

"He couldn't have been involved in the murder. He's an Amtrak car attendant, and according to his sister-in-law his schedule would've put him somewhere between Chicago and Seattle that night." This last bit of information had been provided by Copeland based on Mrs. Alvarez's statement that her brother-in-law hadn't been around that weekend... and a timetable for the Empire Builder downloaded from the internet. And Allison, eager to move on with more pressing matters, had taken Copeland's information at face value and accepted the young officer's promise to follow up by phone with Richard Alvarez.

"And how is that bad news?"

"I guess it isn't, for us. But it is for the defense."

Stack went over to the white board and picked up the eraser. He was about to remove the "man in bar" notation, but something made him hesitate. He drew a line through it instead, then added a tiny question mark.

“I’m so glad you decided to come,” Louise told Jill. “Dio and Marg’s cookouts are fabulous.” She turned her Jeep Liberty onto a tree-lined street in an affluent west-side neighborhood.

They drove past a Mercedes that Jill recognized as Tommy Adair’s. “That’s Tommy’s,” she said. “I’m not sure if he’ll approve of me being here. He’s not one to socialize with the hired help.” Although Jill had worked for Tommy for nearly five years, and the Adairs entertained frequently, she had yet to be invited to their home. She didn’t really mind. It was just the way things were in Drummond.

“That’s his problem,” Louise sniffed. “Since when does he get to decide who’s invited to somebody else’s party?”

Jill was greeted warmly by Margaret Pappas, who strongly resembled her older sister. Both had the same fair skin, blue eyes, and pleasant, straightforward manner. Her wavy brown-going-gray hair was also similar, although Louise’s had considerably more gray and less brown.

A pretty dark-haired girl came up to them. “Aunt Louise, hello!” She hugged her aunt, then extended her hand to Jill. “Hi, I’m Christina Pappas. Tina for short. You must be Jill. Come on, I’ll introduce you around.”

The handoff to Tina was obviously prearranged, Jill thought, but she didn’t mind. As always when she found herself in a crowd, she was grateful that Rennie, her stepmother, had taught her how to work a room. She had become skilled at remembering names and connecting them with faces, and she was an attentive listener. But unlike Rennie, who had thrived on meeting new people—and the more, the better—Jill had never enjoyed large gatherings. If she was to be honest with herself, she was here for one reason and one only: to see Nick Pappas again.

And there he was, standing several yards away beside an older, stockier version of himself who was presiding over a huge grill. Nick glanced toward her, grinned and waved.

"...Stack Ridgeway," Tina was saying, "and his wife, Sherri." Jill tore her attention away from Nick and greeted the couple in front of her. She smiled and addressed them by name, filing them away in her mental Rolodex. She saw an amused glint in the husband's eye and suspected that he'd seen the direction of her gaze.

"Stack heads up the detective division of our local police force," Tina went on. "Jill works for Tommy Adair."

"Tommy's here," Stack said, nodding toward a small knot of people in a corner of the yard. Jill recognized the mayor and his wife, plus the chairman of the county zoning commission.

"Along with her royal highness," Sherri added with a grin.

Debra Adair stood next to her husband, posed with a hand on one hip like the model she had once aspired to be. She was very tall, slim and regal, and at the moment she looked supremely bored. Sherri Ridgeway's "royal highness" comment had been stunningly on point, and Jill couldn't help smiling. Still, it wouldn't be appropriate for her to participate in criticizing her boss's wife, even tacitly. Caught off-guard, she was wondering how to change the subject in a not-too-obvious way when Stack came to her rescue.

"Have you met our host yet? Tina, take Jill over to meet your father."

Earlier that day, Jill had recalled a piece of advice Rennie had once given her. "Remember that old saying, 'easy come, easy go'? People don't value something that's too easy to get. And that's especially true of good-looking guys." And now, as she and Tina approached the two men behind the grill, Jill kept her stepmother's counsel firmly in mind.

"Jill, this is my dad, the legendary Coach Dio Pappas." Tina spoke with such obvious pride and affection that Jill was touched. She greeted the older man warmly and thanked him for his hospitality.

"And I think you've already met my brother, Nick."

Only then did Jill allow herself to look at Nick and smile, murmuring, "So nice to see you again." She turned once more to his father. "Your grounds are lovely," she said. "Did you do the landscaping yourself?"

"Every bit of it," he said, looking amused. "And I sure could have used some help from the agronomist here. Nick, show Jill to the bar and get her something to drink. Beer, wine, soda, take your pick. It's almost time to eat."

That evening, alone for the first time since her arrival, Jill perched on the masonry wall surrounding the upper level of the patio. She was watching the other guests mingling on the lower level when Dio Pappas materialized nearby and spoke to her in his surprisingly warm, mellifluous voice.

"You know," he said, "I used to be a football coach. And every now and then I'd have a kid try out for the team who had a bucketload of talent. A real standout at practice. But in an actual game, not so good.... Did you get enough to eat?"

"Yes, thank you. Everything was delicious."

"Glad you liked it. But as I was saying. Kids like that, I could see in their faces that they were just afraid to get in the game. Maybe the fear was of messing up, or of getting hurt. But if I could help them get past that fear, whatever it was, then they'd be okay." He laid a gentle hand on Jill's shoulder. "The same goes for you, Jill. Don't be afraid to get in the game."

Thank you for the unsolicited advice, Jill wanted to say, but forced herself to smile instead. "I'll keep that in mind. By the way, have you seen Louise? I don't want to keep her waiting if she's ready to leave."

"Last time I saw her she was in the kitchen, gossiping with Marg. But I'll let you in on something: the plan is for Nick to take you home, and I think you should let him. Back in the game, remember?"

"My dad is a force of nature," Nick said as he guided Jill to his red Miata and opened the passenger-side door for her. "He loves arranging things. Being in charge."

Jill smiled. "So I gather."

"And we usually let him, because he's really good at it. Okay to put the top down? It's a beautiful evening."

He was already reaching for the latch, Jill noted. Apparently Coach Dio wasn't the only one who enjoyed being in charge. "Sure, go ahead." And then, because it seemed like a safe subject that would keep Nick talking, she added, "Tell me about your parents. How did they meet?"

He pushed on the convertible top until it folded into place with a click. "Dad moved down from Chicago to coach the high-school football team. He met my mom in the doctor's office where she worked." He settled into the driver's seat, fastened his seat belt, and started the engine. "Both sets of parents disapproved, of course, at least in the beginning. Especially Yiayia and Papou, which is Greek for Grandma and Grandpa. They were really dead-set against it."

"Why?"

"Because they wanted him to marry a Greek girl, preferably one from the old neighborhood." He paused momentarily, checking for traffic as he pulled away from the curb. "For Greeks, especially immigrants like my grandparents, heritage is paramount. They came from the northern part of the country, and Papou used to claim he was descended from King Philip of Macedonia and Alexander the Great. I remember asking

Dad if he actually believed that, but he wouldn't say one way or the other. He'd just shrug his shoulders and smile. And then there was the question of religion." Nick took his eyes from the road just long enough to steal a quick glance at Jill. "I know it's none of my business, but do you belong to a church?"

"No, I don't. My parents were never church-goers, and neither was Kevin. I'd describe myself as a believer, I guess, but no particular denomination. Why do you ask?"

"Because…well, here's the thing. For you—for a lot of people—denomination might not be that important. From my mother's point of view, the important thing is being a Christian. The theological fine points don't matter that much to her. But for Greeks, their religion is a major part of their culture and heritage."

"You said 'their' religion, not 'our' religion. Why is that?"

"Uh-oh. Busted. Good thing my father didn't hear me say that, or my sister, either." They had reached the traffic light at the county highway that led north toward the Juniper Ridge condos, where Jill lived. The light was red, giving him the chance to turn his head and look directly at Jill for the first time since they'd left his parents' house. He realized that he very much enjoyed looking at her.

The light changed. He turned left and accelerated. "My sister wouldn't think twice about identifying herself as Greek, even though she's got almost as much Swedish blood," he said, raising his voice to make himself heard over the road noise. "Of course, she lives and works in Joliet. She attends the Greek Orthodox church there and stays in close touch with Dad's family in Chicago. Our grandparents died years ago, but we have a couple of aunts there and quite a few cousins. Tina's a real chip off the old block. Did you know she's a coach, too? Girls' volleyball. Just at the high-school level for now, but I can picture her moving on to coaching a college team in a few years. She's that good."

"But what about you?"

"Don't misunderstand what I'm going to tell you, because I'm very proud of my Greek heritage. But that said, I seem to take more after the other side of the family. It broke my heart when my Sorenson grandparents sold their land, because I'd always wanted to stay right here in Remington County and farm. And worse yet, I used to go to church sometimes with my mother. My dad didn't like it. In fact, he hated it. But to his credit, he didn't actually forbid it. Religion for him was—and still is, as far as I know—almost as much about being Greek as it is about being Christian. So when my parents started discussing marriage, of course my dad wanted my mom to convert. And because to her it was just another Christian faith, she agreed."

"Then what was the problem?"

"The problem was that the nearest Orthodox church was over sixty miles away. It wasn't an issue at first, but after we kids were born it became one."

"How so?"

"Tina and I were baptized Orthodox, of course, and for my dad going to church on Easter and Christmas was enough. But my mom's concern was how we kids would learn to be real Christians if we hardly ever went to church. She was willing to drive over an hour each way every Sunday to take us to the Orthodox church in Rockford, but Dad…not so much. So Mom started going back to her local Lutheran church and taking us with her. When Tina got to be eleven or twelve, she stopped. Point-blank refused to go. I always thought it was because she picked up on how much it upset Dad. Or maybe because she's got stronger Greek genes," Nick said with a shrug. "We used to go to church summer camp with our Chicago cousins, and I enjoyed it. But when I got home, I'd go right back to Our Savior with Mom. Because I agree with her that it's more about being Christian than what denomination we are. Even though a lot of clergymen wouldn't see it that way."

"That's probably true," Jill said. They were approaching the turnoff into the Villas at Juniper Ridge. "Go left at the next light." While his comments on the religious issues involved in his parents' marriage were interesting, she was more intrigued by another comment he had made. "Tell me something. Why did your grandparents decide to sell their farm?"

"They were getting up in years, and both their daughters were married to non-farmers. And then their only son, my uncle John, was crippled in an accident. He was paralyzed from the chest down. The plan had been for him to take over from his parents, but after that, of course…"

"I understand. Is he still living?"

"No, he moved to Arizona with my grandparents. He died about ten years ago, and they didn't live long after that. My mother said at the time that they must have felt their work was done."

"Oh, I'm so sorry. Louise never told me."

"They'd sold most of the land to developers, including your boss, but kept the house along with a one-acre parcel. When they moved to Arizona, they sold the house to some people who wanted to convert it to a bed and breakfast. But when that didn't work out, the new owners sold it to a Chicago couple who come out here on weekends. It looks like they take good care of it," Nick said, sounding wistful. "I always loved that house when I was a kid."

"Next right," Jill said. "Then the fourth driveway on the left."

He pulled in as directed and stopped. "Nice place," he said as he came around to open her car door.

"Thank you. And thanks for the ride home, too," she said over her shoulder as she moved up the short sidewalk toward her front door.

He'd begun to follow her, then realized he hadn't been invited in. "You're welcome."

She thought he looked surprised. *Pretty sure of yourself, aren't you? Maybe you shouldn't be.* She'd picked up on his remark about wanting to farm in Remington County, and wondered if he had his sights set on running McKinnon Farm, Inc.. While she liked Louise, even trusted her, she could also imagine Nick's aunt trying her hand at matchmaking—with only the best interests of both young people at heart, of course.

When she reached her front door she raised her hand and waved at Nick, still standing in the driveway.

"I get up here from Bloomington several times a year," he called after her. "Can I phone you the next time I'm in town?"

"Sure, if you like," she said. "Good night, and thanks again." She went inside and closed the door firmly behind her.

43

The weather on the Wednesday after the July Fourth holiday was perfect for his purposes: hot and muggy, with a cold front expected to move through later that afternoon. At the end of his workday he went home and changed into the ill-fitting thrift-store khakis and an oversized t-shirt. In the garage, he tossed the old broom into the Explorer's back seat and checked under the front passenger seat for his John Deere cap.

He drove to the Walgreens drug store where Amy Morrison worked and parked in a remote corner of the parking lot, waiting for her to leave. Then he followed her at a discreet distance to the nearby Meijer store where she habitually grocery shopped and, as before, parked far enough away that she wouldn't spot him. He watched until she entered the building. Satisfied, he exited the lot and headed toward the northbound entrance to the interstate. Twenty minutes later, he reached his destination.

On one of his previous visits he'd scouted out the perfect parking place on a lightly traveled street that paralleled the highway. On the east side, closer to Amy Morrison's apartment building, a dense cluster of tall arbor vitae planted close to the sidewalk screened parked vehicles from the view of the building's inhabitants. And on the west side, there was only vacant land all the way to the interstate several hundred yards distant. Best of all, he had only to drive a few blocks north to reach the highway entrance ramp.

He shut off the engine and reached into the glove compartment for the sunglasses he'd chosen to go with this character's costume. They were the cheapest ones he could find, with black plastic frames and dark brown lenses. He'd wrapped a piece of duct tape around one of the sidepieces to simulate a repair, although the glasses weren't broken. He put them on, then reached under the passenger seat for the grubby John Deere cap.

He'd considered wearing gloves but decided that the penniless, mentally-challenged man he was pretending to be would not indulge in a luxury like gardening gloves. And besides, if all went as planned there would be no need to worry about fingerprints. He checked his watch. The Morrison woman was a quick shopper and should be here within half an hour. *The watch.* Like the gloves, a watch would be an incongruous element. He slipped it off and locked it in the glove compartment. He got out of the Explorer, put on the cap, and removed the broom from the back seat. It was show time.

In the stooped, clumsy gait he had practiced, he moved slowly and apparently aimlessly toward the building, stopping every few feet to sweep away some imagined bit of refuse. The heat was oppressive, and he had begun to sweat. He heard thunder and glanced to the west. Towering thunderheads were visible in the distance and were quickly approaching. With any luck, the storm would arrive at the same time Amy Morrison did.

He made his way up the steps at the opposite end of the building from her apartment, sweeping as he went. There was nobody to see him, but it was important for him to stay in character. He stopped at the top of the long flight, standing close to the exterior wall of the building in the shelter of the overhanging eaves, and waited.

Rain had begun to fall when Amy pulled in and parked her silver Mitsubishi Galant in its assigned space. "Shit," she muttered as she got out of the car. "Stupid rain." As she moved around toward the trunk, she caught a glimpse of the man her neighbor Ethel referred to as the Sweeper at the far end of the balcony. She couldn't imagine why he was out in this kind of weather unless he was, as Ethel had said, developmentally disabled. Hunched over against the pelting raindrops, she managed to grab all the plastic grocery bags—three in one hand, two in the other—and shoved the trunk closed with an elbow. It was really starting to come down. She'd just have to make a run for it.

She reached the open stairway and dashed up it, even though she was thrown off balance by the groceries she carried, and was one step away from the top—and the ninety-degree turn toward her apartment—when she saw a flash of movement. *What…?*

Then the broom handle caught her hard in the chest and she was flying backwards, grasping desperately but futilely for the handrail. Her last coherent thought was that the expensive bottle of olive oil she'd just bought would be broken.

He didn't wait to watch her hit the bottom. Instead he swung around and hurried past the neighboring apartments, walking as quickly as he dared but not wanting to attract attention by running. Amazingly, nobody seemed to have noticed anything out of the ordinary. No doors opened, and he saw no curious faces at the windows he passed. When he reached the far end of the balcony, his instinct was to get away as fast as he possibly could. But he forced himself to descend with care because the steps were steep and the rain had made them slick. Once he reached the foot of the stairs he ducked his head and, holding the broom close to his body, sprinted for the shelter of his vehicle.

When he reached the on-ramp to the interstate, he drove north instead of south toward Drummond. It was important to insure that he'd made a clean getaway, so he kept going past the next exit and took the second one, heading west on a state highway and then turning into a residential area where he zigzagged aimlessly around for several minutes before returning to the state road.

Satisfied that nobody was following him, he returned to the interstate and drove home. As always, he entered his garage and hit the remote control as quickly as possible so the neighbors wouldn't notice the out-of-state plates, which he removed as soon the door was fully closed.

He was still on an adrenaline high, shivering from the shock of entering his chilly, air-conditioned apartment when he had been sweating so profusely. A nice warm shower would feel good and settle him down before he moved on to the next order of business, which was disposing of his costume. That was how he thought of the items of clothing he assembled for each of his characters, as though he was acting a part in a play.

After his shower he tossed all the items he'd been wearing into the washing machine and put the baseball cap, stretched over an inverted bowl to hold its shape, in the dishwasher on the steam cycle. He then fixed himself a ham sandwich and washed it down with a light beer while he thought about how to get rid of the khaki pants, t-shirt, cap and broom.

The pants had come from a thrift store, and the t-shirt was an old one of his own. Both were ratty enough to justify being thrown away. Luckily, tomorrow was trash day. He'd put them in a plastic bag and take them to the curb along with his other garbage right before the truck arrived. And he already had a plan for the cap, which left only the broom to be concerned with.

Thanks to his fondness for television crime shows, he was aware of the importance of fiber evidence. Could there be fibers from the woman's clothing stuck to the end of the handle? He retrieved the broom from the back seat of the Explorer and examined it carefully. He saw nothing, even under a magnifying glass, but to be on the safe side he rubbed the top few inches of the handle with some fine-gauge sandpaper. That done, he saw no need to get rid of it right away. After all, there was nothing suspicious about owning a broom. In a few weeks he would buy a new one and throw the old one out with the trash.

He returned the broom to the garage and rummaged in the container where he accumulated plastic bags for eventual recycling. He found one from Sears, which he thought would do quite nicely. Whistling softly to himself, he carried it into the kitchen. When the dishwasher finished its cycle, he donned rubber gloves—a fresh pair, right out of the package—and put the cap into the Sears bag.

As an afterthought, he brought the sunglasses into the kitchen and pulled off the duct tape he'd used to effect the mock repair, removing the residual adhesive with a paper towel doused with Krud Kutter. He considered throwing away the glasses, too, but decided not to. He might want to use them again at some point.

An hour later, he drove ten miles to the shopping mall and entered it, carrying the bag. He went to the store he occasionally patronized—the one specializing in a wide variety of hats and caps—and purchased two new ones to replace the Brewers cap he'd disposed of weeks earlier and the soon-to-be-history John Deere cap. Something edgier this time, he decided, and less mainstream. There was a wider selection on the store's website, but that had the disadvantage of leaving an electronic trail. The low-tech way was better: go in, pay cash, and leave.

That accomplished, he went to the food court and walked through it to the men's restroom, where he entered a stall and shut the door. He reached into the Sears bag, withdrew his rubber gloves, and put them on before taking the Deere cap out of the bag and hanging it on the hook on the back of the door. Finally, he tucked the gloves and Sears bag into the other store's bag along with the two new hats. He listened for voices or other noises before cautiously opening the stall door. Satisfied that he was alone, he exited the stall, pushed the door shut behind him, and returned to the food court.

Whoever found the cap would either keep it or, more likely, take it to the lost-and-found kiosk in the mall's center court. Either way worked for him. Suddenly realizing how tired he was, how drained by the day's events, he went home and fell into bed. Only then did it occur to him to wonder whether the Morrison woman might have survived her fall.

He saw the answer in the next morning's *Drummond Observer*, where the death of Amy Morrison was reported in a brief story on page three rather than the obituary column. There were few details given, and no suggestion that her death was other than accidental.

Stack Ridgeway saw the article, too, but paid little attention to it. While it was always a tragedy when such a young person died, it appeared to be an accident. Besides that, it was beyond the Drummond city limits and therefore outside his jurisdiction. If further investigation was required, it would be done by the Remington County Sheriff's Department under the leadership of Lucas Dean.

Stack had known Dean for years and had always found him cooperative when one of his cases crossed jurisdictional lines. He was also extremely astute. Perhaps, Stack thought, it might help to seek his counsel in the Putnam investigation. A second opinion certainly couldn't hurt, especially since police chief Harry Whitesell was hounding him to get the case closed.

He picked up the telephone, dialed the sheriff's private number, and was rewarded with an immediate response.

"Dean."

"Lucas, it's Stack. Can we get together for lunch? I need to pick your brain."

"Sure thing." It was typical of Dean that he didn't ask for an explanation. "How's twelve-thirty at Frankie's place?"

"Fine. See you there."

Entering the Dragons Den—known as "Frankie's place" by a select few long-time Drummond residents—at the appointed hour, Stack was greeted by the owner, Frank Maloney.

"Hey, Stack," he called out, then laughed at his own joke. "Haystack," he chortled. "Get it?"

"A little early to be drinking up the profits, isn't it, Frankie?"

The grizzled bartender's struggle with various forms of substance abuse had been going on for decades, and he didn't like to be addressed as Frankie except by a small and very exclusive fraternity of which Stack was not a member. Maloney was sober today and had been for several months, at least this time around. But his "Haystack" remark had deserved the comeback, so he let it go.

"Luke ain't here yet. You can wait for him in his booth. It's all the way to the back. I save it for him at lunch time."

Unlike Stack, who liked to keep an eye on his domain from the window table at Pinky's Café across the street, Lucas Dean preferred the dimmer, more private confines of the rear booth at the Dragons Den. He was also a classmate and lifelong friend of Frank Maloney, a famous slugger during their high school years and beyond. Frank had set home-run and RBI records in 1972, his senior year, that still stood. He had eventually worked his way up to the AAA Omaha Royals and stood poised for baseball stardom until his career had flamed out just a few months after being called up to the major-league team in Kansas City.

"Too much wine, women and bong," Frank had deadpanned to the press. He knocked around the minor leagues for a few years but eventually returned to Drummond to help his uncle run the Dragons Den, which was decorated with an assortment of Drummond Dragons sports memorabilia going back to the 1930s. The uncle had died years earlier, and since then Frank had kept the place going with the assistance of a succession of waitresses. The incumbent was named Michelle, and like her predecessors she was rumored to be sleeping with Frankie. She hadn't shown up for work yet, Stack noticed. Frank wouldn't need her until happy hour, when things started getting busy.

On one score, Stack reflected, he had to give Frank Maloney a lot of credit. Although the Dragons Den was one of the most popular watering holes in town, bar fights were virtually nonexistent there. If customers began acting hostile, Frank would fix them with a hard stare.

"Don't make me get my bat," he would say. If they continued, he would pull the Louisville Slugger from its place beneath the bar and brandish it threateningly. Additional warnings were never necessary.

"Want a burger?" Frank called out. His menu was limited to hamburgers, but his customers never complained because he used generous portions of top-quality ground round purchased just that morning at the local Eagle supermarket. The meat was cooked to sizzling perfection and topped with each customer's choice of lettuce, tomato, onion, four kinds of cheese, bacon, or chili, then served on a toasted bun. A wide variety of condiments could be added upon request, and individual bags of chips were available as an additional purchase. Frank never offered French fries, though. In his often-stated view, maintaining a deep-fat fryer was a pain in the ass.

"Thanks, but I'll wait for Lucas."

As if on cue, Lucas Dean blew through the door. A few long-legged strides carried him to the rearmost booth, and he slid in across from Stack.

"Sorry I'm late. Little girl fell down the stairs and broke her neck yesterday. A real bad business."

"I saw the story. Thought it was an accident, though."

"Yeah, but still a bad business. Hey, Frankie," he yelled over his shoulder. "How about some burgers here? Load 'em up. And a couple of Cokes."

"Just lettuce and tomato on mine," Stack added quickly. Dean was well into his fifties but still cadaverously thin; while he could afford to gorge on cheese and bacon, Stack could not. "So what's the deal with the girl?"

"Her parents will probably sue the building management. Actually, I think that's a given. My guys took a lot of pictures last night, but I wanted to see for myself. Talk to the folks who've lived there a while, find out if there was anything that obviously should've been fixed." He shrugged. "The handrail was in good condition, and so were the steps. But the consensus was, they could be slick when it rained. One old gal I talked to said she liked the girl a lot, but they all knew the steps were slippery and she shoulda been more careful."

"Wonder if she'd say that if it was *her* daughter that died."

"Probably not. What'll wind up happening is that the parents will sue, the case will get settled out of court, and the parents will get closure, whatever the hell that means. Along with a big pile of cash that won't bring their little girl back. Now what was it you wanted to pick my brain about?"

"Brian Briggs," Stack said. "Here's the thing that baffles me. He's dumb as a box of rocks, can't find his ass with both hands. So how the hell does he manage to get into the vic's apartment—"

"With a key, of course."

"And you know that how?"

"People talk."

"More than they should, obviously. Okay, so he had a key, and getting in was no problem. But the larger question is, how did he manage to do the deed and get out without leaving a single piece of evidence?"

"I take it none of the surrounding buildings have security cameras."

"Come on, Lucas, this is Drummond, not Chicago." He sighed. "And of course nobody saw him. We are not exactly the city that never sleeps. But it recently occurred to me…"

Frank Maloney approached with their hamburgers and cans of Coca-Cola. He didn't bother with niceties like glasses unless he was serving liquor.

"I started wondering," Stack continued when Frank had gone, "if maybe somebody else was involved."

"Like who?"

"You know we're holding Briggs on a shoplifting rap."

Dean munched on his burger and nodded. "Yeah."

"And the state cops think they'll be able to connect him with a shoplifting ring that operates in several downstate counties in addition to this one. Plus, Tammy Briggs—his mother—is in it up to her neck. She supposedly supports herself by going around to craft fairs, selling those doll clothes she makes. But she also sells other merchandise she gets from Brian. At first she claimed she had no idea where Brian was getting the stuff, because she never asked and he never said. But then she broke down and admitted she figured it had to be stolen, because how else would he get it? Anyway, they'd turn it around as fast as they could. Sometimes they'd sell it directly to customers, sometimes to other vendors, and sometimes to mutual friends."

"Let me guess. The Harvey brothers." Dean and his deputies were well acquainted with the Harveys, who lived south of the Drummond city limits in a disreputable neighborhood known as the Triangle.

"Or friends of the Harveys. And there's another thing." Stack paused to take a bite of his burger. "Damn, this is good."

"Yeah, Frankie gives good burger. Go on."

"Either Tammy Briggs is as stupid as her son, or she's unbelievably devious. She let slip—or maybe it was on purpose, who knows?—that the Putnam girl knew about Brian's involvement with the shoplifting ring. So maybe the Harveys were afraid she'd rat them out. And Briggs's release from jail gave them the opportunity to help him get rid of her, then shift the blame onto him."

"I don't know, Stack." The sheriff sounded doubtful.

"But why else would they not back him up and alibi him for the night in question? Briggs claimed they were driving around hitting some big-box stores, but—"

"Well, there's your reason. Why would the Harveys admit to that?"

"Because we never mentioned what they were supposed to be doing. We just asked if they were together. They could've said 'Yeah, he was hanging out at our place, but we never went anywhere.' And there's another problem. I asked State if they could get us video from the night in question, and they did."

"Shit, man, how do you rate?"

"Easy. I've got a guy assigned to their team as a liaison. So we looked at all the video from all the stores Briggs claimed they hit, and none of 'em showed up. Not Briggs, not the Harveys."

"So Briggs was lying. What else is new?"

"Lying about where they were, for sure. But maybe not about being with the Harveys. They're capable of murder, I'd bet on it. They're some of the meanest bastards I've ever seen. And they're a shitload smarter than our friend Briggs."

"Possible," Dean admitted. "It's quite a stretch, though."

"Yeah, I know," Stack said with a sigh. "But I'm always afraid of developing tunnel vision when I'm working a case. When you don't look at the bigger picture, it's too easy to miss stuff you ought to see."

Jill had just prepared a cup of green tea when she heard the thud of the morning paper landing on her front stoop. She retrieved the paper and carried it and the tea outside onto her south-facing deck, where she settled into a lawn chair.

She usually concentrated on the national and financial news and skipped the obituaries, but today as she turned the page a familiar name in the upper right-hand corner caught her eye.

"Amy Morrison," Jill breathed. "Oh, no." She read the obituary a second time, looking for the cause of death, but learned only that Amy had died at home. She was survived by her parents in Danville, a brother in Champaign, a grandmother in Indianapolis, and numerous aunts, uncles and cousins. *So many people to mourn her*, Jill reflected. *But if I were to die right now, who would miss me?* Her teen-aged half-brothers, perhaps, with whom she kept in occasional contact via email, and possibly her parents, although their involvement in her life was increasingly tenuous.

Her mother had begged off coming east for Kevin's funeral because, she claimed, she had to get the boys ready to start school. Her father had flown in at the last minute, accompanied by a tall, thin, leathery-skinned blonde of indeterminate age who had referred to herself as his fiancée but was not wearing a ring. They had spent just one night in a local hotel before hurrying back to Florida.

She wondered if she should go to Amy's funeral, arrangements for which were still pending according to the newspaper. She'd barely known Amy and would feel like an impostor, mingling with grieving family and friends.

Jill set the newspaper aside and sipped her tea, wishing there were more of a view from the deck. But there was just a rectangle of lawn, which she shared with a neighboring building, and a few frail-looking young trees surrounded by flower beds planted with blooming annuals. The landscaping was cared for by a crew of brown-skinned men who appeared a few times a month, worked diligently, and then departed as quickly as they had arrived. The effect was tidy but impersonal.

The inescapable fact was that she missed the farm. Even though it was being worked by strangers now, under her Agricultural Services arrangement with the First Bank of Drummond, she still felt a strong connection to the land her husband had bequeathed her. She had loved looking out her second-floor bedroom window, from which she could survey the crops throughout their predictable cycle of growth and harvest as summer ripened into autumn.

She was also terribly lonely. Despite her rocky relationship with Jessica, the older woman had been a dependable physical presence in the house; and it occurred to her that Coach Dio's advice to "get in the game" might not be limited to potential romantic involvements. She needed to develop friendships with women as well, and perhaps her own office was a good place to begin. Surely Tommy or Karen, his assistant, could suggest a service club or two that she could join.

Maybe it was due to their difference in ages and lifestyle—Karen was in her early fifties, long married, and the mother of two grown children—but Jill had never felt comfortable with Karen despite working with her for nearly five years. All the more reason, Jill decided now, to approach her for advice. They would probably never be close friends, but at least it would be a starting point.

It was late morning before Jill had the opportunity to chat privately with Karen. "Service clubs," Karen mused. "A lot of 'em are just your typical old boys' clubs, but I could probably suggest a few. Depends on what your interests are."

"My interests," Jill repeated blankly.

"What constituencies you want to serve. The homeless? Old folks? Disabled?"

"That's a good question. I haven't really thought about it."

"Jill," Karen said gently, "is this really about serving the community, or is it about meeting new people?"

"Well…both, actually."

"Okay. Do you have plans for lunch?"

"No, nothing special."

"Then let's go to Chez Marie and check out their lunch specials. Do you realize that in all the time you've worked here, we've never been to lunch together? And if we leave now, we can beat the rush."

When they arrived at the restaurant they were greeted by Courtney Singleton, whom Jill remembered from the trial where they'd both served as jurors. "It's like old home week, girlfriend," Courtney said as she led them to a table. "First that Ryan guy, and now you."

"Ryan Carlyle, you mean?"

"Yes. He was here a couple days ago, and he is just plain creepy." She gestured toward a booth beneath a window. "Will this do for you ladies?"

Jill glanced toward Karen, who nodded. "It's fine. What do you mean, he's creepy?"

"Oh, just something he said. Like it was impossible to hide anymore, because if somebody really wanted to find you, then they would."

"I wonder what he meant by that?"

"I didn't ask him. But it felt like he meant *he* could find *me*."

"Well, you did say where you worked."

"I guess I did, but I never figured he was taking notes." Courtney placed menus on the table. "Gabriella will be your server. She'll be with you shortly." She had started to turn away when Jill stopped her.

"Courtney, did you see in the paper that Amy Morrison died?"

Courtney's eyes widened. "She *died*? When?"

"Wednesday afternoon, I think."

"That's too bad. What happened?"

"I don't know. It didn't say."

"Well, let me know if you hear anything else. I liked that girl." She pulled a business card from her pocket and handed it to Jill. "Here's my number."

Jill glanced at the card: *Lifestyles by Courtney*.

"It's just a little side business," the hostess said. "That's my cell number, but I keep it turned off here at work. So call me after."

Across the table, Karen raised her eyebrows and gave her a questioning glance. "What was that all about?"

"Courtney and I were on jury duty together. And so was Amy Morrison, the girl who died."

"And the other girl was murdered. I saw that in the paper."

"Katie Putnam. Yes."

Karen shivered. "Ooooh, that's weird. Two people involved in the same case, both dead. You be careful."

"I will." Jill remembered why she had never enjoyed Karen's company: the woman enjoyed tragedy far too much. It was time to change the subject. She thought of her former neighbor, Ethan Cameron, and his dog, the one they'd adopted from the Humane Society. What was its name? Rowdy? Yes, that was it. Rowdy. "Children," she said. "And animals, especially dogs."

"What?"

"You asked earlier what constituencies I wanted to serve, and that's it. Kids and dogs."

It was Saturday, quite possibly a good day to catch Jill at the farmhouse. Before leaving home, he thought through what he should take along: out-of-state license plates, of course—Missouri this time—and a dark blue Webster University ball cap. Because he expected to spend several hours in his hiding place, he packed some sandwiches and soft drinks into a small cooler. Finally, he pulled a set of binoculars from a drawer in his upstairs office and hung them around his neck.

"All the better to see you with, my dear," he murmured.

Since the roads in rural Drummond were laid out on section lines, it was a simple matter to approach his wooded hiding place without passing directly by the McKinnon farmhouse. Instead, he drove north on a parallel road until he reached the sign he'd been watching for, then turned west. The road signs bore no names, only numbers, which would add authenticity to his cover story if he happened to be challenged.

He found the now-familiar lane and turned into the wooded tract from which he could comfortably view the McKinnon house, then turned off the engine. He got out of the Explorer, attached the magnetized Missouri plates and put on the Webster cap. He was already wearing sunglasses. Then he checked both of his phones—the BlackBerry and the prepaid disposable—to make sure they were turned on, and set the BlackBerry to vibrate instead of ring. Laying them on the seat beside him, he settled down to wait. The binoculars gave him a good close-up view of the house and driveway.

After two hours his stomach started to rumble, so he took one of the sandwiches out of the cooler and ate it, washing it down with a Sierra Mist. It was warm even in the deep shade provided by the evergreens, whose rich fragrance drifted through the Explorer's open windows. After finishing the sandwich he was very relaxed, perhaps even a bit drowsy, and as a result he never heard the boy approach until he was just a few yards away.

"Hello," the boy said.

Instantly alert, he turned his head and made himself smile. "Hello to you, too," he said genially. "Looks like you caught me." He was grateful for his mirrored sunglasses, which hid the fact that the smile hadn't reached his eyes.

"Caught you what?"

"Trespassing, if this is your property." He kept his tone casual, the smile still on his lips while he sized up the kid. It wouldn't be a problem, he decided, if he needed to take the kid out. He was pretty scrawny. But the dog was something else again. It was a wicked-looking sucker, and big enough to do some damage. "I'm headed for a classmate's house. Long story," he said with a shrug. "And I must've written the directions down wrong. I'm not from around here...but you already figured that out, huh?" He grinned again. "Anyway, I called my buddy, but it went to voice mail. So I'm just waiting for him to call me back."

The kid didn't say anything—just watched him—and the dog was staring at him as if it wanted to rip his throat out. He could hear it snarling, too. Time to bail. He edged his hand, which was out of the kid's view, a few inches to one side and speed-dialed the burn phone from his BlackBerry.

When the burn phone rang, he flipped it open and held it against his ear. "Hey, Jim, 'dyou get my message?...Yeah, that's where I turned, but...oh, *west*. I thought you said *east*. Okay, and then north at...Yeah... Yeah...All right, got it. See you shortly. But stay off the phone in case I need to call you back. Okay, bye." He closed the phone, started the Explorer's engine, and spoke to the boy. "I'm rolling," he said cheerfully. "Wish me luck."

He executed a quick turn, hoping that the kid wouldn't have either the time or the presence of mind to memorize the Missouri plate number, and pulled onto the pavement. He drove west as fast as he dared until he reached the second crossroads, then turned north. He made a few more zigzag turns on rural roads bordered by cornfields, then pulled over, stopped, and removed the Missouri plates. He had already tossed the cap with its block-letter W design onto the floor of the front seat; but now he picked it up and stuffed it into the glove compartment.

Damn! How had he not seen the kid approaching? Good thing he'd had a cover story prepared and his phones ready.

A few miles away, Ethan Cameron was sitting on Jill and Kevin's bench, holding Rowdy's leash. "What was up with that?" he scolded the dog. "That guy didn't do anything to you. He was just lost. How come you were growling at him like that?"

Rowdy nudged Ethan's arm with his nose and licked his hand. "I can't stay mad at you," Ethan said, caressing him. "But don't pull that stuff with anyone else, okay?"

As he walked home, though, Ethan couldn't escape the feeling that there was something not quite right about the man and his story. He couldn't put his finger on it, but for some reason the guy had made the hair on the back of his neck stand up.

"We'd better tell Mom and Dad about it," he said to Rowdy as they walked down the road toward home. "Don't you think?"

His father was in town doing errands, and, rather than wait for him to return, Ethan told his mother about his encounter with the man on Jill McKinnon's property.

When he had finished, she said, "That sounds pretty harmless to me, Ethan."

"I thought so, too, at first. But…"

"But what?"

He shrugged. "I don't know."

Rachel Cameron knew her son was observant and unusually intuitive. "Ethan," she said gently, "what aren't you telling me?"

He hesitated, biting his lip. "Rowdy didn't like him," he burst out. "He growled at him. Not that play-growl thing he does, but a real growl. He had his ears laid back and everything. He even—"

"He even what?"

"You know how hard we've been working with him on heeling? Staying beside us on our left when we walk him on the leash? And he's been doing really good at it, too. But he didn't stay beside me. He got in front of me, between me and the guy."

"Protecting you," Rachel Cameron muttered to herself. Whatever it was about the man that had frightened Ethan, Rowdy had sensed it, too. She reached down and patted him. "Good dog," she said. "I'll tell your dad about all this because I think he needs to know. In the meantime, it's probably best if you don't go up there by yourself for a while."

That night, she recounted the episode to her husband. "It gave me chills, Mark. Dogs sense things about people. That man was up to no good."

"If Rowdy was sensing anything about anybody, it was Ethan. I can understand why it spooked him, seeing somebody there when he didn't expect to, but come on. The guy never approached him, never said anything out of the way, and then he got a phone call and left. I know how much you love dogs, but they do not have magical powers to read the minds of total strangers. Rowdy was just picking up on Ethan's anxiety."

She didn't bother arguing, because she knew her husband wouldn't change his mind. Still, she couldn't get Ethan's words out of her mind: *Rowdy didn't like him.*

Being discovered by the kid had been a wakeup call, that was for sure. He never should have let it happen. Perhaps he should just back off for a while. But there were two things he needed to do right away.

The first was to trade in the Explorer, because too many people had seen it now. There was the black guy, when he'd delivered the flowers, and then the old lady. And now the kid. Black Explorers were common as dirt, but he'd feel safer if he just got rid of it. Besides, he'd been wanting a newer ride.

The other thing he needed to do was to acquire a weapon. Not a gun, he decided; they were too noisy, and there was too much paperwork involved. Plus the fact that he'd never been around guns much, just those few times when his dad had taken him and Chad hunting in northern Minnesota at the ramshackle cottage that Gram and Gramp had owned since the 1950s. It sat on sixty acres of wooded land on the St. Louis River, far out in the middle of nowhere, so they could afford to be casual about taking the occasional deer out of season when it wandered onto their property. The damn things were trespassing, weren't they? And besides, they were hardly an endangered species. They reproduced like rabbits.

Hunting with Chad. He smiled at the memory. If anyone asked, they would always say they were going fishing, not hunting, because summer wasn't deer season. But no matter what they called it, they'd always enjoyed it: the freedom to say, do, eat and drink anything they wanted while his father went directly to his stash and proceeded to get high.

If his father had married Chad's mother, then Chad—his friend and mentor—would have been his stepbrother. Chad was already good with a knife back then and had shown him how to use it. Knives were quiet, and they could be absolutely terrifying. He remembered reading somewhere that most people were more frightened of a knife, if threatened, than they were of a gun. Yes, Chad could help him get a good hunting knife, maybe a clip point knife with a six-inch fixed blade. He'd go up to Milwaukee for a visit next weekend.

Meanwhile, he wanted to take one last swing past the Singleton woman's house before he ditched the Explorer. He'd leave his own license plates exposed this time. Vanity plates were hugely popular in Illinois, but he thought they were stupid. His bore only numbers, which were not likely to be remembered even if anybody noticed him passing by.

The weekend traffic was light, so it took him less than fifteen minutes to reach Courtney Singleton's neighborhood. He turned off the state highway a block before reaching her house, then swung left into the alley behind it. He drew a mildly curious glance from a woman relaxing in a backyard lawn chair a few houses to the west of Singleton's, but there didn't seem to be anybody else around.

He slowed down as much as he dared, watching for the mysterious object he'd seen on her back porch weeks earlier. It was cylindrical, two to three feet high, and he'd thought at the time that it resembled one of those cigarette receptacles businesses often placed by their doors for the use of customers who smoked.

Yes, that's what it was! And it was still there, between her back door and a pair of lawn chairs. Someone in the household smoked, but wasn't allowed to do it indoors. So he—and it was almost certainly a *he*, probably the bad-tempered dude who'd opened the door for the flower delivery—would sit out there on the back porch and smoke whenever the urge hit. He wasn't sure what use he would make of this information, but of one thing he was certain: all information could be important in some way, at some time. He drove on to the end of the block and turned left toward the state highway.

When he reached home, he turned on the television set and stepped onto his treadmill. He ran several miles while watching a previously recorded episode of one of his favorite crime dramas. It was interesting, he thought, that this show—and several others he enjoyed—almost always depicted perpetrators with well-established patterns of behavior that eventually led to their downfall. The dialogue was laden with terms like "psychotic break" and "trigger point," usually uttered by a solemn-faced cast member. If there was one thing that he himself was certainly not, it was psychotic. He did, however, consider "trigger point" an interesting concept. While he wasn't given to introspection, he had occasionally wondered what it was, exactly, that had caused his life to veer off into the direction it had taken since adolescence. Not that it made any difference now, he concluded with a mental shrug, and clicked the remote control to begin another episode. Maybe it would give him some ideas on how to deal with the two women who still eluded him.

Television shows were only entertainment, of course. Many of the crimes depicted were so sophisticated and bizarre that an ordinary person couldn't possibly have pulled them off. Some of the law-enforcement procedures were equally far-fetched, too, at least by local standards. The crime-drama lab technicians were accomplished scientists who had access to sophisticated, up-to-the-minute equipment and ran their own DNA tests, while the Drummond police had to send theirs off to the State Police labs for processing and wait weeks to get results. He'd read about that in the newspaper. Also, instead of a brilliant medical examiner who was alert to the tiniest anomaly, Remington County only had a coroner—an elective position not requiring a medical degree.

On television, he reflected, it would have been a simple matter to set fire to Courtney Singleton's house, with her in it, and make it look like the result of careless smoking. The screenwriters wouldn't have to bother with practical matters like how it was actually done. In reality, it wouldn't be simple at all.

Still, it was something to keep in mind. Luckily for him he felt no sense of urgency, because he'd have to wait until winter—fire season—when cold weather forced the use of unsafe heating methods and drove backyard smokers indoors. The advantages of waiting were obvious. First, some time would have elapsed after the Morrison woman's death. And second, no pattern would be apparent. Death caused by a wintertime house fire was one thing; death due to a fall during a summer thunderstorm was something else entirely. Yes, it was definitely something to think about, although he'd need to keep tabs on Singleton in case there were changes in her employment or routine. Meanwhile, he'd continue trying to track down Jill McKinnon. The farmhouse, and the old gal who lived there, were the key. He was positive of that.

He turned off the treadmill and the television set and went out to the garage, where he retrieved his prepaid disposable phone from the glove compartment of the Explorer. He'd considered storing Chad's number on the speed-dial list but decided against it. The fewer connections between the two of them, the better. Besides, he had it memorized. He punched it in, and when Chad answered, he didn't bother identifying himself.

"Hey," he said. "How about if I come up there next weekend? I need to do a little shopping, and I don't want to do it here."

Jill glanced at the clock. It was nearly eight-thirty, so Courtney should have left work by now. She consulted the business card Courtney had given her and made the call, which went to voice mail. Jill left her name and number, then added a brief message.

"I went to Amy Morrison's memorial service this afternoon, and I promised I'd get back to you if I found anything out about what happened. Call me when you can and I'll fill you in."

She carried her phone and a cup of her favorite green tea onto the deck and settled into a wicker chair. The fireflies were beginning to appear now that dusk had fallen. They were enchanting little creatures, and she'd never seen them until she moved to Illinois. Kevin had referred to them as lightning bugs, she recalled, and the memory made her smile.

That was happening more often lately. Nearly a year had passed since Kevin's death, and memories that used to trigger tears were much less painful now. She sipped her tea and watched the fireflies, wondering if Courtney Singleton would call her back.

It was past nine o'clock when Jill's phone rang. "Sorry it's so late," Courtney said. "I wanted to wait till Kyle left for work."

"Who?"

"My brother. He's had some bad luck lately, so I let him stay here and use my car to drive to work. He's a night-shift security guard at the nuke station. It's not the ideal situation for either of us, but I figure I owe him. He always looked out for me when we were kids growing up."

"Wish I'd had a big brother to look out for me."

"Mixed blessing," Courtney said with a laugh. "But at least he's got a job, even if the ex-wife got the house and the car. And most of the money. So what's the deal with Amy?"

"I met an elderly lady who lived next door to her, and she said Amy fell down the outside stairs at her apartment building. They figured she'd been shopping, and she was trying to carry everything to her apartment in one trip because it was raining. Anyway, she must have lost her footing somehow and fallen. The neighbor said it was a terrible mess. Groceries everywhere."

"That's so sad. Funny how the smallest thing can affect your life so much. Like whether it's raining or not, or maybe you just put your foot wrong."

"That's for sure."

"Oh, and you know what? That Ryan guy came to Chez Marie for lunch *again* yesterday. He didn't say much, just winked at me. And kind of leered, you know? Like he had some kind of secret. After he left I wished I'd asked him if he was the one who sent me those flowers."

"What flowers?"

"A couple of months ago I got this bouquet of white roses from somebody. Card just said 'guess who.' Kyle was *mad*. Deliveryman woke him up ringing the doorbell."

"Which florist delivered them?"

"Don't know. The card didn't say, and Kyle didn't pay any attention to the van."

"And you never figured out where they came from?"

"No idea. Then when that Ryan guy said anybody could find anybody if they really wanted to, it made me wonder if it might have been him."

"That is definitely weird. By the way, I wanted to ask you about your business card. Lifestyles by Courtney. What does that mean, anyway?"

"I sell several lines of merchandise—jewelry, cosmetics, home decor items, stuff like that—at home parties. It's fun. And it helps me make ends meet, you know?"

"I'll keep that in mind, especially the home decor items. I'm living in a rental right now, but I'm planning to build my own place before long."

"Definitely keep me in mind for that, girlfriend."

After ending the call, Jill sat in the darkness and thought about what Courtney had told her about the white roses. She went inside and located the telephone directory, then opened it to the M's and ran her finger down the page: McKay…McKean…McKinnon, J. There were no other McKinnons listed. She and Kevin hadn't thought it necessary to have a separate number for themselves, and her own recently acquired number was unpublished.

Jessica got flowers from a secret admirer, Jill remembered now, *but she thought they were meant for me. I wonder if she could have been right?*

Over the weekend she sifted through her memories of the trial, especially the jury deliberations. Certain remarks that she had, at the time, chalked up to ignorance—if not outright misogyny—now took on a more sinister meaning.

She entered Tommy Adair's office first thing Monday morning, closing the door behind her.

"Tommy," she began hesitantly, "you know I don't like to bother you with anything that doesn't concern work, but…"

"I always have time for you, Jill." This wasn't true, and she knew it, but she appreciated the pleasantry nonetheless.

"I'll be brief. You know I served on the jury for that sexual-assault trial, right?"

"Uh-huh."

"And that the victim was subsequently murdered?"

"Right." His eyes were already straying toward his computer screen.

"Here's what I need to know. If I had some information that might be related to the murder, who should I contact?"

She had his full attention now. "Really? You know something?"

"I'm not sure. But I think it's worth sharing with somebody, just in case. You know everybody in town, how everything works. Who should I talk to?"

"Stack Ridgeway, definitely. I think you met him at Coach's Fourth of July shindig."

"I didn't think you noticed I was there."

"Yeah, I saw you. Sorry we didn't have a chance to chat, but…"

"That's okay, I understand. So can I tell him you referred me?"

"Sure, if you want to, but you won't need to. He'd talk to Bozo the Clown if he thought it would help."

"Should I just call the main number for the police station?"

"He can be hard to reach unless you've got his cell number. Which I do, but he's threatened me with a fate worse than death if I give it out. Why don't you try to catch up with him at lunchtime? He eats at Pinky's most days. And even if you miss him you'll probably see Coach, so you won't go without a lunch partner." His eyes drifted toward his computer screen once more.

Jill took the hint. "Thanks, Tommy," she said, and headed toward the door. He was already tapping away at his keyboard by the time she reached it.

Tommy was right. The pressure Stack Ridgeway was under from the chief of police was steadily increasing. Stack didn't blame the chief, of course, who was merely passing along the grief he was receiving from the mayor and city council.

"Back to square one," he grumbled, contemplating his white board for the first time that day. The item in the lower left corner caught his eye, as it had a few other times lately. Time to make that go away, he decided, and speed-dialed Scott Allison.

"Hey, Scotty, did you ever get hold of that Amtrak employee?"

"Which Amtrak—oh, him. No, Copeland told me he'd left several messages for the guy, but he never called back."

"We need to clear that, one way or the other."

"You want me to send him back over there?"

Copeland was a traffic cop with little experience as an investigator. Sending him back, Stack thought, would probably be a waste of time.

"What's the address? Probably quicker if I go myself."

Twenty minutes later he was ringing Bethany Alvarez's doorbell. "Mrs. Alvarez," he said when she opened the door, "I'm Captain Ridgeway of the Drummond Police Department. May I come in?"

She looked apprehensive, he thought, but stepped back and motioned him inside. "Is anything wrong?"

"Not that I know of, Mrs. Alvarez. I'm just here to follow up on a matter concerning your brother-in-law."

"Richard?"

"Yes."

"He's not in any trouble, is he?"

"We have no reason to think so. We're just trying to locate anyone who might have been a witness in a case we're investigating."

"Oh. Well, there was an officer here last month, and I already told him everything I know."

"And I appreciate that. It's just that we haven't been able to reach your brother-in-law to follow up with him directly."

"That can be hard sometimes. There are some areas out there along his route where the service isn't very good."

She was obviously still nervous about his presence and hadn't invited him to sit, so he had remained standing. He had taken in his surroundings at a glance. The place was shabby but clean. There was no odor of dirty diapers, even though a playpen and a scattering of toys meant there was a baby in the house. His eye fell on what looked like a computer desk, but instead of a computer it was covered with colored paper, assorted stickers and various other items he recognized.

"Are you keeping a scrapbook for the baby?" he asked with a smile. "My wife's a scrapper, too."

She brightened. "We started it before he was born. My mother helps me with it sometimes, but I've still got a bunch of pictures I haven't had time to put in it yet."

"I wonder, do you have a picture of your brother-in-law in there?"

"Maybe," she said with a shrug. She went over to the table and sorted through the stacks. "Here," she said, holding out a three-by-five-inch color print. "That's my husband holding our son. Richard's on the right." But as Stack reached for it, she snatched it away. "It's my only copy."

"That's okay," Stack reassured her, and pulled out his phone. "I don't need to keep it. I can just take a picture of it."

A few minutes later he was out in his Durango, scrutinizing the image of two smiling young men. One was holding a chubby, drooling baby. Assuming things went well, the Sports Fan bartender would recognize the other man as the helpful soul who had taken Katie Putnam home in a taxi two weeks before her death. And if so, they'd track him down and confirm his whereabouts on the night of the murder.

But if not, he wondered, then where, exactly, would that leave them? He glanced at his watch. The Sports Fan wouldn't open for another two hours, so he would just have to wait. In the meantime, he had plenty of time to go downtown for lunch.

He drove back to the station and parked, then walked the four blocks to Pinky's. As he approached, he caught a glimpse of someone seated at his favorite window table. What the heck, he reminded himself, it was a public place. It wasn't until he entered the café that he realized the table's occupants were Coach Dio and an attractive young lady he had met at Coach's cookout. If he remembered right, she was Tommy Adair's accountant. And they were, apparently, waiting for him.

As Stack approached, Coach stood up. "I've already eaten, so I'll leave you now. But I understand Jill has something she needs to discuss with you. I did my best to worm it out of her," he added with a smile, "but she wouldn't tell me."

After lunch, back in his office, Stack dialed Tommy Adair's private number. When his old friend answered, Stack didn't bother with preliminaries.

"Tell me about Jill."

"What about her?"

"She a pretty stable individual?"

"Far as I know she is, and she's worked for me...let's see...five years? Something like that. She lost her husband in Afghanistan last year, but she's handling it well."

"She's not given to flights of fancy or anything?"

"Jill?" Tommy laughed. "That's a joke, right? Shit, what did she tell you?"

"Something she thought I needed to know."

"Okay, fine. Forget I asked. Listen, Jill's all right. I'd say so if she wasn't."

Driving to the Sports Fan half an hour later, Stack thought about what Jill had told him. While he appreciated that she had come forward with information she felt might be significant, he had no idea what to do with it. Even if Ryan Carlyle had been behind the flower deliveries, that was not a crime. And more to the point, there was no tie-in to the Putnam murder that he could see.

The Sports Fan lot was nearly deserted, as Stack had expected this early in the afternoon. He went inside and greeted Josh Dooley, the bartender. Then he took out his phone and pulled up the picture of the Alvarez brothers.

"Recognize either of these guys?"

"Yeah," Josh said. "The guy with the baby is a regular here. His name's Tim. Comes in once or twice a week."

"He an okay guy?"

"Oh, yeah. Just has a couple beers, watches baseball, then he leaves. No problem."

"What about the other guy?"

Josh studied the picture. "I might've seen him here once or twice with Tim. His brother, I think."

Oh, crap, Stack thought. He already suspected what the answer would be, but asked anyway. "Any chance he was the guy that took Katie Putnam home in the cab back in May?"

"No way. For one thing, Tim and his brother are just little guys. Five-five, maybe. Five-six, tops. That guy was taller, probably five-ten, and he had a tattoo of a dragon on his neck. I remember seeing that thing and thinking, man, that had to hurt. I know a lotta guys are really into the body art thing, but—"

"You haven't seen him in here since then, have you?"

"No, but I don't see everyone that comes in. They sit at a table and a waitress serves 'em, I might not even notice 'em. Especially if it's busy. Plus I don't work every shift."

"Well, keep your eyes open. If he comes back, I want to know about it."

"Will do."

For the second time that day, Stack faced the possibility that they'd never identify Katie Putnam's Good Samaritan. Not that he seriously believed the mystery man had anything to do with the girl's death. On the other hand, he needed to eliminate the possibility.

He wondered how many more man-hours it would take to accomplish that goal, and whether it was realistic to continue pursuing it. Allison had already assured him that they'd knocked on every door, and that Alvarez was the only possibility they'd located. Stack had to assume, of course, that the canvassing had been as thorough as Allison believed, and that none of the residents had forgotten—or maybe even lied—

about having houseguests the last weekend in May. And assumptions, as Stack knew, were dangerous things indeed.

His thoughts ricocheted back to his conversation with Jill McKinnon, and he realized there was an angle he hadn't previously considered. Before leaving the parking lot of the Sports Fan, Stack called Lucas Dean.

"I need to see you today. You in your office?"

"Yeah, but only for another hour."

"I'm fifteen minutes out. See you shortly."

The Sheriff's Department occupied much of the second floor of the Remington County Courthouse and Law Enforcement Annex, and Lucas Dean's office was on the southwest corner. He was sitting behind his cluttered desk when Stack arrived.

"I go for weeks without hearing from you, and now you call me twice inside one week. What's up?"

"Amy Morrison," Stack said, dropping into one of the sheriff's guest chairs.

"What about her?"

"Do you happen to know if she—damn, I can't believe I'm asking you this. But when you talked to her neighbors, did any of them mention if she'd had any deliveries recently?"

Dean leaned forward and stared at him. "Deliveries? Of what?"

"Flowers. Or she might've told someone she thought she was being stalked."

"Jesus. Are you serious?"

"Yeah, I am."

"So you're suggesting maybe her fall wasn't an accident?"

"I'm not suggesting that at all. But a couple other women she was connected to got flowers from some mysterious donor, and I was just wondering if she did, too."

"And this is important because…?"

"If I knew, I'd tell you. Listen, I know this is asking a lot, but I wouldn't mind seeing the autopsy report."

"And I wouldn't mind letting you, but I don't see the point. She was one beat-up little girl. Broken neck, fractured skull, multiple internal injuries, any of which would have been fatal on their own. Plus various other broken bones and contusions resulting from a fall down a long flight of concrete steps. She had to be pretty close to the top when it happened, because there were groceries scattered all the way down. Besides the produce and packaged stuff there were broken eggs, a bottle of salad dressing, cartons of yogurt…Jesus, what a mess!"

"Well, I'd still like to see it."

"All right," Dean said with an air of resignation. "I'll email it to you."

"And the pictures from the scene?"

"The pictures, too. Anything else?"

"Not at the moment."

Dean tilted his head and gave Stack a long look. "When you figure out exactly what it is you're looking for, let me know. I might be able to help you find it."

"Thanks, Lucas. I owe you."

"Damn right," the sheriff growled.

The drive up to Milwaukee had gone quickly. He'd made only one stop, at the state line rest area, before pulling into the driveway behind the panel truck Chad used for work.

He found that very little had changed since he'd moved back to Illinois. Chad still lived in the same modest-but-respectable neighborhood and occupied the same small rented house. The yard was large and shady, and there was a single-car detached garage out back. It wasn't fancy, as Chad had often said with a grin, but it was definitely private.

Chad must have heard him arrive, because he called out through the screen door. "Come on in. I got something for you."

He entered the house, following the sound of Chad's voice, and found him in the kitchen. He was a big man, well over six feet and powerfully built, and at the moment he was surveying the contents of his refrigerator. "You got a choice of Rolling Rock or Rolling Rock."

"Rock'll do."

"Here you go, bro." Chad handed him a beer and led the way out the back door onto a covered porch. He gestured toward a haphazard grouping of lawn chairs. "Have a seat. So how you been?"

"Fine." He tried to keep the impatience out of his voice. He'd come up here for a specific purpose, not to hang out and drink beer. Still, Chad would need careful handling. Things hadn't been the same between them since Gram's death…or actually, now that he thought about it, since they'd done the old lady with the dog just a few months before that.

"I was going through some stuff my mom left here," Chad began, then paused.

"Yeah? How is she?"

"The same," Chad said with a shrug. "Still drinks. Still hangs out with the wrong kinda guys. Drunks and losers."

"My dad wasn't a drunk." His father and Chad's mother had been involved in a tempestuous co-dependent relationship for several years before his father's death. "With him it was nose candy. Plus anything else he could snort, smoke or shoot up."

"Yeah, I know. Sad thing, too, because with his brains and family connections he coulda done pretty well for himself. Kinda like your mom did," Chad added with a sly smile.

"Here's to the trophy wife." He raised his beer in mock salute. His mother was a beautiful woman whose looks had enabled her to marry for money, and she had done it twice. The first time was to the son of a successful Milwaukee architect, but she had eventually divorced him because of his worsening drug addiction.

She'd soon found a second husband while vacationing in the resort community of Lake Geneva. Husband number two was a prosperous semi-retired businessman from Farleyville, a small town thirty minutes south of the Illinois state line. He was many years older than she and clearly not thrilled to find himself the stepfather of a young boy whose attitude, as he told anyone who would listen, definitely needed improvement. But, since his bride had full custody of the boy—although she was pleased to permit extended summer visits to Milwaukee every year until his father died—they were stuck with him.

That changed shortly after the end of the boy's senior year in high school. He'd been out celebrating his recent graduation with some friends, including a girl they'd met along the way, when the festivities had taken an unfortunate turn. He didn't understand what the big deal was, but his stepfather had been furious; had kicked him out, in fact. And his mother not only hadn't had the guts to stand up for him, she'd actually agreed with her husband. She'd sold herself for a meal ticket, he thought bitterly, and had to protect her own interests. Luckily Gram had taken him in, perhaps hoping to have better luck with her grandson than she'd had with her son. By that time, her husband and her only child were buried side by side in Graceland Cemetery.

"Do you ever see your mom at all?" Chad asked.

"Shit, no. If she's got no use for me, then I've got no use for her. And as far as they know, I'm still here in Milwaukee."

"Well, anyway, as I was saying. After Mom took off the last time, I was going through some stuff she left in her room. Been there for years. Most of it was junk, and I threw it away. Shit, by the time she comes back she won't even remember she had it. But one of the boxes had your dad's name on it, so I kept that one. Then when you called and said you were coming up, I opened it. And guess what I found."

"What?"

"It was some of your dad's hunting stuff. A couple vests, some gloves, and two knives. Good ones, too. One's a Case Bowie knife with a blade over nine inches long." Chad grinned. "I was tempted not to tell you about that one. The other one's a nice little six-inch Buck."

"Yeah? Can I see 'em?"

"Sure, they're inside. Listen," Chad said after a moment. "You gonna take up hunting again?"

"Might. Haven't decided yet. But couldn't hurt to be prepared, just in case."

"Yeah, well. That depends on what you're hunting for."

He knew where this was headed. "Tell you what. You keep the Bowie, since you like it so much, and I'll take the Buck."

"Hey, thanks, man. Just…"

"What?"

"Just be careful. You gotta ask yourself if the reward is worth the risk."

"Ah, fuck. Is this about the old lady with the dog?"

"We were taking one hell of a chance going in when she was home—"

"She was deaf as a post. Couldn't hear shit without her hearing aids, and not much more with 'em. You know," he went on with an unpleasant smile, "I always thought you felt worse about the dog than the old lady. Listen, I found out afterwards the dog was half blind and almost as deaf as the old lady. Jesus, the thing was fourteen years old. What's that in people years, about a hundred?"

"It wasn't too deaf to hear us when we got upstairs, and she wasn't too deaf to hear it raising hell." The feisty little mixed-breed dog had come storming out of its mistress' bedroom, barking at the top of its voice and rousing its octogenarian owner. When she emerged from her bedroom into the upstairs hallway to investigate the racket, she had unwittingly—and fatally—positioned herself between the intruders and their escape route. "But the point is, you didn't know she had a dog. You shoulda known that. That's what preparation *means*."

"Fine. You win. Let's just say the dog was a learning experience and let it go at that. And besides, it turned out all right. They just figured she tripped over the dog and fell down the stairs. Hit that big cabinet at the bottom and broke her neck. End of story."

"Yeah, okay. But I'm just sayin'. Was it worth the risk? There are very few things worth risking life in prison for."

"I hear you."

"Do you? I'm not so sure."

Two hours later he was back at the state line, in the southbound rest area this time. As he headed toward the men's room he noticed a pay phone. It was funny, he thought, but he couldn't remember the last time he'd seen one. And just a few years ago they seemed to be everywhere.

Although he'd been tempted to simply call the J. McKinnon number he'd found in the phone book and ask for Jill, he'd resisted that temptation up until now. The last thing he wanted was for his telephone number, even the one for his burn phone, to be displayed on caller ID. But calling from a pay phone would eliminate that problem. It was not an opportunity to be missed. He had three or four dollars' worth of change in his pocket—he'd brought it along in case he needed it for tolls—which was certainly enough for the purpose at hand. He had memorized the number weeks ago.

He walked over to the large wall map and pretended to study it while he thought through his approach. He knew that Jill was an accountant, and one piece of information he'd picked up from a business acquaintance recently was that all CPAs were required to meet continuing education requirements on a regular basis. The guy had referred to it as CPE. It was sketchy, as cover stories went, but it would have to do. He took a deep breath and approached the pay phone. *Showtime.*

The phone was answered on the third ring: a female voice, but not Jill's. "Hello?"

"Hello," he responded cheerily. "May I speak with Jill, please?"

There was a moment's silence. "No. She's not here."

"I could call again later. Do you know when she'll be back?"

"No." The voice was rougher this time, the breathing heavy and quick. "I told you, she's not here."

"Oh, has she moved? I met her at a CPE seminar a few months ago, and—"

"There's no Jill here. You have the wrong number."

"I'm sorry to have troubled you," he said, doing his best to sound solicitous. "I don't suppose you know where I could reach—" But before he could finish the sentence, the line went dead.

He left the building and got behind the wheel of his newly-acquired Chevy Tahoe. It was four years old but practically in mint condition, and its pale gray paint job made a nice change from black. He'd probably overpaid for it, but he liked it a lot and had been in too much of a hurry to get rid of the Explorer to engage in a lot of haggling. He started the engine and headed south once more, pondering the McKinnon woman's reaction as he drove.

She was definitely related to Jill. And clearly, she was angry at Jill for some reason. A mother-daughter rift, perhaps, which had led to Jill moving out? Whatever the case, it was all but certain that she knew where Jill was. And since she obviously wasn't going to tell him, he would need to find the information for himself. He had to get inside that house.

Jessica McKinnon sat at her kitchen table, her heart racing. The nerve! Jill had met a man and given him her phone number...when? Hadn't he said it was months ago? And poor Kevin had been gone such a short time then!

She waited for her pulse to slow a bit—it always seemed so fast these days—before crossing to other side of the kitchen and picking up the wall phone. She squinted at her voter registration card, which was affixed with a sunflower-shaped magnet to the side of the refrigerator a few feet away. She had stubbornly refused to add Jill's information to her emergency contact list, which already included Louise and the Camerons. She had, however, jotted Jill's new number on the card next to the name of the precinct polling place. Just in case I ever need to call her, Jessica had told herself at the time, although I certainly can't imagine wanting to.

She punched in the number with far more force than was necessary, and when Jill answered wasted no time on preliminaries.

"You hussy!" she shrieked. "If you've got no respect for Kevin's memory, at least have some respect for me! How *dare* you give out this number to—" She fell silent, gasping for breath and momentarily unable to continue.

"Jessica? What in the world…? I haven't given your number to anyone. Please tell me—"

"Then explain to me, madam, where he got it. He called just now and asked for you."

"*Who* called? What was his name?"

"He didn't tell me his name. He said he met you months ago at a CPE seminar. And when I told him you weren't here, he asked when you moved."

"Oh, my God, Jess. You didn't give him my address, did you?"

"So you do know him," Jessica cried triumphantly.

"Jess, *please.* Just listen to me. First of all," Jill said, striving to keep her voice calm, "I don't go to CPE seminars. I do all my courses online from home. So if this person says that's how he met me, he lied."

"Really," Jessica said, sounding unconvinced.

"And I think—I know this is going to sound melodramatic, but I think somebody might be trying to find me. To track down where I live. So please, do not give anyone any information about me. Not my address, not my phone number, not where I work. Not under any circumstances. Anyone who needs to find me already knows how. Do you understand?"

"Yes. Well, I guess so."

"And as to how he got the number, it's in the phone book. J. McKinnon could mean Jill as well as Jessica."

"Or Joe. We always had it listed with just his first initial because he hated his given name."

"He hated Joe?"

"Joe was only his nickname. His real name was Joachim. He always said he didn't mind being named after the father of the Virgin Mary instead of her husband, but he did mind being asked how to spell it or how to pronounce it. So he always just went by Joe. That's even what I had put on his headstone. Joe McKinnon, not Joachim. I know some people might find fault with that, but…"

"Some might, but I wouldn't. And I'm sorry," Jill added softly, "that the man who called upset you so much. Are you feeling better now?"

"Yes," Jessica said, but she didn't feel well at all. First of all, she wasn't sure she believed Jill about taking those courses online. And second, she was still disturbingly short of breath. Too much excitement, she decided, fingering the emergency response pendant she had faithfully worn ever since Jill had given it to her. Not that she'd ever give her the satisfaction of telling her so. "I'm just a little tired."

"All right, then. Call me any time if you need anything. And Jess? Please make sure your doors are locked."

Good advice, Jill thought to herself afterwards. She checked her own doors and windows, then made a mental note to speak with the office receptionist first thing Monday morning about screening her incoming calls.

When Stack booted up his computer Monday morning he found Amy Morrison's autopsy report in his email inbox, just as Sheriff Dean had promised. There was also a separate message bearing the subject line, "scene pix."

Stack didn't know what he expected to find when he opened the attachments. He was painfully aware, though, that he couldn't spare much time looking. Drummond was not the small, isolated rural community it once had been. As it had grown—and the ever-expanding Chicago suburbs had sprawled westward—problems once limited to the city had begun cropping up here. Each year seemed to bring a small but perceptible increase in crime, and each year the responsibility weighed more heavily on his shoulders.

He glanced at his watch. Exactly twelve minutes remained before he was due at a multi-jurisdictional task force meeting at the sheriff's office. He opened the file containing the scene pictures first. As the sheriff had told him, groceries were strewn all along the outside staircase, most of them at or close to the bottom where the girl lay sprawled on her back. Nothing unexpected there.

Next, he clicked on the autopsy report and skimmed through the dry medical terminology and accompanying photographs. Again, the results were as the sheriff had described: a few catastrophic injuries, any of which would have been fatal on their own, plus several others that, though grotesque in appearance—including compound fractures of both arms—would have been survivable. Stack noted that the girl's extremities and back, including the rear portion of her skull, seemed to have borne the brunt of her fall. Her face was virtually untouched, as was the front of her torso except for a small round bruise a few inches below the hollow of her throat.

Stack took another quick look at his watch. "Damn," he muttered, and closed the file. He was due at Dean's office, which was five blocks away, in four minutes. He'd need to walk fast.

As he turned from the shady side street where the Drummond Police Department was located onto Main Street and strode south toward the courthouse, he reflected on the pictures Dean had sent him and the circumstances of the Morrison girl's fall. Apparently she'd been running up the stairs, slipped, and fallen backwards.

Stack found this difficult to understand. He had been hurrying up a staircase once and stumbled, but his momentum had carried him forward instead of backward. He'd suffered nothing more than some painful bruises to his shins. No, the only time he could recall falling backwards was on the ice, a common hazard in this part of the country. His right foot had shot forward and, unable to regain his balance, he had experienced a classic pratfall that was hard enough to crack his tailbone.

Had his fall happened on a staircase instead of a level surface, he realized now, he would have tumbled backwards down the steps with little chance of catching himself. And yet...wouldn't the riser of the next step have prevented Amy Morrison's foot from sliding forward more than a few inches? The sheriff had said she must have been near the top of the steps, based on the location of her dropped and scattered groceries. More likely, Stack decided, she was already *at* the top, with nothing to stop the forward progress of her foot. Poor kid, he thought. So close to safety. So close to survival.

He bypassed the front entrance to the courthouse and hurried around the block to the rear of the building where the law enforcement annex was located. Greeting some colleagues, he put the matter of Amy Morrison's fall out of his mind.

It was past ten a.m. when he retrieved Jill's message from his voice mail: something about a phone call her mother-in-law had received. He was tempted to ignore it, but, because there was just the barest possibility it was connected to the Putnam case, he didn't quite have the nerve. He listened to the message a second time, then called Jill back and arranged to swing by and see her at noon. Tommy and Karen would both have left for lunch by then and Kelly would be attending the front desk, assuring them of privacy.

"I've been thinking about how to approach this," Stack told Jill as she led him into the small conference room next to Tommy's office and closed the door. "I don't want this to look like an official investigation."

"Really? Why not?"

"For starters, there's nothing to go on except a couple of anonymous flower deliveries and a phone call. But more to the point...well, let me put it this way. When I was a kid, Drummond had under ten thousand people. And now it has nearly forty thousand. But the same families are still in charge of pretty much everything."

"That would include the Carlyles?"

"It would, and they require careful handling." Stack remembered Ryan Carlyle as a teenager: an unpleasant kid with a rebellious attitude, but he'd never been in trouble except for a couple of curfew violations. And Gary Carlyle had been even more displeased with his son for staying out too late than he had been with the police for picking the boy up. "Not just because they're important people locally, but because Drummond is still a very small town in some ways. It only takes a whisper of gossip, whether it's true or not, to ruin somebody's reputation. So we need to make sure that doesn't happen."

Jill nodded and leaned forward, facing Stack across the conference room table. "And you have a plan?"

"Yes. First of all, did you tell anyone why I came to see you today?"

"No, of course not."

"Good. Now, how many of the other jurors' names can you remember?"

"Why? Can't you get them from the court?"

Stack shook his head. "Unofficial, remember? So who do you remember besides Ryan Carlyle?"

"Well, let's see. Courtney Singleton, of course, and—"

"Let's start with the men instead." Then, seeing the light of comprehension in Jill's eyes, he added, "Especially the young white men."

"Brett Petersen, for one. Actually, I think I still have his phone number in my purse."

"Really?"

"Yes, he asked me if I wanted to go out to lunch or something. And I said no, but I had him give me his phone number just in case..." Her voice trailed off. "You know, I'd forgotten about that."

"Hmm. Any chance he could be your mysterious caller?"

"I really don't think so. He hardly seemed like the type."

I've heard that one before, Stack thought. *He seemed like such a nice guy.* Until, of course, the "nice guy" committed a crime.

"You can give me his number before I leave. Who else?"

"Well, there was Jared. What was his last name?" she mused. "I'm usually pretty good with names. Snow," she said suddenly, her face brightening. "Jared Snow. He said he worked for PDQ Print-N-Copy. I remember the name because it's right down the street from my attorney's office."

"Okay, that'll do for a start. Now, here's what we talked about today in case anybody asks. Because of the way the courtroom is set up, the jurors have a good view of everything that goes on. So I wanted to know if you noticed anything or anyone unusual in the spectator area during the trial. Anybody who seemed to be especially interested in the proceedings. Anybody who looked like they didn't belong there. That sort of thing."

"Why, no, I didn't."

"I know," Stack said with a smile. "But that's what we talked about, okay? And that's what I'll be asking these other guys, too. Just to see how they react. Remember, it's unofficial."

Before Stack left, he collected Brett Petersen's phone number from Jill. Outside in his car, he reviewed what they knew about the flower deliveries. It was very little: just that both deliverymen were white males, and one of the vehicles involved was a black SUV. He was glad he hadn't made any promises to Jill regarding when he planned to follow up, because at the moment he simply didn't have the time. For now, he would just file away the information she'd given him and check on these guys later, when he wasn't quite so busy.

54

August had arrived, still and sultry, and with it came the anniversary of Kevin McKinnon's death.

Jessica had hoped for at least a small measure of healing as time passed; but instead, the accumulated weight of so many losses—her husband, her son, her dreams of many grandchildren—had become almost unbearably heavy.

Worst of all was her sense of utter uselessness. There was no longer anyone who needed her, not even Jill. The girl had grated on her, true, but she had also been someone to cook for, keep house for, make a home for. And she had been a link to Kevin, who had asked her to take care of Jill before leaving with his Guard unit for Afghanistan. A fine job she'd done of it, Jessica thought now. She'd chased the poor girl right out of the house, a house that was rightfully hers.

Ah, well. Chances were good that Jill could move back in soon, if she wanted to. Jessica's friend Louise had been nagging her to see a doctor, but what was the point? The increasing heaviness in her chest was less troublesome than the emotional burden she bore. She'd never been a churchgoer, but she still clung to the hope of reunion with her loved ones in some vaguely-pictured afterlife. And even if death brought nothing more than an end to pain, she wouldn't really mind.

Merciful heavens, it was hot! Both of the downstairs window air-conditioning units were running at full capacity, but the temperature inside the house was still over eighty degrees. Hoping it might be cooler outdoors than in, now that night had fallen, Jessica stepped onto the front porch. She flicked off the porch light, which drew swarms of bugs, and sank into her old wicker rocker. Taking a breath of rich country air, she savored the sweet green scent of field corn. It was a fragrance she'd loved ever since she'd come here as a bride. There were acres upon acres of corn growing just beyond her back door, but the men who had planted this year's crop were neither her husband nor her son.

They had done a good job, though. The plants stood tall and straight in tidy ranks, and if all went well—no heavy continuous thunderstorms, no punishing straight-line winds—there would be a good harvest in six or eight weeks.

Jessica heard the phone ringing inside the house. She was tempted to ignore it but, sighing, she pushed herself out of her chair and went to answer it.

A quarter of a mile away, a silver-gray Tahoe was parked in the clearing beyond the row of evergreens. Its owner prowled the tree line searching for the vantage point he'd used before, the one that would let him see past the corn that was now higher than his head and blocked his view of the McKinnon farmhouse. He remembered Chad's warning about weighing risk versus benefit, and he knew his friend was right. But, although the prospect of discovery made him nervous, he was unable to stay away. He had to find Jill, and to do that he had to get inside that house. It was that simple.

He'd been watching his favorite crime drama the night before when one of the main characters used a term that caught his attention. "We need to know what his endgame is," the actor had intoned with a scowl. "If we can figure that out…"

It was at that point that he'd stopped paying attention to the show, which was a rerun he'd already seen. *Endgame*, he repeated to himself. It made him wonder. What was his own endgame? If he managed to eliminate Jill McKinnon and Courtney Singleton, then what?

The girl from Farleyville would be next, he decided. She was a hypocritical, self-righteous little bitch. Everything that had gone wrong in his life since high school was her fault. He hadn't been back since then because it was too small a town, and too many people knew him there. But when the time was right, when he was ready, he'd go back and find her. He'd make her pay.

And after that, why should he go on working at what was probably a dead-end job? He had Gram's money and the cabin in northern Minnesota where he and his father had vacationed with Chad years ago. He'd sold Gram's Milwaukee house for a hefty price but had decided to keep the cabin, even though it was little more than a shack, because he'd always liked its location. It was on sixty acres of mostly forested land, miles from the nearest town, and he could live as he pleased with nobody to bug him. He'd have to winterize it if he was going to live there year-round, maybe install solar panels, too, and go completely off the grid. Well, not completely, because he'd still need internet access to manage his financial affairs. But that was all right. If he was careful enough in disposing of the women, nobody would be looking for him. He could go wherever he wanted, do whatever he wanted. He just had to get rid of the women first.

He found the vantage point he needed, from which he could see the McKinnon house. Elsewhere, the corn blocked the view of the house and road. But here, there was a low area—for drainage, he surmised, since the soil was still damp from a rainfall earlier in the week—separating two cornfields, and it led all the way from the tree line to the edge of the fields nearest the house. *Perfect*, he thought. When the time came, if the stupid old cow ever left her house, he could leave the Tahoe in the cover of the trees and make his way unseen nearly all the way to the back door.

A powerful yard light threw a bright half-circle of illumination that reached from the back of the house past the detached garage almost to the grain drying and storage bins. The house itself was dimly lit, and only at the front of the lower level. The second story was completely dark. As he watched, a light went on at the rear of the house.

Jessica flicked the light switch and answered the telephone. "Hello?"

It was Jill. "Jessica," she began, sounding tentative. "I was wondering…"

Kevin's anniversary date fell on a Friday. Jill had taken the day off from work to spend some time in quiet reflection and to shop for and prepare the dinner she was planning for Jessica. She still found it surprising that Jessica had accepted her invitation, had even sounded pleased about it.

Jessica liked hearty fare, but due to the heat Jill had decided on salad as a main course. She went to the refrigerator and removed the boneless chicken breasts she had baked that morning, now nicely chilled. She sliced them over a base of baby spinach and added grapefruit segments, pine nuts and crumbled gorgonzola cheese, then prepared a citrus vinaigrette dressing to be served on the side along with French bread and whipped butter. And, although she had never seen Jessica drink wine, there was a bottle of Riesling cooling in the refrigerator. For dessert she had purchased a key lime cheesecake to satisfy Jessica's sweet tooth.

The doorbell rang promptly at seven o'clock, and Jill took a deep breath before going to answer it. "Be nice," she reminded herself in a whisper. When she opened the door, she was stunned by how much Jessica appeared to have aged in just the few months since Jill had last seen her. "Jess," she said, smiling to cover her shock. "I'm so glad you came."

"I'm glad you invited me," Jessica replied, and for the first time Jill could remember, the older woman spontaneously extended her arms for a hug.

Jill led her mother-in-law into the great room, where Jessica sank into the cushy leather sofa. Although conversation was awkward at first, it was helped along when Jessica accepted Jill's offer of wine.

"German wine," Jessica remarked. "Did I ever tell you my mother-in-law was German? Bavarian, actually. She was born here, but her parents came over from the old country."

"Why, no. I didn't know that."

"She died when Joe was still in high school, so I never actually met her. But from what I heard, she was quite a character. She insisted on naming Joe after her father. Joachim."

"Oh, yes, I remember you telling me that was his name."

"Joachim was the father of the Virgin Mary," Jessica went on. "Her mother's name was Anne."

"I never knew that before, either, until you mentioned it when we spoke last month. I'm not a churchgoer, but I've read the Nativity story. I don't remember those names at all."

"Well, Marta—Joe's mother—was Catholic. He told me they have a lot of traditions you won't find in the Bible. Beliefs that were handed down by word of mouth. Joe's father agreed to raise their children as Catholic when he and Marta got married, but later on he changed his mind. Told the kids they didn't have to go to church if they didn't want to, so of course they didn't go. Most kids hate going to church. I know I did. Not that my parents were big on church. Joe wasn't either, after he grew up. But sometimes I wish…"

"I know," Jill murmured. It would be nice to have a strong faith to hold onto like Nick Pappas and his family, she thought to herself. "It's interesting to hear these old family stories. Kevin and I never talked about the past that much."

"Young people don't. You talk about the present and the future. Old people like me, we talk about the past because it's all we have left."

"So tell me more about it. What was Drummond like when you were a little girl, and how did you and Joe meet?"

Encouraged by Jill's interest, Jessica launched into a series of inconsequential stories about her youth. Finally, though, she seemed to run out of steam. She paused momentarily and took a deep breath. "I've been thinking about a lot of things lately, and there's something I need to say to you." Jessica set her empty wineglass on the coffee table and looked straight into Jill's eyes. "You made Kevin very happy, and I never thanked you for that."

"And he made me very happy. I don't know if I'll ever be that happy again."

"Someday you will be, I hope."

"So do I.…Oh, my goodness, it's almost eight o'clock. You must be starved."

"To tell you the truth, I'm not sure how much I'll be able to eat. I've got an awful toothache. Feels like one of my molars." She touched her lower jaw. "Serves me right, I guess. I haven't seen a dentist in years."

"Maybe you can chew on the other side. But if you don't mind my saying so, you really should take better care of yourself."

"You sound like Louise. She's always nagging me to get a checkup." Jessica struggled to get up from the sofa. "Give me a hand, will you?"

"Sure." Jill grasped Jessica's hands in both of her own and managed to pull the older woman to her feet.

They reached the dining area, and Jill set out the salad and bread. Jessica accepted another glass of wine and nibbled on a slice of bread and butter; but, although she complimented the salad, she only picked at it.

As Jessica rubbed her jaw, Jill noticed that her mother-in-law's left hand was bare. "You stopped wearing your wedding ring?"

"I didn't want to, but I had to have it cut off. I've put on some weight lately, and my hands swell so bad in hot weather." She dabbed at her forehead with a napkin. "Seems like the heat gets to me a lot worse than when I was younger."

"Jessica, are you sure you're all right?"

"Of course. Well, except for the toothache. And I probably shouldn't have had that second glass of wine. I'm not used to it."

Jessica's wedding ring, Jill noticed, wasn't the only thing that was missing. "And by the way, where's your pendant?"

"At home on my kitchen table. I never wear it when I go out because it only works when it's within range of the base unit." Jessica forced a smile. "And besides, I don't want to look like one of those pathetic old ladies who lives alone with her cat."

Jill smiled back at her. "You don't have a cat."

"Maybe I should get one." She pushed her plate away. "I'm sorry I can't do justice to your meal. It's really good. It's just...I really do think I should go home now. I'll call Louise and see if she knows what to do for this blasted toothache until I can see a dentist."

"I wish you didn't have to leave, but I understand." She really does look ill, Jill thought. "Listen, would you like to take some dessert home with you? It's key lime cheesecake."

"No, honey, I don't think so. But thanks anyway."

Jill watched Jessica walk to her car. She had no idea what surprised her more, her mother-in-law's use of the endearment or her refusal of dessert. Nor did she know what had brought on the change in her demeanor. She only knew that it worried her.

"Phone me when you get home so I'll know you got there okay," Jill called out.

Jessica waved in acknowledgment, then drove away.

He had seen her leave. Although he couldn't be sure from this distance, she seemed to be dressed up—she was wearing a skirt, at least—so she would probably be gone for a while. He'd been watching the place long enough to be confident that she was the only resident, and her departure was an opportunity not to be missed. Even though he was reluctant to leave the Tahoe on what was obviously private property, where its presence would be sure to raise questions if it was discovered, it was a risk he felt compelled to take. He had come prepared, as always, with out-of-state license plates as well as his knife, flashlight, rubber gloves, and the key he'd stolen several weeks earlier.

He waited fifteen minutes before making his way between the cornfields to the back of the house. Once there, out of view of the road, he donned gloves and tried the door, which was locked. Slipping the key into the lock, he let himself in and took a minute to get his bearings. He was standing in a pantry and utility area that led into the kitchen, where he'd entered the last time via the side door—and which was, he had observed, the one the McKinnon woman used.

Then he remembered the high-intensity yard light. Although it was not yet dusk, she might have turned it on in anticipation of an after-dark return. He'd better check now, so he wouldn't be caught in its beam when he left. He poked his head out the door and looked up. Sure enough, it was on. After a few tries, he found the correct switch and turned it off. Good thing he knew about old ladies and how their minds worked, he thought. When she returned and the light was off, she'd just figure she'd forgotten to turn it on. She wouldn't suspect a thing.

In the kitchen, he checked for other lights that might have been left on but found none except for a dim little nightlight above the kitchen counter, next to the stove. No problem there. Surveying the room, he noticed an object he recognized on the kitchen table. One of his grandmother's friends had owned one. He had come across it, and its base unit, while house-sitting during one of her trips.

He picked up the emergency-alert pendant by its beaded chain. He expected to find what he was looking for and be long gone by the time its owner returned, but just in case he wasn't.... He laid the pendant on top of the refrigerator, far enough from the edge that she was unlikely to see it. Smiling, he pictured her consternation when she finally found it. *Why in the world did I put it up there?* she would wonder. It would really mess with her mind, which would serve the old biddy right for being so rude to him on the phone.

Affixed to the side of the refrigerator was a magnetized emergency-contact list. Spaces provided for doctor's information, poison-control center and police and fire numbers were left blank, but there were a few names and phone numbers written in tidy script. He quickly scanned the list. Louise. Camerons. Carol. But no Jill. An assortment of other magnets held up a calendar, a voter registration card in the name of Jessica McKinnon, and a business card for some guy at the First Bank of Drummond's Agricultural Services Division, none of which was of interest to him.

Well, he would just have to keep looking. He began methodically searching the room, hoping to find a card file or Christmas card list that would provide the information he sought. There was a moment's euphoria when he discovered a file box next to a row of canisters, but it contained only recipes.

"Shit," he said aloud. He was beginning to perspire. Damn, it was hot in here. There was an air-conditioning unit installed in one of the kitchen windows, and he could hear another one running elsewhere in the house, but neither seemed to be doing much good.

He moved into the adjacent dining room furnished with an oak table and chairs, a glass-fronted china cabinet, and an old-fashioned sideboard containing table linens and a set of silverware.

The living room was next. The roll-top desk looked promising, but after nearly half an hour of working methodically through the contents of its drawers and cubbyholes he found nothing of any use. Then, climbing the stairs to the second floor, he came to a cluster of photographs hanging on a wall in the upstairs hallway. One of them caught his eye. Because the light was growing dim—he realized with a start that dusk had fallen—he pulled the little flashlight from his pocket, turned it on, and aimed its beam at the photo.

It was unmistakably Jill, standing next to a young man—a brother, maybe?—who had one arm draped around her and the other encircling the woman whose first name, as he now knew thanks to the voter registration card, was Jessica.

"Yes!" he whispered triumphantly.

He quickly assessed the second floor: four bedrooms, one on each corner, and a single bathroom opposite the head of the stairway. He entered each of the bedrooms in turn, but only the largest one at the front of the house appeared to be occupied. Two others were outfitted as guest rooms, and the third was apparently used as a storage room. Judging by the coating of dust that lay on the furniture, none of the three rooms had been used recently.

He was engaged in searching Jessica's room, which was uncomfortably warm despite the chattering window unit, when a flash of light crossed his field of vision. Startled, he looked up just in time to see the headlights of a vehicle turning into the driveway. He took two rapid strides to the window for a closer look. *Damn, it was her!* He pocketed the flashlight and bolted toward the head of the stairs, hoping to escape without being seen. But, even as he rushed down the stairs, he knew he had run out of time.

Then he remembered the knife he carried. Maybe he could still get the information he sought.

By the time Jessica turned off the county road into her driveway she was sweaty, light-headed, and nauseous. The pain in her jaw, which she had initially dismissed as a toothache, had spread down her neck into her left shoulder and upper arm.

She had activated the remote control to open the garage door before she realized that the yard light was off. She had intended to turn it on before she left, knowing it would be dark by the time she got home.

Not that it mattered. There was a light switch in the garage. She pulled inside and parked beside Kevin's F-150, then stopped the engine. She reached up and pressed the remote to close the overhead door, trying to summon the strength to open the car door and get out. She couldn't seem to catch her breath. Maybe if she just rested a minute…

Heart attack. Even as the words formed in her mind, she realized that she had to get into the house and call for help. But she wasn't sure she could make it. For the first time in her life, she wished she owned a cell phone. She pulled herself out of the Town Car, took a step, and felt a crushing pain beneath her breastbone. Gasping, she took another step—then another—toward the side door of the garage and the switch that controlled the yard light. She reached it, flipped it up, and was rewarded by a brilliant flood of illumination.

She started toward the house but had covered only a few feet when the light went out again, and she panicked. Oh, God, what if I fall? Don't let me die here alone in the dark! She struggled to keep going. If she could just get inside to her emergency pendant on the kitchen table, then maybe there was hope.

He had glimpsed her through the window of the darkened kitchen and, seeing her hesitant, stumbling gait, wondered if she had been drinking. But so what? Unless she was totally out of it, she could still tell him what he needed to know.

At last. Almost there. She realized with a moment's terror that she'd left her pocketbook in the car, but thank God she was still clutching her key ring because she couldn't remember if she'd set the deadbolt. She must have, though, because the door refused to budge when she turned the knob. She shoved the key into the lock, twisted it, and pushed the door open.

She smelled the rank odor of male perspiration as soon as she stepped into the house. It reminded her of Joe, but of course it couldn't be. Weak and disoriented, she reached for the light switch next to the door only to have her arm wrenched forcefully behind her back.

Crying out in pain, she was unaware of her keys clattering to the floor or the sound of the door slamming shut, the bolt clicking into place. As he stood behind her, holding both her arms now in a viselike grip, he lowered his head close to hers and spoke into her ear.

"Where's Jill?"

"Let me go," she whimpered.

"Where's Jill?" he repeated.

"I don't know," she managed to say, then slid limply from his grasp and collapsed onto the floor.

He bent over her, glaring. "Drunken old cow," he hissed. "Don't you dare pass out. And don't tell me you don't know, because you do."

"Heart attack," she gasped. "Help me."

He pulled the flashlight from his pocket and turned it on, shining it directly into her face. It was pallid and contorted, bathed in perspiration. Maybe she was telling the truth. Maybe she wasn't drunk after all. "Should I call 911?"

"Yes," she whispered.

"Well, I might," he said conversationally, squatting down beside her. "But first you have to tell me where Jill is." He turned off the flashlight and put it back into his pocket. "So how about it? You gonna tell me?"

Ethan Cameron sat at the small table he used for a desk and looked out his bedroom window, his binoculars at the ready. He was watching for the great horned owl that liked to perch in the maple tree outside his window. It was nearly full dark now, and soon the owl would come out to hunt. Ethan enjoyed watching all birds but liked raptors the best, especially the silent and deadly owl. He sometimes felt bad when he saw the owl carry its prey back to its favorite tree for consumption, especially if the unlucky creature was a cute little squirrel or rabbit. But he was also a country boy who understood that rodents—which they undeniably were, despite their cuteness—would soon overpopulate without the hawks and owls to keep them in check.

He wished that Mrs. Jessica's yard light was on because, even though it was so far away, it provided just enough backlighting to silhouette the owl. He'd seen her drive past the house earlier, headed toward town, so she must have forgotten to turn it on before she left. He hoped she'd get home soon and turn it on, because she always kept it on at night. She'd started doing that when Mrs. Jill moved away. He suspected Mrs. Jessica was kind of nervous about living by herself.

Now that Mrs. Jill's little patch of woods was forbidden to him, he no longer took Rowdy there on walks. Instead, he went only as far as the crossroads before turning for home. Sometimes he'd see Mrs. Jessica sitting on her front porch, and he would stop and visit her for a while. Rowdy liked her, as he did all women, and seemed happy to sit beside her as she stroked his back, running her fingers through his luxuriant coat. Sometimes they chatted, but more often they didn't. Although Mrs. Jessica always acted glad to see him, she wasn't very talkative. When he'd asked his mother for advice on making conversation, she had told him not to worry about it.

"It's enough that you're there, Ethan. She just likes to know she's not forgotten."

Watching the road, wishing Mrs. Jessica would hurry up and come home, he saw a car pass by. It was going the right direction, and, though it was too dark to tell for sure, he thought it looked like Mrs. Jessica's. Sure enough, it slowed and pulled into her driveway, disappearing beyond the dark bulk of the house. Ethan reached for his binoculars. Any minute now, he thought, but the light didn't go on right away; and when it did, it only stayed on for a few seconds.

"That's weird," Ethan said. He hoped she might turn it back on when she went inside and turned on her other lights, but after what seemed like several minutes the house remained dark. "That's not right," he murmured to himself.

He went downstairs and found his mother, who was sewing a dress for his little sister. "Mom," he began.

"What?" She stopped working and looked at him, sounding impatient. He knew she wanted to get Emily's dress done for church on Sunday.

"Mom...I think something might be wrong at Mrs. Jessica's."

"Why?"

"Because I saw her come home, but she didn't turn any lights on. Except the yard light, just for a minute. But no other lights."

"Maybe she was tired and went right upstairs to bed."

"Yeah, but wouldn't she still turn some lights on?"

"She probably did, but you just can't see them from here." She turned away from Ethan and readjusted the pins in the seam she was working on, but he still hovered.

"Mom," he said again.

"*What!*"

"Um...do you think maybe one of us should call her? I could do it."

He's really worried, Rachel realized. "I'm sure she's all right, but I'll call her if it'll make you feel better." She went to the telephone, picked up the handset, and dialed Jessica's number. She let it ring several times, but there was no answer.

He jumped when the telephone rang. He saw Jessica's eyes shift toward it, her lips moving to form the word *please.*

"Ignore it," he said, speaking as much to himself as to her. "Now *where's Jill?* Where did she go?"

Jessica's pain was very bad, and she found it nearly impossible to breathe. Jill must have been right: this man was stalking her. As her strength ebbed, she thought she could hear Kevin telling her to take care of Jill. *Yes, Kevin. Yes, I will.* "San Diego," she muttered hoarsely.

"San Diego, huh? You wouldn't lie to me, would you?" He removed his knife from its sheath and showed it to her, careful to keep it beyond her reach. The crafty old bitch might be faking. He had to be sure.

"San Diego," she said again, the words coming out on a long sigh of escaping breath. Then her head lolled to one side.

Down the road, Rachel Cameron put down the handset and looked at her son. "Ethan, are you sure you saw her come home?"

The boy nodded. "Positive."

"All right. Can you keep an eye on Emily for me while I drive up and check?"

He nodded again.

"And do me a favor," she added. "Daddy's out in the barn, so call him on his cell and let him know I'll be gone for a few minutes."

Grabbing her cell phone, she went to the pegboard near the back door and took down her car keys, plus the house key Jessica had given her for emergency use. Drawn by the telltale clinking sound, Rowdy trotted up and looked at her expectantly. He loved car rides, and Rachel often took him along on her errands.

"Oh, all right," she said. "Come on." Rowdy followed her to the garage, jumping in the minute she opened the driver's side door of her Subaru Forester. She climbed in after him, started the engine, and backed out of the garage. It was still warm outside, but it was too short a drive to Jessica's to run the vehicle's air conditioner. Instead, she opened its large sunroof. As she turned onto the county road she glanced at Rowdy, sitting on his haunches in the passenger seat with his nose pointed skyward, savoring the smorgasbord of odors that entered through the sunroof. Her favorite Eagles CD was loaded in the dashboard player, and Rowdy seemed to enjoy the music as much as she did.

"Goofy dog," she said, smiling, then quickly sobered, wondering what she would find at Jessica's. She hoped everything was fine and her son was mistaken, but she had a sinking feeling that he wasn't. Turning into the narrow driveway, she could see that Ethan was right: every single window was dark. Could the power be out? She pulled up to the side door, shifted into park, and turned off the engine.

He had heard the car drive up. Crouching on the floor beside Jessica, he clutched his knife and growled a warning into her ear. "Not a sound, or you die." It crossed his mind that the warning might be unnecessary, because she didn't seem to be breathing.

There was a moment's deep quiet—no engine noise, no music—before Rachel heard an unfamiliar sound close by. She had opened the driver's side door before she realized what it was.

Rowdy was snarling.

58

Rachel stared at her dog in disbelief, astounded at the transformation in the amiable family pet. His teeth were bared menacingly; his eyes, fixed on Jessica's house, shone yellow and feral as a wolf's in the glow of the dome light. The skin on the back of Rachel's neck prickled as Ethan's words came back to her: *Rowdy didn't like him.*

"Oh, my God," she whispered. What if it wasn't Jessica's car that Ethan had seen? What if…?

Overtaken by a wave of terror, she yanked the Forester's door shut, started the engine, and jammed the gearshift lever into reverse. She backed out almost to the county road, then stopped, breathing hard. She took her cell phone from the center console and speed-dialed the Remington County emergency dispatch number.

When the operator answered, she gave her name and location. "I think there's an intruder in the house," she said, the words coming out in a rush. "Please send someone as soon as you can. I've got a key to the house in case it's needed, so I'll wait at the end of the driveway. I'm in a red Subaru Forester with the engine running and headlights on." And the doors locked, she added mentally, checking to make sure they really were.

She maneuvered the Forester onto Jessica's front lawn to make room for the squad car she hoped would arrive momentarily. Beside her, Rowdy—quiet now—seemed to sense her agitation. He leaned toward her and, as though to comfort her, briefly licked her cheek before returning his attention to Jessica's house.

At first he thought the car had driven away. But when he crept to the window to make sure, he saw to his consternation that it had taken up station at the end of the driveway. *Oh, shit.* Better get the hell out of Dodge. Good thing he'd turned off the yard light almost the minute the old lady had turned it on, or whoever was out there in the car would see him for sure.

The back door, not visible from the driveway, was his best bet. He closed it but didn't take time to lock it as he dashed for the shelter of the nearest grain storage bin. It was about a hundred feet behind the house and, he hoped, beyond the range of the vehicle's headlights. From there, he would be only a short sprint away from the cover of the cornfield and, beyond that, his waiting Tahoe.

When he reached it, his heart still pounding from his narrow escape, he slid behind the wheel and started the engine. He didn't dare use his headlights just yet; instead, he crept to the narrow county blacktop and turned right, away from the road that ran past the McKinnon property, and drove slowly to the next crossroads, where he turned left. Only then did he turn on the Tahoe's headlights and speed away to the north.

He had driven over a mile when he heard sirens faintly in the distance. They were far off to the south, coming from the direction of Drummond, and a minute or so later they stopped. At the old lady's house, no doubt, probably summoned by the driver of the small SUV. But why? There'd been no sound, no movement to give away his presence, and whoever it was hadn't even come to the door. Well, it made no difference now. The old lady was probably dead already, and even if she survived she couldn't describe him. There was no way she could have seen his face in the dark.

He continued zigzagging to the north and east until he found a deserted spot to pull over. He was far out in the country at the top of a small rise, where he could see for miles. There wasn't a car in sight in any direction. He removed the out-of-state license plates and tossed them onto the floor of the back seat. Finally coming down from his adrenaline high, he began to review his actions for any serious mistakes. He could think of only one: he should have locked the back door, since he'd found it locked when he arrived. But there hadn't been time, and because the old gal lived alone—and often left her doors unlocked, which was how he'd been able to get the key in the first place—chances were good that nobody would give it a thought.

The key. He needed to get rid of it, and there was no time like the present. Withdrawing it from his pocket, he wiped it thoroughly with his handkerchief and dropped it into the drainage ditch that lay between the road and a nearby soybean field. It landed with a faint splash.

Lightning flashed off to the west. A cool rain-scented breeze had sprung up, chilling his skin where his shirt, still damp with perspiration, clung to it. Shivering, he got back into the Tahoe. A storm was coming. Looked like his luck was holding, he reflected. A good hard rainfall would wash away any footprints or tire tracks he might have left, assuming anyone even thought to look.

Luck had been on his side up to now. If the old McKinnon woman was dead, it was due to natural causes. There'd be nothing to tie her death to him. And if she hadn't come home while he was still there, he wouldn't know that Jill had moved to San Diego, beyond his reach. No telling how much time he would have wasted looking for her if he hadn't found that out.

Still, he felt a curious lack of satisfaction with the way the evening's events had unfolded. Maybe it was because tracking down and eliminating Jill was a part of his plan—his endgame, he thought with a mirthless smile—and now that part would have to be scrapped. Or maybe it was because he wasn't sure the old lady had told the truth. Would she lie, even at the point of death? She might, he decided, if doing so would protect her daughter.

He had a sudden thought: *the obituary.* If she was dead it was sure to be in the newspaper, along with information on her next of kin. He only had to wait a day or two.

Jill sat slumped across from Louise Engquist at Jessica's kitchen table. "I shouldn't have let her leave," Jill said. "She looked terrible. I should have known there was something going on besides a toothache. I should have—"

"Stop that right this minute." Louise reached out and grasped Jill's hands in her own. "Hindsight is always twenty-twenty. But you know as well as I do, Jessica was stubborn as a mule. I tried and tried to get her to see a doctor, and I told her why. Spelled it out in no uncertain terms. But she wouldn't, and I couldn't make her. At the end of the day, Jill, she was a grownup. Her health was her own responsibility and nobody else's."

"You're right," Jill said with a sigh. "But still…"

"I know." Louise gave Jill's hands a gentle squeeze, then stood up. "Listen, how about if I make us some coffee, and maybe some scrambled eggs and toast? I don't know about you, but I'm starved. I haven't eaten since last night."

"I can do that," Jill said, and started to get up, but Louise pushed her gently back into her chair.

"No. You just sit." Poor kid, Louise thought, and wondered how long it had been since Jill had been taken care of by anyone. Certainly not her parents, Louise reflected. She still remembered Kevin's funeral a year earlier and how shocked she was that Jill's mother hadn't made the trip from California. She'd made some stupid excuse about getting her sons ready for school, as if their father couldn't take responsibility for that. And Jill's own father, Louise recalled, who was retired and short of neither time nor money, had shown up with that ghastly painted-up woman in tow. She'd made it plain that the farmhouse guest room was not up to her standards, so they'd checked into the local Hampton Inn and spent only one night, leaving directly from the next day's funeral service. Louise had wondered at the time why they'd even bothered to attend.

She moved around the kitchen setting out silverware, butter and jelly, watching Jill from the corner of her eye as she did so. She knew the girl had been up all night, first at the hospital—summoned by emergency room personnel, using phone a number supplied by Rachel Cameron—and then, after Jessica was pronounced dead and the necessary formalities had been dealt with, here at the farmhouse. Jill had called Louise at seven that morning.

"I didn't know where else to go," Jill had said. "Can you please come over?"

Louise had thrown on some clothes and jumped in her car, not even taking time to comb her hair. That was one good thing about being seventy years old, she told herself. Nobody paid the slightest attention to how you looked.

She found a carton of orange juice in the refrigerator and poured some into two glasses, then dropped bread into the toaster before setting plates of steaming scrambled eggs on the table.

"I should call Kevin's aunts," Jill said. "And—"

"Later. First, you need to eat."

Jill picked up her fork, holding it motionless in front of her as she stared at the tabletop.

"Eat," Louise urged her gently.

She obediently scooped up a forkful of eggs. "Something's wrong," she said.

"Wrong," Louise echoed. "What do you mean?"

"I'm not sure, but something's missing." She popped the eggs into her mouth, swallowed them, and took a bite of toast. "This is really good. Thank you."

"You're welcome."

"Jessica's emergency pendant," Jill said suddenly. "She said she left it on the table, but it's not here."

"Maybe she picked it up when she got home and dropped it somewhere."

"I know she dropped her keys, because I found them on the floor just inside the door. But no pendant. Her purse is missing, too," Jill exclaimed. "I hadn't thought about it until just now, but—"

"It's probably in there with her other belongings," Louise said, gesturing toward the large plastic bag that the hospital personnel had given Jill. "Maybe the pendant is, too. I bet the sheriff's police or paramedics picked up all her stuff to take to the hospital with her. You can look later, but don't worry. We'll find everything."

After they had finished eating and cleared away their dishes, Jill upended the hospital bag over the kitchen table and quickly sorted through the contents. "Just clothes and shoes," she said. "No purse, no pendant."

"Well, the pendant's small. If the paramedics picked it up, it could have fallen out anywhere along the way. But her purse…I wonder, could it still be in the car? Why don't I go out and have a look?"

Jill shrugged. "Worth a try, I suppose."

"Will I need a key to open the garage?"

"Better take one, just in case." Jill stepped toward the key rack. "The same key fits every lock on the place, so—well, that's funny."

"What?"

"The spare key is missing. Here are the keys to Kevin's truck," Jill said, holding up a key fob with two car keys and a house key, "but there was another ring with just a house key on it. It's been there forever. I think it belonged to Joe."

"Maybe Jessica gave it to someone. The Camerons, maybe?"

"Must have. Well, it doesn't matter." Jill handed Kevin's keys to Louise. "Go ahead and take a look in the garage, if you want to, but watch out for the puddles. That must have been quite a storm last night. I hope it didn't knock down any of the corn."

"It looked fine when I drove by earlier," Louise said over her shoulder as she headed out the side door. "I'll be right back, okay?"

She returned a few minutes later carrying Jessica's handbag. "It was in the car," she reported. "Driver's side door was still open. She must have been—" Louise fell silent, wondering if she was about to divulge information that Jill didn't really need. What did her grandkids call it? TMI?

"She must have been what?"

Jill is a grown woman, Louise reminded herself. She can handle it. "She left her purse behind and didn't shut the car door, so she didn't waste an ounce of strength on things that didn't matter. She must have been fighting like crazy to get into the house and call for help."

"I asked her to call me when she got home, so I'd know she made it okay. And then when she didn't, I tried calling her but the line was busy."

"Calling 911, maybe?"

"Maybe, but the woman at the hospital said the call came in from a neighbor."

Louise shrugged. "She could have been mistaken."

"I guess. But at the time, I thought the line was busy because she was trying to call me. Or maybe she was talking to you about her toothache, because she said she was going to."

"No," Louise said, shaking her head. "I never heard from her."

"So I figured I'd wait a while and try again later. But when I did, it just rang and rang. So I thought about calling Camerons and asking if they'd go check on her, but then the hospital called." Jill sighed. "They said I should come right away. And I was pretty sure I knew what that meant."

Louise gently steered Jill into the living room. "Why don't you stretch out on the davenport for a little while? It's nice and cool in here, and maybe you can get some sleep. I can look for Joe's sisters' phone numbers. I knew them pretty well years ago, so I could even call them if you want. Although," she suggested, "it might be better if we wait until we've made the funeral arrangements. That way we can give them all the information at once."

"Oh, Lord," Jill moaned. "The funeral. I'll have to—"

"You *don't* have to. Not right now, at least. Rest a while first."

"I can't," Jill said. "There's someone at the front door."

60

The front door of the farmhouse was rarely used. Friends and neighbors always came to the side door, the same one that had been used by generations of McKinnons, so Jill was surprised to see Rachel Cameron standing on the front porch. Rowdy sat beside her, looking up expectantly.

"I saw your car," she began hesitantly, "so I thought it would be all right for me to come over for a few minutes. I'm so sorry."

"Of course it's all right," Jill said. "Please come in. You too, Rowdy." At the sound of his name the dog stretched up his head to be petted, and Jill couldn't help smiling.

Rachel chewed on her lower lip, struggling to hold back tears, but made no move to enter. "I owe you such a huge apology," she began. "Well, Rowdy does too. But he's only a dog, so what does he know? It's really my fault."

"Please come in," Jill said again. "I can't imagine why you think it's your fault Jessica had a heart attack." She patted the sofa cushion beside her. "Here, sit. Would you like a cup of coffee? It's still fresh."

"No, thank you." Rachel sat beside Jill. "Down," she commanded, and Rowdy obediently lay down at her feet. "Stay."

"You've trained him well," Jill said. "He's a wonderful dog."

"I'm not so sure how wonderful you'll think he is when you hear what I have to tell you." Rachel drew a deep breath. "The thing is… Ethan saw Jessica drive by on her way home last night. He saw her turn into the driveway, but then when he noticed she hadn't turned any lights on he came and told me. I tried calling her, but—"

"Maybe that was why her line rang busy," Louise suggested to Jill in an undertone.

"—she didn't answer. So I asked Ethan if he was sure he'd seen her come home, and he said he was, so I figured I should run over and make sure she was okay. And Rowdy wanted to come along, because I almost always take him in the car with me. But when I drove up to the side door and stopped, he reacted so strangely. Growling, snarling, staring at the house…it scared me to death. Then I thought maybe it wasn't Jessica that Ethan saw. Maybe it was a burglar instead. So I panicked and didn't go in. All because my stupid dog saw a possum or something."

"You called emergency services, didn't you?"

"Yes, but I didn't go in because I was afraid. And maybe if I had, I could've done something to help her. It was four or five minutes before the sheriff's police got here, and they thought they were responding to an intruder call. So we had to wait even longer for an ambulance—"

"Rachel." Louise had sat down on Rachel's other side and put a firm hand on her arm. "You did exactly the right thing. I happen to know that the sheriff's police are all trained in CPR. Listen, if you hadn't called them there's no telling how long she would have lain there."

"I was glad I thought to bring the key," Rachel said, "because the door was locked, so they needed it to get inside. They went in with their guns drawn…"

"Which door was locked?" Jill asked.

"The side door. Oh, that reminds me. I should probably give this back. Jessica had it made for us after you moved out, but I won't be needing it anymore." She reached into the pocket of her capri pants and removed a key, which she handed to Jill. "They made me stay back, but when they turned the lights on I could see her lying just a few feet inside the door. Things happened pretty fast after that. Another squad car came, and then the ambulance, but I knew from the way they were acting and talking among themselves that she was…oh, God, Jill, I'm so sorry…"

"Hush, now." Jill laid a hand on her arm. "Let's go in the kitchen and have some coffee," she suggested with a smile. "Come on, now. You, too, Rowdy. Maybe you could let him off the leash? He can't go far."

When Rachel unclipped Rowdy's leash, he followed her into the kitchen; but, when she sat down at the table, he trotted past her to a spot near the side door and lowered his nose to the floor.

"That's where they found her," Rachel said in a low voice. "He liked Jessica a lot. Ethan used to bring him to visit her sometimes."

Just then, Rowdy turned toward the pantry and moved silently toward the back door, his head down and hackles bristling. "Rowdy!" Rachel scolded, but he paid no attention. As the three women watched, the dog investigated the area around the back door. Then, satisfied, he returned to the kitchen and flopped down at Rachel's feet.

"That was weird," she said. "I guess he was just checking out who all was here last night. He's a little suspicious of strange men sometimes. We think he might have been abused by one as a puppy. Maybe that's why he reacted the way he did when—"

"When what?"

"Ethan had him out for a walk one afternoon, I guess it was about a month ago. He used to enjoy going over to your little woodlot up the road, Jill, and sketching the different plants he found. He was working on a badge for Scouts."

"Yes, I know. I saw him over there a while back."

"Well, anyway, this one time he found a guy parked there. Apparently he was lost and was waiting for someone to call him back with directions. Which they did, and then he drove away. But according to Ethan, Rowdy didn't react well at all. It scared him, and when he told me about it, it scared me, too."

"Rachel," Jill said slowly, "did Ethan happen to say what kind of car the man was driving?"

"No, just that it was a black SUV. Some boys are really interested in cars, but Ethan's not one of them. Why do you ask?"

"Just wondering," Jill said, but her mind was spinning. A black SUV. Was it only a coincidence?

She waited until Rachel had finished her coffee and left before going into the pantry and checking the back door. It was unlocked, which struck her as odd. Jessica was sometimes casual about locking the side door, but the back one was always locked because it was never used. She returned to the kitchen, where Louise was searching for Jessica's address file.

"Louise," Jill said, "didn't Rachel say that the side door was locked?"

"Yes."

"But why would she—if she didn't pick up her purse or even close the car door, why would she let herself in the side door and then lock it behind herself? That doesn't make sense, especially if she knew she'd need an ambulance. How would they get in?"

"Maybe she came in the back door instead."

"That's possible," Jill said. "It's a foot or two closer, but…" She stood in the center of the kitchen, visualizing the path Jessica would have taken from the back door to the place where, according to Rachel, she had been found lying on the floor—which was very near where Jill had found her keys. She would have had to pass the telephone to get there. Why, if she was so desperate to get help, wouldn't she have dialed 911? "It just doesn't make sense."

"People do a lot of things that don't make sense when they're in that situation," Louise said. "They're in pain, they're disoriented…" She laid a reassuring hand on Jill's shoulder. "Please go lie down now. Rest for a little while."

"In a few minutes," Jill said. She was staring down at the shiny new key Rachel Cameron had given her. It was not the one that had hung beside the side door for so many years. "I want to call a locksmith first."

At Louise's urging, Jill had stretched out on the living room sofa. She hadn't intended to sleep but must have done so, because she was jolted awake after what seemed like only moments by the sound of a male voice coming from the kitchen. She heard Louise's murmured response but couldn't make out the words. *The locksmith,* Jill thought, and stood up, shaking her head to clear it as she followed the hum of conversation into the kitchen.

Instead of the locksmith, though, the man whose voice she had heard was Dio Pappas. He and Louise both turned toward Jill as she entered the room.

"Dio brought us lunch," Louise said, indicating the large bowl her brother-in-law was cradling in the crook of one arm. He also held a brown paper bag.

"Greek salad," Dio said. "Tomatoes, cucumber, onion, olives, feta cheese…and bread to sop up the dressing," he added, brandishing the bag. "I hope you'll like it."

Deeply affected by his kindness and soothing, resonant voice, Jill had to struggle for control before responding. "Thank you. It sounds delicious."

"I'm so sorry about Jessica," he said softly, and this time Jill was unable to hold back the tears. Dio set the bowl and paper bag on the counter and stretched out his arms to her, gathering her into a gentle embrace.

Louise, watching, felt her own eyes well up. She had learned during her long nursing career that when children were very seriously ill or injured, a father's presence was often more comforting than a mother's. Counterintuitive, perhaps, but true. And how long, she wondered, had it been since this poor girl had experienced a father's consolation?

Jill pulled away, embarrassed. "Sorry," she muttered.

"Nothing to be sorry about," Dio reassured her. "Why don't I put this in the fridge for now?" He picked up the salad bowl and opened the refrigerator door, stowing the bowl inside. But, as he closed the door, he saw an unexpected object on top of the refrigerator. It was very close to the back, and even with his height—over six feet—he had to stretch to reach it.

"Funny place for this," he said, holding up Jessica's emergency pendant.

Jill and Louise exchanged glances, but Louise was the first to speak. "We were wondering where it was. Just set it on the counter, why don't you." Hoping to steer the conversation into other channels, she turned to Jill and added, "I found addresses and phone numbers for Kevin's aunts while you were napping. I left them on the dining room table so—"

"Why would she have done that?" Jill burst out. "Told me she left her pendant on the table when she didn't?"

"Oh, honey," Louise said, "it was probably just one of those absent-minded things we older folks do. It doesn't mean—"

Jill was in no mood to be humored. "Her heart may have been bad, but there was nothing wrong with her mind. She was only about five-two, so she couldn't even have reached it." She got up and went over to the refrigerator, standing on tiptoe to survey its top surface. "She must've just tossed it up there when she first got it and left it there. Look at that dust. I'll bet it hasn't been cleaned since I moved out."

Louise shrugged helplessly. "For what it's worth, I really thought she was using it."

"When she was at my place last night it felt like we were finally getting past the...whatever it was that made her hate me. Not hate me," she amended, "but—well, you know."

"I know," Louise agreed with a nod.

"Now, though, it makes me wonder…" Jill's words trailed off into a strained silence, which Dio felt compelled to break.

"Listen, ladies, why don't we break out that salad after all? My body clock is telling me it's time for lunch."

They made desultory small talk while they ate, and Dio, in an attempt to keep the conversation going, asked Jill if she'd heard from Nick lately.

"No. Should I have?"

"Oh," Dio said, sounding surprised and a bit disappointed. "He told me he was going to call you."

"Isn't that what guys always say?" Jill responded with a smile that didn't quite reach her eyes. "'I'll call you,' but they never do."

"He works down in Bloomington, and it's a busy time for him right now." Dio picked up a slice of bread and concentrated on wiping up the last drops of salad dressing that remained on his plate.

Under other circumstances Louise would have enjoyed her brother-in-law's discomfiture, but she was glad when a loud rapping on the door announced the arrival of the locksmith.

"Honestly, Dio," she scolded him after Jill had left the table. "What in the world were you thinking?"

"He really did tell me he was going to call her," Dio argued. "Although…"

"Although what?"

"He didn't think she seemed too interested in him."

"Which means she didn't fall at his feet like girls usually do, and that hurt his pride a little. You know I think the world of Nick. But you have to admit, he's *very* aware of how attractive he is."

"A chip off the old block," Dio said with a grin.

"You must be referring to his ego, because he gets his good looks from his mother. Seriously, Dio, I know they might make a good match. She's an accomplished, attractive, and honorable young woman. And if it's meant to be, it'll happen. Otherwise, it won't. But Nick has to be willing to give the poor girl some time, not to mention some space. Jessica's death has hit her pretty hard."

"Even though they obviously had some issues?"

"Yes, because she was Jill's last real link to Kevin. And her dying on Kevin's anniversary date was another blow. I think," Louise suggested, "considering that Kevin was Nick's friend when they were growing up, you need to let Nick know about Jessica's death. Regardless of what happens between him and Jill, he needs to come down. Not for the funeral, maybe, if it's on a workday and he's as busy as you say. But soon. Next weekend, maybe. He owes that much to Kevin's memory."

After the locksmith had finished his work and left, Jill sat at the kitchen table with Louise and Dio discussing Jessica's funeral arrangements.

"She wasn't religious," Jill told them. "She never even belonged to a church as far as I know. But it doesn't seem right to just bury her without some sort of service."

"My advice," Dio said, "is to do for her whatever she did for her late husband. Chances are pretty good that's what she'd have wanted for herself."

"That makes sense, if I had a way of knowing—"

"The funeral home will have a record. There're only two in town, so it won't be a problem to find out which one it was."

"True," Jill said. "I'll call them."

"And if you'd like me to go along when you make the arrangements, I'd be glad to."

"That's very kind of you, but I hate to impose on your time that way."

"It's no imposition, honestly. I'd be happy to help."

"Let him do it," Louise chimed in. "Dio has quite a knack for organizing things."

62

He had eagerly plucked the newspaper from his doorstep on the two mornings following Jessica's apparent death, wondering if her name would be among the obituaries. When it wasn't there the first morning he was disappointed, though not surprised. *Too soon*, he told himself. But when it wasn't there the second morning, he began to feel uneasy.

By the third morning—Monday—the suspense had become excruciating. What if she wasn't really dead when he left? He opened his front door, reached down and picked up the *Drummond Observer*, and carried it inside. Then, taking a deep breath, he opened it to the obituary page.

Finally! There it was: Jessica May McKinnon. He released the breath he'd been holding and skimmed the two brief paragraphs that followed her name. They contained her date and place of birth, her parents' names, her husband's name and the date of their marriage. Predeceased by…now, there was a surprise. Apparently she'd had a son, Kevin McKinnon, but there was no mention of any surviving relatives, including Jill. Strange, he reflected. Maybe Jill really had cut all ties with Jessica and moved to San Diego. Maybe…but he couldn't escape a nagging sense of doubt.

What if the old gal had survived long enough to tell the police what had happened? If they knew somebody was looking for Jill, wouldn't they keep her name and other information out of the newspaper? It was a disquieting thought.

Funeral arrangements are pending, he read. Maybe there would be more information in tomorrow's paper. Not that it would do him any good, he decided, because going anywhere near the funeral home or cemetery was a temptation to which he must absolutely not yield. Wasn't that a cliché in almost every cop show he'd ever watched? Staking out the funeral to see if the bad guy showed up? But he wouldn't. He was too smart for that.

Jill's first priority on Monday morning was to phone Roy Hanninen, the McKinnon family's attorney, and schedule an appointment for later that day to begin the process of settling Jessica's estate.

"She named you as her executor," the old lawyer told Jill, "even though I suspect she wasn't very happy about it at the time. But I told her that was the only way that made sense, and believe it or not she followed my advice. As for the rest, we'll talk about that when you get here."

Next, Jill met Dio Pappas at the Albright-Stanton Funeral Home, which was located in a converted nineteenth-century mansion in the oldest section of Drummond. She had called this establishment first, guessing—correctly, as it had turned out—that Jessica would have preferred this long-established funeral home to its newer competitor on the north side of town. The third-generation funeral director greeted them courteously and handled the business at hand with smooth efficiency, but Jill was both amused and irritated by the way he virtually ignored her and deferred to Dio instead.

"He played football for me," Dio told her later. "Had to be fifteen or twenty years ago. I don't think he meant to be rude, but he probably still sees me as an authority figure." He glanced at his watch. "I know it's a little early, but why don't I take you to lunch at Pinky's? They have pretty good sandwiches there."

"Sounds good. And I've been thinking about some things that... well...I'd like to tell you about them and see if you think I'm reading too much into them."

When they had seated themselves in a booth at Pinky's Café, Jill told Dio about the flowers delivered to Jessica by a man in a black SUV. She then recounted what Rachel Cameron had told her about her son seeing a black SUV parked where the driver would have been able to watch the McKinnon property, the Cameron family dog's odd reaction to him, and how that reaction was repeated when Rachel parked beside Jessica's house the night of her death.

"One of the things that bothers me most is that Rachel said Rowdy—"

"Who's Rowdy?"

"The dog. Rachel said they think he might have been abused by a man or men in the past, and that's why he seemed so hostile to the guy in the black SUV. But he liked Jessica, so why would he...I don't know. It's just all wrong. The back door was unlocked, but the side door *was* locked even though that's the one she always used. And she hadn't even shut the car door, for heaven's sake."

Barb, the waitress, approached with a smile. "Hey, Coach. Morning, Miss. What'll it be?"

Jill shrugged. Food was the last thing on her mind at the moment. "Whatever he's having," she said.

"Turkey club on sourdough, light mayo, and iced tea. Okay?" he asked Jill.

"Fine. And there's more," she added after Barb had retreated toward the kitchen. "I've been thinking about Jess's emergency pendant. I know what Louise thinks. You heard what she said. But that's not...it just wasn't Jess's way. If she didn't actually wear the pendant, if she was going to lie to me about it, she would've just said it was at home, period. And then changed the subject. She wouldn't have bothered to be so specific about where she'd left it."

"Could be," Dio said thoughtfully. "But sometimes when people fabricate, they think they'll sound more credible by being as specific as possible."

"Sure, if we're talking about other people. But not Jess. I lived with her for years, and trust me. I know."

"So let's assume you're right. Where does that lead you?"

Jill leaned forward and spoke in a low voice. "Honestly? It leads me somewhere I don't want to go." She paused to gather her thoughts. "Suppose there was somebody trying to find me? Why, I don't know. But the flowers didn't work. And the phone call didn't work either, although I'm pretty sure—" Jill broke off when Barb arrived with their drinks. "Thank you," Jill told the waitress with a smile.

"Pretty sure what?" Dio asked.

"I'm pretty sure Jess gave away that I *used* to live there. So what if he was watching the place? And when he saw her leave, on her way to my place, he went inside the house to look for my address or phone number? And he hid her pendant so she couldn't call for help if he was still there when she came home..."

"Those are some major 'what ifs,' Jill."

"I know. But on top of everything else, there was a house key missing. That's why I had the locks changed right away. Maybe Jess gave it to somebody, but I don't think so. She had a new one made for Rachel Cameron, which she already gave back to me. It was a nice shiny new one, but the one that was missing was old. And Louise had one already. Who else would have needed one?"

"Two questions. Do you have any idea who this mysterious person might be? And have you talked to anyone in law enforcement about this?"

"Yes to both. Tommy referred me to Stack Ridgeway, and I told him about some things that happened before this weekend, including the man I suspected. And he said he'd follow up, but..."

"But?"

"I'm not sure he really did. And realistically, Jessica's house is outside the city limits. So it's not even his jurisdiction."

"I see. Well, it just so happens I know the guy whose jurisdiction it's in."

"Is there anyone in town you *don't* know?"

"I'm sure there must be," Dio said with a smile. "But nobody important. And here come our sandwiches, so eat up."

Ten minutes later, Jill had finished her lunch and consulted her watch. "I really should check in at the office."

"Did Tommy have a cow when he found out you wouldn't be coming in this morning?"

"Actually, he was pretty nice about it considering what a busy week we have coming up." She felt a great deal better now that she had shared her concerns with Dio, who not only seemed to take them seriously but also had enough clout to see that they were acted on. She scooted out of the booth and then, impulsively, leaned over to hug the coach. "Thank you for everything. You have no idea how much I appreciate your help."

Stack Ridgeway had entered the café a few minutes earlier and was seated at his favorite window table when Jill left, apparently without noticing his presence. He waited until Dio had paid for lunch and was on his way out before greeting him.

"This is the second time I've seen you with that lady," Stack teased, grinning. "Does Marg know about her?"

"Not only does she know, but she also approves," Dio shot back, sitting down across from Stack. "Maybe you need to know a little more about her, too. First of all, her mother-in-law died Friday night."

Stack's grin vanished. "Did she? I'm sorry to hear that."

"And that's not all. There's more."

Stack listened patiently as Dio repeated what Jill had told him. Stack already knew about the flowers Jessica had received from a secret admirer and the anonymous male caller, who had claimed he knew Jill and asked for her address. He paid closer attention, however, to Dio's account of the SUV Ethan Cameron had seen, the oddly placed emergency pendant, and the missing key to Jessica's house.

"You know, Coach," he said, "that's all interesting, but it doesn't mean much unless Mrs. McKinnon's death was due to something other than a heart attack. Is that your thinking?"

"No, my thinking is that Jill McKinnon is being stalked. And the stalker figured the way to get to Jill was through Jessica. But here's my question for you: what if the stalker was there when Jessica got home? What if he prevented her from calling for help? Wouldn't that be a crime?"

Stack sighed. "That's only speculation, Coach."

"I'm just telling you what I think. What you do about it is up to you."

"I'm glad to hear that. For a few minutes there, I thought you were going to try telling me how to do my job."

"No, because the McKinnon farm isn't in your jurisdiction." Dio stood up and pulled himself to his full height. "So I'm going to pay a visit to Sheriff Dean and try telling *him* how to do *his* job."

"Good luck with that," Stack said. He waited until Dio had left the café before pulling out his phone and sending a text message to detective Scott Allison.

Allison met Stack, as he'd requested, in the parking lot outside the Carlyle Group, LLC, office building. It was a square, unadorned structure in an industrial complex, built for utility and not to impress. Allison got out of his own car and slid into the Durango's front seat beside Stack.

"What's up?"

"Just a routine follow-up call that I didn't want to make on my own." Stack surveyed the lot, noting the vehicles parked there: a beige Ford Focus, a pearl-white Cadillac Escalade, and a dusty black Honda Pilot. "Although," he added thoughtfully, "I might ask you to wait in the lobby while I talk to Carlyle."

"Then why did you want me to come along?"

Stack's eyes lingered on the Pilot. "Be nice to know who owns these vehicles."

"Why not just run the plates?"

"Because I'd rather not. Okay, let's go."

The middle-aged blonde at the front desk greeted them cautiously when they entered. "Hello. Can I help you gentlemen?"

"I'm Captain Ridgeway, and this is Detective Allison from the Drummond Police Department. Is Mr. Ryan Carlyle available to speak with us?"

She looked from Stack to Allison and back again. "Just a minute." She disappeared through a doorway, which she quickly closed. They heard voices murmuring behind the door, then Ryan Carlyle came out followed by the receptionist.

"What?" he barked. His face was set in belligerent lines, Stack observed, probably to hide the apprehension he almost certainly felt. Nobody enjoyed a visit from the cops.

"How do you do," Stack said politely. He didn't show his badge, because his identity was already established and this wasn't about power or dominance. He wanted the guy to feel as comfortable as possible. "Detective Allison and I are just following up on a couple of matters pertaining to the Brian Briggs trial. I understand you were a member of the jury?"

"Yes."

"Then may we ask you a few questions? We won't take much of your time."

"I'll talk to you," he said, stabbing a finger at Stack. He jerked his chin toward Allison, whom he remembered from the trial. "He can wait out here."

"That'll work. Take care of my partner, won't you?" Stack said to the receptionist as he followed Carlyle into his office. This was turning out better than he'd hoped. The ladies loved Scotty, especially the middle-aged ones. They seemed to go for the boyish, clean-cut type. If the receptionist knew anything at all, she'd spill it within thirty seconds.

As soon as her boss was back inside his office, Jackie stopped pretending to focus on her computer screen. "Could I get you some coffee or something?"

"Thanks, but I'm fine." He crossed to the window that faced the parking lot and looked out.

"I'm sorry he was so rude to you."

"Not a problem. Nice Escalade," Allison said with a smile. "Yours?"

Jackie snorted. "Yeah, sure. That's Ryan's."

Allison couldn't miss the hostility in the woman's voice. "And you drive that black SUV, right? Plenty of room for taking the kids to soccer practice."

"The Pilot, you mean? No way. My kids are way past soccer age."

"You're kidding!"

"Oh, no," Jackie said, pleased by his flattery. "They're all grown up. I drive the little Ford. The Pilot's our company car. Ryan uses it to make his rounds. God forbid he should dirty up his precious Caddy."

Allison turned away from the window to face her. "Make his rounds? I don't understand."

She shrugged. "Mr. Carlyle—Mr. Gary Carlyle, that is, not Ryan—owns several local businesses. An apartment complex, a couple of movie theaters, and some other commercial buildings besides this one. Ryan's job is supposedly to manage them, but his father's really the man in charge." She leaned forward and dropped her voice to a whisper. "You know that guy your partner was asking about? That Brian Briggs?"

"Yeah, what about him?"

"Ryan asked Mr. Carlyle to bail him out, so he did. Then Mr. Carlyle brought him over here, and Ryan put him to work sweeping the parking lot. Right out there," she said with a wave of her hand. "When I found out about that girl being murdered, it made my blood run cold. The thought of being that close to a murderer—"

Allison raised a cautionary finger to his lips. "You do realize," he said in an undertone, "that under the law he's presumed innocent until proven guilty."

"Oh, I know that. And besides, not everybody thinks he did it. Mr. Carlyle doesn't believe it," she whispered.

Allison rested his palms on the woman's desk and leaned in as close as he dared. He could hear the rise and fall of voices in Ryan Carlyle's office but couldn't make out what was being said. "Really? How do you know?"

"Because he said so. He went barging right into Ryan's office—oh, my goodness, he was mad!—and when he came out, he told Ryan to his face that he'd murdered that girl. 'You killed that girl. *You* did it. Don't try to tell me otherwise.' Those were his exact words." The voices on the other side of the door grew louder, closer. "Don't let on to Ryan that I told you," she added hastily.

When the door swung open moments later, Scott Allison was once more gazing out over the parking lot and Jackie was busily tapping away at her keyboard.

"Thank you for your time, Mr. Carlyle," Stack said. "I'd appreciate a call if you remember anything that might be helpful."

Carlyle grunted something that might have been assent, then turned back into his office and slammed the door.

"So what was that about?" Allison asked as they crossed the parking lot.

"Did you find out who owns the Pilot?"

"It's a company car. Ryan Carlyle drives it. You gonna tell me what this is about?"

"You're better off not knowing. I expect to get a phone call from the chief within an hour, tearing me a new one." Stack opened the door to his Durango. "You still wondering why I didn't want to run the plates on those vehicles?"

"Ah. Keeping it unofficial." Ryan Carlyle was sure to report their visit to his father, who would in turn complain to the Chief of Police. "There is one more thing," Allison said. "According to the receptionist, Gary Carlyle accused his son of murdering the Putnam girl."

"I can see how he might take that point of view, seeing as how he bailed out Briggs on Ryan's say-so. But I can't believe he meant it literally." He glanced at the black Pilot. So Ryan drives it, he thought. Interesting. "Thanks again, Scotty. We better get out of here before Mr. Ryan Carlyle starts to wonder why we're hanging around."

Stack needn't have worried. By the time the detectives drove out of the parking lot, Ryan Carlyle had retreated into his small private bathroom and was hunched over the toilet, vomiting.

The call from the Chief of Police that Stack had expected didn't happen. He did, however, receive one from Gary Carlyle. It came just as Stack was clearing his desk at the end of the day.

"I understand you paid a visit to my son today," the elder Carlyle said. "I need to talk to you about that."

"Of course. What do you need to know?"

"Not over the phone. I'll be there in fifteen minutes." There was a soft click as the connection was broken.

Typical, Stack thought. Gary Carlyle was a man accustomed to being accommodated, regardless of the inconvenience to other parties involved. Stack glanced at his watch. Based on past experience, he expected Carlyle to keep him waiting beyond the fifteen minutes specified.

Stack called his wife, Sherri, to let her know he'd be late getting home, then speed-dialed another number. Coach Dio wasn't the only person with connections, Stack reflected with a smile. His sister was married to one of the emergency room doctors at the Drummond Community Hospital.

As usual, the call went to voice mail. "Hey, Paul, it's Stack. Please get back to me as soon as you can. It's about a female patient brought in Friday night, a DOA about seventy years old. I need to confirm she had a heart attack."

While he waited for the arrival of Gary Carlyle—or a return call from Dr. Paul Killebrew, whichever came first—he reviewed the information Jill had given him regarding the other young male jurors. He'd have to follow up with them, too, to prove he wasn't singling out Ryan Carlyle.

Brett Petersen was a loan processor at the Remington County National Bank and probably worked normal banking hours, eight or eight-thirty to five. Jared Snow, on the other hand, worked at a twenty-four-hour copy shop. No telling what his hours might be.

Stack considered his strategy for interviewing them, a task he planned to perform himself rather than delegate to Allison. The young detective was a solid investigator, but his skills for reading the subtleties of facial expression and vocal inflection were still developing. Because Stack was primarily interested in the vehicles they drove, his best bet would be to catch them either arriving at or leaving work. Leaving, he decided. That way they wouldn't worry about being late and might be less inclined to brush him off. He'd call the bank and copy shop in the morning and, with any luck, would reach both men to set up meetings.

Gary Carlyle surprised Stack by arriving exactly on time and greeting him courteously. "Thank you for seeing me on such short notice. I know you were probably on your way home. May I?" Carlyle gestured toward one of the guest chairs facing Stack's desk.

"Of course. How can I help you?"

"You went to see my son earlier today. He called to tell me about it, and he was quite upset."

"I don't see why," Stack responded calmly. "It was just a follow-up visit to see if he'd noticed anything unusual or out of the way during the Briggs trial. Specifically, in the spectator area. The way the courtroom is laid out, the jurors have a better view than anyone else except the judge. I've talked to a few of the other jurors already, and—"

"Yes, yes," Carlyle interrupted. "He told me all that, especially about speaking with other jurors. But he seemed to think you had some other motive."

"Really. Such as?"

Carlyle crossed his legs, then uncrossed them. "He feels, and I do, too, a certain level of—there's no other way to say this—a certain level of responsibility for the young lady's death. We put up the bond to have that Briggs animal released. It was Ryan's idea, but I went along with it. Obviously, I had no idea…"

"Of course you didn't. But that doesn't tell me what your son thinks my motive was in coming to see him this afternoon."

"He was afraid. So afraid he got sick to his stomach."

Stack was beginning to grow impatient. "I'm sorry to hear that, but I still don't understand why."

"He's afraid you might think he did it on purpose."

"Did what on purpose?"

Gary Carlyle drew a deep breath, held it, then forcefully expelled it. "Bailed Brian Briggs out of jail so he could kill Katie Putnam."

Stack took his time responding. "And why, exactly, might I think that?"

"From what he tells me, Ryan said some…some intemperate things about the young lady. Her morals. That sort of thing. And they might have sounded like—" Carlyle shrugged.

"Like what?"

"Like…Captain Ridgeway, this is very difficult."

"I'm sorry, but I really am trying to understand. So your son said some things—I'm assuming you mean during jury deliberations?" Carlyle nodded. "And those things sounded like what?"

"They could have been interpreted," Carlyle said, speaking slowly and carefully, "to sound like he hated her. And it's only a small step from there to wanting her dead."

"Frankly, Mr. Carlyle, I think it's a *big* step from disapproving of someone's morals, or even hating that person, to wanting her dead. And another big step from wanting her dead to actually making it happen. Or perhaps I should say, allowing it to happen." Stack studied the man seated across from him for a moment before continuing. "So why do you think it's only a small step? Is there something about your son you're not telling me?"

At that moment Stack's cell phone chirped, and he saw his brother-in-law's name come up on caller ID. "My apologies, but I really need to take this call. It'll be short." He lifted the phone to his ear. "Hey, Paul. Talk to me."

"You were asking about the McKinnon woman, right?"

"Right."

"She had a heart attack, no doubt about it."

"Good to know. But if it's not too much to ask, can you find out if there was any sign of trauma? Abrasions, bruising, that sort of thing?" Stack was acutely aware of Gary Carlyle's inquisitive gaze. *Bet you're wondering if this is about your precious little boy, aren't you?*

"Sure thing. It won't be tonight though. I'll give you a call tomorrow."

"Okay, Paul, thanks." Stack ended the call and turned his attention back to Gary Carlyle. "Well?"

"Well, what?"

"Is there anything about your son that I should know? That you haven't told me?"

"He's not a murderer," Carlyle spoke quietly, almost inaudibly. "I can tell you that with absolute certainty. But he's not—when he was growing up, he had problems getting along with other children. For whatever reason, his social skills just never developed. And children being what they are, they picked on him a lot. Bullied him. His way of dealing with that when he was little was to withdraw. But when he got older, he started acting a lot tougher than he really was. By the time he was in high school he was bigger than most of the other kids, and he could be pretty intimidating. But it's only a front." Carlyle folded his hands and bowed his head, almost as if in prayer. "Ryan works for me," he said, raising his head and looking directly into Stack's eyes, "because he couldn't hold a job anywhere else. Believe me, he tried. He wanted to make it on his own, and his mother and I wanted that for him. But after a while we realized it just wasn't possible, so…"

"Did you ever have Ryan evaluated to try and find out—"

"Only about a dozen times." Carlyle broke in. He spoke with surprising bitterness.

"And?"

"We did get a diagnosis, eventually. We never told anyone what it was because we didn't want him to be labeled, and we still don't. Besides, it didn't do much good except to help us accept the inevitable. And as I said before, Ryan would never cause anyone's death, whether directly or indirectly. It simply isn't in his makeup." Carlyle stood up, signaling that the conversation had ended. "Thank you for your time, Captain. I assume Ryan won't be hearing from you further?"

Stack stood up as well. "Not unless our investigation requires it, sir."

Carlyle blinked. "Am I going to have to speak to Chief Whitesell about this?"

"If you feel you need to," Stack said, pretending indifference. "Although I've already told him about my plans to cast a wider net with respect to the Putnam investigation. Including interviewing the jurors." This was a bit of an exaggeration, since Stack had made only a passing reference to his intentions during a brief hallway encounter with the chief earlier that day. And, of course, he had made sure not to mention any names. That being the case, Stack decided, it couldn't hurt to back down a bit. "But I doubt very seriously that we'll need to speak with your son further. Unless, of course," Stack added with a brief smile, "he calls me. He still might remember something that would help the investigation." He extended his hand, which Carlyle accepted after a barely perceptible hesitation. "Good evening, sir."

He felt a momentary thrill when he saw Jessica McKinnon's funeral arrangements in Tuesday morning's paper, but he was disappointed in the article's brevity. He skimmed through it quickly and found the date, time and place of services. *Memorials to a charity of the donor's choice*, he read, and on the next line, *Online condolences may be sent to the family at…* The web address was that of the funeral home. But there was still no mention of Jill.

There were two possible reasons, he decided. Either Jessica and Jill had been seriously estranged, and other surviving family members were effectively disowning her by omitting her name and city of residence; or—the more ominous possibility—Jill knew she was being hunted and had deliberately withheld the information.

He glanced at his watch. He had a few minutes to spare before leaving for work. He turned on his prepaid disposable phone, located the funeral home's number, and punched it in.

An unctuous male voice answered. "Albright-Stanton Funeral Home, John Stanton speaking. How may I be of service?"

"I saw in the paper that you're handling Jessica McKinnon's funeral services. I'd like to send a card to the family. May I have their mailing address, please?"

"If you'll just send the card in care of us, sir, we'll see that it reaches the intended recipient." As if I'd be dumb enough to give out the address, the funeral director thought to himself. He probably wants it so he can go burglarize the house while everyone's at the funeral.

"Oh. Well, it's just that I went to high school with Kevin"—he remembered the name from the previous day's obituary—"but we lost touch a few years ago. And I live out of town now, so I thought maybe you could help me out."

Stanton's voice took on a slight edge. "As I said, sir, we'll be happy to forward a card if you wish to send one. Or you could visit our online guestbook if you'd rather."

"I might do that. Thank you." The line went dead.

Stanton sat motionless at his desk, thinking about the phone call he'd received from Coach Pappas the day before. It had been just a few hours after they'd made the McKinnon arrangements.

"Don't give anyone Jill's contact information," Dio had told him, "even if they act like they know her. *Especially* if they act like they know her. I don't care who they are or why they want it."

"Jill who?" Stanton had responded, smiling into the telephone. "Never heard of her. And besides, Coach, we have procedures in place to protect our clients' privacy."

"That's great. But if someone does call asking about her," Dio had added, "see if you can get a name or phone number. Then let me know right away."

The funeral director wondered, somewhat belatedly, if the call he'd just received might be one that Coach would like to know about. But the caller had mentioned Kevin, not Jill. And there hadn't been a name displayed on caller ID, just the word "Illinois" and a number—wireless, no doubt—that he hadn't thought about writing down until after the call had ended. And besides, was it really important?

No, John Stanton decided, it was just another former local guy wanting to reconnect with old acquaintances and relive the good old days. The death of a childhood friend, or the friend's parent, seemed to have that effect on people. They wanted to go back and be young again, before death had touched their family or that of anyone they knew. He saw it all the time.

To be on the safe side, though, he posted a note on Jessica McKinnon's electronic file: *No information is to be given out under any circumstances. All queries are to be logged with caller's name and phone number and reported to JS immediately.* That way, Stanton reasoned, Coach Dio's instructions would be complied with even if another staff member happened to answer the phone.

Stack Ridgeway's workday had just begun, but it was already failing to go as planned. Moments after entering his office he'd received a call from Chief Whitesell.

"There's a development in that drug-trafficking case we've been working with the FBI," the chief said. "I need you at the task force meeting. It starts in twenty minutes in the main conference room at County. I'll see you there." The chief hadn't bothered to wait for a response before hanging up.

"Shit," Stack mumbled. The meeting would almost surely suck up his entire morning, and there had been an unpleasant note in the chief's voice that was probably unrelated to the drug case. Stack wondered if Gary Carlyle had been insufficiently reassured after the previous evening's meeting. And if so, had he called the chief and asked him to warn Stack off? It was certainly possible.

One eye on his office clock, Stack speed-dialed Scott Allison. "I need you to go see a couple of guys for me," he said. "I'll text you names and phone numbers in a couple minutes and what I want you to ask 'em. But the main thing I want to know is what they drive. Color and model's good enough. I don't need the year. And also, how they react to your questions. Not the answers so much as their manner."

"Got it," Allison said crisply.

"And Scotty? I know you're busy, but I need this done today. And the outcomes reported directly to me. Orally, not by text. Okay?"

"Sure thing."

"Good man," Stack said.

Fifteen minutes later he was entering Lucas Dean's territory, where he was buttonholed by Chief Whitesell just outside the conference room where the drug task force would be meeting.

"I want the Carlyles left alone," Whitesell said.

"Okay," Stack said, arranging his face into puzzled lines. "But I've already talked to Ryan, like I told you I was going to, and—"

"Like hell you did. You never mentioned his name."

Stack shrugged. "He was only one of several. And I wasn't planning to talk to him again anyway."

The chief gave Stack a long look. "Interviewing the Briggs jurors," he finally said. "That's pretty lame. Why don't you tell me what you're really doing? And why you're doing it?"

"Since you put it that way, I guess I'm grasping at straws. I still like Briggs for the Putnam murder, either by himself or with accomplices. But the problem is, I can't place him at the scene or come up with a single piece of hard evidence. So I was just hoping that one or more of the jurors might have noticed someone in the spectator area who—"

"Stack," the chief cut in, "you do know, don't you, that all the courtrooms are equipped with security cameras? It would be a simple matter to pull the tapes and take a look."

Stack cringed inwardly. *Busted.* "Oh, sure. But sometimes people notice things. And another set of eyes, or even several—"

The chief waved a hand to silence him. "Spare me. I do not, repeat, *not*, want you to continue interviewing the Briggs jurors. That applies to your team as well. Do I make myself clear?"

"Yes, Chief." Stack waited a beat, then nodded toward the door of the conference room. "Listen, I'll catch up with you in a minute. I need to check in with one of my guys."

Hugging the hallway wall, Stack sent a quick text to Scott Allison. "No need to intrvw Petersen or Snow."

The reply came back almost instantaneously: "Alredy sched."

"Cancel," Stack sent back, then pocketed his phone and entered the conference room.

The meeting lasted until nearly noon. When it adjourned Stack lagged several feet behind Chief Whitesell, who was schmoozing with the FBI special agent in charge. Doing his best to ingratiate himself, Stack assumed. But then, that went with the job.

Lucas Dean had also lingered in the conference room. Once the police chief and FBI agent were safely out of range, the sheriff materialized close to Stack's side. "Lunch at Frankie's?"

"Sure." He fell into step beside Dean, whose normally brisk pace was more leisurely than usual. Making sure we don't catch up with the chief, Stack deduced, and wondered why.

"Catch the Sox game on TV last night?" the sheriff asked.

"No, as a matter of fact, I didn't."

"You didn't miss anything. They lost." They walked on in silence until they reached the exit door and stepped onto the sidewalk, heading north. "This guy I know," the sheriff continued, "is a hard-core Sox fan. And he wanted to show his son a good time, so he got Skybox tickets at Comiskey for himself, his son, and a friend of theirs. After the game, they partied for a while and then spent the night at the Hyatt Regency McCormick Place. Back in June, this was."

"Is there a point to this, Lucas?"

"Bet your sweet ass there is," Lucas responded with a chuckle. "The guy and his son were the Carlyles, and who do you suppose the friend was?"

"Chief Whitesell, no doubt."

"Bingo. And the night in question was the same night Katie Putnam was murdered."

"Jesus. How do you find this stuff out?"

"I have my sources. But I'm just telling you, if for some reason you like the Carlyle kid for the murder—"

"Actually, I don't. My interest in him is unrelated to that."

"Unrelated," Dean said, "as in Jill McKinnon and her late mother-in-law?"

"So Coach Dio came to see you. He told me he was going to."

"Yeah, he did. And I promised him I'd follow up."

"You don't really think the old busybody is onto something, do you?"

"No, but unlike you I'm an elected official. Coach has a fair amount of clout in this county, and I need to keep him happy."

They had reached the Dragons Den, and Dean pulled open the door. "Sir Francis," he bellowed to Frank Maloney as they entered the tavern. "Two of your best, and make mine a half-pounder with everything." He gave Stack a light punch on the shoulder. "How about you?"

"Oh, all right. A half-pounder, but no cheese on mine. Just lettuce and tomato." He followed the sheriff to his favorite rear booth. "Now, about Coach. You do know how he fits into all this, don't you?"

"If you mean do I know he's trying to set up his son with Jill McKinnon, then yes. Shit, Coach isn't happy unless he's managing *something*."

Stack felt his phone vibrating in his jacket pocket, pulled it out, and saw Dr. Paul Killebrew's number come up on the display. "You mind, Lucas?"

"Not at all. Go ahead."

"Hey, Paul. Got anything for me?"

The sheriff watched with undisguised interest as Stack listened, the phone held tightly to his ear.

"Really," Stack said into the phone. "Any chance it was the paramedics?"

Several more seconds went by as the doctor answered Stack's question.

"Okay, buddy, thanks. I owe you."

"Anything?" the sheriff asked.

Stack returned the phone to his pocket. "It turns out there was some fairly significant peri-mortem bruising on Mrs. McKinnon's arms, especially the right one. Five distinct marks, like fingers and a thumb. Somebody must have grabbed it pretty hard. The pathologist didn't pay much attention. He just assumed it was due to the way the paramedics handled her when they tried to revive her. But Paul thinks maybe—this might sound crazy, but he thinks the placement of the bruises was all wrong for it to have been the paramedics. And besides, he works the ER and knows those guys pretty well. He said there's no way they would've been that rough."

"Jesus, Stack. You think maybe…?"

"Honestly? I don't know what to think. And anyway, the McKinnon place is in your jurisdiction. So what do you suggest?"

"I suggest—" Dean fell silent as Frank Maloney approached and wordlessly placed two chilled cans of Coca-Cola, dripping with condensation, on the table in front of them. As soon as Maloney turned away, Dean reached out and tapped Stack's soda. "Don't open that for a couple of minutes. I saw him shake it up, probably his idea of a joke. He's a crazy fucker and always has been, even back in high school. But listen. I know the chief has you on a short leash right now—"

"Do you."

"Yeah, I do. Told you, I've got my sources. So what I started to suggest is an after-hours work session at my place. We'll go over everything together. Then maybe tomorrow, if you can carve out a couple hours, we'll take a little ride up north of town."

"The McKinnon place, you mean?"

"Yeah, just to see the layout. God knows, there won't be any evidence worth collecting at this point. Paramedics, friends, neighbors, everyone and their brother's been tromping through that house since the night she died. We wouldn't find jackshit at this late date, even if there was anything there to start with. I think the person I really want to talk to," Dean added thoughtfully, "is that neighbor lady."

"How about the kid?"

"Him, too."

Across the street at Pinky's, State's Attorney Terry Lankowski and Assistant State's Attorney Denise Phelan had just been served club sandwiches when Steve Berglund approached. The defense attorney, looking smug, leaned over the end of their table and placed both hands on its edge.

"I hate to tell you this," he said, "but it looks like my client's alibi for the night of the Putnam girl's murder checks out."

"Not what I heard," Lankowski said calmly. "He claims he and the Harvey brothers were riding up and down the Interstate all night shoplifting. But neither he nor they showed up on the security videos of any of the stores he claimed they hit."

Berglund waved a hand in dismissal. "He already told me he exaggerated that part, about actually going into the stores. What—"

"He lied, you mean?" Lankowski placed a hand to his chest and pretended shock. "No way!"

"What they were really doing was checking out the entry and exit layouts. Access to escape routes, that kind of thing."

"So we're talking conspiracy instead of retail theft, at least for the Harveys."

"That's if there was enough evidence to charge them, which there isn't. But I put my investigator on it, and what she finally came up with is security video from the I-55 rest stop just north of Springfield. It shows Sean Harvey's car, license plate clearly visible, and it's time stamped 2:49 a.m. the morning Katie Putnam died. That rest stop is at least two hours south of here, and if memory serves, 2:49 is pretty close to her time of death. So explain to me," Berglund crowed, "how Brian Briggs could be in two places that far apart at the same time."

"Explain to *me* how you know Briggs was in the car. You got him on tape?"

Berglund blinked. "No, just Darrin. He got out to use the rest room."

"So tell me how that works as an alibi for Briggs?"

"It works because he said they were driving around, and they were. Now we have proof."

"Correction. You have proof Sean Harvey's car was there, and Darrin was there. That's all."

"But—"

"Have the Harveys changed their story? Because according to their statement, they were tired of listening to him bitch about the Putnam girl and the trial. So they dropped Briggs off around midnight near his mother's trailer. And they very wisely didn't tell us what they did after that. But they might have told *him* their plans, then decided not to take him along for fear he'd rat them out later. Which he did," Lankowski said pointedly, "although you're absolutely correct that we can't charge them with anything. If using a rest-area john was a crime, we'd have to jail half the people in Illinois." He picked up his sandwich. "Now if you don't mind, I'd like to eat my lunch in peace."

Denise Phelan watched Berglund leave. "You don't think that's enough to establish reasonable doubt, do you?"

Lankowski shrugged. "Probably not, on its own. But the real problem is that everything we've got up to now is circumstantial."

"We need Stack Ridgeway to come up with something."

"He's been trying to."

"We need him to do more than try. Hell, we know Briggs did it."

"Actually, we don't. We only *think* he did it. And by the way, Denise, in this jurisdiction we don't manufacture evidence to suit our case. If that makes us a bunch of downstate hicks in your view, then so be it."

"I wasn't suggesting that. I only meant—"

"Yeah, I know." Lankowski sighed heavily. "We're all pretty frustrated, myself included. I know Stack was working a theory that the

Harveys were involved somehow, but given what our friend Berglund just told us…"

"No chance?"

"Probably not. I'll call him as soon as we get back to the office. I need to let him know so he won't waste any more time looking in that direction."

Stack was at his desk, trying without much success to concentrate on his work items from that morning's meeting, when he received the State's Attorney's call recounting his conversation with Berglund.

"That's not good news, Terry," Stack said, "but I appreciate the heads up."

Stack replaced the handset, got up from his desk, and walked into the men's room. He splashed cold water on his face and regarded himself in the mirror. The face that gazed back at him looked suddenly older, the lines around his eyes deeper. He realized with a start that he was nearly fifty years old. When the hell had that happened?

"Son of a bitch," he muttered. He'd always considered himself a good cop and a better-than-average detective, but he was no closer to solving that poor girl's murder than he'd been the day after it happened.

He returned to his office and stood before the white board on which he'd charted the timeline, names of witnesses, and other information pertaining to the Putnam case. There had to be something else he could do. His eye fell on the notation near the bottom: "man in bar." He'd drawn a line through it, then added a small question mark. They'd thought they had identified him, but found out later it was the wrong guy. And even if they located him, chances were pretty slim that he'd be able to add any information of value. Stack turned away from the board and went back to his desk.

The phone call had scared the shit out of him initially. But, because years of assiduous practice had made him adept at controlling his breathing and voice modulation, he was reasonably confident that the detective hadn't suspected anything. By the time Scott Allison called a second time, he felt well prepared for whatever questions might follow; so well prepared, in fact, that he couldn't help being a little disappointed to learn that the detective was cancelling their meeting.

By the end of his workday, though, the disappointment had morphed into uneasiness. Why had the detective wanted to see him in the first place? Allison had described the purpose of their proposed interview as "routine follow-up," but what had been the real reason? Even more intriguing, why had he canceled? He'd simply said that the meeting was no longer necessary but had given no reason. On television, a detective might employ such tactics to lull a suspect into letting his guard down. If that was Allison's plan, he decided, it wasn't going to work,

He drove home, went upstairs to his computer room, and opened every drawer in turn, checking for the tiniest scrap of paper that might connect him to any of the dead women. Nothing. Then he combed through his computer files. Again, nothing. But then, there never had been; he had made it a point to keep his search methods low-tech.

Next, he went into his bedroom and pulled out the clothing he'd worn during his fateful visit to the McKinnon farm: jeans, dark blue pullover shirt and sneakers. He'd already washed them all once, but a second time couldn't hurt; and when they were dry, he would deposit them in a charity collection bin along with the already-sanitized baseball cap. He carried everything downstairs, dumped the load into the washing machine, and set the controls.

Next, the sunglasses. He had two pair: the cheap plastic ones he'd camouflaged with duct tape to make them appear broken, and the only slightly more expensive mirrored ones he'd worn when making his deliveries and staking out the farmhouse.

He went to the kitchen drawer where he'd stashed the plastic ones and pulled them out. He'd already removed the duct tape and cleaned off the residue with Krud Kutter. Not good enough, he decided. He dropped the glasses onto the floor and stepped on them, breaking the frames in two places, then threw them into the kitchen trash can. Tomorrow was garbage pickup day. As for the mirrored ones, he would make a trip to the mall and "accidentally" leave them in the food court restroom. He had bought them because he'd thought they looked good on that Carlyle guy, whom he had noticed wearing a similar pair while they were on jury duty, but now it might be risky to keep them. He would buy another pair in a different style while he was at the mall.

That left only the stolen license plates to get rid of. He had been meaning to do that anyway because they were either expired or soon would be, and he had already located an appropriate disposal site. He would scrub all the plates and dump them tonight. He'd hold off on acquiring more until he was sure he would actually need them.

He drew a long breath and let it out slowly, willing himself to relax. Suspicion was one thing, and he might not be able to avoid it entirely. Evidence, on the other hand, was a completely different matter. It was something he could control, and he fully intended to.

Stack and the sheriff sat hunched over a small round table in Dean's office eating takeout deli sandwiches.

"You seem to know a lot about what goes on in my department," Stack said. "And frankly, it makes me uncomfortable."

"Don't you trust me? We're playing on the same team, Stack."

"Whether I trust you isn't the point. The point is that I've lost control of the information coming out of my department."

"It's a small town, Stack. Everybody knows everybody, and unfortunately they see no problem in telling what they know. It's always been that way in Drummond. You should know that. You've lived here all your life."

"But everybody *doesn't* know everybody, at least not anymore. Look at how much this town has grown since we were kids."

"Outsiders," Dean said dismissively. "They came here to work at the nuclear plant or the truck terminal, but they don't count. The same few families run Drummond that ran it forty years ago. Or a hundred years ago, for that matter."

"Which includes the Carlyles, of course."

"I went to school with Gary Carlyle. Hell, I was probably one of the few friends he had back then. He wasn't a bad kid, just unusually reserved. Still is, actually. After he came home from college he married a girl from his church, a real wallflower. Not bad looking, but extremely reclusive. To this day you hardly ever see her out in public. My wife says she has agoraphobia. All things considered, I guess it's not surprising

Ryan turned out the way he did. He supposedly has some kind of personality disorder."

"If being a dickhead is a personality disorder, then yeah. I agree," Stack said around a mouthful of pastrami on rye. "It's interesting that his father has two good friends in law enforcement—you and the chief—but according to Jill McKinnon, he didn't have a good word to say about our police force."

"We're his father's friends, not his. Let's leave it at that."

"And since you've refused to out your informant inside my department, how about we get back to the business at hand?"

"Okay, let's look at this logically. Do you think there's a connection between the Putnam murder and this possible stalking thing?"

"Yeah, I do."

"But why? Because if Briggs did the Putnam girl, he couldn't be the stalker. He was out on bail for less than seventy-two hours before your guys picked him up again."

"True," Stack said. "But I still think it's related some way."

"Then how, specifically? You said the McKinnon girl came to see you before her mother-in-law died. She thought she might have information about the case. What was it?"

"The flower deliveries. The black SUV. What Courtney Singleton told her...she got flowers, too. The stuff Carlyle said during the trial."

"Okay, but those are separate incidents. What made the light bulb go off inside her head that made her think they were related to Putnam?"

"Amy Morrison's death." Stack paused briefly. "Are you sure that was really an accident?"

"I don't see how it could've been anything else. Tragic, yeah, but still just a coincidence. They do happen, you know. So let's look at this piece by piece. We know Briggs couldn't be the stalker because he's been in jail all this time. And we know Carlyle couldn't have killed Putnam because he was in Chicago. So where does that leave us?"

"Wait a minute. When Gary Carlyle came to see me yesterday, he told me he was afraid I'd think Ryan bailed out Briggs so he could kill Katie Putnam. But the idea never entered my head until he suggested it. Maybe that's what *he* thought might have happened." Stack set down his sandwich and pushed it aside impatiently. "Those plans to go to Chicago had to be made at least a few days ahead of time. Skybox tickets aren't that easy to come by. And Briggs had already been in jail for weeks waiting for a new trial. So why, on the same day he knew he'd have an ironclad alibi, did Ryan suddenly decide they should bail him out?" He leaned forward, his eyes boring into the sheriff's. "And consider this: according to Jill McKinnon, she, Amy Morrison and Courtney Singleton were the only young single women on the jury. And they also voted to convict Briggs, which had to piss off Carlyle. If he hated Katie Putnam—his father's term, not mine—then that hatred might have extended to those three girls as well. So there's your connection."

Dean stared at him. "You're serious, aren't you?"

"Damn right I'm serious."

"Listen, Stack. With his father's connections, Ryan could've found out anything he wanted to know about Jill McKinnon in five minutes flat."

"That's true." Stack remembered without checking his notes what Jill had told him about the remark Ryan Carlyle had reportedly made to Courtney Singleton: that if somebody wanted to find her, they could.

"Then why would he need to go through all that bullshit with the flowers and the phone call and staking out her place?"

"So nobody would remember him asking about her. So there'd be no trace in his computer history. Technology's great, but unfortunately it tends to leave a trail."

Dean drummed his fingers on the table. "That's an interesting theory. Listen, if you want to come with me tomorrow afternoon when I visit Mrs. McKinnon's neighbor—what's her name?"

"Rachel Cameron."

"—okay, when I visit Rachel Cameron, you're more than welcome. But I strongly suggest you not tell your boss or anyone else what you're really doing. Anyone asks, you're helping me follow up on some tips related to the drug thing."

"What tips would those be, exactly?"

"Oh, I'll think of something. Seriously, Stack, you want to be very careful here."

"I intend to be. And Lucas?"

"Yeah?"

"If the chief gets wind of this, I'll know who told him."

Their visit to the McKinnon farmhouse the next afternoon was brief and businesslike. Alerted by a phone call from Stack that morning, Jill was present when they arrived. She greeted Stack briskly and offered her hand to the sheriff.

"How do you do," she said. "Where would you like to start?"

"I'd like to follow the route your mother-in-law would most likely have followed from the garage into the house."

Jill led them into the kitchen, out the side door, and onto the gravel driveway a few steps away. "As you see, the driveway leads back straight from the road, along this side of the house, and back to the garage," she said, gesturing toward the detached garage.

Stack estimated the distance to be about thirty feet from the side door. "May we see inside, please?"

"Of course. Jessica would have used the garage-door opener in her car," Jill explained, "but we'll go in this way." Using a key, she opened a door at the rear corner of the structure and let them in. She flipped on a light, illuminating a beige Lincoln Town Car and a dark blue Ford F-150 pickup. "This is—was Jessica's car," Jill said, indicating the Lincoln. "My late husband drove the truck. I've thought about selling it, but…"

"Tell us again how the car was found the morning after Mrs. McKinnon's death?"

"The driver's side door was open. Her handbag was on the front passenger seat."

"Were the keys in the ignition?"

"No, I found them on the floor the next morning. I'll show you where when we go back inside."

"The overhead doors were closed, correct?"

"Yes. And thc door we just came in was closed but not locked."

"So she must have come out this way, not through the overhead door."

The men turned to gauge the distance from the garage to the back and side doors of the farmhouse. Stack glanced at the sheriff, who was sketching the arrangement of house, garage and other outbuildings. "What do you think? Back or side?"

"Back might be a little closer, but it's off at an angle and she would've had to cross the yard. See the bushes?" The sheriff gestured toward some low shrubs at the edge of the back yard. "Normally, I'd say the side door. But if she was in a hurry to get inside..." He shrugged. "Hard to say."

"She always used the side door," Jill said. "But we can go in the back if you like." She led the way to the back door, into the house and through the pantry. "There's the phone," she said, pointing. She continued on for several feet, then stopped near the side door they had exited a few minutes earlier. "If she came in the back, she'd have had to pass the phone to get here. According to Rachel Cameron, this is where she collapsed. Or at least that's where the paramedics found her. And the next morning I found her keys there, next to the wall." Jill pointed again, this time indicating a spot about two feet from the door.

"I see." Stack nodded and glanced toward Dean. "Anything else?"

"Nope, I think we're done. Thank you," he said to Jill. "It was a pleasure meeting you."

The two men got into Dean's Suburban and drove the quarter-mile to the Cameron farm. Rachel met them at the front door, holding onto the collar of a medium-sized black-and-brown dog.

"It's okay, Rowdy," she murmured. "Go to your spot." She released her grip on his collar, and he trotted obediently to a corner of the living room and lay down on a braided rug.

"He'll be fine," Rachel reassured them. "Come on in."

Stack noted that while the dog's eyes remained fixed on them, alert and watchful, he didn't seem to regard them as a threat. Taking his cue from his mistress, Stack surmised. "Good-looking dog," he said.

"Yes, he is," Rachel said, and gestured for them to sit down. "Now tell me how I can help."

"We need to know exactly what happened the night Mrs. McKinnon died. What you saw and what you did."

Rachel recounted the details of that evening: Ethan's fear that something was wrong at Jessica's house, her phone call to Jessica that hadn't been answered, her arrival at Jessica's, and Rowdy's reaction.

"It scared the daylights out of me," Rachel said. "I thought maybe instead of Jessica, Ethan had seen a burglar drive in. Later on, after I had a chance to think about it, I realized that didn't make sense."

"Why not?"

"Because there was no car in the driveway, and a burglar wouldn't have parked in the garage. But at the time, I didn't think. I just reacted."

"A good reaction, as it turned out. You called for help."

"Yes, but I know every second counts when a person has a heart attack. Maybe if I'd gone inside right away..."

"It wouldn't have mattered," Stack said gently. "Now, you were inside your car with the headlights on. You're sure you didn't see any sign of anyone else in the house or on the grounds?"

"No, but it was dark. My headlights only lit up the driveway as far as the garage."

"So there's no way to know what your dog was reacting to. An animal, maybe? A possum or raccoon?"

Rachel shook her head. "I have no idea, because he's usually so easygoing. Standoffish with strangers, especially men, but never hostile or aggressive. And I remembered what Ethan told me about how Rowdy didn't like the man they found on Jill's little parcel up the road."

"That reminds me," the sheriff said. "We'd really like to speak with Ethan, too. Is he at home?"

"Yes," Rachel said hesitantly, "if it's really necessary. But he's only a boy."

"Sounds like he's an observant one, though. Would you call him, please?"

Rachel went to the foot of the staircase. "Ethan," she shouted. "Come on down here, would you?"

The boy appeared so promptly that Stack couldn't help smiling. He must have been lurking at the top of the stairs, eavesdropping.

"First things first," the sheriff began. "Tell us about the man you saw parked on the McKinnon property. This was when?"

"Couple weeks ago. It was on a weekend, so maybe closer to three weeks."

"Can you describe him for us?"

"Not really. He was wearing a cap and a pair of sunglasses, the kind that reflect. So I couldn't see much of his face."

"What was he doing when you got there?"

"Just sitting there. He kinda had his back to me, like he was looking out the window."

"Then what?"

"He turned around and saw me and said he was lost. He was waiting for a friend to call him back with directions."

The sheriff leaned forward. "And did he ask you for help?"

"No, but I knew not to get too close in case…well, you know. Then I heard Rowdy growling, and it bothered me."

"Why?"

Ethan shrugged. "Because I never heard him growl at anyone before."

"Okay," the sheriff said. "What can you tell me about the vehicle?"

"It was black. Bigger than mom's, but not as big as yours."

"Did you notice the make or model? License number, maybe?"

"I don't pay much attention to cars. There's so many kinds, it's hard to keep track. The license…I don't think it was an Illinois license. They've got all those different ones for conservation and stuff, but it didn't look like any of the ones I've seen before. I'm sorry," he said, sounding embarrassed. "I didn't know it was going to matter."

"That's all right."

"And besides," Ethan went on, "I was watching Rowdy and wondering what he was thinking. There was just something wrong about the guy. I don't know what it was, but it seemed like Rowdy noticed it too."

"But the man left right away, correct?"

"Yeah, he got a phone call and left pretty fast."

"All right, Ethan. Now tell us about the night you saw Mrs. McKinnon come home."

"Not much to tell," the boy said. "I was upstairs in my bedroom watching for the owl and wishing she'd left her big yard light on. Then she drove into her driveway and a minute later the light went on. Then it went off again. And she didn't turn on any lights inside the house, so I went downstairs and told Mom."

"I wonder," the sheriff suggested, "if you'd mind showing us the view from your window?"

"Sure," Ethan said. "Come on." He took the stairs two at a time, trailed by the sheriff, Stack and Rachel. At the top of the staircase he made a right turn into his bedroom. "There," he said, pointing.

Although the view was partially obstructed by a large maple tree outside his window, the McKinnon farmhouse was clearly visible.

Noticing a pair of binoculars on the boy's nearby desk, Stack picked them up. "Do you see a lot of birds from up here?"

"Oh, yeah. I especially like to watch for the owl. When Mrs. Jessica turned her light on at night, it was like the tree was silhouetted—" The boy stared at the binoculars Stack was holding. "Binoculars," he said suddenly. "I remember now. That's what didn't seem right. He had binoculars hanging around his neck."

Stack set the binoculars down on Ethan's desk. "You're sure?"

"Yeah, pretty sure. When he turned toward me he let go of them, but I could still see the strap they were hanging from. And he put his hands down where I couldn't see them." Ethan glanced at his mother. "A kid I know at school, his family moved here from Chicago. And he's always telling the rest of us we should watch people's hands. Make sure we can see their hands."

"Streetwise kid like that," Dean said with a wry grin, "you want to make sure you can always see *his* hands. So then what?"

"Like I told you before. His phone rang, he answered it and talked to somebody for a couple minutes. Then he left."

"Going which way?"

"West. And he kept going straight at the crossroads."

"Good job, Ethan," Dean said. He glanced at Stack. "We done?"

"Far as I'm concerned. Thanks very much, Ethan."

The two men got into the sheriff's vehicle. "I think we ought to take a look up there," Dean said. He turned north and drove past the McKinnon farm, then turned right at the crossroads.

"There," Stack said, gesturing.

Dean slowed the Suburban to a crawl and turned onto the bumpy dirt lane. He stopped the engine. "House should be right over there," he said, pointing. "Can't see it from here, though. Normally you could, because the trees aren't that thick. But the corn's too tall."

"Maybe it's grown since three weeks ago."

"You spend too much time in town," Dean retorted. "Farmers planted early this year, so the corn woulda been just as tall three weeks ago. Hell, it's already starting to ripen."

"Then what about the binoculars?"

"What about them? Even if he had 'em—"

"You think the kid was wrong? Or maybe just making it up?"

"Shit, I don't know. But the point is, he couldn't have seen the house from here whether he had binocs or not." The sheriff heaved a sigh.

"You think we wasted our time coming up here?"

"No, because now we can tell the Coach and the McKinnon woman that we checked everything out. We'll get credit for being diligent, and that'll be the end of it." Dean started the Suburban's engine and shifted into reverse.

I wish I felt as sure as you do, Stack thought. He felt his phone vibrating in his pocket and pulled it out. "Dammit," he grumbled when he saw the number displayed on caller ID, but when he answered the call he kept his voice carefully neutral. "Hello, Chief." Beside him, Dean shifted back into park and set the brake.

"Where the hell are you, Ridgeway?" the chief demanded.

"Up on the north side of town with Lucas Dean."

"Dean! What the hell are you doing with him?"

"We got a tip about a possible drug buy. We—"

"It takes you *and* the sheriff to check out a possible drug buy?"

"Gimme that phone," Dean demanded, grabbing it from Stack's hand. "This is Dean," he said into the phone. "Stack's with me because there was a question of jurisdiction. We're right at the city limits. Kid saw a vehicle where it shouldn't have been, with the driver acting suspiciously. He thought it might be a drug buy."

"So is it?" the chief sounded somewhat mollified.

"Don't know yet. Got somebody approaching the vehicle right now. We'll have to get back to you." The sheriff snapped the phone shut. "And that's how it's done, my friend."

"Okay, smartass, what do I tell the chief about our supposed drug buy when he asks me? And trust me, he will ask."

"Damn, do I have to come up with all the lies? Just tell him it was a local citizen meeting his boyfriend to set up their next tryst. And since no crime was committed and the aforementioned local citizen is married and still in the closet, you feel morally bound to keep his name out of it."

"You're a warped bastard, you know that?"

The sheriff jammed the Suburban into reverse and backed out onto the pavement. "It's one of my best qualities. You ready to head back to town?"

When the sheriff delivered Stack to the Drummond Police Department, both men saw Chief Whitesell watching from his second-floor window.

Stack had just entered the building when the chief materialized and followed Stack into his office, shutting the door behind them.

"I'm sure," Whitesell said, "that our friend provided you with a cover story for your little excursion. And I'm also sure it involved discovering a leading citizen in some sort of homosexual encounter, so don't waste my time by repeating it." Stack's jaw dropped, and the chief smiled.

"I've known Lucas Dean for forty years. He's a homophobe and always has been. So whenever he tells me some tale about catching someone *in flagrante*, I know it's a crock of crap." The chief sat down in one of Stack's guest chairs and patted the seat of the other one. "I think it's time for you to tell me what's really going on, don't you?"

Stack took a deep breath. The chief was his boss, after all. "Most of what he told you was true. We did get a tip. It did involve a car that was parked on private property. And it was in Lucas's jurisdiction."

"You said 'we' got a tip. Does that mean you, or does that mean him?"

"It means both of us, from two different sources." Stack wasn't normally a name-dropper, but, given the chief's political sensibilities, he decided to make an exception. "I heard about it from a woman who was referred to me by Tommy Adair. Lucas got it from Coach Pappas."

"Well?" the chief demanded. "So what about the car? Who was in it?"

"Don't know. By the time we got there it was gone."

"Dean," the chief barked. "That lying weasel! Why didn't he just say so?"

"He was afraid you'd think we were wasting our time. And maybe we were. But—"

"But what?"

Stack fought back a momentary urge to tell the chief everything: the unexplained bruises on Jessica McKinnon's arm, the black SUV whose driver might have been watching the McKinnon farm, and the possible connection to Ryan Carlyle. "But," he said with a shrug, "since Adair and Pappas are both influential local citizens, we felt it was prudent to check it out. Which we've now done, and we can tell them so. End of story."

Chief Whitesell studied Stack's face. "About Lucas Dean. Did he by any chance tell you not to trust me?"

"As a matter of fact, he did."

"He tells everybody that." The chief's face twisted into a reluctant grin. "And I would give you the same advice about him. I may be a political animal, but so is he. The only difference between us is that I don't have to get re-elected, and he does. Listen," the chief went on after a momentary pause, "I know you've been under a lot of pressure to connect that Briggs bastard with the Putnam girl's death. The City Council's constantly on my case about that. But I've reviewed the case file from top to bottom, and I don't know what else we could've done. Besides, he's not going anywhere. Lankowski will send him up on the theft charges, and while he's serving his time for that..." Chief Whitesell shrugged. "Who knows, we might get lucky."

"I hope so. We've never had an unsolved murder in Drummond. Of course, there haven't been that many murders, period."

"That might change unless we get a handle on this drug thing. We used to be so far off the beaten path that we never had to worry about stuff like that. But you bring in new industry and new people, pretty soon you find out you've also brought in a lot of problems you never used to have." The chief stood up. "We've got two interstates, so it was just a matter of time before the drug traffickers discovered Drummond. I'm serious, Stack. We need to get a lid on it, and I expect you to make that your top priority until I tell you otherwise." The chief moved to the door but didn't open it. "Just so we're clear, I don't want to hear any more about you hassling the Briggs jurors. I'm not stupid, Stack. I understood from the get-go that it was just a cover for investigating Ryan Carlyle. Take it from me, there's no way he's involved in the Putnam thing. I've known him since he was born, and I'll admit he can be obnoxious. But he's all talk and no action. So put that out of your mind."

As soon as the chief was out the door, Stack checked his messages. The first—and the briefest—was from Scott Allison: "Call me."

Stack speed-dialed Allison. "Hey, Scotty, what's up?"

"Can you talk?"

"Sure," Stack responded.

"Listen, it's about those two guys I was supposed to see yesterday. The ones you told me to cancel."

"You did cancel, didn't you? Shit, the chief will have my ass if—"

"I didn't talk to 'em, if that's what you mean. But I was supposed to see 'em when they got off work, so I had to find out their hours. Jared Snow works the seven-to-three-thirty shift at PDQ Print-N-Copy, and Brett Petersen works seven-thirty to four at the Remington County Bank. So last night, I got to thinking it couldn't hurt if I happened to be close by when they got to work this morning. Maybe check out their rides."

"Either of 'em see you?" Stack asked brusquely.

"Course not," Allison said, sounding miffed.

"Okay, okay...I don't suppose either of 'em drives a black SUV, do they?"

"An SUV, yeah. A gray Chevy Tahoe. Other one's a maroon Toyota Corolla."

"Gray," Stack repeated, sounding hopeful. "Like charcoal, maybe? Could it pass for black?"

"No, it's way too light. I think my wife would call it dove gray."

"Oh, well. I appreciate the effort." Then, struck by the note of pride in Allison's voice when he had referred to his wife—a very attractive young woman to whom he had been married less than two years—an unwelcome thought occurred to Stack. If memory served, the bodacious Mrs. Allison was related some way or other to Sheriff Dean's wife. Her niece, maybe, or cousin. Not that the exact relationship mattered. Extended families were close in Drummond, and the longer they'd been here, the closer they seemed to be.

"By the way, Scotty...you don't talk about your work to your wife, do you? I mean, the cases you're working on, stuff like that?"

The fractional hesitation before the young detective answered told Stack all he needed to know. "No, of course not. Well, maybe sometimes," Allison amended, "but just in general terms. No names or anything."

"That needs to stop," Stack said.

"But she'd never tell—"

"It needs to stop," Stack repeated sternly. Then, in keeping with his practice of following a reprimand with a compliment, he added, "And listen, I appreciate your follow-up with Petersen and Snow. That was good thinking."

After ending the call, Stack sat at his desk and pondered the morning's events. He empathized with Jill McKinnon's concerns, but there were often unanswered questions surrounding an unexpected death. That did not mean a crime had been committed. The police chief's instructions had been clear and unequivocal. It was time to give the drug interdiction effort his full attention.

73

The day of Jessica McKinnon's funeral was typical of late August: muggy and stiflingly hot. Considering the weather, and the fact that Jessica's service was being held on a weekday, Jill was surprised by the number of people who attended, even joining the procession to the cemetery. The majority were older women who remembered Jessica from many years earlier, and several of these expressed hurt feelings that Jill didn't recognize them from Kevin's funeral the year before.

As if, she thought. I never saw them before or since, until today. Still, she did her best to respond graciously. "I'm so sorry," she told them. "I was totally in shock at the time. But I truly appreciate that you were there for Kevin. And thank you for coming today."

Family members were in much shorter supply. Joe McKinnon's sister Doris was too frail to make the trip from Florida, but Carol, the younger sister, had driven down from Rockford. Her two sons, Kevin's cousins, had not come with her.

"They were afraid to take the time off from work," Carol confided. "The job market being what it is these days, it seems like companies will use any excuse to fire people. I retired last year, so I don't have to worry about it. But ask for the day off to go to your aunt's funeral? That might be enough to cost your job. So why take the chance when there could be a dozen people lined up waiting to replace you? And at lower pay, too."

Dio Pappas gave a similar reason for Nick's failure to appear. Dio, Margaret and Louise lingered at the farmhouse after Carol and a handful of other guests had departed, helping Jill clear away the leftover food and dirty dishes.

"I was hoping he'd make it," Dio said, "but he's really busy at work right now. And with a brand-new crop of college grads out looking for jobs, well…you know how it is."

"Unfortunately, I do. It seems like fewer employees are expected to do more and more work these days." Even Tommy, her own boss, was feeling the pinch. New home construction had slowed to a crawl, which meant lot sales had fallen off as well. He had very reluctantly terminated Kelly, the receptionist, which meant that Jill was now assisting Karen, Tommy's executive assistant, with telephone and reception duties in addition to her regular tasks. "So please don't worry about it, because I really didn't expect him to come."

Dio draped an arm around Jill's shoulders and gave her a squeeze. "I appreciate your understanding, especially at such a difficult time. But he did tell me that he was planning to come up Saturday morning and spend the weekend."

"I'm sure you'll enjoy seeing him," Jill said.

"I'll tell him hello for you, if you like."

"Of course," Jill said in a neutral tone.

Louise exchanged a glance with her sister. They needed to drop the subject of Nick. "Jill," Louise asked, "I know it might be a little soon, but have you thought about what you're going to do with this house?"

"Actually, I have. Kevin and I used to talk about building a new house up the road, but his first choice would have been to renovate this one if Jessica would've allowed it. That way we could leave his little patch of woods alone. He loved playing there when he was a boy," Jill said with a misty smile. "He told me how he used to pretend he was a pioneer or an explorer. And he was hoping that when we had kids—" Jill's eyes filled with tears that threatened to spill down her cheeks, and she fought to hold them back. "So," she continued after a moment, "to answer your question, I'm going to do exactly what he wanted because it's what I want, too. Gut this house and rebuild it with up-to-the minute green technology, and leave the little woods for kids like Ethan Cameron to enjoy. Or mine, if I ever have any. I'll leave the little bench Kevin made, too. It's right where our great room would have been if we'd built a house there, and I always hated the idea of having to move it. But it made sense to lay out the house that way because the view from that particular spot is great. You can even see this house from there."

"Good for you," Margaret said. "I think that's a wonderful idea." She caught Dio's eye and gave him their time-to-go signal, which he acknowledged with a barely perceptible nod.

"We'll be on our way," Dio said. "But before we leave I should tell you I had a call from the sheriff. He told me he and Stack didn't find anything to indicate foul play with respect to your mother's death. He sounded pretty confident."

"That's good," Jill said. "I guess. But…"

"Yes, *but*. Be careful, Jill. Don't be afraid to trust your instincts."

Jill hugged them, then followed them out to the driveway and waved as they drove away.

"Dio," Margaret said as they turned south and headed back toward town.

"What?"

"Jill's obviously still pretty tender over losing Kevin, and Jessica's death has brought it all back again. I think we might want to back off a little bit, trying to get her and Nick together."

"By 'we' I assume you mean 'me,' correct? Because you didn't seem that crazy about the idea to begin with."

"I never saw the reason for us to get involved, that's all. Nick is perfectly capable of finding his own girls."

"True," Dio conceded, "but he only seems interested in a pretty face, and Jill is a lot more than that. She's easy on the eyes, sure, but she's got *substance*."

"She's also got some fairly serious baggage, and I don't know how well Nick would deal with it."

"Meaning?"

"I say this with love, but our son has kind of a big ego. And the idea that Jill loved somebody else first—on some level will probably always love him—I'm just not sure how he'd handle that. And besides, she's not Greek. I know how important your heritage is to you."

"Not important enough to keep me from marrying you. Besides, Nick's the product of a mixed marriage. He knows it can work if the people involved are committed to it."

"Mixed marriage? You make it sound like I'm a Hottentot. Which I was, in your parents' eyes."

"Oh, but such a lovely Hottentot. Besides, you agreed to convert."

"And I did, at least to start with, but we both know how that turned out. Seriously, Dio, I don't want to push them on each other. I realize she owns a farm, which is a big thing in her favor because Nick's always wanted a farm of his own. But doesn't it seem just a little *mercenary* to you, especially since she's such a recent widow?"

"I would have thought it was just one more reason to get them together," Dio said. "Nick would do a wonderful job of running the place."

"But you saw the way she nearly broke down talking about Kevin. And it almost made me cry, too, hearing how they used to sit on that little bench and—"

"The bench," Dio broke in. "I need to check something out before it gets dark." At the next crossroads, he swung his Buick Lucerne into a U-turn. "The sheriff said they couldn't see the house from there because the corn was in the way," Dio explained, "but Jill said you could. I need to find out who's right."

Five minutes later, Dio cautiously nosed the Lucerne off the pavement and into the narrow, rutted lane. He shut off the engine, and they got out.

"Looks like the sheriff is right," Margaret said as they approached the line of evergreens. "I can see through the trees, but I can't see the house. Just corn."

Dio turned in a slow half-circle. "There," he said, pointing. "Come on." He moved several yards to the left of where he'd parked the Lucerne, stopping when he reached the bench. "Son of a gun," he murmured. "Look there."

Margaret joined him and followed his gaze. From where they stood, the McKinnon house was clearly visible through a gap several feet wide between two cornfields.

"Are you going to tell the sheriff?"

"No, I don't think so. It was obvious when I talked with him earlier that he's already washed his hands of the whole thing. I think I'll tell Stack instead. It's out of his jurisdiction, and there's probably nothing he can do. But he does seem to take it seriously, at least a little bit. Which is more than I can say for the sheriff."

"Is there anything else we can do?"

"I wish there were, but at this point, probably not. I've already given Jill my best advice. She needs to be careful."

By Saturday he had almost convinced himself that Allison's presence so close to his workplace, just one day after the detective had made and then canceled an appointment to talk to him, was simply a fluke. Allison, whom he'd recognized from the Briggs trial, had been parked half a block away, sipping a cup of coffee and, as near as he could tell, had never even looked in his direction. There was a bakery nearby, so perhaps Allison was simply enjoying coffee and a donut before beginning his shift.

He had carefully ignored Allison and pulled into the parking lot behind his workplace, then entered the building as usual. A few minutes later, when he'd ventured a cautious look through the small window in the rear door, Allison was gone. He didn't appear to have returned since then, either. Still, it was disquieting.

Best to lie low for a while, he told himself, even though the need to find Jill McKinnon never left him. In fact, it was stronger than ever. He constantly repeated his mantra, *be patient*, but it seemed to be losing its power.

As a distraction, he decided to check out the new shopping center at the Commons at Juniper Ridge. There was a restaurant there featuring cuisine from all over the world—some Japanese, a little Indian, and a smattering of Thai—that might make a nice change of pace.

The lunch rush was nearly over by the time he arrived. The hostess showed him to a booth near a window overlooking the parking lot, and he had just opened the menu when he heard a familiar-sounding female voice coming from the booth directly behind him. It took him a few seconds to recognize the voice as Jill's.

He wanted to laugh out loud. After all the time he had spent trying to track her down, here she was back-to-back with him, not more than a couple of feet away. She seemed to be chatting with a lunch partner. If he listened carefully, maybe he would overhear something useful such as where she was living now.

When the waitress came back to take his order, he'd barely glanced at the menu. Not that it mattered, because he had never been a picky eater.

"I want that," he said in a low voice, pointing to an item at random.

"The rice noodle stir fry?"

"Yes."

"Anything to drink?"

"Pepsi."

"Anything else, sir?"

He shook his head. "No," he murmured, willing the waitress to go away so he could hear what Jill was saying.

The topic of conversation was green technology, specifically solar and wind power, and Jill's male lunch partner seemed to be monopolizing the discussion. He was droning on and on about something called the Twin Groves Wind Farm.

Shut up! He wanted to shout. *Let Jill talk!* And then, as if in response to his unspoken demand, Jill spoke once more.

"I couldn't have one of those gigantic commercial towers, but I'd like to look into installing a small wind turbine out back by the grain bins," she said. "Just big enough to provide the power I'd need for the house and..."

At that moment a couple with four loud, unruly children made their noisy way past his table, drowning out the conversation behind him. He shot the parents a dirty look, but neither of them paid any attention. By the time the family had moved on, the conversation behind him had turned to another subject.

"...back to work?" he heard the man ask.

"Monday," Jill said. "Tommy's getting impatient, especially since we've been shorthanded lately. I wish I had more time to spend on getting the farmhouse renovated, but my job has to be my first priority."

"Dad says the real-estate market around here isn't so hot."

"That's true, but we're still doing better than a lot of other areas."

He was so intent on the conversation behind him that he was startled when the waitress set his lunch order in front of him. "Rice noodle stir fry," she announced, "and a Pepsi. Will there be anything else right now?"

"No," he grunted. He knew the waitress would think he was an ill-mannered jerk, but he didn't care. He only wanted her to go away.

"Then I'll just leave this for you now. You can pay up front whenever you're ready. Have a good day." She slid his lunch check onto the edge of the table and turned away.

Finally, he thought. *About freakin' time!* Aware of movement behind him, he ducked his head and watched from the corner of his eye as Jill and a young man passed by on their way out of the restaurant.

They stopped at the cash register. The man paid, he observed—were they on a date?—but, as they walked out the door and into the parking lot, they didn't hold hands. Nor did Jill take his arm. He did, however, open the passenger-side door of a small red convertible for her.

He would have liked to follow them in case they were headed back to Jill's, but that wasn't an option. Still, he had learned some very important things: Jill still worked in the area. She now owned the farmhouse, which she was planning to fix up and probably move into when it was done. She had also mentioned someone named Tommy, presumably in reference to her boss. Although the name rang no bells at the moment, he would keep it in mind.

Then an idea occurred to him that was so stunning in its simplicity he couldn't believe he hadn't thought of it sooner: most working women went out to lunch. While he himself did not—or at least hadn't up to now, preferring to carry a lunch from home and eat in the break room—there was no reason he couldn't start. Sooner or later he was bound to run into her, maybe even strike up a casual conversation if the opportunity arose. He would find her. It was just a matter of time.

At the moment, though, he was still concerned about that detective showing up on his doorstep earlier in the week. It was time to think about developing a Plan B in case he needed to get out of town. Perhaps he should pay a visit to Chad and see if he was still in touch with that guy who specialized in providing new identities. His stuff didn't come cheap, but it was top quality and worth every penny. It wasn't something to call or text Chad about, either. An in-person visit would be required.

He ate his stir-fry quickly, barely tasting it, and drank his Pepsi. After he paid his bill he walked out to the parking lot, got into his Tahoe and pointed it north, towards Wisconsin.

Nick Pappas closed the car door for Jill and came around to the driver's side. As he slid behind the wheel he gave her an admiring glance. She was wearing a pair of trim-fitting white capri pants and a pale pink t-shirt with floral appliqués, and as the breeze ruffled her shoulder-length dark hair he caught the faint scent of oranges. She was, he realized, one of those women with a gift for looking wonderful with little obvious effort.

"Want to take a ride down to Twin Groves with me? Check out the wind farm?"

"How far is it?"

"East of Bloomington on Route 9."

"I don't know," Jill said as she buckled her seat belt. "That's a pretty long drive just to look at a wind farm. Mendota Hills is a lot closer."

"That's true, but it's a beautiful day for a ride." The earlier hot weather had moderated, with temperatures in the low eighties and minimal humidity. "Is there anywhere else you need to be right now?"

"No," she said, but he heard the note of hesitation in her voice.

"Are you sure?" he asked with a smile. "You don't sound very sure."

That earned him a smile in return. "I'm sure," she said. "Really."

"All right, then." He put the Miata in gear. "There's some sunscreen in the glove compartment if you want it. I'd hate for you to get sunburned."

"Good idea." Jill opened the glove compartment and removed the squeeze bottle of sunscreen, which was less than half full. She wondered how many other women had used it.

Given Coach Dio's obvious matchmaking efforts, she hadn't been completely surprised to receive a call from Nick that morning. He'd apologized for missing Jessica's funeral, pleading work demands, and there had been no reason to refuse when he suggested lunch. Even an afternoon car ride seemed innocent enough. But the impression she'd formed at their previous meeting—that he was a little too sure of his appeal to women—still lingered.

"I remember you telling me you knew Kevin," she said. "From Future Farmers, wasn't it?"

"Yeah. I was so envious of him living on a farm. My mother's parents farmed, and I grew up wanting to follow in their footsteps, but—well, I told you all that already. They sold the place and retired. So I did the next best thing, went to ag school and became an agronomist. I have several areas of interest, but I specialize in combating pest infestations in ways that don't harm the environment."

It was rather revealing, she thought, that he had immediately turned the conversation from Kevin to himself. "Listen, Nick," she blurted, "there are times when I need to talk about Kevin with someone who knew him, and it was just too painful with Jessica. I was hoping you could tell me some things I might not know about him."

"I'm sorry," he said. "I didn't mean to…" Didn't mean to what? he wondered. Although his mother had cautioned him just this morning about trying to move too fast with Jill, he hadn't taken her seriously. But perhaps his mother was right, and Jill needed a friend more than she needed a boyfriend. "Let's start over. I was two years behind Kevin in high school, but I remember how worried he was about paying for college."

"Yes, he told me. He tried hard, but his grades weren't quite good enough to make the cut for any academic scholarships. And he didn't play sports, either. Well, I take that back. He ran track and cross-country. But he wasn't a star, so he was never offered any athletic scholarships. And his parents made just enough money that he couldn't qualify for needs-based aid."

"Yeah, I remember how discouraged he was about that. And then he was so happy when he found out about the National Guard scholarship program because—" Nick broke off abruptly, remembering too late that Kevin's membership in the Guard had resulted in his death.

"He told me his recruiter warned him he might really have to go to war, even though we weren't in one then. But of course he never imagined...he'd just started his senior year in college when the September 11 attacks happened," Jill said after a momentary pause. "We didn't know each other then, of course. We met a few years later, after his unit came back from a deployment to Iraq. He told me at the time he was never in any real danger, and we always figured the fighting would be over before he got called up again." They had reached the southbound Interstate, and Jill gazed at the ripening cornfields as they raced past. "He was in a *communications* unit," she burst out. "He wasn't supposed to die! He wasn't regular Army! He was just a farmer from a little town in Illinois that nobody ever heard of. Nobody else from Drummond was over there, and hardly anybody in town even knew *he* was over there. Or cared, for that matter. There was a flurry of attention when he was killed, of course, people bringing food and all that. But it didn't last. We were so completely isolated, Jessica and I. It's a blessing I had my job, or otherwise I can't imagine what I would've done."

"I'm so sorry," Nick said. "I had no idea."

"Nobody did, either then or later." She reached out and lightly touched his arm. "Hey, listen. I didn't mean to make you feel bad. I just needed for you to understand. My plan now is to move forward with rebuilding the house, and I want to use the best environmentally-friendly methods available. So if you have any ideas on how to do that, I'd like to hear them."

"Count on it," he said. "Although to be honest, I'd rather have you ask my advice on running the farm."

"Except I don't actually run it. I let the bank handle everything."

"But you've got all the equipment, even your own grain bins. Of course you could run it."

"Are you kidding? I have a full-time job, and I don't know the first thing about farming. Kevin did all the actual work. All I ever did was keep the books."

"You could hire me to manage it." He hadn't realized he was going to say the words until they had escaped his lips and were hanging in the air between them.

"There's just one problem, Nick," she said after a brief but chilly silence. "I don't think I could afford you."

"It was just one of those random thoughts," he said quickly. "I didn't mean for you to take me seriously."

"That's okay," she responded with a smile. Then, to gloss over the awkwardness, she changed the subject to one which was, she was sure, his favorite. "Tell me more about your work."

It was growing dark when they returned to Drummond. By that time, Jill knew a great deal more about what Nick did for a living. She also knew that she was strongly attracted to him despite his apparent self-absorption—and that, while some women might find physical attraction an adequate basis for a relationship, she wasn't one of them. When they reached her condo, she thanked him for lunch and the drive but didn't invite him in. Instead, she smiled and waved as he backed out of her driveway and drove away.

She closed the door and turned on the lights. The Juniper Ridge condos, planned and begun while the real estate market was still hot, were not selling well. Hers was one of only two on her block that were occupied. There were two other finished units, both listed for sale, one of which was a model. There were four other buildings still under construction. She had planned to enjoy a glass of white wine on her deck, but—suddenly aware of her isolation and the darkness beyond the property line—she decided against it. She remembered Coach Pappas' words: *Be careful.*

A security system would be a good idea, and surely Tommy would allow her to install one at her own expense. She would make the call on Monday.

Stack closed his eyes and took two deep breaths, savoring the not-quite-autumn fragrance of the warm, still air as he lounged beside his wife in a glider on their wide front porch. Their home in one of Drummond's oldest neighborhoods was only two blocks away from the smaller house of similar vintage where Stack had grown up. Both were century-old, two-storied dwellings with massive trees out front whose vast canopies provided deep shade over yards that now exhibited the slightly unkempt, going-to-seed look of late summer.

With every year that passed, Stack took more comfort in the sense of place provided by his old neighborhood. Drummond might change around the edges, but here, deep in its heart, the rhythms of life scarcely varied from year to year. It was this beloved heart that he was sworn to protect from the twin scourges of hard drugs and spiraling violence.

The drug-interdiction campaign and the steady volume of lower-profile crimes provided more than enough work to keep him busy. For that reason, he cherished his rare leisure hours. But now, with the grass cut and the sidewalks swept—when he should have been able to relax and let his mind drift—he was annoyed to realize that his thoughts kept returning to his previous morning's encounter with Coach Dio.

The view of the McKinnon farmhouse from beyond the cornfield was unimportant in the greater scheme of things, but Coach couldn't seem to grasp that. He had planted himself in front of Stack's desk and, displaying the single-minded determination that had marked his entire playing and coaching career, had simply refused to move until Stack had heard him out.

The coach was deaf to pleas that the McKinnon property was outside Stack's jurisdiction, that Sheriff Dean had investigated and declared himself satisfied with the outcome, and that there was nothing to be gained by pursuing the matter further. Finally, in desperation, Stack had promised he would think about it.

"Fair enough," the coach said, nodding, then turned and left.

It was a promise Stack had not intended to keep, at least not right away, so he was irritated to find himself actually thinking about what the coach had told him. Not just the cornfield, but the event that had brought Jill McKinnon to him in the first place: Amy Morrison's death. It nagged at him like a mosquito bite that was nearly healed but hadn't quite stopped itching.

His thoughts jumped to the conversation he'd had with Lucas Dean on that same subject weeks earlier. It hadn't registered at the time, but the sheriff had been very quick to dismiss the Morrison girl's death as accidental. In the same discussion the sheriff had said there'd almost certainly be a lawsuit, which would be settled out of court. The railing and stairs at Amy Morrison's apartment building had been a little on the steep side, perhaps, and slick when it rained, but in good repair. So how did he know there'd be a lawsuit, Stack wondered, unless he had already spoken to the building's owner? The question hadn't occurred to Stack before, but now he realized he wanted to know who owned the building. The name Gary Carlyle drifted into his mind. He was rumored to own half of Drummond, including several rental properties. Could that building be one of them?

Not now, he decided, and with a deliberate act of will forced the cornfield from his mind. Instead he focused on Sherri, still seated beside him, and how fortunate he was to have married this magnificent woman. He caught a whiff of the floral-scented bath products she'd used that morning combined with the faint, earthy aroma of garden soil. The combination was intoxicating. He reached out to caress her arm.

"You smell wonderful," he murmured.

She turned her head and gazed into his eyes, smiling. "Hold that thought, honey," she said with a wink. "The kids are home, and I need to get dinner going." She rose and started into the house.

"Hey, Sherri?" he called after her. "Do you still pay our property taxes online?"

She stopped in the doorway and turned to look at him. "Yes, why?"

"Just wondering if you've got the County Assessor's website in your favorites."

"Sure I do. Why?" she asked again.

"Just something I want to check on later."

Visiting the assessor's website was a shot in the dark, but it might be a source of some interesting information. If he plugged in the building's address, which he already knew, then the name and address where the property tax bills were sent should pop right up. Of course, it might be a land trust or an out-of-state business entity, which wouldn't be much help. But it was still a shot, and—since the sheriff and chief of police had both warned him off—one he preferred to take from his home computer instead of the one in his office.

Just off his and Sherri's bedroom was a small sitting room they used as a home office. Stack booted up the computer, pulled up the County Assessor's site, and moments later was staring at the tax record of the building where Amy Morrison lived. The owner was listed as a limited liability company, the name of which Stack copied onto a sheet of scratch paper.

Next, he navigated to the Secretary of State's corporate and LLC search site. When it came up he clicked the LLC button, keyed in the company's name and pressed Submit. The record appeared almost instantly, revealing that the company's manager was Gary Carlyle.

"Yeah, baby!" Stack exulted. "I knew it." But even as he spoke the words, he had to wonder: what, exactly, did he really know? And did the building's ownership have any true significance?

He knew that Gary Carlyle and his son, Ryan, were sheltered under the protective umbrella of local law enforcement. Chief Whitesell had been pretty straightforward in telling Stack to leave the Carlyles alone, and Sheriff Dean had already admitted that he and Gary Carlyle had been friends in high school. He had also strongly cautioned Stack about investigating a member of the Carlyle family. "You want to be very careful here," the sheriff had said.

Stack also knew that both the chief and the sheriff honestly believed that Ryan Carlyle was innocent of any wrongdoing, and both men had known Ryan all his life. But the question Stack had to ask himself was this: could he afford to blindly accept their judgment, which was so likely to be biased?

It was an interesting conundrum, but one to which he couldn't afford to give much thought at the moment because the drug problem would have to take precedence. School had started the previous week, and there were already rumors circulating that a local middle-schooler was distributing methamphetamines.

It was a function of his age, Stack realized, that he was having trouble processing the notion of a middle-school student dealing drugs. Back in his own middle-school days, the worst offense he'd heard about was a classmate caught smoking in the boys' restroom. In high school there had been occasional underage drinking, and he knew of a classmate who'd found his parents' stash of pot and experimented with it when the parents were away. But hard drugs? Never.

Priorities, Stack reminded himself. One of his daughters was in eighth grade, the other a sophomore in high school. His most pressing duty at the moment was to keep them and their classmates as safe as he himself had been while growing up in Drummond. Everything else would have to take a back seat, at least for the time being.

Three weeks went by before Stack found the time to follow up on the matter of Amy Morrison's death. At the end of yet another interagency task force meeting, he caught Marcus Dean alone and nudged him into the alcove where the building's vending machines were located.

"I want to talk to some of Amy Morrison's neighbors. Can you help me out?"

"What the hell for?" The sheriff sounded irritated. "She fell down the stairs, period."

"Okay, so she fell. But I still want to find out if she had any unexpected deliveries or if anybody seemed to be watching her place."

"You're going off the reservation here, Stack," the sheriff said in a low voice.

"I realize that. But I can't get past the idea that there's some kind of connection. It's been bugging the shit out of me."

"Oh, for crying out loud." Dean sighed deeply. "Listen, if it'll help you get this business out of your system, stop by my office later. I'll give you copies of all the interview notes."

"Actually, I was kind of hoping you'd come with me."

"Jesus Christ! You don't want much."

"I'd do the same for you, Lucas. And you know it."

The sheriff sighed again. "All right, I'll go with you. Seven o'clock tonight okay?"

Stack blinked. "Tonight?"

"I'm booked solid for the next week. You want me to go, it needs to be tonight. Up to you."

"Sure, okay."

"See you then. I'll pick you up."

By seven-twenty that evening, the two men were pulling into the parking lot of the apartment complex where Amy Morrison had lived. Sheriff Dean guided his Suburban into a parking space and shut off the engine.

"Like I told you earlier," he said, "my guys did a pretty thorough canvass at the time. Seems like everyone kept pretty much to themselves here. Couple people said they'd seen the girl coming or going, but they didn't know anything about her. Nobody knew anything, nobody saw anything. The only person who even knew her name was Ethel Lindsey, the next-door neighbor. Older woman, I'd guess around eighty. You want my opinion, she's the only one worth talking to."

"Okay. But if it's all right with you, I'd like to take the lead."

"Deal."

The two men climbed the steps and turned to the right, past the door to the apartment that had once been Amy Morrison's. The next one belonged to Ethel Lindsey. Stack rang the bell.

The woman who opened the door looked frail, but the blue eyes behind bifocal lenses were alert and intelligent. "Why, Sheriff Dean," she said with a smile. "What a nice surprise. Please come in." She stepped back from the door, extending her hand to Stack as she did so. "I'm Ethel Lindsey. And you are?"

"Stack Ridgeway, Mrs. Lindsey. Drummond Police Department."

"It's 'Miss,' but that's another story. Now, Sheriff, the last time you were here we spoke about Amy Morrison, poor thing." She gestured toward a grouping of two mismatched chairs and a sofa. "Please sit down."

Stack sat down on one end of the sofa. The sheriff settled into a leather-covered wing chair, while their hostess perched on the edge of an old-fashioned platform rocker.

"So," she asked, "what can I do for you gentlemen this time around?"

"I'm just following up on a case that might have a connection to Amy Morrison," Stack began, "and I was wondering if—"

"Oh, dear. Is this about the lawsuit?"

"What lawsuit?"

"Against the building management. I've already been interviewed about it. Just the other day, this was."

"No, it's nothing to do with any lawsuit. What I was wondering is—"

"People are so sue-happy these days. Nobody wants to take responsibility for their own carelessness anymore. But I interrupted you. You were wondering…?"

"This may sound like an odd question, but I was wondering if you were aware of any unexpected deliveries Amy might have received. Specifically, flowers."

"She didn't mention any. But of course that doesn't mean there weren't any. Why do you ask?"

"Two young ladies Amy was acquainted with might be victims of a stalker, and we—"

"Victims! Are they all right?"

"Yes, they're fine."

"Oh, thank heavens. But then why did you call them victims?"

"Because stalking is a crime, even if nobody gets injured. So there were no flowers or other deliveries that you know of," Stack continued. "Did you notice anyone hanging around, maybe watching her apartment?"

Ethel shook her head. "No, not that I recall."

"No one who seemed out of place, who didn't belong here?"

"Well," Ethel said thoughtfully, "there was the Sweeper. But I wouldn't say he didn't belong here, because he was staying with his mother."

"The Sweeper. Who's that?"

"I don't know his name. That's just how I thought of him, because he always had a broom in his hands. Sweeping. He was a young retarded man…oh, I'm sorry. That's not an acceptable word any more. What are we supposed to say instead? Developmentally delayed? But anyway, he told me he was staying with his mother in the next building over. Just temporarily, until she could find a new place for him. And I guess she did, because I haven't seen him for a while."

The two men exchanged glances. "How long ago was this?" Stack asked.

Ethel shrugged. "I don't really know. It's been several weeks, at least."

"Could you describe him?"

"Well, he was young. Probably in his late twenties, and not very big. Taller than I am, of course," she said with a smile, "but most people are. And thin. He was wearing baggy old clothes that just hung on him. He had brown hair, although I couldn't see much of it underneath that ratty old John Deere cap. And I couldn't see his eyes at all because of the sunglasses. I could never forget those sunglasses. They were held together with a piece of duct tape. Poor soul, he always looked like something the cat dragged in."

"So how long was he around here, and how often did you see him?"

"I saw him three times, or maybe four, over a few weeks' time. But I only spoke with him once when he was sweeping right in front of my door. A couple of other times, he was sweeping the balcony of the building across the way. The one where his mother lives."

"And you know his mother?"

"No, I don't, but he pointed out where she lives. And besides," Ethel said with conviction, "he couldn't have been a stalker. He never bothered anybody. All he did was sweep. He just kept sweeping back and forth, hunched over his poor old worn-out broom."

"And you didn't notice anybody else?"

"Not a soul."

"Well, then," the sheriff said, "I think that's all we need." He glanced at Stack. "Unless you have something else?"

"No...well, yes. One more thing. Do you remember what time of day it was when you saw him?"

"Of course. It was in the afternoon."

"Always?"

"Yes, because I spend mornings sewing in my spare room. I make prayer quilts for my church. So even if he was out there, I wouldn't have seen him."

"I see." Stack rose. "Well, thank you for your time, Miss Lindsey."

"You're welcome. Good luck with your case."

The men descended the steps, crossed the parking lot and got into the sheriff's Suburban before either one spoke.

"You think there's anything there?" Stack asked.

"I doubt it. I know of one residential facility and a couple of training sites for the disabled that closed this year. This Sweeper guy might have been one of the displaced residents."

"Yeah, maybe. Hey, if he was staying with his mother, wouldn't the rental office have a record of it?"

"Probably not, especially if it was just temporary."

"But the mother *might* have told them, in case of emergency. What if he got locked out or something?"

"I'll bet you five bucks she didn't. People like to keep their personal stuff personal."

"It's possible, though. I think I'll call Jackie in the morning and ask."

"Jackie who?"

"I don't know her last name, but she works for Gary Carlyle. His bookkeeper or assistant or something."

"And how does Gary Carlyle figure into this?"

"He owns the building, Lucas. But then, you already knew that, didn't you?"

"I did," the sheriff said wearily. "And it's just one more reason I think you're insane for believing Ryan Carlyle had anything to do with anything. Shit, he wouldn't have to stake out Amy's apartment. All he'd have to do is pull up her record in his office computer. And remember, the Lindsey woman said this Sweeper fellow was just a little guy. Ryan Carlyle is over six feet tall and weighs two hundred pounds, easy."

Dean was right, Stack realized. "Yeah…but I can't help feeling like I'm overlooking something. I can't put my finger on it, though. I need to think about it some more."

"Think about it all you want, my friend, but from now on leave me out of it. If you get something solid, call me. Otherwise, you're on your own."

"Understood."

They rode the rest of the way back to town in silence. Stack stared out the window as a single question kept circling around in his brain: *What am I missing here?*

Maybe thinking about it was a waste of time, and he should just stop. He would call Jackie in the morning and see if he could get a line on either the Sweeper or his mother. If so, he'd follow up; if not, he'd just let it go. After all, he had plenty of other work to do.

Over a month had passed since he'd seen Jill at the World Class Grill. Although he'd made it a point to eat lunch out every weekday since then, either at the World Class or other northside restaurants he thought she might patronize, he hadn't caught so much as a glimpse of her. He'd even gone to Chez Marie once, even though it was a bit pretentious for his taste, and been greeted by hostess Courtney Singleton.

"Well, hello," she had said with a warm smile. "I haven't seen you in a while."

He had pretended confusion and glanced at her name tag before returning the smile. "Oh, Courtney. Hi. From the trial, right?"

He had been so tempted, as she led him to a table, to ask if she'd seen anyone else from the jury—Jill, maybe? He didn't want to take the risk, though. He hoped she might volunteer some information along those lines, but she didn't. Oh, well. At least he knew that Courtney was still around, working at the same job. He wondered if she still had a live-in boyfriend. He needed to find that out one of these days, but there was no rush. Her turn would come.

And besides, the more time that elapsed the better it was for him. People's attention spans were short. A girl fell down a flight of stairs —yesterday's news. An old lady had a heart attack, or maybe it was a stroke. Who cared? Even the Putnam murder was quickly receding into the distance in the public's rearview mirror. He'd overheard a couple of people talking about it over lunch the previous week, and their conclusion was that of course Brian Briggs had done it and would be brought to justice one of these days. Then their conversation had turned to Washington politics.

He was just returning to work from his lunch break when he glanced out his car window and saw Jill walking quickly along the sidewalk. As he watched, she entered a professional building housing several attorneys' offices.

He parked in the lot at the rear of the building where he worked. It was unfortunate that his workstation didn't offer a view of the street, which meant he wouldn't be able to watch for her to leave. He would have liked to see how long she stayed in the building. Did she work there, or was she just running an errand?

For some reason he'd formed the impression that she worked on the upscale north side, although she'd never actually said so. But maybe she worked right here in downtown Drummond. And if that was the case, she'd probably eat at closer-in places like the Downtown Deli, Consuelo's, or Pinky's. And, starting tomorrow, so would he.

Coach Dio Pappas had always loved early October's crisp temperatures and bright blue skies. In recent years, fall weather triggered a bittersweet nostalgia for football seasons of years past, of golden autumns when he was a participant instead of an observer. Still, he had decades of good memories to cherish. He was a lucky man, and he knew it.

He pulled open the door to Pinky's Café and made his way to his favorite stool at the rear of the café. It was taking him longer than usual these days because of the pain in his right knee, the one that had been so badly injured during his college days. His doctor had been urging him to have the joint surgically replaced, and he had finally agreed—with the proviso that the operation be delayed until January.

"I refuse to be cooped up inside while the weather's nice," he had insisted. "When it's cold and snowy out, I won't mind." An equally important factor was his wife's planned retirement at the end of the year; he wanted Marg, a nurse with nearly forty years' experience, to be home with him full time while he recovered. Still, he was beginning to question the wisdom of his decision. The knee was growing more painful by the day. Even Melissa, the waitress, had noticed that he was limping.

"Hey, Coach," she greeted him. "How's the knee?"

"So-so. How's everything with you? How's Colton?" Colton was Melissa's infant son.

"He's great. He got his first tooth this week."

"How old is he now?"

"Six months and growing like a weed. What'll it be?"

"Got chili today?"

"Sure."

"Then I'll have a bowl of chili, no cheese or onions, and a side salad."

"Balsamic vinaigrette dressing, right?"

"You got it."

Coach was savoring his chili—the best in town, even better than Consuelo's—when he heard Melissa's sudden intake of breath. He looked up in time to see her turn away from the cash register and duck into the kitchen, where she held a brief whispered conversation with Barb, the other waitress.

"Okay," he heard Barb say as she left the kitchen carrying a lunch order, which she placed in front of a patron seated near the front door.

Melissa returned to her station near the cash register, her face flushed.

"What's wrong?" Coach demanded.

"Not now," Melissa said in a low voice. "How's the chili?" she asked in a more normal tone.

"It's fine." As he ate he watched Melissa, noting the way she kept her head down except when she was accepting payment from customers. Even then, she looked up only when absolutely necessary.

He finished his chili and pushed the bowl aside. "Got any pictures of the baby?" he asked Melissa.

"I'll bring some tomorrow." She fidgeted with her order pad, shooting quick corner-of-the-eye glances toward the front of the café. Then, as Barb approached, Melissa vanished into the kitchen.

"I'll take that for you, sir," Barb said as she slipped behind the counter. She accepted the money the customer—a young man, Coach noted, who looked vaguely familiar—held out along with his lunch check. Smiling, she handed him his change. "Thank you, and have a nice day."

Barb waited until the door had shut behind the customer before poking her head into the kitchen. "He's gone," she said.

Melissa closed her eyes and exhaled. "Thanks, Barb."

"So now," Coach said, "tell me what's wrong."

"That guy," Melissa began.

"The one who just left?"

"Yeah, him. I didn't want him to see me. I was afraid he might recognize me."

"But why?"

"Because he once threatened to kill me, that's why." Melissa stepped to the register as an elderly couple approached to pay their bill. She waited until they were out of earshot before continuing. "I was born in Drummond and lived here most of the time I was growing up. When I was fourteen my parents split up. My mom moved to Farleyville and took me along. It was a bad time for me. I was an outsider, I didn't know anybody, and I got into kind of a bad crowd. So anyway, I was out with a couple other girls one night and I met this guy. He was older than me, and I thought it was pretty cool he noticed me. I wasn't cute—I was kinda fat back then—and boys never noticed me before. So I ditched the girls I was with and went off with him and his buddies. Of course it was dumb, but I didn't know that then. I was only fourteen. I was just looking to have some fun, but not the same kind of fun they wanted." Melissa shook her head and looked away. "When I told 'em that, the other guys seemed okay with it. They were like, hey, she's just a stupid kid. Let's take her back where we found her and dump her. But not him. He didn't want to take no for an answer. He kept trying, but I wouldn't let him. He called me some names you wouldn't believe. He even threatened me. And when I still wouldn't, he beat me up. Then his buddies—"

"His buddies were still there while this was going on? And they allowed it?"

"Yeah…but I think they were afraid of him. I heard one of 'em say he was a mean sucker, except he didn't say 'sucker.' Anyway, they told him to leave me alone and they should get out of there before somebody came along and caught 'em."

"And where was this, exactly?"

"In the pool house at his parents' place. They weren't home."

"And then what happened?"

"Him and one of his friends drove me home. He told me I better not tell anybody what happened, because if I did he'd kill me. And I believed him, too."

"But you did tell somebody?"

"Wait a minute," Melissa said. The lunch rush was nearly over, but a late-arriving customer had taken a seat at one of her tables. After she had taken his order, she returned to her station behind the counter.

"Did you tell anybody?" Coach asked again.

"I had a split lip and two black eyes, and my arms were all bruised up. You think nobody would notice that? So my mom asked what happened, and I told her. She said I should have known better than to go off with a bunch of older boys."

"Did she call the police?"

"No way. She went to his parents and told them what happened. She found out his so-called father was really his stepfather, and he wanted rid of him. So they gave my mom some money that was supposed to be for my doctor bills, but she must have kept it for herself because she never took me to a doctor. School was out for the summer, so I stayed home until I healed up. Anyway, they promised my mom they'd send him out of state to live with his grandma so he wouldn't bother me anymore. She let them buy her off," Melissa said bitterly. "I came back down here to live with my dad after that, but I quit school before I graduated and came to work here. That was over six years ago."

Stories involving bullies were nothing new to Coach. He had heard dozens of them in his decades of working with high-school students. He had also seen various anti-bullying programs come and go, some of which had even seemed to help a little. Still, despite the best efforts of teachers and administrators, bullies remained an unpleasant fact of student life. And outside of school, in situations where faculty members were powerless to intervene, a student's first line of defense was his or her parents. For that reason, Coach was both angered and distressed by Melissa's account of her mother's actions.

"Are you sure that was him?"

"Oh, yeah. Trust me, that was him."

"But even if he recognized you, do you honestly think he'd harm you after all this time?"

"I hope not, Coach, but I don't know. I think he really would have killed me if those other guys hadn't been there."

"I'm sure it'll be fine. Don't worry." He dropped a ten-dollar bill on the counter. "Keep the change."

"Thanks, Coach," she called after him. "Take care of that knee.

He left the café and stepped onto the sidewalk, frowning. "I've seen that guy before," he muttered under his breath. He knew Farleyville's general location—about an hour's drive to the northwest—but couldn't remember ever being there. It was much smaller than Drummond. Its high school was classified as 2A, while Drummond's was 4A, so the two schools had never been sports rivals. He regretted not asking Melissa for the man's name, then realized it wouldn't have helped. He had a good memory for names as well as faces, and if he had ever known a person's name it would usually come to him, even though it sometimes took a while. But for the young man he had just seen, there was no name buried in his memory bank. Of that much he was sure.

He barely managed to contain his excitement until he was out of the restaurant. He had gone in hoping to see Jill, but she was of little importance to him now that he had stumbled on the ultimate prize: the bitch from Farleyville. She was older and a lot thinner, but he had recognized her the moment he saw her.

Returning to work, he found it difficult to stay focused on his duties. His mind kept replaying the moment he had spotted her behind the cash register at Pinky's. How in the world had he not encountered her sooner? He had eaten lunch at Pinky's during the trial, back in April, and she hadn't been there then. But that didn't matter. What mattered was that he had finally found her, and this time she would not escape.

He wondered if she had seen him. He didn't think so, but he couldn't be sure. As a precaution—so she wouldn't feel threatened, even if she had recognized him—he would watch her from a safe distance, at least to start with. Then, once he knew where she lived and had learned her routine, he would develop a plan. *Be patient.*

The first order of business was to figure out what her working hours were. Because he had worked in downtown Drummond long enough to be thoroughly familiar with its layout, that shouldn't be difficult. There was a small employee parking area directly behind Pinky's and its next-door neighbor, the gift shop. This rectangular area was bordered on its south end by an alley and on the north by a commercial building that occupied the corner of Main and Second Streets and housed Mason's department store and a ladies' shoe store. To the east, on the other side of a low masonry wall—barely more than a curb—was a free city parking lot. Since most downtown businesses closed at 5:00, the lot was only lightly used in the evenings. It would be an ideal spot from which to keep watch on the rear employees' entrance to Pinky's, assuming he could avoid being captured on video by security cameras belonging to Pinky's other next-door neighbor, located just across the alley to the south: the Remington County Bank.

The chances of that, he knew, were reasonably good. The 140-year-old bank building had a rear entrance that could be used by customers as well as employees, but no drive-up lanes. Its ATM machine, added at a much later date, was built into the south wall of the structure facing First Street. The bank's security cameras there concentrated there, for the safety of walk-up users, while the rear entrance was covered by a single camera pointing almost directly down. He would simply have to select a parking space beyond the range of that camera. He would also need to survey the area for other cameras, although their use in Drummond—except by banks—was still rare.

Lucky for me, he thought.

Karen rose from her desk and approached Jill's. "Can I ask you something?"

"Sure."

"Are we going to be okay? The business, I mean."

"Of course we are. Why do you ask?"

"Well…lot sales were slow all summer, especially in Juniper Ridge."

Jill lifted one shoulder in a slight shrug. "But it's a great location, especially with the shopping center beginning to take off. It'll be fine."

"I hope so," Karen said with a sigh, and held out an envelope. "This came in today's mail. It's a maturity notice for the Juniper Ridge development loan."

Jill accepted the envelope and laid it aside. "No big deal. That's why Tommy's at the bank right now. We'll pay the interest and renew the loan. It'll be fine," she said again.

"I've been worried sick ever since Kelly got let go. What if Tommy decides he doesn't need me, either?"

"Not much chance of that." Although Kelly had answered the telephone and run occasional errands, her primary function had been to serve as eye candy for Tommy's builders. She had become a luxury that Tommy could no longer afford. Karen, on the other hand, was a workhorse. "You're busier than ever, especially with the Juniper Ridge promo."

Tommy had engaged a graphic artist to design a promotional package for Juniper Ridge consisting of printed brochures as well as an enhanced website. Karen had been assigned to coordinate the project, which was now in its final stages.

"And I've enjoyed it. It's been fun to do something different. Oh, that reminds me," she went on. "You know Don and I are going on vacation next week. Leaf-peeping in southern Missouri."

"I've heard it's beautiful down there."

"It is. We love it. But the thing is, the CD with the computer files for the brochure should be here tomorrow. I've heard PDQ is good, so I'll drop it off with them for printing as soon as—"

Jill's phone, which was lying on her desk within easy reach, began to ring. She picked it up and saw her boss's number displayed on caller ID.

"Excuse me," Jill cut in. "Yes, Tommy?"

"Do you have a copy of the Articles of Incorporation for Juniper Ridge in your computer?"

"Of course."

"Can you email them to Carl here at the bank?"

"Sure."

"Okay, great. I thought he already had them, but he says they don't. I guess the loan processor needs them."

"Give me his email address and I'll have them there in a few minutes." She maximized Outlook and keyed the information Tommy gave her directly into her contacts list, then read it back to him. "Is that right?"

"Yeah. I've been a customer here for years," Tommy added, "and they never used to be this picky." He sounded cranky, but Jill realized this last comment was not directed toward her. He was registering his displeasure with the bank loan officer in whose office he was currently seated.

Jill had already located the necessary file and attached it to an outgoing message. "It's on the way," she said, and clicked Send. "Let me know if he needs anything else."

She ended the call from Tommy and turned to Karen, who was now sitting in one of Jill's guest chairs. "Sorry about that. Now, what about PDQ?"

"They'll need a few days to turn the order around. They can call the designer if they have any technical questions, but they'll still want a contact here and Tommy won't want to be bothered. So can I give them your name?"

"Sure, go ahead."

"Thanks." Karen plucked one of Jill's business cards from the holder on her desk. "I appreciate it."

A few miles away in downtown Drummond, Brett Petersen was at his work station in the processing department of the Remington County Bank when a new email hit his In box. It was a forwarded message from the bank's senior commercial lender and contained the Juniper Ridge articles he'd been waiting for. Brett had his computer mouse poised over the attachment when the sender information appended to the bottom of the message caught his eye. He scrolled down to read it.

"Jill C. McKinnon, CPA," he mumbled under his breath. "Controller, TBA Enterprises." Brett had processed loans for several Adair entities besides Juniper Ridge, but TBA was not one of them. He had never heard of it. Could it be some sort of holding company? Not that he cared, because below the name of the company was the only information that interested him: Jill's office address, phone, fax, and email. The only thing missing was her cell number.

82

Jill gazed out the office window, wishing she could spend the day outdoors savoring the warm Indian summer weather. She hoped Karen, who by now was relaxing at a resort in southwest Missouri, was enjoying some spectacular fall foliage.

How long since I've had a vacation? Jill wondered. I haven't had any time off this year except for jury duty and Jessica's death. Those were hardly vacations. This might be a good time to ask Tommy about taking a few days off after Karen returned. He was in a jovial mood this week because they'd closed on the sale of one of the spec units in Juniper Ridge and made a decent profit on it, even after paying off the construction loan. They also had a potential buyer for a second unit, possibly thanks to the updated Juniper Ridge website. It was already receiving hits. The brochures would be distributed to local real estate agents, banks, and mortgage brokers and, ideally, generate even more interest.

Jill frowned. Now that she thought about it, the brochures should be done by now. She located the number for PDQ Print-N-Copy and dialed it. When a woman answered, Jill identified herself and asked about the status of the Juniper Ridge brochures.

"I'm not sure," the woman said. "Hold on, and I'll check."

A minute later, Jill heard a man's cheerful voice. "Hello, Jill? This is Jared Snow. Your brochures are in the folding machine right now. We'll have them packaged and ready for you first thing tomorrow morning."

"Excellent. Can I pick them up between eight-thirty and nine?"

"Sure thing, or I can deliver them if you like."

"Thanks, but that won't be necessary. And Jared? Can you leave one out for me to look at before I sign off on the order? Karen left me the proof copy the graphics guy gave her so I'd know what they're supposed to look like."

"Of course, but we take pride in our work. I'm sure you won't be disappointed."

After ending the call, Jared removed Jill's business card from beneath the paper clip that attached it to the job order and tapped it against his desk. *TBA Enterprises. Tommy-something-Adair. I should have known.*

Stack Ridgeway returned to his desk after yet another task-force meeting and began working through his voice mail messages. They were all routine except for one from a caller who identified herself only as Jackie.

"Um, yes, this is Jackie? From the Carlyle office? I don't know if you remember, but you asked me to check on something for you?" Stack's finger had been poised over the Delete key, but he immediately pulled it away.

"I told you I couldn't give you any information because of the privacy thing, but then I had an idea. I watched for the rent to come in for the apartments in that building, and when I posted the payments I looked at the tenant profiles. I finally got the last one this morning. Call me after five-thirty on my cell, okay?" She gave the number, then hung up.

He waited until almost seven o'clock to call her. "Hello, Jackie? Stack Ridgeway."

"Oh, hello. I was starting to wonder if you'd call me back."

"Actually, I was glad to hear from you. Did you have something for me?"

"I'm not sure. I thought—well, you must be looking for a woman old enough to have a grown son. So when I posted the rent receipts, I pulled up the tenant information records and looked at their date of birth."

"Good idea. So…?"

"Most of our renters are young. Either singles or married couples just starting out. I only found two people over thirty-five in that building, and one's a man. The other one's a woman named Delores Griffin. She's fifty-two."

"Delores Griffin," he repeated. "Which apartment is she in?"

"Three. It's on the ground level. But listen, I'm not supposed to give out any information about our tenants. It would cost me my job."

"Your secret is safe with me. And Jackie? Thanks for your help. I really appreciate it."

I can either lie awake all night wondering, he told himself, or go up there right now and settle this Sweeper business one way or the other. "Sherri," he called out, "I need to take a little ride up the road. I'll be back inside an hour."

As he drove north he contemplated how to approach the Griffin woman and decided that, in this case, the direct approach was probably best. He parked, located her apartment, and rang the bell. He sensed rather than saw an eye on the other side of the peephole and held up his badge.

A heavyset black woman opened the door. "Can I help you, sir?"

"Are you Delores Griffin?"

"Yes," she said. "Is something wrong?" She sounded more curious than frightened.

"No, ma'am. There was a young man around here a few months ago that went around with a broom, sweeping. Do you know who I'm talking about?"

"No, I never saw anyone like that."

"Oh. Well, I was told he might live here."

"Someone told you he lives *here*? You mean *this* apartment?" She shook her head, laughing. "Nobody lives here except me and Bootsie. That's my cat."

"I see. Well, I'm sorry to have troubled you. Good night, Ms. Griffin."

He glanced across the parking lot and saw that the lights were off in Ethel Lindsey's apartment, so he went back to his car and drove away.

He called her the next morning. "Miss Lindsey," he began, "I'm sorry to bother you, but I have another question about the man you referred to as the Sweeper. I assumed he was white because you didn't say otherwise. But I didn't ask, and I should have."

"Yes, Captain, he was white."

The timeline for Katie Putnam's murder had been erased from the white board in Stack's office weeks earlier and the board put to other use, but he taken a picture of it with his phone and emailed it to himself. He pulled up the picture now and studied it, then was struck by a sudden thought. He opened the computer file containing Amy Morrison's autopsy report and carefully reviewed both the written report and the photos. He picked up the phone and dialed Lucas Dean's direct number.

The sheriff answered promptly. "Yeah, Stack."

"Do you still have the Morrison autopsy pictures?"

"Probably. Why?"

"There was a little round bruise on the girl's upper chest. It was the only mark on that part of her body. It just occurred to me…it could've been made by the end of a broom handle."

"What? Are you nuts?"

"No, listen. She fell backwards, right? There was a lot of damage to her skull, her back and her extremities, but her face and the upper front part of her torso were completely unmarked except for that one little bruise. How do you suppose that happened?"

"Who the hell knows? She was carrying sacks of groceries, shit went flying everywhere. She could've fallen on anything small and round."

"But how, when she landed on her back? And remember that Sweeper guy Ethel Lindsey told us about, the one who was supposed to live in the building across the way? Well, I checked. The only woman in that building old enough to have a grown son never heard of him."

"So *she* says."

"No, Lucas, I believe her. She's black, and according to Ethel Lindsey the Sweeper's white."

Dean was silent for a moment. "Do I understand correctly that you went back up there, without *me*, to question people in *my* jurisdiction? What the hell did you do that for?"

"As I recall, you told me to leave you out of it unless I had something solid, and then call you. Which is what I'm doing now."

"I can't talk about this now," the sheriff finally said. "Let me get back to you later."

Stack hung up the phone, wondering if the Dean was about to rat him out to the chief. While it wasn't likely, he couldn't rule out the possibility. Better if he hears it from me, Stack decided, and walked down the hall to Chief Whitesell's office. He paused at the doorway. "Can you give me five minutes?"

The chief sat motionless while Stack, seated across from him, told him about Ethel Lindsey, the Sweeper, and the bruise on Amy Morrison's chest.

"This is County's case, not ours. So why are you involved?"

"Because I think there's a connection to the Putnam murder."

"How so?"

"It struck me as really odd that in both cases there was a guy who showed up out of nowhere and then disappeared. In both cases he said he was visiting in the neighborhood, but we couldn't track him down. And in both cases, nobody could give us a good description of the guy."

"Back up a minute. You lost me. Who was the guy in the Putnam case?"

"Two weeks before she died, she met a guy in the bar where she used to hang out. She got drunk, and he took her home in a cab. He told the bartender he was visiting his brother in the subdivision across the street."

"We know anything about him besides that?"

"We talked to the bartender and a couple of Putnam's friends that saw her there that night. They couldn't tell us much, just that he was an average-looking guy between twenty-five and thirty. Katie's friend Jennifer thinks his name was Brad, or it could've been Chad. The only thing they all remember is that he was wearing a Milwaukee Brewers cap. And the bartender said he had a dragon tattoo on his neck."

"That's pretty tenuous, Stack." He folded his hands and rested them on his desk, a mannerism which, Stack had learned long ago, meant his boss's patience was wearing thin. "Don't tell me you've given up on Brian Briggs. He's still the logical suspect."

"I haven't given up on anybody, Chief. And," he added as he stood up, "I don't intend to. Thanks for your time."

The past few days had been busy as well as rewarding. Not only had he found that hated bitch from Farleyville, but Jill McKinnon as well. He had decided to start with Jill because he wanted to give the other one—he never thought of her by name—enough some time to relax and let her guard down.

At the end of the workday when Jill's workplace address had, almost literally, fallen into his lap, he drove straight to TBA Enterprises. The business occupied half of a sleek single-story brick-and-glass structure across the street from a large grocery store. *Piece of cake*, he thought with a smile. He parked in the store's lot and settled down to wait.

At a quarter after five, he saw Jill leave the building and get into a black Impala. When she pulled into the street he trailed behind at a respectful distance; but, as they approached the county highway leading north, he noticed that she seemed to be checking the rearview mirror with increasing frequency.

Perhaps she suspected she was being followed. The cap and dark glasses he wore would prevent her from recognizing him, especially when three car lengths separated their vehicles, but there was no point in arousing her suspicions. He slowed, dropping farther behind her, and turned right at the next side street. There was a quick-stop store on the corner. It would be a good place to pick up the tail the next afternoon.

It took two more workdays, each time following her on a different segment of her drive home, but he finally saw her pull into her driveway.

The garage door was almost, but not quite, fully closed when he drove past. The buildings on her street were clearly brand new, and there were two "for sale" signs on the block. Both were from the same agency. He made a mental note of its name, then drove back to town. It was time to find the other one.

He knew Pinky's was open until 7:00 p.m. With any luck, the bitch worked until closing. He had already spotted a rusty Honda Civic, at least ten years old, that looked like the kind of vehicle she would drive. He parked at the end of the lot farthest from the bank's security camera. He felt safer there even though night was closing in, and the lot was not well-lit.

Luck was with him. The back door of Pinky's opened shortly after seven, and a small figure stood silhouetted in the light over the rear door. She surveyed her surroundings, her gaze settling on the Tahoe. She ducked back inside, then reappeared a moment later with a man right behind her. The cook, maybe, or the manager. Whoever he was, he stood in the doorway while she walked over to the Honda and got in. Then he went back inside and shut the door.

He watched the Honda as its engine started, its lights went on, and it pulled into the alley. Then it turned left onto Main Street. *Interesting*, he thought. Suspicious little bitch must have spotted my car and realized it hasn't been here before. Well, that was no problem. He'd seen her head south, so tomorrow night he would park a couple of blocks away. He'd find a place where he could see her go by and pick up her trail. He'd also make sure she became accustomed to seeing the Tahoe. It would become part of her landscape.

Stack wasn't sure whether or not he was surprised to receive a call from Sheriff Dean suggesting a lunch meeting at the Dragons Den. The sheriff might be devious and cynical, but he was still a law enforcement officer and, in Stack's opinion, a shrewd one.

"I'll be there," Stack had said. He hadn't asked what the sheriff wanted to discuss. He was pretty sure he already knew.

The sheriff was already waiting in the rear booth when Stack arrived. "That thing we talked about last week," Dean said in a low voice. He hunched over the table, his face barely a foot from Stack's. "That bruise. It might be what you thought."

"Really. And what led you to that conclusion?"

"Same thing as you. Just plain logic."

"Okay, so where do we go from here?"

"Good question. Hey, Frankie," the sheriff bellowed. "You gonna get us some burgers, or what?"

"Keep your friggin' shirt on," Frankie shot back. "They're coming."

"Here's what I think," Stack said. "We're looking for a guy who took Katie Putnam home in a taxi two weeks before she died. And we're looking for a guy who was sweeping in front of Amy Morrison's apartment. Then there was also a guy who delivered flowers to two different women, and a guy who watched and maybe broke into the McKinnon farmhouse. We never identified any of them. What if they were all the same guy?"

"Putnam and Morrison, possibly. But the others, I'm not so sure. Where's the connection?"

"The connection has to be the trial. That's the only thing that ties them together. And something else occurred to me, Lucas. God bless my wife, because she put her finger on it without even realizing it."

"What's that?"

"We got invited to a costume party for Halloween. But when she told me about it, she called it a masquerade. Now think about this: when Ethel Lindsey told us about this Sweeper character, she mostly talked about what he was wearing. Ragged old clothes, John Deere cap, broken sunglasses. It was a *masquerade*, Lucas. He even had a prop. A worn-out old broom, remember? So anybody who saw him would have a lot of stuff to focus on besides what he actually looked like. Not that they could see a lot, considering the sunglasses and the cap."

Frank Maloney approached, bringing their hamburgers and two cans of Coke. "Seen a lot of you here lately," he said to Stack.

"Yeah, well, don't get too used to it. All this red meat is bad for my cholesterol."

"You get just as much cholesterol across the street."

"Yeah, but the waitresses are prettier."

"Bite me."

"Nicer, too," Stack said to Frank's departing back.

"You have to admit," the sheriff said with a grin, "there's a certain ambience here that Pinky's doesn't have."

"Thank God. Now here's another thing," Stack continued. "The guy at the Sports Fan, the one who took Katie Putnam home two weeks before she died. Everybody noticed his Brewers cap, and the bartender was fixated on his dragon tattoo. But you know what I think? It was probably fake. One of those temporary ones. They're everywhere right now, this close to Halloween, but you can find 'em any time of year. Misdirection, right? They notice the hat, the tattoo, but not the face."

"And now that you mention it, didn't the delivery man with the flowers wear a cap and sunglasses, too?"

"And so did the guy the Cameron kid saw. Not that it proves anything, because baseball caps are common as dirt. And so are sunglasses. But even so…"

"You still think Ryan Carlyle is connected with this?"

"No," Stack said with a sigh. "Mostly because of what Ethel Lindsey said about the Sweeper's size. Small and thin. The guy might've been taller than she thought, because he went around all hunched over. If he stood up straight he might be several inches taller. But there's no costume in the world that could make Carlyle look thin."

"So where does that leave us?"

"I'm glad you said 'us,' Lucas. I'm hoping you'll back me up."

The sheriff nodded. "What do you need from me?"

"Help me convince the chief to rescind his order."

"Which one?"

"The one telling me to stop investigating the Briggs jurors. Because if it's not Ryan Carlyle, then chances are pretty good it's one of the others. And there were only two young white guys on the jury besides Carlyle."

"You mean to tell me you didn't go ahead anyway?"

"I would've done it in a minute if I'd thought he wouldn't find out. The chief is all over everything my guys and I do. Hell, we can't run a license plate without him knowing. He's paranoid about that stuff. So afraid somebody'll complain they're being targeted, harassed, whatever. Like Gary Carlyle did. I need to convince him there's some plausible reason, or otherwise I'm shit outta luck."

"You can count me in if you think it'll help," the sheriff said. "Although the chief isn't one of my biggest fans. But Morrison was on my turf, and so was old Mrs. McKinnon."

"Who also had some unexplained bruising, if you'll recall."

"That's right, she did. Now let's eat. Be a shame to let these burgers get cold."

On Saturday morning he visited the real estate agency that had the Juniper Ridge listings and approached the first person he saw, a middle-aged woman.

"Hello," he said politely. "I wonder if you could tell me something about the Juniper Ridge condos? I'm just renting now, but I'm thinking of buying. Mortgage rates are so low that it seems like a good time."

"It's a very nice development." The woman reached into a drawer and pulled out a brochure, which she handed to him. "We just got these in."

He glanced at it, then folded it and put it into his jacket pocket. "Actually, I was hoping someone might show me one. I noticed one on Poplar Grove Way—"

The agent prided herself on her ability to distinguish at a glance between buyers and lookers. This man was definitely just a looker, and therefore not worth her time. "As it happens, there's a model unit that's open every weekend from ten to three. You're more than welcome to go over and take a look."

"Really. Thank you," he said coolly, letting her know he was aware of the brush-off. He would have preferred to be driven to Juniper Ridge in somebody else's car, so Jill—if she happened to be home—wouldn't spot his Tahoe. On the other hand, a real-estate agent might begin asking questions he would prefer not to answer.

He drove to Juniper Ridge and parked around the corner from Jill's unit, where the Tahoe would be out of sight. Wearing a red Illinois State ball cap and aviator sunglasses, he approached the model unit on foot. It was identified with a yard sign that hadn't been there at the time of his earlier visit and read simply, "Model now open." He entered and was met by an attractive thirty-something woman.

"Hi, there," she chirped. "Welcome to Juniper Ridge. Would you please sign our guest book?"

He noticed that there was only one other entry on the page. Business must be slow. He picked up the pen provided and entered his name as Chad Winters. Although he often introduced himself as Chad when he didn't want to reveal his own name, he never used his friend's real last name of Somers. *Honor among thieves*, he thought with a smile. He wrote "unlisted" in the space provided for his telephone number.

"Feel free to look around," the agent said. "Let me know if you have any questions." She stayed near the front door, probably lying in wait for more promising prospects. Apparently she had written him off almost as quickly as her colleague back at the office had done.

"Are all the units the same, or are there different floor plans?"

"They're all the same, but we offer optional basement finish for anyone who needs more living space."

"Thanks." He wandered from the great room into the kitchen, then climbed the stairs to the second floor. "Nice," he murmured as he moved from the loft into the large master bedroom at the rear of the unit. He poked his head into the master bath, then retraced his steps through the loft and entered the smaller front bedroom. From the window he had a clear view of Jill's unit across the street. He was interested to note that it backed up to a green space, with the nearest houses several hundred feet beyond. And if all the units were alike, there would be French doors at the rear opening onto a deck. *Promising*, he thought to himself.

Shifting his gaze to the front of her unit, he noticed a small sign beside her front door. He couldn't read it from where he stood, but he recognized it immediately and knew what it meant. She had an alarm system.

He trotted down the stairs, letting the displeasure he felt show on his face.

The agent met him at the bottom of the staircase. "So what do you think? Isn't it lovely?"

"I guess," he said. "But I noticed the place across the street has an alarm system. Is there a problem with crime here?"

"No, this is a very safe area."

"Then why have an alarm system?" he persisted.

"I'm sure it's just a precaution." Her eyes had drifted away from him and were now focused on a fashionably dressed silver-haired couple coming up the walk. "Thanks for coming by."

Although he was irritated by the woman's curt dismissal, it had saved him from wasting any time or effort deflecting a sales pitch. Reaching the Tahoe, he unlocked it and settled himself behind the wheel.

"Damn," he muttered. Jill McKinnon had an alarm system, and Courtney Singleton had something even better: a live-in boyfriend. At least he assumed the guy was still there, but this wasn't the time to try finding out. Perhaps he should take a step back and reconsider his priorities. McKinnon and Singleton weren't that important to him now. Instead, he would concentrate on getting rid of the bitch from Farleyville. From now on, he would focus only on that goal and block out everything else. What was that phrase of his grandmother's? *Tunnel vision*. Yes, that was it. But for some reason he had never figured out, she had made it sound like a bad thing.

He turned on his disposable phone and punched in Chad's number. When the call went to voice mail, he left a carefully worded message.

"Hey, it's me. I'm just checking on that package we talked about. The one with the old stuff of my dad's. Let me know when it's ready for me to pick up. Thanks. See you."

He knew Chad would figure out that the word "package" referred to his new identity documents, which he would need before moving on with the next—and final—phase of his plan.

Melissa served Dio the fruit plate he had ordered for lunch instead of his usual soup and sandwich. "Going on a diet?" she asked with a smile.

"Sort of. I'm planning to have one of Frank Maloney's burgers for dinner tonight, and I'm going to get it with the works. Bacon, cheese, everything. So I'm having a light lunch to compensate."

"How come you're not having dinner at home tonight? You and your wife have a fight?"

"Silly girl. No, Marg's out of town. She and Louise took off for a girls' getaway this morning. They've been doing it every October for several years now. It started because she thought I got too preoccupied with football." He chuckled. "Imagine that, a football coach preoccupied with football. So she informed me she needed a break, and she wanted to take her sister along because the anniversary of her husband's death was coming up and she was feeling low. They went up to Galena for a long weekend and stayed at a bed and breakfast, went antiquing... just girl stuff. So now it's become a tradition. They leave on a Thursday morning and come back Sunday."

"Sounds like fun. Do they always go to Galena?"

"No, it's somewhere different every year. This time it's a B and B in a town near Milwaukee. It's run by a nurse and her husband, which is why they picked it. They'll get a discount."

"That's nice. Maybe someday I'll have a chance to do stuff like that."

"I hope so," he said, but he didn't feel very hopeful. A high-school dropout with a dead-end job, a baby and no husband wasn't likely to enjoy a bed-and-breakfast getaway any time soon. "By the way, have you had any problems with that fellow from Farleyville?"

"No, he hasn't been back. I saw a different car out in the parking lot a few days after he showed up, and it kinda freaked me out at first. But it's been there off and on for the past several days, so I guess it's okay. I see it sometimes when I leave work. It's always in the same spot."

"It might belong to someone who lives around here. A lot of these old buildings have apartments on the upper floors."

"Maybe," she said with a shrug. "I told my mom I was nervous about seeing him in here, and she told me I should be more nervous about where I live."

"Is it a bad neighborhood?"

"I live in the Triangle. I know it's got a bad reputation, but it's not *that* bad. At least, not if you belong there. My boyfriend's lived there all his life, so people watch out for him. And for me, too."

"That's good," Dio said. "But keep your eyes open."

He paid for his lunch and hobbled back to his car. His knee was killing him. If it wasn't at least a little better by dinnertime, he'd have something at home and skip the burger at Frankie's place, even though he craved the male companionship he would find there along with the red meat. The major league baseball playoffs were underway, and the Yankees were playing tonight. Most of the yuppy crowd would be up north at the Sports Fan, which boasted several high-definition screens, but Drummond old-timers remained loyal to Frank Maloney and the single 19-inch television mounted above the back bar. It should be fun.

He had finally worked out a plan of attack. It was risky, but the need that drove him, now that he'd found her, was overwhelming. And besides, there was no alternative. The bitch lived in the Triangle, and while she was in there she was untouchable. He had been in Drummond long enough to know that nobody willingly entered the Triangle who didn't belong there. Even law enforcement didn't go in without backup.

The only time and place she was vulnerable was when she left work. The fixture over Pinky's rear door illuminated the steps descending to the parking lot, but, except for a few scattered pools of light at the periphery of the city lot, the rest of the area was dark. It was also nearly always deserted, especially Sunday through Thursday nights.

When he left work Wednesday afternoon, his coworkers thought he was leaving on vacation. "Have a good time," they had called after him.

"I will," he'd replied with a grin. "See you a week from Monday." But of course they wouldn't, because he wasn't coming back. By the time they realized that, he would be long gone. He would also have a different name, because Chad had called to let him know his new identity documents were ready.

He had gone home and packed a few essentials—a change of clothes and some basic toiletries—in a sports bag. He opened a desk drawer and removed the small fireproof box containing his important papers. He swathed it in bubble wrap, then stuffed it into a UPS overnight box he had obtained earlier in the week. He thought about including the key to the box, which was on his key ring, but decided against it. If anything went wrong, Chad wouldn't let a small thing like not having the key keep him from opening the box. He took the package to the local UPS office and addressed the airbill to himself, in care of Chad at his Milwaukee address. He paid in cash.

Then he had returned and methodically combed through his remaining belongings. Except for his laptop and prepaid phone, there was nothing else he would need, nothing he would regret abandoning. Clothing, furniture...it could all be easily replaced when the time was right.

He spent much of the next day going over his plan, examining it for weaknesses, searching for any previously undiscovered ways to reduce the risk. He had never attempted anything quite so daring before, but he was up for it. He tossed the sports bag onto the front passenger seat and placed the laptop on the floor. He stowed the prepaid phone in the glove compartment.

He dressed in sweatpants and a hooded sweatshirt layered over a flannel shirt for warmth—no cap, which might fall off, and no sunglasses because it would be dark—and laced up his running shoes. At 6:30 p.m., he got into the Tahoe and clicked the remote control to open the garage door. Backing out of the driveway, he pressed the remote control again. He felt strong. No, he realized, he felt *invincible.*

At that moment Dio was sitting at the bar in the Dragons Den, watching the news on a Chicago station and waiting for the baseball game to begin. He had finished his cheeseburger, which he had enjoyed every bit as much as he'd expected, and was now sipping from a can of ginger ale. There still wasn't much of a crowd, although there might be once the game started. Dio hadn't lived in Chicago for decades, but in a sense it was still his home. So when the newscaster switched from Chicagoland news to national stories, he stopped paying attention. He did, however, look up at the screen at one point and catch part of a story about a trial somewhere on the East Coast. Who was on trial—and for what—escaped him, but he did hear the newscaster say that the jury had been deliberating for three days and had still not reached a verdict. There was a significant possibility of a hung jury.

For some reason, the term "hung jury" made him think of Jill. He hadn't seen or heard from her in recent days and wondered how she was doing. He also wondered if Stack Ridgeway was making any progress in his investigation. He hadn't seen Stack for a few days, either.

The pre-game show started. Dio watched for a while, mildly interested, but—though he would never have admitted it to Frank Maloney—he found baseball rather boring, especially compared to football. Besides, he was having trouble keeping his mind on the sportscasters' commentary. There was something buzzing around in his brain, some fragment of an idea he couldn't quite get hold of.

Then he glanced across the street and noticed that the dining room lights had gone off in Pinky's Café. At that moment, he knew where he had seen the man from Farleyville: it had been right there at Pinky's. Like Jill, he had been on the Briggs jury. He had been the man whose body language Dio couldn't read. And it was one of the men on the Briggs jury that Jill suspected—

He stood up quickly, his knee objecting to the change in position, but he barely felt it. If he hurried, he might be able to catch Melissa before she left the building.

He waited silently behind his gray Tahoe. It had been parked in the same space nearly every night for a week, just beyond the low barrier that separated the two parking lots, so that it would become part of the landscape. He had huddled in the back seat, invisible in the darkness, and watched her leave the café. She was less cautious every night; he could read it in her body language. Now it was just a matter of not blowing it, not betraying his presence by motion or sound, until his quarry was too close to evade him.

As he watched, fidgeting with the heavy-duty plastic trash bag and extension cord—a makeshift garrotte—in the kangaroo pocket of his sweatshirt, the back door of Pinky's opened a foot or so. A woman appeared, silhouetted in the narrow shaft of light as she looked both ways, scanning the parking lot behind the building. He held himself motionless as her gaze passed over the Tahoe. Then, apparently satisfied, she called a brief goodnight to someone inside: the owner or manager who, he now knew, would remain there for at least another hour.

She emerged from the café, shut and locked the door behind her, and began walking quickly toward her battered Honda Civic. She had less than 20 feet to cover, and he could tell by the way she held her right hand that she had her car key at the ready. Timing would be critical. If he made his move too soon, she might evade him. Too late, and she might reach the haven of her vehicle. He tensed, gathering himself for the assault. *Now!* he catapulted himself from behind the Tahoe and bounded forward, running silently on the balls of his feet.

Dio had nearly reached the entrance to the parking area off the alley when he heard a thump and a quickly stifled scream. Following the sound, he saw Melissa in the grasp of a man wearing a hooded sweatshirt. He had apparently grabbed her from behind, pinning her against her car with his body while he covered her head with what looked like a plastic trash bag. He yanked the drawstring and pulled the bag tightly closed, then his right hand captured hers and twisted it violently.

Momentarily transfixed, Dio saw light glinting off something that fell from Melissa's hand—her key ring—and landed with a soft *ching* on the pavement. It was a small thing, but enough to galvanize him into action.

In the fraction of a second that it took Dio to launch himself at the man who was assaulting Melissa, the sixty-three-year-old coach with the blown-out knee was transformed—at least in spirit—into the muscular star linebacker he once had been, charging his opponent with ferocious determination. The bad knee protested with a dizzying jolt of pain, but Dio ignored it as he sprang forward and tackled the assailant from one side, jolting Melissa from his grip. She tore the bag from her head, gasping for breath.

"Go!" Dio yelled to Melissa as his momentum carried both men to the ground. "Go!"

In a football game, the whistle would have blown. The play would have been over, and both men would have stood up and rejoined their teams. But this was no game. The man in the hooded sweatshirt was fighting back, and he had a knife.

Dio glimpsed Melissa still standing a few feet away, watching in mute horror. "Run!" he shouted. "Get help!"

Melissa's head swiveled left, then right. Run, but where? The back door of the café was locked, and she'd lost her keys. The police station was several blocks away, and the sheriff's department not much closer. Then she heard a burst of music, a man's laughter, and she knew where to go. She dashed into the alley and from there onto the sidewalk. Flying across the street with no thought for traffic, she flung open the door of the Dragons Den.

"Help!" she cried out, but nobody seemed to hear her. The attention of every man in the place was riveted on the television set, its volume turned up loud enough to reach even the rearmost booth. She darted over to the bar and grasped Frank Maloney's arm. "There's a guy beating up Coach Dio behind Pinky's. You gotta help him!"

"Michelle!" Frank barked at the waitress. "Call 911!"

He grabbed his baseball bat from under the bar and rushed toward the door. As he charged across Main Street and into the alley he heard grunts, then a terrifying shriek, and he could just make out the shape of a man in a hooded sweatshirt, his back toward the alley, crouching astride the supine form of Dio Pappas.

Jared Snow heard the wail of sirens in the distance, but—if he was very quick—there was still enough time to finish the job and escape. *Invincible,* he told himself. *I am invincible!* He raised the knife, preparing to strike one final blow. It was only at the last second that he glimpsed a blur of motion and sensed the faint disturbance in the air near his head. *What the hell...?* It was his last thought before the Louisville Slugger wielded by Frank Maloney—the Drummond Dragons baseball star whose home-run record had remained unbroken since 1972—found its mark.

Just before noon on Friday, the chief entered Stack's office and closed the door.

"I appreciate you not saying 'I told you so,'" the chief said.

Stack shrugged. "No problem."

"So it was Snow. Did you suspect him?"

"Not at first. After I ruled out Ryan Carlyle, I was leaning toward Petersen."

"Because…?"

"Jill McKinnon told me he hit on her during the trial, and it seemed to tie in with that thing about the flowers. But after I thought about it, that was probably more about casing their houses than anything romantic. And then too, it seemed like whoever was doing all this, he wouldn't want anyone to link him with her. To say, 'Oh, yeah, Jill went out with him a couple times.' Plus the fact that Petersen works for a bank. They would have done a background check before they hired him."

"But you ran a check on both of them, and Snow came up clean, too."

"We'll keep digging. I bet if we look hard enough, we'll find some dirt on him. And I plan to start with that guy who left a voice mail on the phone we found in his glove compartment. It was something about getting the package he sent." Stack sighed. "But as things now stand, we still can't connect him to anything except last night's attack. The techs went over his apartment with a fine-tooth comb and didn't find a damn thing to link him to any of the women."

"Any of the witnesses ID him?"

"Lucas showed his driver's license picture to Ethel Lindsey in a photo lineup, but she couldn't pick him out. Neither could the Cameron kid. Scott Allison did the same with the Sports Fan bartender and Katie's friend Jennifer. We struck out there, too."

"Struck out," Chief Whitesell said with a grim smile. "Good thing old Frankie didn't. Looks like he may have done us all a favor."

"He feels worse about it than I would've thought. Keeps saying he didn't mean to kill the guy."

"Tell him not to feel too bad, because I had a call from the hospital a little while ago. Snow's on life support, waiting for a team to come in and harvest his organs. Creep actually checked the donor box on his driver's license. How's that for irony? As his last act on earth, he's going to save some lives."

"So where does this leave us with respect to the Putnam murder? I'd bet a month's pay he did it, but I can't prove it. I'd like to be able to call Katie's aunt and tell her the case is closed."

"Sorry, Stack, but you can't do that. You said it yourself, you can't prove it. Brian Briggs is up before Judge Meyerhoff next week on the retail theft charges, and they'll stick. Once he serves his time for that, it'll be something else. Even if we can't put him away for Putnam's murder, which I grant you he probably didn't do..." The chief spread his hands, palms up. "The guy's a total loser, and he'll be in and out of jail the rest of his natural life. And you know what? I'm not a damn bit sorry for him. I'm only sorry for his victims."

Dio Pappas drifted into wakefulness, screwing his eyes shut against the lights. *Too bright. Turn them off.* He heard a voice nearby, female and unfamiliar, but his brain was still too muddled by painkillers to let him make out the words. Then he heard another voice close to his left side, and this one he recognized. *Marg.*

"He's in and out," Margaret Pappas said.

"Well, that's to be expected. He's on some pretty heavy medication. We'll start backing down the dosage…"

The not-Marg voice went on speaking. While Dio struggled to understand what it was saying, the meaning escaped him. He heard Marg answer the unknown voice, expressing what sounded like understanding and agreement. But not fear, so there must not be anything to worry about. He lay there with his eyes closed until the murmuring voices fell silent, then opened his eyes and turned his head to the left. Marg was still there, reading a book. She looked up, saw him watching her, and smiled. He went back to sleep. The next morning—his fourth in the hospital—he was moved from intensive care to a regular room. They had him up and walking a few steps before the day was over.

He had attracted a large number of visitors due to his popularity and the circumstances of his hospitalization, and while he was in intensive care they had congregated in the ICU waiting room. During the first anxious hours, the atmosphere had been somber and the voices hushed. But once Dio was out of danger, the mood had turned jovial. Even the news that Jared Snow had not survived his traumatic brain injury failed to affect the happy ambience, especially when it was learned that Frank Maloney would not be charged in Snow's death.

After his move to Two North, the surgical wing, Dio began holding court in the mezzanine lounge because hospital rules strictly limited the number of people he could have in his room. The lounge overlooked the hospital's main entrance and was an ideal location for Dio to monitor his visitors' comings and goings.

It was from this vantage point that Dio spotted Tommy Adair and Jill McKinnon entering the lobby. As Dio watched, Tommy approached the white-haired volunteer at the reception desk while Jill waited a few feet away.

Nick had come in just behind them. A lifelong student of body language, Dio couldn't help noticing the way Nick seemed drawn to the girl as though by gravitational pull, the way he bent his head toward hers.

Dio leaned close to his wife, who sat beside him with her ever-present paperback book.

"Marg," he whispered, gesturing toward their son and the young woman beside him, "do you think she'll convert?"

ACKNOWLEDGMENTS

I would like to express my deep appreciation to three special men who, at different times and in various ways, helped me craft this story.

First and foremost, **Lyndon Rich**: Beloved husband, enthusiastic cheerleader and number-one fan, he has been a source of unwavering support. Through nearly forty-five years of marriage, he has been my rock.

Second, **Harry Diavatis**: Playwright, actor, director, friend and classmate at Vallejo (California) High School, Harry christened the Coach Diogenes Pappas character and helped me keep him true to his Greek-American heritage. Since Harry played college football and is a retired athletic director, it's anybody's guess how much of Coach is really Harry. He would probably say, "Only the good parts."

Third, **Charlie Spooner**: Also a VHS alumnus, Charlie is a gifted storyteller and poet who not only provided encouragement and feedback but also served as my baseball consultant for the Frank Maloney character.

My heartfelt thanks to all.

Normal, Illinois
October 2010